D1610312

BLITZ HARVEST

Recent Titles by Peter Leslie from Severn House

ACTION IN THE ARCTIC
BALTIC COMMANDO
FLAMES OVER PROVENCE
THE MELBOURNE VIRUS

BLITZ HARVEST

Peter Leslie

This first world edition published in Great Britain 1999 by
SEVERN HOUSE PUBLISHERS LTD of
9–15 High Street, Sutton, Surrey SM1 1DF.
This first world edition published in the U.S.A. 1999 by
SEVERN HOUSE PUBLISHERS INC of
595 Madison Avenue, New York, N.Y. 10022.

British Library Cataloguing in Publication Data

Leslie, Peter
        Blitz harvest
        1. Suspense fiction
        I. Title
        823.9'14 [F]

        ISBN 0-7278-5440-2

Typeset by Palimpsest Book Production Ltd.,
Polmont, Stirlingshire, Scotland.
Printed and bound in Great Britain by
MPG Books Ltd, Bodmin, Cornwall

Author's Note

Internment is a weapon used by governments in wartime to protect their own citizens against the actions of residents or foreigners sympathetic to the enemy. After the 'Fifth Column' scares provoked by 'Quisling' traitors involved in the fall of Norway, the British Government, as it had in 1914, decided under Article 18B of the Defence Regulations to sequester potential security risks, members of the British Union of Fascists and others considered likely to assist the enemy. Three major and several minor camps, mainly of existing built-up property, were requisitioned in the Isle of Man through which many thousands of internees passed at various times between 1940 and 1945. Refugees from Europe were also detained there until they could satisfy the tribunals that they were not Nazi spies infiltrated undercover from the occupied countries.

Such geographical, geological, urban or domestic details as correctly described in this reconstruction are reproduced by kind permission of Manx National Heritage. Inadvertent inaccuracies and fictional variations are of course the author's own.

Special thanks for valuable information are due to Ms Andrea Roberts, Library Assistant of the Manx Museum in Douglas, Isle of Man, and Ms Cathy Stanley of Lloyds Bank Offshore Centre in Douglas.

Prologue

Secret Entry

Nicholas Hart had been flat on his face, crawling through the stifling dark of the tunnel for more than an hour, before the first roof-fall blocked his way. His eyes had grown used to the aching and total absence of light; the illusory kaleidoscope of brightly coloured spots transmitted to the optic nerve from his retinas had long since subsided. Protestingly, his body had accustomed itself to the coffin-like dimensions of the passageway. Even his groping hands no longer flinched away from the unseen creatures scuttling across his flesh. But now he could go no further.

The first puff of damp air against his cheek had been followed at once by the sliding, soft thump of the fall. His outstretched fingers burrowed immediately into the obstruction now blocking the blackness ahead. He lay listening to the hoarse bellows of his own breathing and the small ticking sounds of earth and gravel pattering down on to his wrists.

Hart twisted his head. The tunnel was only eighteen inches high and so narrow that it required a tremendous effort to get his arms back to his sides once they had been stretched ahead. And stretched they must continually be, for the tunnel had been pierced through hard sand criss-crossed by seams of prehistoric alluvial gravel and there was always a certain amount of spill to shovel away behind him before he could proceed. Even a small subsidence directly overhead could bury him alive – and if the fall that narrowly missed him was more than two or three feet thick, the escape would be out of the question anyway: there was no room to turn round and the exertions of backing out more than a hundred yards would almost certainly cause another fall behind him. Apart from which there would no longer be any means of getting the spill out of the way.

It was a crazy idea anyway, the whole operation. Whoever heard of a clandestine agent tunnelling his way *into* a bloody prison camp! And what chance did the agent have of getting away with it when the prisoner he was supposed to spring didn't even have a clue that he was coming?

He rolled over on to his left side until his right shoulder was jammed against the tunnel roof, then forced his right arm down to pluck the flat wooden scoop from the hip pocket of his overalls. Inching the hand back against the coarse sand of the wall, he stretched out once more and began to scrape away at the slope of rubble in the darkness ahead. When he had dragged the scoop towards his face three or four times, he transferred it to his left hand and rolled laboriously over again, shoving the sand and earth down the length of his body with his right. With total lack of vision and no idea how far ahead the fall was blocking his progress, it was despairingly nerve-wracking work.

By the time he'd executed the manoeuvre a dozen times and had scrabbled the soft, friable spill further back still with his feet, Hart was drenched in perspiration. The overalls he wore to protect his prison clothes made him unbearably hot. The limited air in the tunnel was dank and foul, and his own body effectively cut off the entry of more from outside. With the reduction of oxygen and the exertion of working in so confined a space, his overtaxed lungs were soon pumping at twice their normal rate. He lay listening to the blood thundering in his ears as the sweat rolled down between his shoulder blades and soaked into the garments around his waist.

Almost weeping with frustration, he was agonisingly aware of the ever-present spectre of claustrophobia and the panic situation it could provoke. His shoulders ached abominably. His pulse rate was ridiculous and he felt deathly sick. For an instant he lowered his cheek to the cold floor of the tunnel and tried to steel his nerves.

Only ten feet above him there were bricks and mortar, perhaps roots and then stems and leaves already. And above the leaves was the night sky, scattered with stars. There had been a cool breeze blowing off the sea when they lowered him into the tunnel, floating the sounds of the guards' voices across the compound. Could he be under the wire yet? Were the stalks above trodden flat by military boots?

Only ten feet . . . but how many tons of sand and gravel could you get into ten feet? Hart's lips twisted into a grin. Depended on the area, of course. Simple maths . . . though figures had never been his thing. Surely that couldn't be the tramping of feet he could hear? No, of course not! Be your age, man. The blood, trying to force its way through your own arteries and veins. Poor bloody blood: trapped in a tunnel, just the way he was! Hey, that wasn't bad: bloody blood. Trust Nick Hart, always ready with the snappy catchphrase!

Consciously, he tried to still the onset of . . . what? Hysteria? Some kind of psycho-intoxication? Was it the blood, though? Could it be the outflow? The tunnel was charted not too far from an underground drainage stream for some yards beneath the camp perimeter. The current wasn't exactly in the Amazon class, fanning thinly over the sandy beach on its way to the sea where it emerged not far from the tunnel entrance, but he had always thought they were running a risk, going that close. He had of course been overruled ("Not your show, old boy. Leave it to the professionals, eh?"). But he had in fact never heard the running of water when they were digging the thing. But there were lights then, so he might not have noticed. This eternal darkness exaggerated everything! It would be just his luck if the damned stream burst through to flood and drown—

Steady! Hart told himself. Hold on, there! Breathing hard, he resumed his shovelling.

Ten minutes later, he unbuttoned the cuff of his overalls, pushed up his left sleeve, and looked at the luminous dial of a watch strapped far up his forearm, near the elbow. The phosphorescent figures swam vividly into his view, big as the face of a church clock in the Stygian black, almost blinding him with their relative brilliance. The hands stood at eight-forty. Smothering a curse, Hart began frantically to dig again. "Finger out – or we'll be late for the party," he muttered aloud.

The trite phrases, strangely comforting in the walled silence of the unseen tunnel, calmed his nerves. Panting, he scraped and pushed and spilled, rolled back and shovelled again as his breath grew shallower and faster, his body hotter and wetter. It was a risk, carrying the watch at all, Webster, his control, had told him severely. But Hart had felt able to insist. As long as it wasn't immediately visible, it was a risk that had to be taken, for timing was the essence of the plan. If he wasn't out of the tunnel within a half-hour either way – at any rate before the bloody camp concert ended – he might as well abandon any hope of contacting the man he was briefed to get out of there. And no contact meant no escape. Mission aborted – and all hell to pay!

Lamplighters working for Webster had constructed the tunnel – anonymous professionals entrusted with such preliminary intelligence work as stakeouts, video surveillance, the bugging of sensitive premises, provision of safe houses and secure transport. Everything that must be one hundred percent spot on before the man in the field enters the red sector.

The route ran beneath the camp buildings, then for thirty yards underneath an open space used as a barrack square for roll-calls, addresses by the commandant and certain permitted leisure activities. A quarter of its length – the part nearest the stream – had modified an abandoned warren or badger's earth, where the animal burrowers had selected subsoils easy enough to excavate but dense enough to withstand pressure. The final exit – or entry for the inmate destined to escape – was concealed in a shrubbery of rhododendrons and spotted laurel.

The last couple of feet, mainly soft sand, had been left for Hart to scrape away.

He had been with the lamplighters when work on the tunnel started. They had located the old earth easily enough, but it had taken them three weeks to enlarge and strengthen it even this much . . . and still there were no props and no roof supports at all. It had been hell, too, to dispose of the spill virtually under the eyes of the perimeter guards.

Lack of props had worried Hart less than lack of light the first time he had crawled into the uncompleted tunnel. But this time Webster had been adamant. "Be a bad show, psychologically," he said, "having the place lit up like a fairground. Only underline the claustrophobic element once you're on your tod in there. Besides, think of the risk if one of the guards—"

"But they're using a bloody lamp to dig the tunnel!" Hart had protested. "A fucking great bulb on the end of a spool of flex, for God's sake!"

"Yes, old boy. But we're working in daylight, aren't we? Don't forget your show will be after dark. You don't want some unexpected gleam or other to stick the buggers on to you. Remember, the contact who wised us up on the old earth hasn't been near the site since the buildings were put up. You never know what could have happened since."

"You mean . . . ?"

"I mean stoats, weasels, water rats, bloody rabbits even – anything could have dug down into the old earth and make a crack that would let out the light."

"Yes, but surely—"

"Could be so small that you'd miss it from inside," Webster interrupted. "But the bloody guards would notice it if they saw a

chink of light under their feet, wouldn't they?" He shook his head.
"Sorry, old lad: it's no go."
"Couldn't I crawl up almost to the exit in daylight, using a lamp,
than wait until it was dark to dig my way out?"
"What? Wait three hours in that drainpipe without moving? You'd
go off your perishing rocker! Apaft from which, I doubt if the air
would last that long . . ."
And so Hart had no light after all.
But he was blocked, he did feel claustrophobic, he felt as if he
was going off his perishing rocker just the same! Here he was, only
halfway through, and the roof had fallen in . . .
He dragged up his sleeve again. Twelve minutes had passed and
the wall of earth blocking his way seemed as solid as ever. Hart
began to despair. If there had been only the smallest, tiniest glow,
anything to indicate what he was up against . . .
The fear was no longer of failure, of the mission abandoned; it
was now a sickly, gut-wrenching terror that he was never going to
get out of the fucking tunnel alive, mission or no sodding mission!
He groaned, choking off the sound in his throat. There was a
ringing in his ears. The cramped and agonising movements of his
arms had become automatic. He was aware now only of the cold,
dark pressure of the earth around and above him, relentless and
forbidding.
And of a cold, light pressure on the hot and tingling skin of
his face.
There was a current of air cooling his wrist; his groping fingers
touched nothing.
A quarter of an hour later, he began worming his way forward
again into the dark.
For the third time Hart glanced at the watch face. The hazard
was passed, but in a sense he was only back where he started: the
situation had changed from hopeless to merely desperate. He was
still entombed beneath thouands of tons of earth, the discovery of
his exit menaced by men with guns, his race against time threatened
by the possibility of further falls. The glowing figures represented
his sole link with sanity . . . but they also underlined the difficulty
of his position, for it was now ten past nine. And if he wasn't clear
of the tunnel by a quarter to ten . . .
Once more he steeled himself to think of nothing but the few
dark inches immediately ahead, nothing but the next shift of knee
and hip and elbow.
The air had suddenly become moister and there was a dank smell

overpowering the pervasive odour of drains that had for the past few minutes been manifesting itself. The floor of the tunnel dipped unexpectedly downwards and its surface grew wet. There was, too, a subdued drumming, a distant vibration competing with the pulsing of blood in his ears. He must be lined up with the stream, approaching the further line of perimeter wire with its guard dogs and its gun tower and its searchlights.

It was when the drumming was at its loudest that the roof collapsed for the second time.

Hart was half-smothered in damp earth and sand. There was a weight across the small of his back, his legs were buried and his mouth and nose were full of dust. Choking, he struck out like a swimmer in a nightmare, flailing his arms through motionless waves.

When the initial panic subsided, he realised the fall was not as bad as he feared. Most of it had landed behind his knees, and one hand was already through the obstruction, beating at the space in the tunnel beyond. Forcing a passage for the other, he clawed aside the fallen earth and dragged his body painfully forward, squirming from side to side to dislodge the debris from his back. A few minutes later he was in the clear once more, negotiating the sudden sharp curve in the passageway that signalled his perilous odyssey must almost be over.

He bared his sweating arm and looked at the watch. It was almost nine-thirty.

He should have been out in the open before now. But there was still a chance, there were only a few more yards to go. If luck was with him . . . if the plan of the camp was accurate . . . if nobody saw him cross the open ground . . . if the damned concert hadn't ended ahead of schedule and the planned electricity cut coincided with his exit and covered his approach . . .

If . . .

Hart had been to the very end of the tunnel once before, the day the lamplighters had completed it. He had actually seen the daylight streaming like a blessing over the sand barrier he would have to sweep aside before he emerged. But he hadn't dared peer through the screen of leaves beyond. Even operatives in the red sector must resist the urge to tempt providence!

This time, though, he was going to make it. And the relief would be the keener for having been deferred.

As he hauled himself up the steep incline leading to the exit, he forced himself to slow down, fearful that the gasp of his lungs dragging at the fresh air might give him away to a passing guard.

With streaming eyes, he shouldered his way past the sandy ridge, over the crumbling edges of the hole, and crashed out among the bushes hiding it.

Christ, he was *out*!

Hart was drunk with the sheer effect of space. The sweet, cool, moist night-air whistled past his cracked lips. The stars wheeled about his head. The distant roar of waves, the sound of music and boisterous laughter from a building on the far side of the compound, charmed his ears. In his nostrils there was the scent of leaves and of sap and of green things growing. He was trembling all over and it was nine forty-three.

Overhead lights, flooding the compound with brilliance, died. The masked lamps faded, turned momentarily orange, vanished in the sudden dark. Hart shivered, fancying himself for an instant back in the tunnel.

Then the stars pricked out the sky. There was a chorus of groans, shouts and laughter from the building where the concert was being held. The music dissolved into silence.

Branches creaked. Leaves rustled. The one Englishman in the camp who knew Hart was coming materialised at his side. Brass buttons gleamed in the gloom. Against the night sky, the tall, domed silhouette of a policeman's helmet manifested itself.

"Good show," the newcomer murmured. "We have two and a half minutes before they're due the Anthem and the audience streams out to get home before Lights Out. Follow me and I'll put you next to your bird. He skipped the concert. Don't blame him, it was bloody Wagner. You'll find him third hut on your left . . . but after that you're on your jack."

"Fine," Hart replied. "Full speed ahead. Talking of Lights Out, how long before the compound illuminations come on again?"

"Six minutes minimum, eight maximum, according to the saboteurs."

"We're on our way," Hart said. "One bird flies into the cage, two fly out. Wacko!" He followed the contact out of the shrubbery and across the dark, deserted compound.

9

Part One

Genesis of a Spy

One

"Build a tunnel to get myself *into* a concentration camp, sir?" Nicholas Hart had repeated in astonishment some weeks before in London. "Surely you can't be serious?"

The Special Services colonel on the other side of the desk had smiled faintly. "Not precisely a *concentration* camp actually," he replied. "Internment is perhaps the better word. But this is something of a one-off job: nothing is quite what it seems."

He was young for a colonel – a dark, handsome man with a sensitive face and hair touched with grey over the ears. He didn't look like an army officer at all, especially an officer connected with cloak-and-dagger activity. More like a don at one of the more go-ahead universities. Or maybe an art critic, the owner of an antiques shop, or one of the more superior journalists. He had in fact been a research chemist before the war.

But then nothing about this rather odd unit overlooking Regent's Park was what it seemed. Hart, a captain in the Oxford and Buckinghamshire Light Infantry, had expected to find himself in some seedy office around the corner from Whitehall when he was urgently called away from his comfortable posting in Northern Ireland, told he was seconded to Special Services, hurried to a Dakota transport at RAF Aldergrove and passed to a dispatch rider at Heston later that morning. Now here he was in a pleasant library on the first floor of Cumberland Terrace – a lofty room whose bowed Nash windows, criss-crossed with anti-blast adhesive, framed a view of grassy slopes bordered by trees whose branches were already misted with Spring green. Although the day was quite mild, a real fire crackled in the grate. A white fur rug was spread in front of the hearth, and comfortable leather chairs stood around a low table strewed with magazines. More like a Harley Street specialist's waiting room than a Duty Officer's den, Hart thought when he was ushered in.

The colonel, it was true, sat behind a desk, but the only publication on it was a copy of *The Studio*, and there was neither a file nor a filing cabinet to be seen.

Hart had no idea why he was there. The rakish lieutenant-colonel with green Intelligence flashes, who had dined him at Belfast's Grand Central Hotel the previous evening, had told him only that he possessed one – no, two – attributes that nobody but he in the whole wide world could claim. Attributes that made him, and only him, tailor-made for a particular, important show.

Intriguing, but the lieutenant-colonel refused point-blank to reveal what these attributes were. "Best left to the johnnies who'll be briefing you, old lad," he had said. "Only set all the wrong hares running if I was to let on. It's kind of a special do: much the best if you approach it with an open mind, what!"

The colonel in Regent's Park, whose name was Adam Nichols, seemed no more eager than this first contact to reveal the secret. The first thing he said, after they had shaken hands – itself something of a break with tradition, Hart thought – was: "So far as your personal file is concerned, the most important item I can recall at the moment is that you prefer vodka to gin. Is that so?"

"Er – yes, sir," Hart replied. "If that's possible."

"Anything is *possible*," said Nichols. "Most of our work consists in proving this when previous estimations had considered success unlikely. So far as vodka is concerned, fortunately some rather good stuff came my way recently. One of my chaps just back from Warsaw." Another smile. "Having this kind of show to run does have its advantages from time to time. What do you like with it? Lime? Tonic?"

"Just ice, sir, thank you," Hart said, wondering again precisely what kind of show it was that he was to be involved in. Whatever it was, it was going to be a sight different from his work in the sleepy country town of Antrim – explaining to his fast-paced conscripts the finer points of the infantry training manual in the rough country among the Sperrin Mountains on the far side of Ulster's Lough Neagh.

Nichols had pressed a switch on a small bakelite box sitting at one end of his desk. "Mason," he said into a grille at one side of the device, "a large vodka and ice for my guest. The usual for me."

"Very good, sir," a tinny voice had said from within the box. And a few minutes later Hart had found himself grasping a wide, low glass of heavy Waterford crystal filled with the most generous measure of vodka he had ever seen, while his new CO began explaining some of the background underlying this new and mysterious posting.

"I'm not going to bore you with details, Hart," Nichols began. "But we do still have agents in the Reich – and according to some

14

Blitz Harvest

of these bods, something rather, well, discomforting seems about to break here in the home country."

"Not for the first time," Hart said. "You mean stepped-up raids? Gas attacks? One of these much trumpeted 'secret weapons' of Hitler's?"

"No." Nichols held up his glass and scrutinised the afternoon sunlight slanting through the whisky it contained. Beyond the window, Hart could see a YMCA mobile canteen serving tea to the crew of a sandbagged anti-aircraft gunsite in the park. "More in the line of Fifth Column activity," the colonel continued, transferring his gaze back to his visitor. "But something that could prove to be deuced damaging for the war effort as a whole."

"Propaganda, sir? Disinformation?"

"Something much more positive – or negative for us. *Information* to be precise."

Hart sipped his vodka and waited. He supposed something factual would emerge eventually.

Nichols drank, replacing his tumbler carefully on the chased-leather top of his desk. "In a nutshell," he said, "it seems – despite all the sweeps and the rolling up of supposed Nazi sympathisers here – that there still exists in this country a ring, a network of 'sleeper' agents, installed by German Intelligence long before the war, equipped with unimpeachable cover identities, genuine businesses and jobs, and instructions never, ever to show any interest in, or enthusiasm for Hitler, National Socialism or Germany in general. They have been accepted, these . . . people . . . as normal, ordinary citizens or legal foreign residents, showing no interest in politics or international ructions. Their job has been to lie low, keep their noses clean – and wait for the big one, whenever that happens to arrive."

"Very efficient, very thorough," Hart commented. "Very Teutonic. And the big one . . . ?"

"Well of course it could have been after the Battle of Britain in 1940 – if we hadn't won that one and Germany continued with Operation Sea Lion and invaded. But at this moment in time, naturally, it has to be the Second Front."

"I see."

"I very much doubt it," Nichols said with a pleasant smile. He drank again.

"Yes, sir."

"You know, of course," Nichols said, "that Stalin has been bellowing at us for months to open this so-called Second Front

15

and draw German troops west to relieve pressure on Soviet forces in the Ukraine. You know, everybody knows, that the only feasible second front available to us is a seaborne invasion of the European mainland."

"Yes, sir."

"And you know, we all know, rather better than the man in the street, what colossal problems of logistics, of transport, of arms concentrations and exercises and planning such an operation has to involve."

Hart nodded. The colonel continued: "At least a year's evaluation of the options open to such planners is required before consideration of the forces and the means to be employed is even put on the agenda. Once it is on, you can add another six months before a believable invasion force exists even on paper."

"Yes, sir, indeed. I can imagine." Another sip. The vodka really was exceedingly good. It was the Polish Wyborowska brand, flavoured with a particular long grass esteemed by buffalo on the great central plain. The YMCA canteen had disappeared in the direction of a barrage balloon site on the far side of the slope.

Colonel Nichols grinned. He drank whisky. "Not to worry, Captain Hart. The point of this rigmarole is finally at hand!"

Hart thought it best to say nothing.

Nichols said: "So this, the planning stage, is the big one. And according to our information, the ring of secret sleepers is to be activated specifically to gather information – any and all information possible – on these preparations for the invasion. I know you're not an I-Corps type, but you must be aware of the spooks' credo: that every slightest, tiniest detail, perhaps insignificant in itself, can combine with all the other apparently insignificant details to furnish a global, collated picture that's . . . well, panoramic. If these unknown sleepers all over the country, note every smallest troop movement, each senior transfer, all rail and air freight manifests – even a change in the calibre of ammunition ordered from a particular factory – this can help with the composition of the plot's final aim: a blueprint of the invasion scheme delivered to Berlin by intelligence analysts before the first landing craft even leaves port!"

Hart opened his mouth to comment, but the colonel held up a restraining hand before he could speak. "Time now," Nichols said crisply, "to cut to Scene Two. You will have been told, I imagine, that you are the possessor of two advantages which fit you, more than anyone else in the entire world, for a role in this scenario?"

"Just that," Hart said. "And not a single bloody phrase more!"

Nichols laughed. "Somebody – for once – was obeying orders!" He pressed the button on his intercom and said: "The same again, please, Mason," then turned back to Hart. "The first of these . . . talents . . . is that you speak perfect German – with a Bavarian accent. Right?"

"Well, yes, I suppose so," Hart said. "As a geologist and cartographer in civil life, I happened to live for three years in the mid-thirties in Munich – part of an international survey mapping parts of the Zugspitze foothills."

"Quite. Now I could probably find a dozen other blokes who spoke kraut with a Bavarian accent if I rooted about long enough among the brutal and licentious soldiery here. But how many could I find who combined this with your second, more important attribute?"

"Which is?" Hart demanded, intrigued now in spite of himself.

"This," Nichols said. He slid open a drawer of the desk, took out a cabinet-size photograph, and handed it across to Hart.

Hart scanned the print. A snapshot portrait, head and shoulders, enlarged, a little grainy. He was looking at his own face, ruminative, snowcapped mountain crests in the distance.

He studied the photo again. His square chin, wide, well-defined lips, nose a little prominent, eyes slitted against the sunlight below thick brows and the thatch of pale hair.

"Funny," he said. "I don't remember this being taken. No recollection at all. I don't recognise the peaks behind. And as far as I recall, I never had a jacket with a leather collar like that when I was in Munich."

"That doesn't surprise me at all," Nichols said. "The picture isn't of you. The subject is a man known as Axel Hunzinger. He is a Nazi spy. And it was he who organised and installed the secret sleeper network here of which I have been talking."

17

Two

"**B**ut that's incredible!" Hart exclaimed. "I mean . . . well, astounding."

"It *is* remarkable," Colonel Nichols agreed.

"I could understand somebody else – even someone who knew me well – mistaking this for me," Hart said, gazing at the photo. "But, Christ, I *myself*, even now can't believe it's *not* me! Dammit, I can practically recall what I was thinking from the expression on my . . . on this . . . face!"

"That is precisely why you, and only you, can be so helpful to us." Nichols held out his hand, took the photo, and replaced it in the drawer.

Hart said: "I suppose, in some way or other, you want me to take this merchant's place. Is that it?"

"On the contrary, we want you to help him re-establish his own place," Nichols replied.

Hart stared at him.

"Before I explain that, I'd better fill you in on the how and the why," said the colonel.

"It might be a help!" Thankfully, Hart accepted a second vodka from a white-jacketed orderly and settled back in one of the leather chairs.

"The powers-that-be are convinced that this fellow Hunzinger would, at this moment, be activating his sleeper ring," Nichols told him. "If he was in a position to do so."

"And he's not? Where is he then?"

"He's here. That is to say he's in the UK. Unfortunately the security people were too efficient when the balloon went up, and they nabbed him along with all the Nazi sympathisers, members of the British Union of Fascists, folk with foreign-sounding names and suchlike. Together with the so-called enemy aliens and Mosleyites – and Sir Oswald himself for that matter – Hunzinger is at the moment incarcerated as a security risk in the 18B internment camp on the

Isle of Man. Counter-intelligence would be happier if he was out of it and free to roam around."

"You mean . . . free to contact these sleeper johnnies and put them to work?"

"Exactly."

"So the boys in blue could round them up once they'd been identified – and before they could start furnishing Adolf with all your apparently insignificant details?"

"That's right."

Hart smiled. "But you *don't* want me to take the blighter's place in the camp . . . which is obviously the first jape that springs to mind?"

Nichols pushed back his swivel chair and rose to his feet. He was quite tall and sparely built. He strolled to the window and stood with his back to Hart, staring at the shadows of trees now lengthening across the grassy slope. "The trouble, of course," he said, "is that Hunzinger is *not* free to roam around. And there's no way of freeing him that we can think of that wouldn't instantly cause him to smell a rat. Quite a few of the people with funny names have in fact been released from the camp after thorough screening; many of them have joined the British forces. But pardons, sorry-chum-our-mistake and that kind of caper would never work in Hunziger's case: he simply wouldn't wear it. The man's a skilful, experienced agent after all. He'd simply accept the freedom and lie low, steering well clear of the sleepers."

"Who would do what?"

"Presumably be activated by Berlin. There must be a control or a cut-out somewhere that we don't know about. It's only if Hunzinger does it himself that we can roll up the ring. Because we do know about him – and if he *didn't* suspect a set-up, genuinely felt the coast was clear, he could be kept under very discreet surveillance and every contact he made duly logged."

"In fact you're stuck for a plausible reason to have him sprung?"

Nichols took a short pipe and a tobacco pouch from his jacket pocket and began filling the bowl with a practised thumb. "Actually," he said, "we think we've found one."

Hart frowned. "Well, that's good. But . . . ?"

Nichols produced a box of Swan vestas, struck a match and held the flame to his pipe. "Nothing," he said, puffing smoke, "that originates . . . or seems to originate . . . or could even remotely be suspected to stem from any British, Allied or even neutral source . . . would be of the slightest use. Not the slightest. We are all agreed that there's only one approach that would have a respectable chance of success with our man."

"And that is?"

Nichols swung around to face into the room. "Hunzinger must be sprung from the camp illegally," he said. "And the springing must be done – or he must absolutely and firmly believe it to be done – by his own people. By agents, that is to say, of one of the Nazis' own intelligence services. With the precise aim of ensuring that he is able to activate his ring."

Hart's face registered astonishment once more. "I say, that's a bit of a tall order, isn't it?" he observed mildly. "I mean how can you possibly—?"

"Fake it, you mean? Because obviously we can't do it for real? Not so tall, really." Smoke plumed upwards in the direction of the high ceiling. "Not when you have the escaping prisoner's own brother on hand to plan and organise the break."

"His own *brother*?" Hart's jaw had dropped. "What on earth are you saying—?"

"His twin brother," Nichols said. He swept an arm towards Hart in a theatrical gesture. "Meet Zoltan Hunzinger of the Third Reich Foreign Intelligence Service," he declaimed.

Three

"Not as far-fetched as you might think, Hart," Adam Nichols said. The young captain had been rendered speechless by his announcement. "Hunzinger does have a twin brother. But the two haven't met since they were seven years old. They were born in Munich but the family split up at the end of the First World War – Dad remaining in Germany with Axel and *Mutti* emigrating to Australia with Zoltan and her down-under boyfriend."

"OK," Hart said. "But even so . . . I mean how in the world could I possibly . . . ?"

"You miss the point," Nichols said. "Axel knows he has a twin brother. With the extraordinary coincidence of this unfakeable resemblance, and in his present situation, he has no earthly reason to think you're *not* that brother. I mean it's not as though you'd be rigged up with some tricky disguise or cosmetic surgery. By some genetic accident you *are* as damned well alike as two peas in a bloody pod! We've a lot more evidence than that photo – most of it on film – to prove it."

"Very well. But even so . . ."

"A great deal of material has been amassed. An enormous dossier. You're going to school for a month, Hart, to live breathe and sleep Zoltan's first seven years – plus the life in Australia afterwards. Axel, don't forget, doesn't *know* anything about this. He doesn't know as much as we do; the two have never been in touch. He can't fault you on facts because by the time you meet you will in fact know a sight more about Zoltan's life than he does!"

Hart, who had been pacing agitatedly left and right since the colonel's original revelation, sank bank into one of the leather chairs. "I'm sorry, sir," he said, "but I think perhaps I need another drink, although the sun's still high over the yard-arm! I'm sure you have a lot more to tell me."

"You can say that again!" Nichols turned back to his box. "Mason – once more with feeling!"

"Right away, sir," the box quacked. Mason, a suave sixty, glided in

21

with a tray, distributed the drinks, collected the empties and vanished as silently as he had appeared.

The colonel abandoned his desk and took a chair beside Hart. He laid his pipe in an ashtray. Blue smoke hazing the big room drifted in layers towards the sunlit window. "Before I start a run-down in detail," Nichols said, "I'm aware that you must be seething with questions. So let me short cut some of them by dealing with objections before you raise them." He leaned back in the chair. "The most important, of course, is the basic premise – that he'll accept you. Well, there you'll simply have to take my word for it. And the word of all the shrinks and backroom boys who've been working on the idea." He drank whisky, picked up the pipe again. "When, looking the way you do, you turn up with a believable story relating to his present situation and his undercover work, no man, however suspicious by nature, could dream up a scenario more plausible to explain your appearance. At that time; at that place. Are you with me?"

"I suppose so, sir." Hart still sounded dubious. "But what *is* my – er – scenario? Why am I there? What am I doing in England? How do I know he's in the Isle of Man?"

"That's all taken care of. Part of the dossier. Your cover's been extensively worked out. In brief, you yourself have been sprung from an aliens' internment camp in the outback and spirited here by German intelligence – precisely with the idea of persuading him to quit the camp and let you help him activate the sleepers."

"They know about the twin brother thing, then?"

"They know everything," Nichols smiled. "Or so Axel will believe in the circumstances!"

"No, but . . . I mean, you're not actually latching on to a genuine, *existing* plan dreamed up by the Nazi intelligence wizards?"

"Of course not. Even we have our limits! But it seemed the most satisfactory way to explain your appearance – like a demon king in a pantomime – after more than thirty years. And to convince him he should follow you out of the camp."

"You say follow me out. You already said quit the camp. I assume the details of that form part of this dossier you keep quoting? I mean, I can't just show up at the main gate, announce myself as his long-lost brother, and say 'What about taking a stroll to the mainland'?"

Nichols nodded. "The dossier, as you say." And it was then that he revealed the plan to construct the tunnel – so that 'Zoltan' could get in and, as fast as possible, the two brothers get out.

It took a while to overcome the young officer's incredulity. A little longer to persuade him that the idea was even valid. Mason had been summoned yet again when at last Hart said: "I hope you're not expecting me to dig the bloody thing myself!"

"No, no. Hitler's overseas handymen will do that for you. Or so Axel will think. In fact it will be done well in advance by ours. We'll shunt you in a couple of times while they're working on it, so you'll know the form and could believably have been involved."

"How is this camp organised? The usual POW-type hutments and all that?"

"Very oddly, as it happens." The colonel's pipe had gone out. He cradled his glass in both hands and leaned back again, crossing his legs. Rather loud red-and-blue checked socks below the immaculate uniform trousers, Hart observed. "There was a camp there in the fourteen-eighteen," Nichols said. "Place called Knockaloe, on a stretch of moorland in the middle of the island. Hutments and so on, as you say. But it's a very different story this time. Perhaps because they were in more of a hurry, Fifth Column alarms and so on. Maybe because it was more urgent and more security risks were involved. I don't know. Anyway, this time our masters made use of existing property, most of it in built-up areas, some of it actually in town centres."

"Good Lord! Do you mean to say . . . ?"

"One tends to say 'The internment camp on the Isle of Man', but there are at least three main sites and several offshoots. There's one at Peel, a small fishing village on the west coast, another at Port Erin – bottom left-hand corner of the map, as it were. And here, the entire peninsula has been cut off – with barbed wire, watchtowers and all – from the main part of the island. This is mainly where women internees are held."

"Which is the one I have to fish my brother out of?" Hart asked.

"The main one. In Douglas, the capital. Once the 18B regulation was enforced, the government requisitioned and wired off half the seafront promenade to house and feed those whose loyalty was thought to be less to King and country than even further overseas!"

"So the camp's actually incorporated in the existing town?"

"Yes. Sounds crazy, doesn't it? Looks pretty odd too, as I say. All those long and dreary lines of terraced grey boarding-houses called 'Sea View' and 'Mon Repos' with gimlet-eyed landladies, ketchup on the tables and cardboard signs in the window announcing *Vacancies!*"

"No vacancies now, I guess!" Hart said.

"No. Quite a number of the 18B's have in fact been released –

23

it was sufficient at the start to have a Berg, a Stein or a Mann in the name to get nabbed – but it's still pretty well a house-full. Very strange sight too. Halfway along the prom this great double wall of barbed wire; in some places the roadway itself is cut in two laterally, wired straight along the middle to keep people away from the beach. Some of the garden squares behind are partitioned that way too. But the oddest thing of all is that the landladies of half the boarding houses have been retained in place, paid by His Majesty's government to feed the inmates as if they were bloody holidaymakers!"

"They'd probably be better off, gastronomically, if they really were in a POW camp," Hart said sourly. "But you're telling me – you are actually saying that this is where you plan to dig a *tunnel* – under a concrete and macadam esplanade, through brickwork and cellars and past gas and electricity and drainage conduits? I said before: surely you have to be joking!"

"Only the first part is beneath buildings," Nichols said mildly. "The place has been well surveyed, I promise you. The promenade is quite high up. The entrance is beneath it, and the beach is out of bounds to the general public there anyway. Municipal 'works' can cover a multitude of intelligence sins. After the first line of houses, the tunnel will run beneath a square – an old public garden turned into a compound. You'll even find your hutments there between the Victorian terraces if you look hard enough. Right now, Axel – maximum security, you see – is lodged in one of them according to the latest reports."

"I wouldn't expect to spend too much time looking," Hart said. "So assuming I get the bugger out, what's the form after that? On second thoughts, that seems an even tougher nut to crack!"

"Details can wait, but this is one case where – so far as your relations with Axel are concerned – you play it entirely by ear. It would be idiotic for us to lay down hard and fast rules when we haven't the faintest idea how he's going to react to you. You help him as much as you can, secretly taking note of the individual sleepers as and when they are contacted."

"And helping you?"

"An absolutely zero profile – for the moment at any rate. Don't call us; we'll call you! If necessary it can wait until you have dossiers on the whole network."

"Right. But you say details can wait," Hart objected. "There's one detail, though – perhaps the most vital – that I must have a ruling on straight away. Before I even start thinking about the job."

"Let's have it, then. That's what this meeting is for."

"Help him as much as you can, you say. Take details of the sleepers. This presumably means we shall be gadding about all over the shop. The two of us. Right?"

Nichols nodded. "Naturally. Or that's what we hope."

"Well, how?"

"How?"

"In what manner, sir? Wartime England isn't like Nazi territory, with identity checks on every street corner. Even so, security is pretty tight – especially if anything rum appears. And here you have two bods as alike as . . . well, identical twins . . . roaming the bally country. Why? What are we *supposed* to be doing? As far as the constabulary, military police, wardens and suchlike are concerned. Who am I to them? What am I doing? Why aren't I in uniform? I imagine they won't be in on your little charade?"

"Certainly not. The more people who are, the greater the risks of a leak. Obviously. The mission revolves around a very tight nucleus: myself, my intelligence chief, your control – and of course the lamplighters concerned with the tunnel." Nichols began reloading his pipe. He smiled. "So far as general avoidance of the law is concerned, ask advice from your brother – he's an expert! He did in fact have a genuine business here before the balloon went up. Import-export, somewhere in South Wales. Camera parts, especially lenses, I believe."

"From Germany and Japan, of course?"

"Where else? He'll be able to look after himself, if you ask me. If not, kraut intelligence – which is to say us – will have provided you with stuff to cover him."

"Yes, but even if he's one hundred per, who the hell's his buddy? Am I supposed actually to be his twin brother, *really* just arrived from Australia?"

"No way." The colonel struck a match and sucked in smoke. "That would, I agree, be pretty rum! The first time your identity card was asked for, the law would probably call in counter-intelligence. Be a turn-up for the books if *you* were booked as a suspected foreign spy!"

"Very droll," Hart said. "So what does A do?"

"There we – and you – are fortunate. This double identity bit can cut two ways. The spin of the coin, you know. And every coin has two faces. If you can pass for Axel, evidently Axel could pass for you, right?"

"Well, yes, of course. I mean I suppose so. But . . . ?"

25

"And, despite what you said, you will in fact be in uniform."
Hart looked astonished. "I will?"

"Certainly. We – and therefore supposedly Nazi intelligence – have found the perfect cover for you." Nichols paused, shook out his match, dropped it in an ashtray, exhaled smoke. "You'll pose as – forgive me – an unimportant junior officer, in England on a course from his quiet billet in rural Ulster," he said. "Name of Captain Nicholas Hart, Oxford and Bucks Light Infantry, at present based in Antrim."

"Good *Lord!*" You're not telling me, sir, that my cover as Zoltan is my real self?" Hart laughed aloud. "During the whole of this mission I'm impersonating one Nick Hart? My God, that's really something! Not too hard to carry off, either. I see what you mean by coins. Bit of a heads-I-win-tails-you-lose situation, wouldn't you say!"

"With two extra advantages," Nichols smiled. "One – nobody can possibly claim that your papers are faked, that the cover is . . . just a cover."

"And two?"

"Well, you see, both sides of the coin again. It's certainly no sweat for you to 'pose' as young Captain Hart from Northern Ireland. But because of the likenesses, *your* identity can equally well be used as a cover by Axel Hunzinger. If a situation demanded it."

"Christ! Tweedledum and Tweedledee – Alice's predicament: no, *you're* part of *my* dream!"

"If you happen to be separated physically, there's even the possibility of there being two Captain Harts operating at the same time."

"I'd better order a second uniform at once."

"It has already been attended to. You can collect it from Gieves tomorrow afternoon."

"My God," Hart exclaimed. "You people think of everything!"

"Like PG Wodehouse's perfect butler," Nichols said, "we endeavour to give satisfaction, sir."

Four

I n Regent's Park it had been a pipe. The first impression Nick Hart registered, pushing his way through the swing doors of Belfast's Grand Central Hotel was the pervasive smell of cigar smoke. This was less because of the wealth of Ulster businessmen frequenting the restaurant there than the prevalence of American army officers, steadily increasing since the first landing of US forces in Northern Ireland in 1942.

Hart's control, Webster, was to be the same raffish lieutenant-colonel who had originally sought him out in Antrim and sent him to see Adam Nichols in London. He held no cigar or pipe, but there was a Balkan Sobranie black Russian cigarette with a gold tip between his lips when Hart found him nursing a large brandy-and-soda in the hotel's spacious lounge bar.

The Oxford and Bucks subaltern hadn't known it at the time, but Ian Lindsay Webster, DSO and Bar, MC, was something of a legend in cloak-and-dagger circles. At the time of the German breakthrough at Sedan in May, 1940, he had been a major in the Intelligence Corps, linking Lord Gort's British Expeditionary Force with the French 4th Armoured Division, led by a Colonel Charles de Gaulle. He had won the first DSO riding with one of De Gaulle's regimental commanders during the operation north of Laon that was the sole successful counterattack of the entire defensive campaign. Adrift in the chaos of Dunkirk, he had stolen a Stuka dive-bomber and flown it home for evaluation by RAF technicians. Subsequently he had played a secret part in an abortive attempt to prevent the disastrous Royal Navy attack on demilitarised French warships at Mers-el-Kebir after the fall of France. Later still he led a commando raid to sabotage powerful Nazi gun emplacements threatening submarines and surface craft passing through neutral waters south of Sweden. That had won him the Bar to his DSO.* It was rumoured that the Military Cross was

* see Peter Leslie's *The Catapult Ultimatum* and *Baltic Commando*, also published by Severn House.

the result of a discreditable one-man invasion of occupied Holland, ostensibly to survey the disposition of Wurzburg Bowls controlling the radar servicing of Luftwaffe night fighters – but an ancillary result of which was the appearance of Polish vodka and Dutch gin in Colonel Nichols's cellars. Webster in fact got results. The reverse side of his particular coin was the fact that the man was a womaniser, a hard drinker, capable if he thought fit of disrespecting orders, not following the form and turning his back on any and every kind of bullshit.

Webster, then, was an individualist, a rakehelly, buccaneering one-off type who had always played the war his own way – and, until he had been picked up by Special Services, unfailingly a headache to his traditional, form-filling regimental superiors. 'That *bloody* man Webster,' they would say. 'What in hell kind of tomfoolery has he got himself into now?'

It was perhaps to quieten down his more extreme exploits that he had been promoted to lieutenant-colonel and made controller rather than man in the field.

He was leaning back in a stuffed armchair, beneath a palm in a corner of the lounge, when Hart sought him out, the brandy balloon cradled in one hand, the exotic black and gold cigarette scissored between strong fingers of the other.

He was in mufti – a Harris tweed sports jacket with beige cavalry twill trousers, suede desert boots and what the young captain recognised as an MCC tie. He was the sort of man, Hart thought, who would undoubtedly have gone in first wicket down! A hitter, with graceful wrist play, but a man of quick decisions, able to take chances if he considered the odds favourable.

Nobody, though, could possibly have taken Webster for a civilian. The hawk face, with a strong chin, deepest eyes and a thin, dark chevron of moustache was reminiscent of such current movie adventurers as Errol Flynn, Colman, Donat, Brian Aherne and Melvyn Douglas. Nick Hart approached him with some trepidation – his reputation had gone before him, and he was clearly not the relaxed, easy going type charac-terised by Colonel Nichols – but Webster put him at ease instantly with a crisp: "My dear chap! Do sit." And an imperiously raised finger with the order: "Waiter – a large vodka and ice for my friend!"

"Did you have a good flight?" he asked once the drink had been served.

"A little bumpy," Hart admitted. "There was a Hun – a Heinkel, I think – strafing a coaster not far off the Isle of Man. Some of the ship's flak came uncomfortably close!"

"Nothing like having a close-up of your next field of operations,"

Webster enthused. He sank a large gulp of brandy. "Talking of which, we're going to be, as it were, closeted together for a month while you go back to school and Fearless Frazer here fills you in on spookery and how to seem Australian."

"Fearless Frazer?"

"My way of distancing my real self when I'm not a hundred percent certain of what the fuck I'm supposed to be doing!" Webster said genially.

"I'm sure it'll be a pleasure, sir," Hart, the amateur, said politely.

"It'll distance me from you too if you don't drop the 'sir' crap while we're working together."

Hart grinned. "Be my guest," he said.

The school turned out to be a small house rented on the outskirts of the county town of Antrim.

For the moment, Hart remained in his official billet at Hall's Hotel in the small town's main square, although the infantrymen's daily manoeuvres were now supervised by another officer. An entire hotel built for the pre-war coach-party trade, the Massereene Arms, had been requisitioned as quarters for the soldiery, and this, like Hall's next door to it, boasted a fairly new dance hall annexe built out behind it on stilts above the shallow river fording its way towards Lough Neagh.

Hart had already become attuned to certain . . . specialities . . . particular to Ulster as well as to the adjacent – and neutral – republic of Eire, still known in certain quarters as 'The Irish Free State'. Mainly because of the large Catholic population in each country, these specialities revolved around the imposition of draconian laws and regulations with severe penalties for those ignoring them – for all of which the dogmatists responsible had thoughtfully provided the (legal) means of avoidance and/or evasion.

Divorce, for instance, was forbidden to Catholics on pain of excommunication. A divorced person, 'guilty' or 'innocent' according to the lay judiciary, was not permitted to remarry. There was, however, the possibility of the annulment of an unsuccessful marriage, for which a Papal Dispensation was required. But a partnership annulled had theoretically never existed. So the parties thereto had never officially been married – therefore, logically, could not be said to be 'divorced', and were therefore free to be joined together in Holy (and legal) matrimony.

The same elasticity pertained to the matter of the (legal) consumption of alcohol. The Sabbath, both Protestants and Catholics were agreed, was the official Day of Rest. Joy must therefore be restricted and fun if possible prohibited. The serving of alcoholic beverages on Sundays was as a result forbidden by law in both countries.

With, nevertheless, certain specific exceptions. Decrees framed before the days of mechanised transport recognised that a person who had travelled on horseback from Kerry, say, to Monaghan might reasonably be in need of refreshment on arrival. He might legally, therefore, be served – even if it be during the Lord's Day. But who was 'he'? The exception must be defined.

The definition arrived at was that he must be 'a bonafide traveller'.

And what was a bonafide traveller? Simple. A person having the means of transport.

This regulation explained the exceptionally large car parks provided by Irish road-houses and country hotels and the high concentration of motor vehicles, bicycles, horses, jaunting-cars and sidecar combinations outside public houses in the towns at weekends.

It would have been simpler, as Webster confided to his pupil, to say that drinks could be served on Sundays – except to pedestrians. But this would hardly have accorded with local tradition.

His delight in the public disregard of the Sunday law was equalled only by his reaction to weekday conditions at Hall's Hotel, his drinking base.

The place boasted, apart from its upstairs dining-room, two bars and a residents' snug. The permanent residents included the local bank manager, a couple of commercials, and officers from the army, the navy, the Fleet Air Arm and the RAF at Aldergrove, where 502 Squadron, Coastal Command, was based, most of them with their families. To these every evening could be added American civilian technicians attached to a USAAF maintenance unit at Ballymena and good-time girls with men from infantry, armoured, SAS and transport units in the neighbourhood. Until the official closing time at ten o'clock, therefore, the place could be said to be jumping.

Curiously, though, although closing time had been called, very few of the customers seemed in a hurry to leave. By eleven o'clock, when the low-ceilinged rooms were thick with cigarette and cigar smoke and the roar of conversation at its height, the number of uniformed non-residents customarily exceeded the number of rooms in the hotel in a ratio of about four to one – every one of them with (at least) one glass at hand.

Occasionally – about once a week as a rule – the phone in the office beside the locked front doors would ring a little short of midnight. To the landlord, who answered, the heavily accented voice of the local Royal Ulster Constabulary superintendent would announce apologetically: "Bob, I'm sorry to be troubling you, but the high-ups are at us again: we have an order to raid you tonight."

"That's all right, Herbie. What time would you be thinking of calling round?"

"Whenever it suits you, Bob. Would a half-hour be too soon?"

"Thanks, Super. A half-hour it is."

And then, when the officer and his four or five men had been ushered into the office: "So what will it be then – a drop of the creature?"

"No thanks, Bob. No, not when we're on duty. You know."

"Sure, well take the bottle, boys – and pour yourselves one on me when you're home."

"The best, Bob. And thanks again . . . Now if maybe we was to take a wee look, eh?" And the officers in their dark uniforms would move respectfully away towards the dining-room and bars, leaving their chief with the landlord.

"Will you not be persuaded, Herbie, while the boys are busy? Just a quick one, then?"

"Well, perhaps a wee drop. Thank you kindly, Bob."

The interior of the hotel, meanwhile, had briefly been a scene of frenzied activity. The instant the knock on the door had sounded, the two potboys and Sadie, the sharp-tongued but much-loved dining-room waitress, had hurled themselves among the crowd of drinkers, snatching away glasses and vanishing behind curtains and through doorways. Many of the non-residents, unaware that this charade was traditionally played out three or four times a month, protested – some of them forcibly.

"Hey, what the hell you think you're doing?"

"Gimme back me bloody glass, boy: I hadn't finished that!"

"Jesus Christ, can't a guy even find time to—"

And Sadie's acid reproaches: "All right, sir, all *right*! You'll be getting it back for God's sake. Just sit still a minnit, you . . . 'Tis only the polis: if you'd please stay quiet . . . this one'll be on the house anyway, sir."

As the policemen entered the first bar, Sadie herself might well be lying flat on her face up the covered stairway, pushing a tray loaded with brimming glass out of sight around the corner of the landing above.

But the law knew better than to pry. The officers remained discreetly in those premises where alcoholic beverages might be expected to be consumed. If none were to be seen during their cursory inspection, they could dutifully return to the office where the sergeant would tell the superintendent: "Nothing to report, sir."

It was after all no business of his to comment on the abnormally large number of men and women sitting around doing apparently nothing in the hotel's public rooms.

Webster, who insisted that his protégé's 'schooling' should be tempered with suitable off-duty relaxations, found similar pleasure in the night-life of the city. There was also a certain shrewdness in his insistence on the joys of drinking and whoring and kicking against the pricks. Webster might be insubordinate and disrespectful of the top brass, but he was a good judge – had indeed proved himself a splendid leader – of men. And there was good reason, plenty of good reasons, for ameliorating the sheer drudgery of the young and inexperienced Nick Hart's forcible subjection to the mass of material – Australian and German – forming Zoltan Hunzinger's background.

"I must tell you, sir, for the umpteenth time," he protested, "that I have no experience, no knowledge whatsoever, of intelligence work, as I tried to explain to Colonel Nichols. I cannot possibly be expected to retain this . . . this morass of personal detail about a man I never met. The brother will be able to catch me out time and again!"

"That's just where you're wrong, old boy," Webster said mildly. "However little you know, however little you remember of what I'm feeding you, it'll be more than Axel knows. That's the joy – the lucky chance – of this mission. He doesn't bloody *know*. If the mind goes blank, you can improvise, and he won't be able to contradict you."

"What about those first seven years?"

"What about them?"

"I forget the pet-name of our nanny, or I've never been told it . . . I score zero on why Fritz or Franz seemed to prefer him to me. Or vice versa. I can't complete some story he half recalls. What then?"

"On recollections of childhood, his memory can be as much at fault as yours. Again, you improvise. You bluster. You attack him and tell him he's a silly cunt who can't even remember the colour of your mother's eyes!"

"Which was?" Hart needled.

"Hazel!" Webster said triumphantly. "With blonde hair."

And after such exchanges, he would say: "You're trying too hard, laddie. Bravo . . . but relax! You'll find that a few genuflections at the altar of Bacchus, plus the occasional dipping of the old wick, have a wonderfully rejuvenating effect on the memory cells. I know: I've always tried it!"

Apart from a series of cheap dance halls which could be hired by the night – and the big municipal ballroom which had been requisitioned and turned into the American Red Cross leisure centre – the red-hot night-life of wartime Belfast was concentrated on two self-styled nightclubs, the Embassy and the Four Hundred. Each of these occupied the first floor of a business block in the town centre; in each, the 'members only' restriction was limited to the handing over of a small sum of money and a three minute wait while a card was filled in. Both of them provided small, driving, American-style, surprisingly good jazz groups. Customers in either of them could dance until one o'clock in the morning (three on Fridays but only midnight on Saturdays, otherwise they would be intruding on the Sabbath). Males who did not bring their own partners had a surprising choice of shopgirls, mill workers, girl students, abandoned housewives and mothers selling their daughters for a box of K-Rations, a carton of Lucky Strike or a hip flask of unobtainable whisky. They could also drink unlimited quantities of Indian Tonic or Coca-Cola. But they could neither eat nor partake of wine or spirits. For what was common to each club – no surprise to the patrons of Hall's Hotel, Antrim – was the fact that neither had a licence to provide or sell booze.

In the Embassy, the management thoughtfully provided dark brown tinted tumblers in which the soft drinks were served so that the brutal and licentious soldiery could conceal the methylated spirits or whatever they poured in from their hip flasks in an effort to befuddle and remove any moral scruples from the local talent they wished to violate.

"Absolutely extraordinary, old boy," Webster pronounced. "The only two reputed hot spots in town – and you can't get a bloody drink! Still, we'll go; the talent's not bad, and if your hip pocket's wide enough for a second flask, we can serve ourselves under the table."

Hart nodded. It was already six months since his unit had been posted to Ulster. "Back to the hotel," he said wryly. "No *bottles* must be visible, right? But what we swallow is private!"

Webster laughed. "There are more things in heaven and earth, *mon capitaine*," he misquoted, "than can be found in your Protestant licensing laws! Happily, most of them are female – and it is our duty to discover which has the most to offer among the birds perched in the Embassy tonight."

But by one of those unforeseeable quirks of fate unknown to the Prince of Denmark, the bird with whom they happened, all unaware, to share most of that evening with was to have a vital influence on

33

their professional relations – and indeed on Hart's mission itself – in the not too far distant future.

She was a big, fleshy girl with wide, smiling eyes who could well have been forty but in no way showed it.

On first sight, she reminded Hart of the poet's Russian love 'whose friendly breasts uncorseted' gave promise of pneumatic bliss. Beneath this prominent feature was a small trim waist that was still somehow soft and pliable, and billowy hips. Her legs were admirable and her auburn, shoulder-length hair was secured at the nape with a black velvet bow.

She wore a black knee-length skirt, a white shirt with a deep collar and a waisted jacket knitted from some sage-green woollen mixture. Very simple, very chic. But the thing that immediately impressed both men was the global effect visually of those clothes. She was one of those women who had the gift, without seeming to try, of looking always as though everything she wore had been freshly ironed and folded less than half an hour previously; she herself could have stepped straight, as they say, out of the bandbox. The white shirt, you knew, would be crisp, the creases razor sharp, the long points of the collar pristine. This was a girl who would never have dark patches under her arms, her skin would be cool and scented, her stockings never wrinkled or laddered. "My word!" Webster enthused as they installed themselves at a vacant table beside the dance floor. "Just feast your eyes on that, my boy! I wouldn't mind wading barefoot through those calm waters, and that's a fact!"

She was dancing at the time with an American airforce major – decorously, but with a certain rhythmic fluidity of hips and shoulders that hinted at a sensuality waiting to be unchained. To their surprise, she seemed to be unaccompanied, for at the end of the dance she thanked the officer politely and returned alone to the table next to theirs. Quite openly she unzipped a leather shoulder bag the same green as her jacket, took out a small silver flask, and emptied it into her glass of coke. She lit a cigarette, raised the glass, and drank.

Webster was not a man to allow such an opportunity to pass unused. He produced his own flask, laid it momentarily on the table, and raised his glass, smiling, in her direction. "Welcome to the Club of Illegal Trades," he said.

She turned to face them – not just the head, but shifting the whole sexy weight of her, the hourglass voluptuousness that the French would delight to term *pulpeuse*, in their direction. "Ridiculous, isn't it?" she said. "All these men from America and New Zealand and Canada and wherever, here to save our European bacon—" a sweep of a graceful arm to include all the uniformed men in the club – "and they can't even get a legal drink when they're off duty!"

She had a slight accent which Webster couldn't place at first, the voice low and melodious. "Scandalous!" he agreed. "Let me offer you one on our particular house." He slid the flask along the bench seat towards her.

She smiled. But before she could answer, Eddie Freeman, the leader of the jazz group, stamped them into a fast flagwaver and a blare of trumpet, trombone and tenor improvisation, coupled with the pounding of jitterbug feet on the floor, rendered sane conversation impossible until the end of the set.

Her name, she told them when the band took a break, was Zelda. She was Austrian by birth but acquired British nationality through marriage to an army officer working for the Control Commission in the twenties. He was now what was called a gentleman farmer in Kent. "Which simply means," she said, "that he's the one whose wellingtons don't get muddy when it's calving time or the hay has to be baled." She was in Ulster for a few days only, representing her husband – who seemed to be something of a big wheel – at a conference in Stormont, the local parliament.

Hart, who was sitting on the far side of Webster – and like him wore civilian clothes – leaned forward over the table to face her directly. "I reckon the difference in farming practice between this province and Kent," he began, "if that's what you're discussing, must be—"

He stopped in mid-sentence. Zelda's jaw had dropped. Her eyes had widened in something very like horror, but which could simply have been extreme surprise

"What is it?" Webster asked. She was staring bemusedly at Hart's face.

"Not true!" she gasped. "I mean it can't be; it's simply not possible. I just don't believe it!"

"Is something wrong?" Hart was mystified.

"It's the . . . I mean, your *face* . . ." She floundered, unable to find words.

He put up a hand to touch his cheek. "What's wrong with it? Have I cut myself shaving?"

"No, no. Nothing's wrong. Forgive me." She collected herself. "It's just that something's . . . too *right*. There's a resemblance . . . it's uncanny, a total likeness to . . . well, someone I know . . . Someone I knew."

Both Webster and Hart hesitated. Each realised what must have happened. By some absurd, completely unforeseeable coincidence, they happened to have picked on someone who must know – or have at some time known – Hunzinger. There was a risk that the whole careful structure of Nichols's plan could be damaged, triggered off in advance, pre-empted – if they didn't play their cards right. Right now.

But which card? The King's man . . . or the Knave?

There were only two options: play it straight, an odd coincidence that this officer looked like someone this woman had known; or, since neither of them was in uniform, jump the gun on the mission and present Hart as the Australian brother – arrived perhaps from the German Embassy in neutral Dublin.

There was a risk, though – tiny but present – that it might have been Zoltan himself and not Axel that she knew. The senior man decided straight away on the former choice.

"Rude of us not to introduce ourselves," he apologised. "My name is Webster. This is Captain Nick Hart of the Oxford and Bucks Light Infantry, at present stationed in Antrim. A night on the jolly old town, don't you know!"

"But I'm sorry not to be your absent friend," Hart added with his most charming smile.

Zelda's features relaxed. She returned the smile. "My fault entirely," she said. "Stupid of me. But the likeness is so exact that I was taken by surprise."

"No problem," Webster said. "An opportunity, happily, for us to offer you another drink." He held up the flask.

"Well, that's kind," she said, holding out a hand. "And fortunate, for mine's already empty!"

When the second flask was innocent of whisky, Webster said "Shall we dance?" and Zelda rose at once, sliding into the embrace of his right arm with a brilliant smile. Hart was very conscious nevertheless of the fact that the woman's disconcerting regard returned time and again to his face during the entire set of slows – and Webster was an expert dancer. What could there have been so special, so significant to a county farmer's wife, apparently happily married, in a friendship – an affair? – with an immigrant importer of camera lenses? Surely something more than the fact that, presumably, each of them spoke German? Perhaps dialogue during the next slow might offer a clue. It would be natural after all for him, the sosie, to pose the odd question about his lookalike.

But when the band rocked into a slow-drag version of *There'll Be Some Changes Made* and he rose to say politely: "My turn now, I think!" she shook her head.

"I'd love to," she said. "Really. But I have to leave now. As I told the officer I was with when you came in, I have a date. I promised to meet a girlfriend at the Four Hundred at midnight."

"A girlfriend?" Webster crowed. "By Jove, that's a piece of luck: we'll make it a foursome, eh?"

She smiled again. "If you like."

"But first we'd better haunt the lower quarters of the town in search of products emanating from distilleries across the water."

"That's all right," Zelda said. "The doorman at the Four Hundred is a friend – and Irish whisky, specially Bushmills from County Antrim, is quite drinkable, you know!"

"The Four Hundred it is," Webster said. "If the doorman here is friendly enough to raise a cab with enough fuel left in its gasbag to get us there."

The friend was called June. She was a sweater-girl – a slender blonde wearing a straight white pleated skirt with gold high heels and tight blue wool plastered to full breasts worthy of a magazine cover designed to raise the morale of enlisted men.

June was a dancer with a variety company doomed to stay at the Empire Theatre for the duration, since return traffic to England was restricted to service personnel and their families and functionaries on 'official business'.

She was in fact a joy to dance *with*, in what might be called a civilian way – as Hart soon found out, since Webster carefully (perhaps selfishly?) engineered the party in such a way that his protégé was not coupled in any sense of the word with the potentially dangerous Zelda.

The dancing time too was of course restricted, since the club was obliged to close at one o'clock. But there were enough slows in the final hour for the two couples to establish a corporal contact that was as sensuous as it was promising.

Fortunately for them all, the friendliness of the doorman extended to the furnishing of an address – that of a hotel, conveniently nearby and open all night, where the night porter could be bribed to supply liquor, and where Captain Nicholas Hart was enabled to sample other, more lustful joys supplied by the busty yet willowy form of his dancer.

Part Two

Night Flight

Five

Webster slumped in the passenger seat of a rented Ford Anglia parked without lights on the seafront promenade in Douglas, Isle of Man. He was watching the serrated silhouette of the steep slate roofs and chimneys crowning the Victorian boarding houses that formed the outer ring of the internment camp complex, dimly visible against the faint illumination rising from the masked lamps in the compound. It was fifteen minutes short of ten o'clock, and a cool night wind, blowing off the sea, rocked the small saloon on its springs.

If all had gone well, Hart should be out of the tunnel by now, waiting in the bushes to be led to his quarry. Webster hoped the agent in policeman's uniform, one of Colonel Nichols's lamplighter crew, would have no difficulty locating the German who was to be spirited away from the camp. Hart would have very little time to establish his spurious identity, persuade Hunzinger to follow him and lead the man back to the concealed tunnel entrance.

Webster had confidence in the young man. His success passing the month-long crash-course in the twin brother's background had been remarkable. Everything should go according to plan – just so long as nothing untoward happened to shake Hart's own confidence in the vital first hour of the meticulously mapped-out escape.

Webster uttered a small sound of satisfaction. The boarding-house skyline had vanished against the starry curtain of the sky. The lights in the compound had gone out.

He sat up straight, thumbing the catch of a stopwatch. The crash of waves on the beach below was momentarily drowned in the cry of voices from within the camp as the music in the concert hall faded into silence.

Hart had eight minutes maximum in which to convince Hunzinger and get him to the shrubbery. Little time for an amateur to bring off the most vital coup of the entire mission!

Webster bit his lip, imagining his protégé's desperate delve into his memory to liberate the words with which he had been programmed; his struggle to perfect the air of conviction which must manifest itself

41

normally from his assumed personality. He wouldn't have to try too hard, Webster thought, to get across the urgency of the situation! Mentally, he followed Hart across the compound, in among the bushes, persuading his shadowy companion, indicating the tell-tale opening barely visible against the dark earth.

The rooftops were visible again. The compound was once again illuminated. This time Webster's satisfaction was verbal. "Good show!" he said aloud, He clicked the stopwatch.

Seven minutes forty-five.

He hoped they had at least made it as far as the shrubbery, even if they were not yet in the hole.

Meanwhile there were things to do, last minute checks to make, arrangements to confirm for the nth time. He climbed out of the car, closed the door quietly, scrutinised the promenade. Ahead of him requisitioned terrace houses, boarded up and uninhabited, stretched bleakly away to the twelve-foot-high double barrier of barbed wire marking the camp perimeter. Behind, no light penetrated the blackout masking the bow windows of the few buildings still occupied between the camp and the square. Faintly, from an upper floor, the strains of dance music drifted. Further away, lower down, he could hear a radio voice, a hint of laughter. Webster strode to the promenade railings, vaulted nimbly over, and dropped to the wet sand of the beach below.

The tide was out; he could distinguish parallel lines of white, frothing shorewards against the dark. Water creamed towards his feet, receded, and surged in again as he strode towards the wired off sector below the camp. The sound of the waves grew louder; a gust of wind flung spume against his cheek. They should be well into the unlit tunnel by now. He crossed his fingers, willing the sandy roof not to collapse.

The tunnel exit was four hundred yards along the prohibited area, shielded by a breakwater where the strand banked up near the outflow culvert, well below the barred roadway. The two runaways were to spend the night in an abandoned beach hut already provided with a valise containing a change of clothes and papers – supposedly supplied by German intelligence agents – for Hunzinger. Nobody among the camp officials was aware of the plan. Nichols had been adamant. "There's not to be the least hint of a put-up job," he said. "It's not only got to look like the real thing: it's bloody well got to *be* the real thing. If there's the merest suspicion of a bogus set-up, the faintest doubt cast, then someone will talk, the gossip will spread and the whole operation could be kaput. The camp authorities will treat it as a prison break, call in the police and army intelligence (none of whom will be in on the scheme), and start investigations in the normal way. It will be evident anyway that the tunnel was dug from the outside. All the evidence is there. There's no place for the spill inside the camp, for instance. It will be assumed – correctly – that it was spread over the beach. There will be nothing to show that anyone inside the camp knew about the attempt, least of all the escaper himself. That's true anyway. It will be assumed, equally, that someone urgently wanted Hunzinger out. That's true too – but we hope they'll think *that* someone was Jerry. That's what Hunzinger's got to think, after all. We've fabricated a lot of evidence to convince him!"

"Yes, that's all very well," Hart objected when Webster reported the conversation. "But if it's *known* that Hunzinger's been sprung, surely there'll be a public scandal? You know: Boche super-spy evades top-security jail. The papers will make a meal of it! How can Axel and I go swanning around all over the country if every cop and MP has seen a Wanted photo and is on the lookout for him? Especially as there will be two of him! A hue and cry like that—"

Webster interrupted, shaking his head. "Not to worry," he said. "The Admiral will receive a special directive from Winston to prevent that."

"The Admiral?"

"He's the Chief Censor. Boss of the Censorship Division at the Ministry of Information. No story can be printed in any British publication unless it's been submitted to – and passed by – the boys working for him. The Admiral will slap a dead-stop, operative for at least two weeks, on any mention whatsoever of 18B, the Isle of Man, Hunzinger himself, probably spies in general." Webster laughed. "That'll keep Fleet Street guessing. They'll wonder why, of course – but they won't be able ask the question in print!" Another chuckle. "Too bad – especially since they'll be sitting unawares on the angle of the two admirals."

"The two . . . ?"

"Another of our twin-set, specialised coincidences! In the left corner, Admiral Thompson, the Chief Censor – controller of what you may and may not read. In the right corner, Admiral Canaris, controller of Hitler's *Abwehr* – the military intelligence service hungrily awaiting the information Hunzinger's sleepers hope to unearth. What you may or may not reveal, in fact."

"And Canaris is the supposed mastermind . . . ?"

"Canaris, supposedly out of favour with Himmler at the moment, nevertheless directs from neutral Lisbon the worldwide spy network extending from Europe to parts east. All the spook names you have been fed, the chaps supposed to have organised the jailbreak, the tunnel and your Australian flight, they're all genuine agents on the Canaris payroll. That's why Axel is going to swallow your story: he knows them all; or at least knows of them by reputation."

Peter Leslie

"So why isn't at least one of them here to congratulate him on his escape?" Hart asked.

"Personally you have no idea. If he raises the point, nobody tells you anything. Sensitive territory perhaps? The need-to-know story – and if you don't know, you can't tell. So play the cards you've been dealt and shut up, eh? Hunzinger is enough of an old hand to know that secret services are . . . secretive."

Hart sighed. "I suppose so," he said.

Webster himself was now stealthily approaching the most 'sensitive' part of the off-limits beach, the curve of sand in which the tunnel exit and the old hut were located. He had to check the lock, the contents of the valise, the papers, then make himself scarce before the tunnellers arrived. They should be at least halfway through by now, with no alarm raised, and it was essential that Hunzinger didn't see him. At the same time he wished to be in a position to observe the two men together – if only to judge from the evidence available how successful, how convincing and persuasive, the substitution of Hart had been.

Treading warily through the soft sand, Webster became aware of subdued male voices somewhere in among the forest of barbed wire overhead. Probably a couple of army sentries on patrol sharing a forbidden cigarette on some sheltered corner of the promenade. Best to take no chances, though. He moved in closer to the brickwork below the railings.

Not too close, though: the prevailing winds were easterly; there could be fine shingle or dried wrack piled up at the foot of the wall deep enough to draw attention to a clandestine footstep.

He was outside the cabin. The lamplighters would have oiled the door hinges and the lock; blacked out the grimed windows. Webster turned the handle: the door swung noiselessly open.

So far, so good. You could usually rely on Nichols's men.

He sidled inside, closed the door silently and switched on a pocket flashlight. The blackout was in place. So was the valise, behind a rickety card table and a pile of folded deckchairs.

The place smelled of yesterday's summers – sundried wood and dust, peeling paint, perished rubber and linseed oil. He emptied the contents of the valise on to the table.

A change of clothes for Hunzinger. An RAF flight-sergeant's uniform for Hart. Papers in zipped pochettes. Emergency food supplies – two boxes of American K-Rations (a nice touch, Webster thought) together with a flask of Steinhaegger schnapps.

And, below the false bottom of the valise, a Walther '08 automatic pistol together with a long-barrelled Mauser, each loaded and with a spare clip.

44

Nichols had been against the weapons, but Webster had insisted. "No intelligence service as efficient as Jerry's," he urged, "would dream of deposing a kit for spies behind the lines in enemy country without a spot of self-defence available. Be reasonable, Adam: you'll have to leave it to Hart to make sure they're not used against our own cops or MPs. He's a reasonable type after all."

"I'm not happy about it," Nichols persisted. "You know what they say: if guns are available, people will use them."

"Not professionals, not if they can help it," Webster argued. And then, inconsequentially: "They really confirm the genuineness, the true kraut quality of the kit. They're both pre-Great War designs. You know: spooks are not real soldiers; give 'em the outdated stuff!"

Nichols shrugged. "Whatever you say." A sudden smile "Perhaps they'll jam anyway!"

Webster replaced everything in the valise. Ten out of ten for the lamplighters. He pushed it back behind the table and let himself out of the hut. The wind had freshened; the incoming tide looked rougher.

Earlier reconnaissance had revealed a place ten or twelve yards beyond the beach hut where the brickwork below the promenade was faulty and a concrete buttress had been added to shore up the sidewalk and railings above. Webster secreted himself behind this and settled down to wait.

It was not far short of midnight when he heard the first hint of voices.

The soldiers on the terrace above were no longer audible. News bulletins and radio music from the inhabited houses had been swamped by the increased roar of waves. The wind now whistled through the multiple strands of perimeter wire.

Webster stiffened at the first murmur drifting his way from the tunnel mouth. It was at once followed by a scrape of shingle, what could have been the soft fall of earth. Webster craned forward, trying to make out moving shapes, dim figures against the dark blur of buildings at the far end of the strand. He would have time to overhear only the briefest of exchanges before the two fugitives were inside the hut.

It must have been hell, he thought, trying to coax a man unprepared for it, and doubtless unused to eighteen-inch passageways, through the unlit calvary of the old badger's earth and the confined tunnel that followed it. And indeed the first words he actually made out – in German of course – were Nick Hart's: "Thank God you had that flaming pocket torch! I don't know if I could have faced a second traverse in the total dark!"

And then Hunzinger: "Why in all that's holy didn't you bring one yourself?"

The first trap, Webster thought. Hart's voice was a light tenor; the German's much deeper, almost mellifluous. Was that believable, genetically, morphologically, in the case of identical twins? If it wasn't, there was nothing they could do about it now.

"I wanted to bring one," Hart was saying. "But Korsun wouldn't hear of it."

"Korsun?"

"The Canaris man who organised the whole thing."

"Don't know him."

"You wouldn't, Axel. He's new. Rowed in by Himmler from the Pacific sector," Hart said calmly.

Bully for you, boy! Webster thought. The two figures were distinguishable separately now, stepping up on to a decrepit veranda at the front of the hut. "How many people are they holding in there anyway?" Hart asked. "Hundreds, I suppose?" It seemed a reasonable question to be posed by a man just arrived from the other end of the earth.

"Thousands," Hunzinger replied. "A certain percentage have been released – they were a trifle hasty at first – but there are still two thousand three hundred in the forty-eight houses around Hutchinson Square where I am . . . where I was, that is! Mostly us. The Italians were released when Mussolini capitulated. One house is set aside for the Finns."

"The *Finns*?" Hart's voice was a model of astonishment.

"They came in with us after Mannerheim squashed the attempted invasion by the Bolsheviks."

Hart was at the door, fumbling in the dark for the lock. "What's the food like?" he asked.

A laugh. "It could be worse – if you have a lively imagination! The joke is, it's actually prepared and cooked by the landladies who were the original owners of the boarding houses! The Englanders pay them to continue just as if they were still catering to the holiday trade!"

"My heart bleeds for you," Hart said feelingly. Hunzinger's reply was inaudible: they were inside; the door closed.

Webster breathed a sigh of relief. He had heard enough. It was going to be all right – at least as far as Hunzinger's acceptance of his 'brother' was concerned. From the little he had heard, it was already clear that a relationship had been established. Bravo Nichols, bravo Nick Hart!

Bent double, Webster sped past the darkened hut and hurried towards the stretch of inhabited promenade where the Ford was parked. If he hadn't handed it in at the hire company headquarters by eight o'clock in the morning there'd be a whole extra day to pay, and he'd be torn off an enormous strip by Nichols's Accounts Department.

Six

Axel Hunzinger's instinctive reaction when Nicholas Hart first appeared in his hut had been as exaggerated – overdone almost to the point of comical – as Zelda's when she saw his face at the Embassy Club. The eyes widened as if in fright, the jaw fallen open, the voice quavering.

"*Gott in Himmel!*" he stammered. And then in English: "No, it cannot be. This is not possible, not to be believed! And yet . . . surely one explanation only could be . . . ?"

"Yes," Hart said calmly. "I am Zoltan. There is no mistake. It is good to see you . . . brother . . . after all these years."

"B-b-but I do not understand. I mean, how could you possibly—?"

"The admiral wants you out," Hart cut in. "I have been sent to get you out. But we have very little time, a matter of seconds only. You must follow me at once. There is a tunnel. No questions, please. I explain later." The huts were gaslit, and his eyes were screwed up a little against the flaring light after the darkened compound and the blackness of his journey. Perhaps, too, some obscure gut reaction told him that the deception might have a better chance of success if Axel didn't at first see his 'real' face.

But Hunzinger, a professional schooled to take quick decisions, was convinced: the likeness was sufficiently extraordinary, the situation incredible enough, to still what could in other circumstances have been suspicion or doubt. "Very well," he said crisply. "We go."

He looked once around the hut – there were six bunks, the other five inmates presumably being at the concert – then snatched up a flashlight and moved towards the door.

Hart eased it open, nodded, and they moved swiftly out into the dark. Seizing Hunzinger by the elbow, he guided him at a half-run to the shrubbery.

They had just plunged in among the leaves when the overhead lights in the compound blazed to life behind their masks. "Very efficient," Hunzinger approved. "But I see what you mean by a matter of seconds! How did you organise the cut?"

"We have friends," Hart said. "But it had to look like nothing more than a temporary fault."

He was on his knees, crouched low, parting branches. "This is the tunnel," he murmured. "But I warn you: it is no more than forty-five centimetres high. The exit will be head-first, very slow, uncomfortable and claustrophobic. Give me the torch and I will lead the way."

Hunzinger handed the flashlight over and Hart ducked down to crawl into the hole. "Believe in me, Axel," he said.

His last wry reflection, as the shouts of the men streaming from the concert hall faded and the cold stillness of the underground passageway took over, was: *Thank God the bugger doesn't realise that final remark was a prayer and not an encouragement!*

Although it was almost two hours before they emerged, sandy, grazed and sweating, on the beach, it was nevertheless enormously comforting to Hart to have another human being – even a potentially dangerous one – behind him during that second emotionally tense traverse. He hated to think of what it must have done to Hunzinger, unprepared for the shock of seeing a twin brother, totally unready for the subterranean hell that followed.

The tunnel nevertheless provided an unexpected and wholly welcome respite for Hart himself.

For once he felt it safe to switch on the torch and they could exchange low-voiced confidences, the question-and-answer marathon began.

It was then that he realised fully how right Colonel Nichols had been to risk everything – the success, the existence even, of the entire mission – on a single throw of the dice: the belief that the likeness would be enough to convince Axel Hunzinger that Hart was his brother.

And the two hazardous hours inching forward underground were enough for virtually all the really vital points – how Hart came to be there, how the escape was organised, what he had been doing for the past twenty years – to have been raised and replied to without Hart's face being visible and any possible doubts or anxieties revealed.

Once this hurdle – the acceptance of Hart's supposed identity – had been overcome and left behind, the mission had become a totally different ball game. There was no longer any question of who was who. They knew each other; they were just two team-mates engaged in an undercover operation, each of whom could rely on the other to offer the maximum assistance.

And if any queries or doubts should ever suggest themselves to

Blitz Harvest

Hunzinger, he had only to look searchingly at his companion to have them scoffed at.

It was almost with pleasure that Hart saw for the first time around a curve in the tunnel the evidence of the first roof fall that had nearly finished him on the way in. In the fading light from the torch, the scratched and shovelled and spread mounds of sandy gravel appeared to block the hard floor practically up to the level of the arching roof. But Hart knew how far the obstacle stretched; he had after all been here before. "Spot of trouble ahead here," he muttered. "But it's no more than a few yards – never completely blocked."

And this time he forced himself forward with all his strength, pushing the friable material ahead, bludgeoning his way through rather rather than wasting his time and strength scraping it back and distributing the spill behind him.

Journey's end this time was auditory rather than tactile. Despite the sea wind, there was no cool current of air to soothe their heated skin, just the blessedly familiar, advancing and receding boom of breaking waves to signal the end of their odyssey.

Their mood inside the beach hut – although for different reasons in each case – had a quality of almost joyous intoxication. The batteries of Axel's torch were almost exhausted, but Webster had left them his own flashlight. In its faint illuimation, with a near hysterical glee, they changed clothes, consumed the rations, drank the schnapps and kept watch in turn for the oncoming dawn.

By the time the sun rose, they were on a side road approaching Douglas from the north. Clothes they had worn in the tunnel had been dropped into the sea from a rocky spit beyond the beach. The K-Rations containers had been buried in the sand. The schnapps flask was at Hart's hip.

Hunzinger, in a suit of sober clerical grey, wore horn-rimmed spectacles and carried the valise with a selection of shirts, underclothes, socks and European toilet articles inside. His English, accentless and gramatically perfect, was as good as Hart's Bavarian – if a trifle pedantic at times: there were too few Can'ts and Don'ts and Isn'ts in his vocabulary for his speech to be truly demotic, and Nichols had wisely identified him in the papers provided as a Swiss member of the International Red Cross – Doctor Eduard Valder, at present on a fact-finding mission to check the well-being of Allied prisoners-of-war.

The name – not German enough to raise suspicion – and the role suited his appearance perfectly: a serious Swiss (aren't they all?), rather boring, probably from the French-speaking part of the country. Hunzinger himself had been much amused – and impressed – by it. "This Korsun of ours," he had said during the night. "A man of talents, eh?"

Hart, adopting a long, loping stride, walked a little way ahead as if he wished to get shot of the German's company. To hide as far as possible their physical similarity, he had – thanks to Webster – darkened his hair in the hut with a quick rinse and attached to his upper lip a believable moustache to support the RAF flight-sergeant image.

The first test, traumatic for each of them, came a few minutes past seven-thirty, when they were approaching the Granville Hotel on the Loch Promenade – in fact directly behind a row of houses which had been one of the first internment camps as long ago as 1940. They were about to turn into a street which would lead them to the Sefton Hotel and the Gaiety Theatre when they saw the police patrol: a sergeant and three constables blocking the sidewalk beside a black Wolseley saloon parked at the foot of a gentle rise.

Hart continued his approach at the same pace. It would have been suicidal to turn back, to hesitate, to attempt to bolt or even cross to the other side of the road.

Much of course depended on whether Hunzinger's absence had been noticed – and, if so, whether or not the tunnel had been discovered and an alarm raised. In any case the only possible way to handle the situation was to play out their roles as convincingly – and as innocently – as possible.

The sergeant stepped forward as they drew near. Two of the constables spread out behind him and the third sidled past to station himself behind. The uniformed driver, wearing a peaked cap with a black and white check hatband, got out of the car.

"Sorry to trouble you," the sergeant said, eyeing the oddly assorted couple with disfavour, "but I must ask you where you are going and what you are about at this hour of the morning? Just routine, sir, you understand—" this to Hunzinger—"but we have to ask also to see your identity cards."

One of Hart's party pieces, elaborated during his Northern Ireland posting, was the affectation of a robust, only slightly exaggerated Ulster accent. He used this now.

"That's all right, Sarge," he said. "Gentleman's car conked out on the way down from Ramsey." He fished in the breast pocket of his uniform and produced a pay book. "He's lookin' for the quickest way into the town centre." He held out the document. "He has business in

Port Erin, sure, and I promised I'd put him on the road to the bleedin' station."

Hart knew that there would be a broken-down hire car somewhere on the road between Glen Affric, Laxey and the outskirts of Douglas. Webster was that efficient. There was an internment camp at Ramsey and another at Laxey. Female internees were housed in Port Erin at the south-western extremity of the island. It was perfectly feasible that a Red Cross official could be on his way there to check living conditions after visits to the other two towns.

The sergeant had flicked a cursory glance at the pay book and studied Hunzinger's papers at much greater length. Now he handed both of them back. "OK, Flight," he said. "We're going that way ourselves. We'll see that the good doctor gets his train."

"Be glad if you would," Hart said. "I'm already fuckin' late meself. Should have clocked in at the Raf station behind Central bloody Prom a half-hour ago! Thanks for the help, copper. And good day to you, sir."

Raising a nonchalant hand to Hunzinger, who bowed stiffly, he lumbered away.

There hadn't even been the need for a verbal signal indicating one of their agreed fallback routines. Perhaps the alarm at the camp had not yet been given – the first roll-call, Hunzinger had said, was not until nine. If it had, the police had certainly not been called in yet, otherwise any foreigners, even neutrals, would sure as hell have been hauled in for questioning and a double-check.

Hart and his escaper were in any case genuinely on their way to Port Erin, where a boat would be waiting to take them off the island that night. They were in fact planning to go there by train.

Hart possessed a left-luggage ticket which would give him access to a second valise and a set of civilian clothes with his own ID. All Hunzinger would have to do once he was dropped at the station would be to wait until he saw his twin in his new role, then board the same train – in a coach as far away from Hart as possible. Port Erin was the terminus anyway.

Everything in fact – or so Hart thought as he approached the station – had been taken care of.

Seven

The Isle of Man Railway, linking Douglas with Port Erin in the south and Peel on the west coast, was opened to the public in 1873. A northern branch, crossing the mountainous interior to terminate at Ramsey, was completed six years later. But even in the mid-forties, seventy momentous years further on the narrow three foot gauge track, with its short, squared-off coaches and archaic side-tank locomotives, remained sufficiently 'quaint' an anachronism to attract quantities of tourists, military as well as civil. Hart, using it professionally in the build-up to the internment camp escape, found it fascinating. He had never ridden on the Talyllin Railway in Snowdonia or the miniature Romney, Hythe and Dymchurch line on the south coast, so the toytown approach to the rolling stock, the doll's-house compartments in which the head of a seated man almost touched the ceiling, seemed to him so out-of-this-world as to be practically dreamlike. The trains on the Douglas-Port Erin branch – complimented in the press not long before the war on achieving 'an average speed of as much as twenty-five miles per hour' – did not roar through the rural countryside; they trundled.

The one that Hart took was hauled by a splendidly preserved two-four-two Beyer Peacock tanker complete with a tall smokestack and a magnificently burnished silver dome. With the name *Tynwald* (the Manx parliament) blazoned ahead of its cab, the loco pre-dated the line itself by several years.

Hart's destination – and Hunzinger's – was in fact Port Erin, but they had agreed to leave the train at Port St Mary, the stop before, and complete the journey, separately, on foot. There was no point hanging around the terminus for several hours when they didn't plan to embark in the boat left for them until after dark.

There were two other arguments against their going openly into that part of the peninsula, even furnished with the right papers to get them through the barbed wire barrier sealing it off from the rest of the island. The first concerned the credibility of the counter-intelligence plan as explained to Hunzinger. Were it really an *Abwehr* conspiracy organised by Canaris and his men, was it really likely that, having spirited their spymaster away from one internment camp, they would leave the means for his final escape within the territory of another? The second related to Hunzinger's bogus role as a Swiss Red Cross investigator.

Less than two years previously, a committee from the International Co-operative Woman's Guild had reported favourably on ·living conditions for the women and children behind the wire. It was entirely possible therefore that a visit from a second authority, unannounced, might stimulate unwelcome questions to which there could be no persuasive answer – especially as the camp was operated and guarded by the British Home Office and police authorities rather than the military responsible for all the other sites.

Webster had brought up both points at the planning stage, but was overruled by Colonel Nichols. "The objections are absolutely valid," he said. "But they must take second place to the choice of boat we have to leave for you. Clearly, this must be manoeuvrable, powerful and fast if you're to avoid or outrun coastguard or naval patrols not in on the scheme. But we can hardly run in such a craft in the middle of a national emergency and unload it for you to 'steal' in one of these tiny fishing ports! It would, to say the least of it, start folks talking. It's got to be a boat that's already there – and one, moreover, that will not at first be missed (though Hunzinger doesn't need to know that)."

The sole suitable craft was within the internment camp perimeter, Nichols said.

It was laid up for the duration in a locked boathouse at the seaward margin of an expensive property whose owners had moved to the mainland at the outbreak of war.

The boat had been unshrouded, checked over, tanked up and readied for the voyage by Nichols's lamplighters. The hinges of the boathouse doors had been oiled, the exit left unlocked. But the entrance to the property itself was indeed within the wired-off camp area.

It was agreed therefore that Hart, using his own genuine identity, should go past the sentries once darkness had fallen, ostensibly for a meeting with an official whose name had been supplied by Nichols. But that once he was out of sight of the police guarding the perimeter he should race to the property, scale the outer wall and hurry down to the inlet where the boathouse was located. Once he had started the motor, he was then to head out to sea, coasting back shoreward to pick up Hunzinger from a rocky spur jutting out on the far side of Port Erin Bay.

"I'm not entirely happy about this," Hart confided truthfully to

Hunzinger. "But I guess it was difficult enough for Korsun and his team to find any boat at all in a situation – and a place – like this!"

"They have done very well this far," Hunzinger said. "We cannot expect a welcome party bearing banners with the *Führer's* image – especially within an internment camp!"

The east wind freshened still further during the day, and by mid-afternoon waves dashing against the rocks bordering the harbour at Port St Mary were flinging shellbursts of white skywards to mask the grey façades of the seafront houses.

The peninsula bifurcated into two lobes at the southwestern extremity, not unlike those of Land's End and the Lizard in Cornwall. Port St Mary lay to the east of this double outcrop and Port Erin to the west. It was across the neck of land between them – the narrowest part of the promontory as a whole – that the camp barrier extended. They crossed it some way inland, where the ground began to rise towards the hilly interior.

Port Erin was strung out along the lip of a curve of scrub-covered high ground, steep enough to be termed a bluff but not high enough to qualify as a cliff. Below it, fishing boats lay drawn up on the sandy beach of the bay between high-water mark and the deserted huts and cabins of pre-war holidays.

It was easy enough to remain undetected among the clumps of bushes and craggy outliers of this slope as the light faded and the sky became overcast with cloud cover sailing menacingly overhead from the southeast. They had snatched a sandwich and a beer beneath the steep slates and domed cupola of Collinson's Cafe in the town centre as soon as they arrived – the first time they had openly shown themselves together since they left Douglas. Now there was nothing to do but wait and watch the waves grow rougher on this side of the island until it was time for Hart to make his run for the camp perimeter and the boat.

He decided to fill in the time with a rundown of his plans for the night and the following day. It would at least prevent more intimate conversation possibly raising points he might find it hard to reply to.

It did that. But at the same time replies from Hunzinger himself raised points – and difficulties – for which Hart, and the agents who had programmed him, were totally unprepared.

The agreed plan, after the boat prepared by counter-intelligence had been 'stolen', was to make, during the night, for the low-lying mainland coast near Southport, where the estuarine tide recedes almost a mile and individual figures on foot could abandon a low craft and wade ashore virtually unseen along outflowing streams cut through huge banks of hard sand. And where Hart already had secret preparations for Hunzinger's integration in English civilian life well advanced.

The German was, had always been, in favour of a maritime escape and the sea voyage.

But to Hart's horror he strongly disputed the choice of destination. "No, no, my brother," he objected. "Here for the first time you are in a mistake. We must head not east but west. The Embassy of the Reich in neutral Dublin must be our goal."

Hart stared at him, aghast. This was entirely unforeseen. "But . . . but Axel," he began. "I have already explained. We – Canaris and his men – have made arrangements, contacts. Safe houses, comunications, signals . . ."

The German shook his head. "I have studied maps, Zoltan," he said. "The nearest landfall is Dundalk Bay, less than fifty miles from here. And in Eire. From Dundalk we can be safely in Dublin within the hour."

"Southport," Hart urged, "is no more than twelve to fifteen miles further. And we can land, especially at daybreak, almost certainly unobserved. My arrangements—"

"The arrangements can be changed, replanned. The safe houses will still be there . . ."

"I have cover – a perfect set-up – organised all the way to—"

"From the Embassy," Hunzinger interrupted, "I can get back in touch with my superiors in Berlin. Not from England. I shall need instructions on how and when to continue my work; what the Englanders call an update must be supplied to me."

Hart was in a quandary. The reasoning was entirely logical . . . from Axel's point of view. But it was entirely at variance with his own instructions – and there was no way he could contact *his* superiors. Apart from which, he doubted whether he had been sufficiently well programmed to pass muster as a genuine German operative at a Nazi Embassy – even if spoken for by Axel, who had himself been out of a touch a long time. Worst of all, Berlin intelligence might very well know for a fact that the real Zoltan was still in Australia. Himmler kept track of everything. His experts would in any case be suspicious of a sophisticated escape plan – even if it was said to derive from Admiral Canaris – launched entirely without their knowledge.

"But Axel," he said desperately, "we already *know* how your work is to be continued – I have the most specific instructions . . . your agents, the so-called sleepers, must at once be activated. Korsun and the Admiral have done everything possible . . ."

"No," Axel Hunzinger said. "We go to Dublin."

Hart said no more. He was cast, evidently, as a fervid Nazi sympathiser, rowed in because of his relationship and because he was supposedly a twin, but definitely playing second string to the professional spymaster. In the scenario as written he dare not push too hard, however good his case. To overdo it would be to risk compromising the credibility of his own cover.

"Just as you say, Axel," he conceded.

"Good. Then as soon as you pick me up we head west. At least it will save us from making a tour of this island's entire – and well policed – outline, no?"

"Yes, Axel," Hart said again.

Eight

The boat was a lean, twenty-five foot teak and mahogany speed-ster with a half rail over the decked bow and a short roofed section immediately behind the windshield. According to an unsigned, unattributed card attached to the wheel by a cord, the craft was powered by twin-screw one hundred and fifty hp diesels and the fuel tank, which registered full, held ninety gallons. The craft resembled an American racer known as a Lancer, which Hart had been familiar with on Cornish holidays before the war, but he could see in the light of Webster's torch that the brass plate screwed to the instrument panel bore the name of a Swiss shipyard on Lake Geneva. Smart work, Nichols! he thought as he studied the switches and levers and dials.

Reaching the boathouse had been more difficult than he bargained for. For a start, the property was no longer uninhabited. Evidently it had been requisitioned since the lamplighters had passed by to service the speedboat. It was now, according to a notice displayed between the ornate gate-posts, a Kosher House, reserved for practising Jewish internees and their families.

Hart swore. There were two uniformed policemen on sentry duty outside.

Despite the fact that he was in civilian clothes, he had had no difficulty passing the guards at the screened entry in the wire barrier. His papers and confirmation of a supposed appointment with the official in the administration block had earned him no more than smart salutes and a polite: "About three hundred yards, sir. Past the first two rows of houses and turn right. It's the second building on the left, the old town hall."

Hart had of course left the road once he was out of sight of the wire. He had memorised the web of lanes and footpaths that could lead him to the big clifftop mansion without too much exposure on the public streets. He decided to improvise once he saw the guards, using a variant of the planned stratagem which had gained him entry to the camp. It didn't work. And not only because this time he possessed no document citing a specific name.

57

Once he was visible to the guards, he continued his approach at the same pace. To do anything else in a private cul-de-sac would be asking for trouble . . . and questions.

As he drew near, the taller of the two policemen – they wore tin hats and carried rifles – moved to block the pass-gate in the tall wrought iron *portals*. "Sorry, sir. You can't come in here," he said stolidly.

"Why ever not? It's not Lights Out for another hour. I have an appointment—"

"This is the Kosher House. Jewish families only."

"I know that, man. I have to see Doctor Hirschfeld on a matter of importance."

"Sorry, sir. We have our orders."

"For God's sake! I have a message. The Home Office think they may have made a mistake: there's a chance he may be released next week. I've got to see him before I catch the last train back to Douglas."

"It's Saturday, sir," the shorter man intervened suddenly.

"So?"

"The Jewish Sabbath," the officer blocking the gate explained. "You know – no music, no theatricals, no funny books. And especially no business."

"Blast!" Hart had no difficulty summoning up an irritation he genuinely felt. Any delay could have disastrous effects on Hunzinger, exposed in the open, waiting for the boat to take him off. "Look," he said. "It's literally only for a couple of minutes, but I simply must have a word."

"More than our job's worth." The shorter man shook his head. "Very particular about their religious rules, the Jews."

"They complain," his companion said. "You'd best go back to admin and ask there, sir."

"I'll do that," Hart said angrily. He swung around and strode rapidly back along the lane.

It curved away after a hundred yards and he was out of sight of the police, but the property was surrounded by a ten-foot demesne wall topped by broken glass and three strands of barbed wire inclined inwards. Apart from the damage to his clothes and the risk of gashing his hands, the time involved negotiating this was simply out of the question in the circumstances. On tiptoe – he wore leather soles and the ground was hard – he began to run.

The wall continued, snaked away among trees, plunged downhill and crossed a slope of grass and heather. The sounds of the sea – waves breaking, explosions of froth and spume, the swash of receding gravel – grew louder. Wind whistled through the hilltop scrub.

Nowhere was there a suitable tree, an out-thrust branch, a rock from which to jump so the damned wall could be crossed!

The wind was chilly but Hart was sweating as he stumbled and ran. The wall led him right to the edge of the bluff – and even here, as it dipped down towards the shoreline and buried its brickwork in the turf, it was terminated by a *cheval-de-frise*: an iron half-circle spoked on the outside to deter intruders.

Cursing aloud now, the words snatched away by waves and wind, Hart tried to manoeuvre himself around this, hand over hand outside the wicked spikes, feet scrabbling on the soil beneath. But the lip of the bluff crumbled away. Clods of earth, small stones and a shower of gravel pattered away into the dark, leaving Hart hanging from the ironwork, his legs swinging out over the lines of white surf, bicycling in space, all of his weight dragging at his arms.

He attempted desperately to hoist himself up high enough to regain a foothold, but failed. After the third attempt he was obliged to let go and slither twenty feet down the steep slope, where a rock projection broke his fall.

It wasn't dangerous in terms of a cliff. But scrambling up again in the dark, with roots breaking off in his grasp, his feet slipping and always the friable surface cascading away, left him completely exhausted by the time he finally made the top.

But at least he was now on the inside of the property.

The boathouse, though, was on the far side, where the land sank down nearer the ragged rocks at the water's edge – and the route through the gardens he had been given was of course useless. With a completely different orientation, he had to find greenhouses, negotiate a terraced Dutch rosery, skirt a vegetable garden, a stable block and a tennis lawn and, ultimately, locate steps cut down through a shrubbery to the inlet where his boat should be. All of it at differing levels, with varying slopes and surfaces, in total darkness. He could hear distant voices but no light escaped through the mullioned windows of the massive three winged block with its monolithic Queen Anne chimney columns. It would be two hours before the moon rose, even if the cloud mass allowed its illumination to appear.

Hart wrenched his ankle once, treading on a step that wasn't there. He fell twice, stumbling over unseen obstacles, grazing the knee of his other leg. He was crossing the unused tennis court when he was hit.

He was hurrying – there should be at least fifty or sixty yards of open country ahead! – when a violent blow in the pit of the stomach

Peter Leslie

felled him to the ground and winded him completely. The grass of the lawn had grown long, the net had been removed . . . but the wire from which it had hung was still tightly stretched between the posts, and he had walked straight into it!

He had originally, of course, intended to use Webster's flashlight, but had prudently ruled that out once he knew the house was occupied. And although he was on the alert for the unexpected, the brutal effect of his collision with the wire was so extreme that he cried involuntarily aloud as he fell.

At once light, dazzling, blossomed from the dark bulk of a building – the stable block? garages? – higher up the slope above the court. Illuminated in a jerked open door, Hart saw the silhouette of an elderly, heavily bearded man wearing a hard-brimmed black hat. "What is it . . . ? Who is there . . . ? Don't you know this is private property?" a voice called angrily. And then, over one shoulder into the interior: "There is somebody prowling about in the grounds!"

Gasping for breath, Hart scrambled to his feet. He had meant – perhaps hoping to be taken for another Jewish internee who had missed his way – to call out some Hebrew or Yiddish greeting. *Shalom*, was it? *Musel-tov?* But in his consternation the wires got crossed and instead he yelled *"Insh'Allah!"* at the lighted doorway . . . and fled. Which just happens to be an Arab expression.

"Moishe!" the old man screamed. "There are Arabs at the bottom of the garden!"

Hart blundered past spiny stems, crashed through rhododendrons. At last he knew where he was; he was on his planned route. He took the steps down to the boathouse two, three at a time.

From behind and above there was a confused hubbub of voices, angry, scandalised, scared. They were calling the police at the gate. They didn't want the Sabbath desecrated. They were organising a search of the grounds. All the shutters must be closed, at once.

Despite the rude double-awakening from his isolated entry through the dark, Hart allowed his panic to dissolve, the thudding of his heart to decelerate, his panting breath to quieten once he was inside the creosote-smelling shelter of the closed boathouse. Even if all forty or fifty of the mansion's inmates flooded out into the gardens with flaring torches, the creek with its shrouded craft would be about the last place, he supposed, a search would reach.

Except that the speedboat, polished wood winking, brass and glass glittering in the light of his torch, was very much unshrouded at the moment.

Easing himself sideways along the plank walkway to the exit, he pushed wide the doors on their oiled hinges. Water swirling through from the inlet sucked at the wooden piles supporting the structure, rose and fell along the banks, rocking the slender craft against the lines retaining it.

Hart stepped down into the cockpit, his weight tipping the flat-bottomed hull from side to side. He moved in beneath the windshield canopy.

Dials and counters gleamed in the torchlight. Switches shone. The phosphorescent needle of the ship's compass swung beneath the glass of the binnacle housing. He reached out to touch the padded wheel.

Past mishaps forgotten and however rough the sea, Hart was already excited at the thought of piloting the thoroughbred Lancer – as he liked to think of the craft: it brought him a step nearer reality.

But what the hell was reality in this crazy charade of double identities? He caught sight of his face reflected in a shaving mirror hanging from a windscreen pillar. Yet it wasn't his face at all! The unfamiliar hair – he had yet to wash out the dark stain – the silly moustache . . . this was the face of Zoltan Hunzinger, a spy's brother from Australia. But he wasn't Zoltan either – any more than he was Axel!

So whose were the features staring at him from the mirror? Where was Captain Nick Hart in this confused and confusing pantomime?

Well, at least he had a boat to drive! His hand tightened on the wheel.

Concentrate on the positive. E-lim-inate the negative as the song said. No past, no future – at least for the present. And the present was what counted.

Hart took a deep breath. He emerged from the cockpit and cast off. The boat rose and fell gently as the tide swilled in. Back behind the windshield, Hart took a last look at the instrument panel, shone the torch on labels and pictograms, clicked switches.

He stabbed the starter button with a decisive finger.

The boat heaved as the twin diesels amidships shuddered . . . then burst to life with a shattering roar. The rakish bows lifted fractionally from the water.

Almost deafened in the confined space of the boathouse, wary of the immense power trembling beneath the duckboards, Hart dropped a hand to the knob of the lever and eased the machinery into gear, manoeuvering at the same time the throttles.

Behind him, churned water gurgled and slapped as the screws threshed.

So what the hell, Archie! He slammed the throttles open wide.

61

The bows lifted abruptly. The motors howled – and Hart's Lancer arrowed between the open doors to vanish into the night, towing a creamy double wake.

Christ, Hart thought – a double wake, twin screws, three men with the same face! Every damned thing in this crazy mission was a multiple . . .

He eased the wheel this way and that, feeling for the delicacy of the speedboat's response. The flat stem smacked hard into the advancing waves, sending sheets of spray over the narrow hull, flattening the surface of the sea.

It was rougher than Hart expected. Wind shrilled over the water, scooping foam from the crest of each swell, whining through the aerials. The boat creaked and shuddered, staggering with each impact as he drove her hard at the crumbling combers.

When they were half a mile offshore he spun the wheel to head northeast, parallel with the coast.

Now, broadside-on to the rising tide, the craft wallowed and heaved, rising and falling with a sickening speed as each wave surged past. Hart gripped the wheel with steady hands, staring to starboard. It was an odd sensation just the same for a man used to holiday boating and the coruscating necklace of shore illuminations etched glittering against the night.

Here all he could see to locate his position was the distant, wavering line of white which marked the breaking waves, and an occasional pale flurry of foam as an extra large one smashed into jetty or rocks.

Luckily the wind dropped and the sea calmed a little once he was within the shelter of the northerly point framing Port Erin Bay. The spit where Axel Hunzinger would be waiting plunged straight into deep water – they had reconnoitred in detail that afternoon – but it was tricky navigational work throttling back, coasting, feeding tiny bursts of power to the engines as the deck rose and fell beside the steep rock face – even when Hart had finally and decisively found the right place in the dark, even with the help of the shadowy figure waiting there. The net-webbed cork floats draped over the counter had thudded several times against the rock face and both men were wet through before Hart finally managed to drag his passenger aboard.

He backed off instantly, opened the throttles wide, and headed straight out to sea.

"You took your bloody time!" Hunzinger complained.

Nine

The boat was probably capable of forty knots, Hart thought. But with following seas – they were heading due west – threatening to poop them at any moment, handling her was tricky, especially for an inexperienced pilot. The deep-troughed rollers surging past them, occasionally lifting the twin screws clear of the water, reduced progress to an awkward series of sinking decelerations alternating with sudden bursts of speed. And this bounding stop-and-start advance was further complicated once they were clear of the thirty-seven mile shelter provided by the mountains of the island.

Here, violent currents from the north, channelled through the narrows separating Belfast Lough from the Stranraer peninsula in Scotland, raged into the Irish Sea to complicate still further the turbulent surface conditions.

With each fractional change in the wind, the steep swells rolling towards Ireland were now menaced by transverse crests speeding southward, whipping spray from the crumbling whitecaps to shower the cockpit with icy water every time the hull shook to a lateral impact.

The speedboat's timbers shivered and groaned, the engines roared, the light craft's entire frame shuddered at the assault of the sea each time the bows smacked down into the heaving maelstrom.

Wrestling with throttles and wheel, Hart concentrated all his attention on the unseen dangers welling around them from the dark. The white crests criss-crossing the rise and fall of the black surface provided his only indication of the direction from which the next attack might come. Axel Hunzinger crouched down below the windshield, teeth chattering and arms wrapped around his cold, wet body. In such conditions speech – let alone conversation – was impossible. In any case, such time as Hart could find for reflection must be consecrated to the one burning question overriding even the handling problems of the Lancer.

How in hell was he going to handle the situation once they landed in Ireland?

There were only two options: take a powder, run out on Axel, vanish into thin air and abort the mission; or, soldier on regardless.

If he quit, the operation, clearly, could never be restarted. Things had already gone too far. A second attempt, however far from the original plan, would never convince a man like Hunzinger. It was all very well, nevertheless, glibly to say soldier on. But under what conditions, especially in Dublin? With what contacts? In what direction? All that Webster and Nichols would know for sure, would be the fact that the two of them had left the island. And after that?

The deluge! Hart thought wryly, feeding maximum power to the diesels as the boat sank into a particularly frightening trough.

There was no fall-back plan based on an Irish landfall. It might be ages before word of their arrival filtered through to Regent's Park. Even then, they would have no way to contact him – or he them. The options he would have to choose between, assuming he was at the Embassy, still asumed to be Zoltan, were a closed book. There was no way, no way whatever, that he could divine, guess, predict, foresee or dream up a scenario which could fill him in on any situation he might have to face.

Gritting his teeth, Captain Hart did his best to help the Lancer forge on through the tumultuous dark.

It was when the storm of howling wind and water was at its height that the battering, thumping, creaking inferno of noise within the cockpit was joined by an insidious, more sinister sound. Hunzinger heard it too. In the light of the binnacle he gestured towards the stern.

Off the port quarter – the steady, intrusive throb of powerful marine engines.

"Shit!" Hart shouted. "That sounds like something official and fast – must be one of the navy's bloody coastal patrols. The hell with navigation: we'll have to make a run for it!"

And indeed, silhouetted against a faint radiance diffused by the still-rising moon, each time they lifted to an especially large wave they could distinguish half a mile astern the dim grey outline of a rakish power boat.

Too small for a naval corvette, too big for an MTB, the craft could have been some kind of coastguard cutter or patrol boat. "No lights," Hart yelled, "so it can't be Irish!"

There was, however, no doubt that the Lancer had appeared on the ship's radar screens – or that it had in fact taken up the pursuit. Inexorably, the thudding of the engines increased in volume; the creaming bow wave etched itself menacingly against the dark as the sharp stem plowed into the heaving deep. Distantly, garbled by the effect of the raging weather, they heard a voice from a loud-hailer relaying orders. "Identify and be recognised. Or heave to until we are alongside.

"Hold tight, Axel," Hart shouted. "This time we're giving her all she's got! It's about now anyway that we should be shifting a few points south to line us up with Dundalk."

He jammed the throttles as far forward as they would go.

The bellow of the engines rose to a scream. The boat leaped forward like an arrow released from a bow, careening wildly to port as Hart spun the wheel.

Skating crosswise now from crest to crest, they rocketed away as the cutter's loud hailer boomed unintelligibly again. Seconds later a belch of flame stabbed the dark above the chaser's well deck, followed almost at once by the thump of gunfire. They heard the shell shriek overhead, saw the white tower of water rising, falling, a quarter of a mile ahead. Then the second explosion.

"The next one will be astern, bracketing us," Hart observed. "Small calibre stuff, but uncomfortable if you happen to get a direct hit on the third!"

The cutter fired again. Another seething column of foam and steam jetted skywards after the billow of flame, and the beam of a searchlight split open the night, restlessly sweeping the waves. The gun layers would be seeing them big, centred on the radar screens; now they were trying for a visual, making the third round definitive,

An unidentified light craft was sunk with all hands by one of our coastal patrols early today, west of the Isle of Man. The boat, buffeted by heavy seas, had failed to answer requests to . . .

Hart was zigzagging the speedboat crazily now. They found the crest of a seventh wave, sped southwards along its remorseless advance, slipped back helplessly into the trough, zoomed obliquely up a wall of water to a following crest, held that for almost half a minute, then swung through a hundred and eighty degrees to ride the tide head-on. The compass needle swung wildly.

"Well done, Zoltan!" Hunzinger called. "You must have spent your school holidays on the Great Barrier Reef!"

Hart grinned over his shoulder. It was the first time since they'd left the tunnel that the man had made a remark that was even mildly lightweight. And it was true that the Lancer's antics had begun to caricature the manoeuvres of an Australian surfer. He was beginning to enjoy himself.

The third shellburst was a near miss, a violent shock wave threatening to cant the craft over and capsize it as the pale column hurled skyward by the detonation collapsed into the sea.

The fourth was astern again and the fifth even further away. Hart was racing them sideways along a trough, using the full hundred and fifty hp of each motor to keep them temporarily sheltered by two gigantic crests. Hunzinger had discovered two Mae West life jackets in a locker and shrugged himself into one. Now he helped Hart, wrenching at the wheel, into the other. "Just in case!" he shouted into the Englishman's ear. Hart grinned again; held up an approving thumb.

The pursuers fired a sixth round, but they didn't see it burst – and the gunfire was no more than a distant thump punctuating the hammering of the sea.

They had outdistanced the coastal patrol.

"Thank God for the lamplighters!" Hart said in English. As he had hoped, the boat was a gem.

"What was that? What did you say?" Hunzinger was at his side, clinging on to a bracket at the end of the instrument panel.

"Nothing. Just a stray thought," Hart replied hastily. *Watch it, Jack! Just remember who you are . . .*

He reduced speed slightly, riding the current again, allowing the Lancer to advance with the tide. He hadn't the slightest idea where they were. During the flight from the attacker, twisting this way and that, speeding, slowing as the lightweight craft was tossed around by the sea, he had lost not only all sense of direction but also the remotest idea of how far south the encounter might have taken them. Were they far enough down to line up with Dundalk, with Drogheda even? Or could they still be north of the Ulster frontier, which was at the same latitude as the Port Erin peninsula?

"I think we'd better head west again," he advised Hunzinger. "The Mourne Mountains actually mark the border. We should be able to make those out clearly enough, even if we have to hang around until dawn. We wouldn't find it so easy to make Dublin if we were hauled ashore by the British army – especially if the coastal patrol has reported already."

"You are driving, Zoltan," Hunzinger replied. "Do whatever you think best."

What Hart thought best of course would indeed have been to run ashore at Kilkeel or Newcastle and rejoin his unit by Lough Neagh. But that mustn't be what Zoltan thought best. He swung the boat enough to starboard to steer due west again.

Stars had begun to prick out the darkness overhead. The dense cloud cover was beginning to break up. Soon the risen moon sailed into sight through a gap in the massif, silvering the wilderness of white foam and waves in which they pitched and wallowed. If it remained visible, they should be able to sight the mountains when they were still some way offshore.

Inundated by icy spray, Hart battled on. Hammered by the furious seas, stern squatting deep and gunwales awash every time the bows lifted, the Lancer forged ahead.

They could see now in the wan light that the waves, small perhaps compared with a South Pacific ocean swell, were just the same, between fifteen and twenty feet from trough to crest – big enough to dwarf their small craft and engulf them at the slightest misjudgement on the pilot's part. In this cauldron of howling wind and water, it was as much as Hart could do, preventing them falling beam-on to the huge seas racing at them from the north; caught like that, they could be capsized by a breaking crest in an instant.

Catastrophe, when it struck, nevertheless took them completely unawares.

It was some freak effect of nature – a vortex of wind and waves, schooled perhaps by abrupt alterations in the levels of the seabed; by the heights and declivities of distant landscapes – that created a momentary tornado as dangerous as it was spectacular.

It was as though the ocean had been stirred by a giant, destructive hand. The waves whirled, doubling in height, breaking up into precipitous slopes crossing and recrossing the surface as the gale whipped foam from their crests. Time and again a huge comber would rear up behind the stern, its towering lip crumbling into froth, lifting the high-speed craft inexorably onward – only, as Hart struggled with the wheel, to go hissing past, dropping them into the trough until the next one surged up. Soon, too, the rain came, sweeping across the wild seascape in seething bursts.

It was a mountainous wave, racing obliquely across the current, that finally trapped Hart. He had just swung the wheel to starboard and, before he could correct, the bows reared almost vertically up the menacing slope towards the creaming crest. At the same time a second roller, advancing in a contrary direction, hollowed, curled and broke over the counter in a flurry of foam with a sound like another shellburst.

Pushed out and over from above, forced downward from below, the speedboat leaped clear of the whirlpool and crashed down on to its back, spilling the two men into the raging deep.

Seconds later the tornado had passed, spiralling crazily onwards towards the south.

In the relative calm after its furious passage, the capsized Lancer floated upside down in the swell, at the mercy of wind and weather. Hart and Hunzinger, supported by their inflated Mae Wests, struck out for the wreck and eventually reached the inverted hull. In a debris of floating cushions, ship's papers, duckboards and unidentifiable baulks of wood, they attempted to heave themselves up on to the savaged timbers and regain their breath.

But the boat, technically flat-bottomed in that it possessed no keel, was nevertheless built with a curving under-surface too slippery and slick for it to be used as a raft: the streamlined surface offered nothing to hold on to, no angle into which a foot or a hand might be wedged. The survivors were forced to remain immersed, supported on arms and elbows as the derelict swirled and yawed. It was too late in the year for them to suffer from hypothermia, but it was an extremely uncomfortable night, especially when the cloud front hid the moon again and the dawn seemed a century away.

The two of them were half dead from exhaustion when a small ship heading east sighted them soon after daybreak and lowered a boat to rescue them from the hulk.

Their saviour was a 1200-ton collier outward bound from Dun-Laoghaire. But there was no chance, not the slightest hope in bloody hell, the grizzled skipper told them, that he would put about and land them back there – whatever the inducements offered. "I have to file a route with the Admiralty," he said, "complete with chart coordinates, ETA – the bleeding lot. And there's hell to pay if I don't follow it to the letter. In any case, if I'm off course we risk getting blown out of the water!"

Wrapped in a steamer rug and sipping hot coffee with brandy in the wheelhouse, Hunzinger asked querulously: "Where then – if it's not on the official secrets list – are you actually bound for?"

"Fleetwood," the captain told him, "Where else would I be shipping a cargo of Irish fucking coal in bloody wartime!"

He turned to stare at Hart, who appeared to be convulsed with near-hysterical laughter within the warm cocoon of his blanket.

"What is it?" Hunzinger demanded. "What *is* it, Zoltan? What's so funny?"

Hart shook his head helplessly. "Nothing," he choked. "Just a thought. Forget it."

Fleetwood, the port just north of Blackpool, was less than twenty miles from Southport, where he had originally hoped to land them!

Part Three

Spreading the Net

Ten

There were, of course, a lot of formalities once they landed. Fleetwood is a small port. Naturally, therefore, the dock police, customs and immigration officials, coastguards and the military security people were officious, pen-pushing types – minor functionaries playing everything by the rule book, demigods scared of making decisions in case they were blamed. The kind of men, inevitably, who get shunted off into the less important postings requiring less initiative. Who are of course more difficult, more obstructive, more bloody-minded as a result because this is the simplest way to increase their own self-importance.

The problem for them in this case was – which rule book were they to consult?

In the matter of security risks, Fleetwood was less concerned about a seaborne landing of Panzer forces or a mass paratroop invasion than the infiltration of an occasional member of the Irish Republican Army, which had been active in the area before the war.

But two men, clearly not Irish, with no luggage, no passport, no papers at all, picked up from a wreck in the middle of the Irish Sea? Two men with a *speedboat*, for Pete's sake! What the devil did they think they were at? And what should be done with them?

Who the hell could they be anyway? Shot down German airmen? Unlikely, with English Mae Wests and British labels on their clothes (they were actually wearing dungarees contributed by the collier's crew, but their sodden garments had been put ashore and inspected).

Ah, but if they were German *secret agents*, spies, surely they would have been equipped with UK equipment as a matter of course, wouldn't they?

Members of the underworld, then, smugglers perhaps?

What about – stroke of brilliance from the coastguard officer – escaped fascists from the camp on the Isle of Man?

It was here that Hart frowned and exchanged glances with Hunzinger. Bit near the knuckle, eh? And the Manx authorities would by now have discovered the tunnel and alerted the local

71

police and military that at least one internee really had escaped. The problem would have to be resolved before these idiots thought of phoning Douglas to check.

"Why don't you accept us as we are?" he protested to the dock police officer and the immigration official. "Why not simply ask and we'll tell you what you want to know. You already asked where we were going and why. We told you: from Holyhead, Anglesey, heading for Kilkeel on the Ulster coast. We were badly filled in on the met and got overtaken by a storm."

"Why a speedboat for such a long voyage?" the policeman said.

"Precisely because it is speedy. We were in a hurry. We weren't to know about the bloody gale."

"Where was the boat's port of registry?"

Hart bit his lip. The first major black he had put up. It was probably Douglas, but he hadn't checked the letters and figures at the stern which indicated its origin. "Birkenhead," he said glibly. Registrations along the busy estuary between Liverpool and the open sea would take time to check, especially when they had no details and the Lancer certainly wouldn't have been salvaged yet.

"You say you have an import-export business in – Wales?" The officer glanced at his notes.

"I don't just say it: we do have. Hartzmann Brothers, optical instruments. Zurich and South Wales. We have a factory on the new industrial estate at Abergavenny."

Make it as far away as possible, but consistent with an Anglesey embarkation. They had worked out their story on the way to Fleetwood. Play it for real, or the apparent real. Keep as close to the truth as possible. Swiss neutrals, hoping to profit from the war, cutting it perhaps a bit fine, but what the hell – business is business, no?

"You could have reached Northern Ireland much more easily on the regular passenger route from Holyhead, or even Heysham or Liverpool," the immigration man observed.

"True," Hunzinger admitted. "But—" he cleared his throat – "well, only the military or those 'on business of national importance' qualify for the NI Pass permitting you to book a passage on those routes. We have business there, but apparently it is not considered important enough by the powers-that-be. It is to us, though. So we decided to risk – er – bending the rules a bit. We'd go anyway, but under our own steam, as it were."

"You were breaking the law in fact," the policeman said severely.

Hunzinger shrugged. "That's arguable," Hart put in. "As I understand it, the law is that you must have the necessary pass in order
to book a passage or, subsequently, to board a boat on any of those
routes. I have never seen it stated that it is illegal for British citizens
to be in Northern Ireland."

"Nonsense," the immigration officer said. "That's a point that
won't hold water at all. It's perfectly clear, by implication, that it
is the passage between the two . . . territories . . . that is forbidden
to those without passes."

"That was the point as far as our boat was concerned," Hunzinger
said. "It wouldn't hold water either."

Nobody smiled.

"This 'business' you say you had," the man from Military Security
interposed, pronouncing the word as if it was unclean. "Of what
precisely does it consist?"

"Something I should have thought might be considered of national
importance," Hart said angrily. "We sell precision optical instruments.
There's this company just outside the Harland and Wolff shipyard in
Belfast that manufactures accessories – some components of which
come from a branch in Dublin. If they could supply us with certain
infra-red equipment, we would be in a position to submit a design for
a vastly improved bomb-sight which would be invaluable on night
raids." It was pure invention, an improvisation to gain time – pretty
lame, Hart thought, when technical questions came to be asked. But
it was the best he could do in such unforeseeable circumstances. The
important thing was to get them the hell out of there before such
questions were put.

"Such a deal," Hunzinger was saying, "might well have brought us
a very important contract with the War Office or the Air Ministry."

Oh, yes? Bloody war profiteers, then! You could see the prejudiced
opinions forming behind the stolid faces. *Probably Jews, at that!*

"In my opinion," the security official said, "such negotiations could
perfectly well have been conducted by telephone. Or even by letter.
The Post Office still works, you know. Even in wartime."

Exactly, Hart thought. Staffed in the main by clerks as obstinate and
stupid as you. That could well have been the reason why we decided
to take a boat! But this was not a reflection he felt himself able to
make aloud.

"Not in our opinion," Hunzinger was in any case retorting. "In
business the personal approach is always essential."

"If the trip was so important," the policeman said, "and the . . . deal
. . . so vital to you, I can't understand why there were no papers, no

documents of any sort, on either of you. Surely you would have been
carrying specifications, invoices, reports as well as official letters and
your ID?"

"We had put them in a locker under the instrument panel, all of
them. For safety."

Hart turned to the immigration official. "Talking of rights of passage, you hesitated when you said 'between the two *territories*'. That
is a word normally used to distinguish separate countries. Northern
Ireland is as much a part of the United Kingdom as Scotland or
Wales, with the same citizens and the same passports. I fail to see
how a government can legally ban one portion of such a kingdom to
any section of the population holding valid passports."

"In a State of Emergency," the security man snapped, "the government can ban any damned thing it wants to!"

One of the telephones on the scarred desk in the harbourmaster's
office was ringing.

The dock policeman scooped up the receiver and recited some
extension number. "Who?" he said. "Where . . . ? At Downpatrick,
you say . . . ? Well, yes. Yes we have. This afternoon." He listened
for a while, stony eyes sweeping over the dungareed survivors. Then
he exclaimed: "What! You did . . . ? Yes, very interested indeed . . .
How's that again? *German* ones you say?" He had been perched with
one hip resting on the desk. Now he rose slowly upright, eyes still fixed
on Hart and his companion. "Yes. Yes we will: all the necessary . . .
Thanks again, mate. Much obliged."

Slowly, he replaced the instrument on its cradle. "That was the
coastguard station at Downpatrick," he said. "One of their patrols
sighted your capsized boat early this morning. It's just been towed
into the creek and righted. They found no locker under the instrument
panel. But trapped there in front of the gear lever was a valise."
A pause, held for effect. And then, triumphantly: "Beneath a false
bottom, they found two automatic pistols of kraut manufacture!"

He slid open a drawer in the desk and took out a Webley pistol. "One
move in the wrong fucking direction," he said, waving it towards Hart
and Hunzinger, "and you're two dead men we fished out of the sea!"

Turning to the security man, he said: "There's no cuffs in here.
Bring round a Bedford with a jeep escort right away, Dan. We got
to get these birds down to the station PD-bloody-Q!"

The action, if there was going to be any, had to be in the next few
minutes. Once they were hand-cuffed and behind bars, Hart realised,
there was no way of saying how long it would be before they were

released. When they were, it would have to have been through Webster or Nichols, and it could be some time before news of the arrest filtered through – even though they must have warned counter-intelligence to be on the lookout. In any case, it would be difficult after that to maintain the Zoltan identity, however discreetly the release was handled. Hunzinger, too, would certainly have been recognised after the alert from the Manx police and military.

In a nutshell, if the mission was to have any chance of continuing, they must avert at all costs any possibility of an 'unofficial' release from custody, which could only sow the seeds of suspicion in a mind as professional as Hunzinger's.

None of this could be confided to the spymaster of course. It would have to be enough to emphasise that they must free themselves before they reached the police station.

The one ray of light was that, since they were evidently assumed to be German spies anyway, they might as well speak German between themselves. It was unlikely that any of these clods, Hart thought, would be familiar with the language – and in any case it was a chance worth taking: it could hardly make things worse than they were at the moment.

How beautifully tailored, the ironies of life, he reflected. A monumentally complex operation had been designed to place him in a position where he could pose as a German spy, the aim being to flush out other German spies. And here they were with the entire mission at risk – because they had in fact been mistaken for . . . German spies!

Or, to put it more simply: Sod's Law again.

"Whatever we do," he murmured to Hunzinger, "it's got to be quick, it's got to be effective, it has to be decisive. Also it's got to be pretty well now."

"Agreed," Hunzinger said. "Once they have us inside any building that is secure, with senior officers at hand, we might as well take singles to Douglas right away!"

"A dockyard's likely to offer more cover than most places," Hart said. "A lot of space – but plenty of different obstacles to dodge behind."

He glanced out of the window. As he had thought: cranes moving on gantries along the outside of a warehouse, a siding with lines of open railway trucks, coal bunkers and stacks of timber.

"I shall follow your lead, Zoltan," Hunzinger said.

"It had better be while they transfer us to the transport," Hart told him.

"Better call up the Duty Officer, have him come to the station right away," Military security was suddenly brisk and businesslike. *In the case of suspected persons . . . the most senior authority available . . . first having effected an arrest.* It was all there in the book.

With the gun-carrying dock police officer and the coastguard, he closed in on the two suspects. The immigration man picked up the telephone and dialled a number. The customs official stayed by his side. He was admin, a civilian; he wasn't concerned with the physical stuff.

From outside the harbourmaster's office, revved up engines and a squeal of tyres announced the arrival of the escort. "All right, you two – down the steps and into the truck. And no funny business," the policeman said. "And don't forget I'm right behind you." He jerked open the door and nodded towards a flight of steps slanting down to the ground.

A swift glance was enough for Hart to take in the immediate scene.

Facing the office a Bedford truck with a canvas top and an open jeep were drawn up below, the jeep in front and the Bedford immediately behind it, each with the motor idling. The driver was behind the wheel of the jeep; a driver and two tin-hatted soldiers with slung rifles stood below the canvas flap at the rear of the truck. A sergeant was approaching the steps.

Beyond, perhaps thirty or forty yards away, two bunkers of coal separated railway tracks sunk into the macadam surface of the dock. One of the lines curled away towards the siding, where a shunting locomotive was manoeuvring a string of closed vans towards the warehouse cranes. Nearer, but off to the right, overalled workmen were gathered outside a glassed-in cabin presumably the command post of a foreman or overseer.

Cool air spiced with the odours of fish, tar and the gritty sting of coal dust blew in through the open door. The background noise included hammering, the mutter of a donkey engine, shouting dockers, a distant siren and the clatter of buffers.

Flat planks slung between two wooden baulks formed the steps leading from the office to the dock.

"That ladder's not wide enough to take two side by side," Hart said in German.

"Understood," Hunzinger replied.

"Get on with it," the policeman said roughly, prodding Hart with the gun barrel. "And no bloody talking." He shoved Hart down on to the first step, shouldering the German into a position immediately behind. After that, followed by the security man and the coastguard,

76

he lumbered down with the Webley rammed between Hunzinger's shoulder blades. Very unprofessional, Hart thought. There were nine or ten steps. He took the first three. The sergeant was waiting below.

Warily, Hart continued. When there were five men on the steps – three representatives of the law and the two fugitives – he turned to look over his shoulder.

"I said get on with it," the policeman rasped. "Rear of the bloody truck."

"Now!" Hart yelled.

A great many different things happened in a very short time after that.

Hart was on the last step but two. As the words left his mouth, he leaped violently forward and up from this already slightly raised position – not, as might be expected, towards the men filing down the steps but towards the unarmed sergeant. Cannoning into him at chest height, he knocked him completely off balance, spun him around, and shoved him in the direction of the soldiers standing a few yards away at the back of the truck. The man staggered into the group, spilling them sideways before they could unsling, let alone aim their rifles.

Hunzinger, the professional, had meanwhile profited from the policeman's ignorance of the gunner's basic maxim: never stand too close when you have the drop on someone. Consciously relaxing the tones of every muscle in his frame, he dropped like a stone into a sitting position, at the same time wrapping both arms around the officer's calves and pulling his legs from under him. Before he was sufficiently recovered to raise the gun, Hunzinger had squirmed around and dropped from the steps to the ground. Bounding upright, he sprinted away.

Hart was already on his feet and running off to the left. "The workmen!" he shouted.

Hunzinger caught on at once and veered his way. If they were among the dockers, nobody could shoot.

The soldiers and the sergeant had righted themselves. Shouting, they raised their rifles. The jeep driver was standing up on his front seat. Military security and the coastguard had jumped down to hare after the German. A single shot cracked out from the furious gunner.

Hart's spur of the moment plan – if such it could be called – was based on three facts.

There was plenty of cover; he was a fit man and so was Hunzinger; and the Webley pistol – it was a .455 Mark 6 revolver – was heavy, fired only six shots, and was inaccurate at anything over fifty feet except to a trained marksman firing at a fixed target.

77

He was aready level with the outer circle of men, who were apparently listening to a diatribe from an official in the cabin. Hunzinger was closing up. "The bunkers!" Hart panted. "Circle to the left . . . keep these between us and the truck."

Hunzinger nodded without speaking. They ran on, scattering the dockers. Some protested, some, alerted by the gunfire, tried to grab them, others shouted angrily without knowing why.

The men from the harbourmaster's office ran out past the jeep and the truck, aiming to cut them off as they left the dockers behind and turned towards the bunkers – then halted as they realised they would be blocking the riflemen's line of fire, and the sergeant waved them angrily back. The policeman with his Webley had raced round to the far side of the Bedford.

Hart and Hunzinger, only partly screened by the dockers were now zigzagging frantically, only thirty yards from the first bunker . . . twenty . . . ten. A rifle shot echoed across the yard, then another. There was a rattle of bolts, a third sharp report. The two men dashed on.

From the far side of the truck two heavier shots resounded. The fugitives were in full view of the policeman, but the heavy, half-inch slugs from his six-round revolver were unable to carry the distance or else flew wide. Hunzinger and Hart vanished behind the slatted wooden sides of the first bunker. For an instant they were visible in the gap between the two, then the line of shunted trucks ran back below the crane gantry and they were lost to sight among piled crates, a trolley loaded with mail sacks and the dockside timber stack.

For the first time now, someone – the sergeant perhaps? – had taken charge of the pursuit. Orders were shouted. The soldiers with the guns moved towards the warehouse; the two drivers headed for the goods trucks; the men from the harbourmaster's office fanned out between them, approaching the dock. On the far side of the basin, white smoke jetted skywards behind the red funnel of a coaster and the siren brayed again.

For the first time Hart realised the sky had clouded over and a few drops of rain had started to fall. They heard it pattering among the ironwork as they soft-footed alongside the vans shunting below the cranes. Over the moving buffers they could see the chase closing in. There was nothing for them to fear: they knew the fugitives were unarmed.

"There! Between the trucks, below the third crane," someone yelled. "Going left."

The advancing line changed direction. Hart and Hunzinger crouched down and ran. "What they won't expect," Hart hissed, "is for us to go back where we started. You know . . . into the jaws!"

Hunzinger nodded again. There was no need to speak; better to save the breath.

As Hart had hoped, the line of trucks screeched to a standstill with a diminishing rattle of buffers. Almost immediately, he heard the sudden accelerated puffing of the loco, and the train jerked into motion in the opposite direction. Jumping up on to one of the heavy couplings, he risked raising his head and saw – again as he had surmised – that points had been switched and the tanker was now pushing the vans out to join a dozen wagons loaded with coal waiting at the far end of the siding.

Hart's move had been observed, however. A hundred yards behind them, one of the riflemen had swarmed up on to the roof of a barred cattle-truck at the end of the line. Two shots rang out as Hart dropped back to the tarmac between the lines. One round ricocheted off an iron bracket strengthening the sliding door of a van; the second thunked into the woodwork of the door itself, stinging Hunzinger's face with small splinters.

The two of them were running now to keep up with the goods vehicles. "Too close," Hart gasped. "If he jumps from roof to roof fast enough, he'll be able to enfilade us on the curve. We make it on the buffers until we hit the outer limit of the bend, right?"

"Good thinking," Hunzinger replied. Hoisted up by Hart, he scrambled on to the nearest buffer, crossed the heavy linked coupling, then reached back to help the sprinting Englishman. Hart fell forward between the two vans, pulled himself upright, and settled on his side of the coupling. Astride the steel projections, the two of them rode uncomfortably out on the curve leading to the shunted coal trucks.

Clanking, rattling, creaking, the unsprung goods wagons trundled towards the outer limit of the curve, which was just behind the harbourmaster's office and about fifty yards away from it. Sheltered between the two tall weathered timber ends of the vans, they would be safe until the line of wagons took the sharpest part of the bend, but at that point – if the rifleman had had the sense not to come too near – they would temporarily be visible and in his sights. The rest of the pursuit, too, would be racing up behind between the warehouse and the railway lines now that their quarry had been located again.

Hart was upright once more, leaning for support against the shifting planks of the leading van. He peered towards the harbourmaster's office. No sign of the customs or immigration officials. They must have run to join in the chase after all.

He clutched Hunzinger's shoulder, steadied between the swaying chassis of the two vans. "Another hundred yards," he shouted as the train rattled outwards on the curve. "There's a plate-layers' hut which should shield us temporarily."

Hunzinger nodded. The vans careened slightly as the bend sharpened. Hart, watching on the outside of the curve, stared ahead with narrowed eyes. "Now!" he called for the second time.

It was a difficult jump. The train was now going at about fifteen miles per hour. They had to leap sideways one after the other to clear the ends of the two vans, then hit the ground running if they were not to overbalance and fall.

One after the other they leaped as the wooden hut slid into sight, Hunzinger first, then Hart.

The German landed well, slowed down, but missed his footing and tripped over a signal wire running beside the line. He rolled over and fell.

Hitting the ground just behind him, Hart reached down, seized the back of his dungarees and hauled him to his feet as he ran past. They came to a halt on the far side of the hut – and froze there for a tenth of a second.

Two railwaymen stood facing them, one holding a short iron bar, the other a heavy wrench. "Where the fuck you think you're goin'?" the older man demanded, moving forward. "What the hell's happening here?"

The younger man had raised his wrench.

The fugitives, after the initial shock, reacted fast. Hart stepped up to the man who had spoken. A case here for the unarmed combat course Webster had insisted upon. "Sorry about this. Really sorry," he said. But before the second phrase was out of his mouth, his right hand, held flat and hard as a plank, had whipped up and smashed a wicked blow across the railwayman's Adam's apple. Choking, his eyes bulging wide, the man scrabbled for his savaged throat and fell to his knees. Gagging for air, he folded forward and writhed in the dust.

Hunzinger's reaction, less scientific, was equally effective. Balancing on his toes, he swung around to lash out with one foot at the younger man's crotch. As the ferocious kick struck home, the man's breath exploded in a sudden yell as he doubled involuntarily up. The wrench dropped. His hands fled, clawing at his massacred genitals. Hunzinger caught the wrench low down, straightening to slam the heavy steel tool with all his strength against the man's temple.

He fell at once to collapse across his companion's prone body.

Hart and Hunzinger were running again, haring across the fifty yards that separated them from the harbourmaster's office.

But the hunt was now in full cry. Spilling through between the moving vans, spreading across the goods yard, speeding their way – at least a dozen, Hart thought. The two riflemen were trying to keep their balance on the roofs of different vans approaching the runaways. A bullet gouged the tarmac between Hart's feet; another scuffed wood from a telegraph pole behind Hunzinger; a third tore away part of the heel on one of his shoes, almost throwing him to the ground.

They were twenty yards from the office building. A ricochet shrilled skywards from an iron pipe projecting through the roof.

Ten yards.

The pursuers were further away. Apart from the gunners and the dock policeman husbanding his three remaining rounds, they could see the sergeant, the four remaining dock officials, a few stevedores and dockers from the warehouse heading their way, trying to cut them off.

Plus the two military drivers.

And this was the whole point of Hart's roundabout. In the sudden excitement of the escape and the chase, the Bedford truck and the jeep had been left unattended.

Hunzinger and Hart dashed past the front of the wooden office building. Confused shouting from the following crowd increased in volume as the pursuers took stock of the situation and realised Hart's intention. They changed direction, still hoping to cut them off. The sergeant was out ahead, running fast. The soldiers with the rifles had jumped down from the vans to take up a steadier firing position from solid ground, but now some of the hunters were between them and their targets.

The runaways were level with the military transport.

The engines had been idling, ready for the urgent convoy to the police station, when Hart and his companion made their break. Since then the motor of the Bedford three-tonner had choked into silence. But the jeep's four-cylinder Willys was still turning over sweetly.

"In we go!" Hart yelled. They leaped to the front seats of the open utility and he seized the wheel, slamming the short lever into gear.

Treading hard on the pedal, he sent the jeep careering around in a tight circle, missing the steps to the deserted office by inches. With engine howling and exhaust crackling, they roared across the tarmac towards the inner margin of the dockyard.

Through the rain now slanting down to polish the surface, Hart's last view of the pursuit was of the policeman, standing aside as the others ran, uselessly emptying his heavy handgun in their direction. Shortly after that the chassis shuddered to a couple of heavy blows, and seconds later the windshield shattered and fell from its frame. Last word from the riflemen, he supposed. Luckily, apart from a flying glass scratch along one of his cheeks, neither of them was touched.

Then he was twirling the wheel to skid them around the corner of another warehouse and they were at the start of a long, wide avenue bordered by parked vans, lorries, delivery trucks and long distance trailers from which forklifts were ferrying crates and sacks into a loading bay.

At the far end of the straight a guardhouse stood beside the closed dock gates. And here they profited from the luckiest thing of all.

With no clear idea of how he was going to react, Hart sped towards the exit and the sentries posted on either side. He was perhaps a hundred yards away when the gates – tall, timber-framed rectangles backed with corrugated iron sheeting – were dragged open by two soldiers to admit a camouflaged Humber staff-car flying a Command pennant. The ATS girl driver had a uniformed sergeant-major sitting beside her. Behind, an elderly, red-tabbed staff officer lounged on the rear seat. He was smoking a cigarette in a long black holder.

Presumably, Hart thought, the 'most senior person available', arriving to question and then oversee the incarceration of the two captured spies. He braked, sliding the jeep sideways a little on the treacherous surface. The sentries saluted; the officer raised a languid hand in reply; the Humber accelerated into the dockyard.

Then came the miracle. Seeing the familiar Duty Officer's jeep heading for the exit, the sentries decided to save time: instead of closing the gates and then reopening them according to the rules, they held them open and waved the jeep through.

For the second time, Hart floored the pedal and they roared past before the soldiers realised the occupants were civilians in dungarees and not men in uniform.

Hunt punched Hunzinger on the shoulder and let out a yell of delight. They were out in the street! They were free! There was nothing to stop them taking the first turn to the right and racing away to his safe-house near Southport!

Eleven

Twenty miles is no great distance to cover in a jeep with a full tank on a rainy day – even when the route lies through the industrial outskirts and holiday playground of Blackpool, and the more genteel residential spider-web of Lytham St Annes. Even when the jeep is a hot one.

But when the full tank has been holed near the bottom by a 13.9 gram, nickel-jacketed .303 bullet fired from a Short Lee-Enfield Mark III military rifle . . . well, then the journey risks becoming tedious, if not interminable.

Nick Hart knew of course that an alarm call would have been put out at once, the moment they were clear of the dockyard, and all MPs and civil police would be on the lookout for them. But one jeep is much like another, all of them in the same dun camouflage tint. Also he reckoned they should have taken the turning for Blackpool before the alert would have been sounded, so with luck the chase would additionally have to cover the routes to Manchester, the Lake District and Halifax. There was, too, an advantage in the fact that the identification number plates of military transport carried far more letters and figures than civilian vehicles – which should make instant recognition of a speeding jeep more difficult.

Finally, they had found a khaki army greatcoat on the rear seat, and Hart had given this to Hunzinger to wear, hoping he might at first sight be taken for an officer driven by an overalled motor pool mechanic.

It helped when they pulled into the forecourt of a closed filling station and put up the hood. But at anything over twenty-five miles per hour, the rain – falling heavily now – whipped in through the space where the windscreen had been to sting their faces and obscure much of the road ahead. Realistically, Hart thought they'd be lucky to make the far side of Blackpool before they would be forced once more to abandon ship.

In fact, they were fortunate to make the outskirts of the town.

Passing an industrial estate busy with lorries and delivery trucks between the serrated roofs of factory buildings, Hart was aware with sudden and unexpected force of the lack of response from his accelerator pedal. The jeep was losing way. The booming of the exhaust had ceased. He floored the pedal. The motor coughed . . . caught for an instant, surging the utility forward with a roar . . . died again. Hart stabbed the pedal. He engaged the starter. The Bendix whirred but the lack of response was total. The only sound now, as the jeep slowed, was the buffeting of wind around the canvas hood and the greasy hiss of tyres on the rain-wet asphalt.

Hart flicked a swift glance at the fuel gauge. He swore. The needle was hard against *Empty*.

Spinning the wheel, he wrenched the lever out of gear to free the transmission from the drag of a useless engine and steered them over a shallow pavement into the car park of a modernistic pub. The jeep coasted to a halt between a shiny station wagon and a flat-bed truck loaded with barrels of beer.

"Must have been one of those last three shots from the tommies," he said when he had inspected the damage. "That's torn it a little too soon."

"What do you suggest now, Zoltan?" Hunzinger asked.

Hart stared at the pub. It was of the roadhouse type – flat roofed, concrete, with cinema-organ scallops and swirls framing the entrance porch. Through mullioned windows yet to be blacked out he saw a brightly lit bar caparisoned with holidaymaker furniture and fittings, panelled walls with silk-shaded bracket lamps, hunting prints, a pinball machine. The long bar with its gleaming brasswork and glass was disguised as a fairground kiosk. Young women in red checked dresses and aprons moved swiftly among tables, wheelbacks and banquettes styled in 'Ye Olde' reproduction oak. They must be readying the place for the evening trade, Hart thought.

And at that moment two men wearing leather aprons emerged from a side door and approached the beer truck. "Opening time's not for another bleedin' hour, mate!" one called out, seeing Hart.

"Thanks, we know," Hart replied. "We'll wait." He nodded towards the jeep. "Run out of juice, anyway!"

He turned to Hunzinger. "So far as what we do now is concerned, we have two options. Either we walk – and it's a pretty long hike from here. Or we do wait. Then we go into the pub, order ourselves a beer and a sandwich and – once we have some change in our pockets – take a bus."

"You don't think going into the bar, or aboard a bus for that matter, is a trifle . . . risky?"

Hart shrugged. "No riskier that anywhere else. In the circumstances."

Such money as they carried on them had been returned, along with their sodden clothes, on the collier. But it was all in waterlogged banknotes, many of them in £5 or £10 denominations. No coins had been recovered. The clothes were still at Fleetwood, but luckily they had stowed the folding stuff into their dry dungarees.

"Looking the way we do," Hart explained, "offering a banknote to a bus conductor – or at a railway station ticket office – would be asking for trouble, suspicious in itself. Even if the cops and the military weren't on the lookout for us."

"Yes," Hunzinger said. "I see."

"We'll keep the wads hidden," Hart said. "Take out two single one-pound notes, and pay with them. I'll apologise to the barman, say it's all I have, and explain that it's wet because some bastard swiped my mac at lunchtime – and all my change was in that!"

The two deliverymen had prised open the metal flaps of a trap against the wall of the building. Now they laid planks from the tailboard of the truck to the ground and began rolling the barrels down one by one, to be lowered into the hands of cellarmen waiting below the opening.

"Meanwhile," Hart said, "we might as well get back into the jeep until they admit us to the bar. It'll hardly be picked up here: the back is to the road, and there'll be other cars parked on either side of it pretty soon."

"Yes." Hunzinger smiled wryly. "After all," he said, "no runaway criminal in his right mind would stop at the first pub he came to for a sandwich and a drink, would he?"

As it happened there was no problem at all. A factory whistle across the road blew. A crowd – at first in twos and threes and then in a flood – surged across the roadway, heads bent against the driving rain. A queue five or six deep had formed outside the pub porch before the doors even opened. The barman and three barmaids were so busy taking orders behind the long counter that Hart's soggy note was scarcely looked at. One of the girls concertinaed it, drew the edges sharply apart to test the quality of the paper, and slammed it into the till. "Two pints and two ham," she called over her shoulder, then spilled coins on to the bar and closed the drawer. "Thanks, dear. Cheers!"

Hunzinger was treated in a similarly perfunctory manner when he ordered another round and proffered the second note. The place was soon crammed with customers, surging the length of the bar as they shouted their orders, filling every chair, table and bench below the ritzy pink wall lights. The noise was deafening. Over a blare of dance music – Glenn Miller, Artie Shaw, Ambrose – the ringing of the pinball machine and the clatter of plates and glasses, several hundred male and female voices joked, argued, yelled, laughed – in a far corner of the big room even sang – in a roar of conversation that broke like angry surf against the walls.

Backed into a niche below one of the loudspeakers, Hart placed his mouth close to Hunzinger's ear. "Walpurgisnacht, eh?" he said. "Time we got out of here. Meet me by the jeep in five minutes." He shouldered his way through the throng of drinkers and vanished through an archway beneath an illuminated sign announcing *Toilets.*

When he rejoined the German, he appeared around an outside corner of the building, wearing a knee-length grey raincoat. "Shame, really," he excused himself. "Probably belongs to one of the staff . . . but I left a couple of quid stuffed behind the same peg."

"Zoltan, you go too far!" Hunzinger expostulated. "I suppose you to be practising your command of the celebrated Englander sense of humour: absurdity in the face of adversity, no?"

Hart himself, on the top floor of a bus heading for St Annes, wondered if in a sense he *was* finding that he had almost progressed too far – at least in the matter of identification with his false alter ego. Slightly at first – it had started outside the Kosher House in Port Erin – increasingly during the sea chase, and strongly when faced with official stupidity in Fleetwood, his reactions had become less those of an actor, more and more instinctive. Much as a thriller writer can find himself faced with a minor character shouldering his way to the forefront as his book progresses, Hart was finding that the gut reactions of the pretend Zoltan risked eclipsing his own!

Eluding the dockyard soldiers, flooring the sergeant and the plate-layers, his instinctive emotions, and the actions they provoked, had genuinely been those of a wrongdoer, frantic to escape the law. The adrenaline fuelling the flight in the jeep had been stimulated by a real fear of authority – not by a cold appraisal of the dictates of his mission.

There was an additional complication in the fact that – if only as a companion in adversity, as the man himself had said – he was beginning quite to like Hunzinger.

Watch it, soldier, he told himself (they were travelling on separate buses). *Remember your duty and where your loyalty lies! This man is an enemy, on the other side: his own mission is to help destroy your country. Remember that your job is to destroy him.*

The safe house was actually on the northern bank of the deep Southport estuary, in a St Annes suburb known as Lindsell. It was on the corner of a long street of identical red brick semi-detached residences with bow windows and steep slate roofs. The wrought iron gates and railing enclosing the pygmy front garden had been removed for melting down as base material for munitions, but there were still two laurel bushes beside the threadbare pocket lawn. And an aspidistra between the white lace curtains of the bow window . . . as there was in the house next door.

The place was perfect. The archetype of depressed Victorian gentility. Two old ladies with a Yorkshire terrier, perhaps; or one who took in lodgers. Anonymity personified, in any case.

In the other half of the semi, there were in fact two old ladies, *habituées* who spent most of each day peering out between the curtains, but they were pensioned off counter-intelligence staff and their job was precisely *not* to comment or report on the activity of those who came and went at Number 147 next door.

Cars were parked along each side of the street, several of them painted the dull khaki camouflage colour obligatory for all persons entering military targets or defence sites. In one of them, Hart fondly hoped, a member of Colonel Nichols's lamplighter brigade should be slumped down unseen, outposted to report the eventual arrival of Hunzinger and himself. They hoped.

At any rate, Hart imagined, they would by now know the two of them had been fished out of the Irish Sea – and at least echos of their Fleetwood exploit should have reached Regent's Park!

He walked down the narrow concrete passageway leading past the side of the house to the backyard. In a tumbledown shed outside the kitchen door, he felt in the darkness for the hiding place of the keys he knew would be there. Everything else they needed – supposedly left there by the fictitious Korsun and his Nazi agents – would be indoors.

Quietly, Hart let himself in, checked the blackout, and switched on the lights. The place smelled stale, dusty, unused, with a hint of linoleum polish in the background. Tomorrow they would open the windows.

He had of course been here before, with Webster during his crash Zoltan course. But he checked over as a routine what he expected to be there.

Food, drink, toilet articles. Two changes of clothes and two cover identities for Hunzinger. A couple of Walther PPK pistols with amunition (not to be used, but to give the German confidence: it was unthinkable that a safe house team would leave the place without arms for their men in the field). A British army uniform and cover identical with Hart's own – plus the most refined of all the Nichols's subtleties: the photo on the supposedly bogus Captain Hart's papers was not of Hart himself, but a copy of the Axel Hunzinger portrait Nichols had produced in London!

The thinking here was that 'Korsun', unable to find a picture of the real Zoltan because he was in an internment camp in Australia, had sensibly made use of an existing one of the twin brother.

The same delicacy of deceit flavoured a secret message left for Axel, ordering him to activate his sleepers. This was in code, but a genuine Nazi code Axel would know and could decipher, in fact provided by the British School of Cryptography at Bletchley Park after they had broken the enciphering system of the famous German 'Enigma' machine.

The only thing left for Hart to do was supply a dead letter drop with a brief report of what had happened to the two of them since the tunnel episode, together with his opinion of how the mission was progressing so far – with particular emphasis on the success or otherwise of the Axel-Zoltan relationship. He would have to attend to that in the morning, while Axel was otherwise occupied.

There was a code knock on the front door. Axel himself, whose bus had left Blackpool later than Hart's, had arrived.

And now, suddenly, the professional manifested himself too.

Throughout the tunnel escape, the boat drama and the Fleetwood evasion, Hunzinger had been an easygoing, almost unobtrusive companion, allowing Hart to take the lead, make decisions, play senior partner. The twin brother would have reconnoitred the terrain; he would know the score. Why waste energy competing when he could relax and play follow-my-leader – so long as the leader knew what he was doing. Which, so far, he apparently had done.

But once he had safely arrived, as it were, on the field of play; once he was in a position to act, the real Axel Hunzinger picked up the reins.

Rapidly, methodically, he went over every inch of the safe house – supplies, equipment, arms, accomodation. He studied the architecture, the arrangement of rooms, alternative entrances and exits. He went outside to familiarise himself as far as he could in the dark with the layout of adjoining gardens, walls and streets. Then he went upstairs to the bedroom assigned to him and decoded his instructions.

"Excellent," he said crisply when he returned. "This Korsun appears to be efficient. But we are already late: I should have contacted the agents I have to brief days ago. We must start work at once, tomorrow morning."

"What do you propose?" Hart said. "Can I help in any way?"

"You will have to." The voice was controlled, decisive. "We shall work together. But at the start, until the operation is under way, we must split up and act independently to make up for lost time. I will take one group of contacts, you another. I will supply you with names, addresses and recognition codes. You will alert each agent, instructing him to stand by and await orders from me."

"And how exactly," Hart ventured, "I mean in what physical role do you intend us to act?"

"The agents I shall alert myself," Hunzinger said, "will be those I know well, individuals who would not fail to recognise me however I appeared, in whatever role I choose."

"And myself?"

"The likeness is quite remarkable," Hunzinger said. "Almost uncanny. Quite good enough to persuade those I know less intimately or have scarcely met. You, my friend, will profit from this genetic coincidence; you will *be* Axel Hunzinger."

For an instant Hart was silent. Then he said: "And you too?"

"Not at all," the German said. "Let us not confuse the issue: some of these agents already know one another. Any hint of two Axels could lead to unnecessary questions. For myself, I propose to utilise this other cover and play the role of this—" he glanced at the documents – "this Captain Nicholas Hart."

Twelve

The message had to be short. It must fit on to a scrap of paper small enough not to be noticed beneath the strap of Hart's wristwatch – and thin enough when folded to be wedged into a crack between the wooden back of a public seat on the pavement and its iron support. The text must therefore avoid repetition of anything Webster and Nichols should already have picked up or guessed from reports filed by services ignorant of Hart's mission. The coastguards, for instance, would certainly have to report their patrol's unsuccessful attempt to intercept, then sink the speedboat. The Fleetwood harbourmaster, aided by dock police, would have been asked for a detailed account, citing witnesses, of the fugitives' escape. Fleetwood and Blackpool civil police would have opened a dossier quoting possible witnesses from the pub and the industrial estate where the damaged jeep had been abandoned. And, since supposed spies were concerned, the military would surely have alerted Special Branch and MI5 counter-intelligence. By now, Hart thought, the hue and cry in the immediate area could well be frantic enough to cause them acute embarrassment. It was fortunate that Hunzinger had considered *his* mission in an acute enough state to warrant them working individually, at least at first. Any two men of their age and apparent description seen travelling together risked at least questioning by an alert local constable or squad car team.

Given the circumstances, Hunzinger would of course know this as well as Hart himself, but it didn't make the immediate future less chancy.

To keep the safe house safe, they would even have to leave separately – one perhaps in daylight, through the front door, the other after dark, over the garden wall. The desk in the parlour had naturally been equipped with plenty of large-scale maps and street plans of the vicinity.

The public seat used for the drop was on the far side of the main road to Southport, facing an area of sand dunes behind the beach where a small nine-hole pitch-and-putt golf course had been laid out. South of the dunes and just before the estuary was a freshwater playground known as Fairhaven Lake – an extensive stretch of water with an island in the middle and a cabin from which diminutive sailing boats and skiffs could be hired even, as with the golf course, in times of national emergency. Perhaps the two leisure pursuits were considered useful factors in the maintenance of civilian morale during a time of shortages. In any case the seat – which was in full view of the safe house – was a reasonable place for a man to rest his legs for a couple of minutes, with the golfers and the yachts as an additional distraction.

Once they had retired for the night, Hart started to compose his message. It was to be printed in tiny capitals on a cigarette paper – preferably a single line, but two or three could, at a pinch, be used.

Hand machines for rolling cigarettes, together with tins of tobacco and Rizla papers had been left in each bedroom. The tobacco – this week's deliberate mistake – was German. Nichols was a perfectionist: he knew the most experienced of agents could make one error. Bully for him, Hart thought: human frailty could be one more small link in the chain of Hunzinger's belief in the existence of the Korsun team.

Hart slid a rectangle of paper from the orange packet. Several more had emerged and been discarded before he was satisfied with his message. He at once chewed up and swallowed the discards: no sifting through vacuum sacks or the contents of wastepaper baskets on this trip! The two lines he eventually came up with read:

BLAME FREAK STORM SALVAGE OP. SORRY DOCKYARD FIASCO DUE LOCAL SILLYCOPS. BROTHERHOOD ACCEPT-ABLE SO FAR WORKING SEPARATELY NOW.

There was of course no sign-off and no destination or recipient cited.

If Hunzinger decided to send him out in daylight, it would be no problem for a man still in view to stop to light a cigarette or hoist a foot on to the seat to tie a loose shoelace. He might even sit down for a minute to watch the boats, if only – possibly watched himself? – to check obtrusively that no tail was evident. If he was to be the nightbird, on the other hand, the drop would be even less of a problem.

Meticulously, Hart folded the paper lengthwise three times, then leapfrogged the thin oblong over and over, compressing it hard with his thumb until he had a tiny wad.

He stowed it beneath the watch itself, then tightened the strap by one hole.

He had been briefed on the location of three fallback letterboxes – one nearby and two in London – to be used only in extreme emergency either by Webster or himself. But because messages might have to stay hidden there for some time, these would be a great deal more difficult to service unseen, even if he were to be free of Hunzinger's hawk-like surveillance.

*   *   *

The difference in Hunzinger was remarkable, evident from the moment he left his bedroom at dawn the following morning, more noticeable even than it had been the evening before. Despite the long-lost brother syndrome, Hart found himself in the position of a cadet caught between the imperatives of a sergeant-major and a battalion commander.

Hunzinger performed the routine necessities – shower, shave, teeth, hair – with teutonic efficiency. He removed the blackout, dressed, brewed artificial coffee, cooked a dried-egg omelette, placed rusks, butter, marmalade and the health ministry substitute for orange juice on the kitchen table, and ate a silent breakfast. Afterwards, in the front parlour, he spent a half-hour juggling words, letters and figures around on a sheet of paper, but although Hart passed behind him several times and glanced over his shoulder the scribbles conveyed nothing to him. Acrostics or some private code, he imagined, supplying names and addresses from memory, out of his head.

Even after three or more years in an internment camp. Astonishing!

What was more remarkable still to the Englishman was simply to watch the man himself.

Wearing a uniform indistinguishable from Hart's own, he presented a picture, an image that seemed to Hart virtually hallucinatory. It was of course the uniform that underlined and emphasised the extraordinary facial likeness which itself he had somehow by now come to accept.

This morning, though . . . this was the total substitute! It was as though, standing in front of a mirror, his reflection had stepped out and proceeded to live a life of its own; an old Marx Brothers variety act played for real!

Hunzinger-Hart had finished playing with his paper. He went into the kitchen, held a lighted match to it, and flushed the ashes down the sink with hot water.

"Very well, Zoltan," he said tersely, returning to the parlour. "I have decided. Today I shall leave myself. You will remain here until after blackout. I shall give you three addresses and three messages, which you will commit to memory and then destroy. After dark you will leave here and visit each address and deliver each message in the order I shall give you. They are some distance apart. You will not be able to complete the task in a single day. We shall meet again, therefore, here. The day after tomorrow. Towards the end of the afternoon."

"Understood," Hart said. "That is all I have to do: deliver the messages? It would not be possible, if the message is short and apparently innocuous, to telephone?"

"Don't be a fool, Zoltan. Korsun, wisely, has intalled no telephone here. That is because, in wartime, no telephone line is secure. None. My sleepers are deeply buried. It is most unlikely that their lines could have been interfered with, but not impossible. The Englanders, never forget, are not beginners in the intelligence game. Calls, after all, can be traced."

Hart nodded. "I understand," he said, trying to look crestfallen.

"Also, most importantly, it will be your appearance that guarantees the authenticity of the message. To these less important actors in the play, do not forget, you will *be* me." He uttered a short, dry laugh. "Ironic, no? The authenticity of a communication guaranteed by a fake!"

Hart nodded. "English humour again?" he ventured.

Hunzinger nodded. Point taken – but no need to confirm. No comment. No smile necessary.

He said: "The message itself, the precise wording I shall give you, will be all you have to remember. Otherwise, less said the better. The message will in any case simply instruct those whom you contact to get in touch with the more important players I shall be seeing myself. After this we shall have to journey south, where most of the principals are. And there we will work together."

"Whatever you think best, Axel," Hart said.

"Sit down now." Hunzinger produced another sheet of paper, a pencil. "Write down exactly what I tell you. Memorise it word for word, then destroy the paper as I did mine."

For five minutes he spoke in English. Measured tones, neutral delivery, BBC pronunciation, repeating spelling or whole phrases when necessary. When he had finished he read what Hart had written, nodded, approved with the single word: "Good."

He repeated none of the instructions. It should not be necessary. He picked up his peaked army dress service cap and set it at a slightly jaunty angle on his head.

Again Hart marvelled at the efficiency of Webster's men. They had even removed the circular wire stiffener from the crown of the cap, so that the top now had the softened, faintly floppy (and strictly non-regulation) outline favoured by the more rakish, unconventional young officers.

"I shall leave now," Hunziger said. "Until tomorrow afternoon." Unexpectedly, surprisingly, he held out his hand. Hart shook it. The grip was firm, dry, forceful.

Hunzinger left the house carrying simply the leather briefcase which had been left for him. Money, Hart supposed. Credentials, maps, ID, perhaps even shaving tackle if he was going to be away all night. Later he discovered that one of the Walther automatics was also absent.

Watching – over the aspidistra – the man stride away towards the main road and the lake, Hart noticed that one of the cars in the line parked across the road – a camouflaged one, he thought – had been driven away. Lamplighters, withdrawn after reporting the arrival of the expected guests, he imagined.

It was up to him now to make a difficult decision.

Splitting up the way they had, deprived him of noting the names and addresses of the more important agents Hunzinger himself was to contact in the next thirty-six hours. There were only two choices open to him: follow Hunzinger secretly and note exactly where he went; or grin and bear it.

The more he thought about it, the more the risks involved in tailing the German seemed to him unjustifiable. He had no idea where Hunzinger was heading, even in St Annes. The buses? A train? Taxis? A car hire firm – if he could find one? By the time he himself could leave the house, even though the nearest main road bus stop was half a mile away, the spymaster would be long out of sight.

And if he did, miraculously, regain contact?

Since he didn't have even a clue to Hunzinger's first destination, he would obviously have to stay close. And a single glance his way from Hunzinger would blow the impersonation plan wide open, would kill the entire mission, with its months of meticulous preparation, stone bloody dead.

Hart shook his head. No way. Not after all he had been through. Not when the target had so unquestionably accepted the unbelievable, the existence of Zoltan-Hart.

It would have to be hoped that Hunzinger's important trio would be unable, on their unmasked own, to do much intelligence harm – and certainly nothing on the scale of his original scheme as a whole. Better still, according to Hunzinger himself, the lesser fry Hart was to contact would be familiar with the names and addresses of Hunzinger's initial contacts – and might conceivably be persuaded to reveal them once they themselves had been rolled up.

OK, decision taken – for better or for worse. Nevertheless, Hart had to break his big brother's rules and leave the safe house anyway. He had an important telephone call to make.

Before he slipped out, there was one minor investigation, nothing directly affecting the mission, that he was anxious to make. He had seen a dictionary on a small bookshelf above the writing desk in the parlour. He took it down and began riffling through the entries under letter H.

Here it was. **Hallucination:** *the apparent or alleged perception of an object or a person not actually present.*

Quite.

Thirteen

Before he attempted to get in touch with his three sleepers, Hart had decided that he must at all costs contact his own control and demand the use, as soon as possible, of an unidentifiable fast car with enough petrol coupons to make all three addresses in a single round trip. This way, if he could get the car soon enough, while Hunzinger was still away, he should be able to handle the whole job in one day – tomorrow if possible – which would leave him free the day after to make whatever investigations he thought necessary before the German's return that evening.

Without the car, however, if he was obliged to use public transport, it would be as much as he could do to visit those addresses and be back in St Annes at the same time as Hunzinger the day *after* tomorrow! Half an hour in front of the LMS and GWR train timetables was enough to prove this without any doubt. And that was without allowing for delays, derailments due to enemy action and cancellations due to shortage of locomotives or rolling stock.

The addresses in fact were in places as far apart as Preston, Shrewsbury and Brecon – the county town of the tourist region just west of the Welsh border country. The sleepers, according to the information he had memorised, were respectively a small-time newsagent, the rector of a boarding school for girls evacuated from London and an antiquarian bookseller.

Hart slipped out of the safe house just before eleven, thankful there was no telephone there through which Hunzinger could check whether or not he remained in all day as instructed.

The St Annes post office was in a row of small shops near a four-star hotel fully booked by government officials, factory owners and other civilian customers in 'reserved occupations' – that is, legally absolved from the necessity to answer the call-up and wear uniform. Hart threaded his way through the crowd inside and shut himself into a telephone box. He fed pennies into the slot of the machine, dialled a two figure code, then a seven-figure number he had been given by Webster. The receiver at the other end was lifted immediately after the first ring. A female voice announced the sole word: "Listening".

He pressed the button labelled A, waited for the coins to be accepted within the box, and said carefully: "The absent heart grows fonder still."

After a slight pause – the correct code having been recognised – the voice recited another, different seven-figure number, repeated it slowly, then hung up.

He dropped in more coins, dialled the number. This time a male voice replied.

"Direct Supply—" again a pause – "Limited. May I have your order, please?"

Hart presed the button again. "Blackpool – Lytham St Annes," he said without preamble. "Urgent delivery. A fast, reliable saloon. Fuel for the circuit Blackpool, Preston, Shrewsbury, Brecon, Blackpool. Three-fifty miles minimum."

"And the names, sir?"

"Nicholas for Webster."

"Please hold on," the voice said.

The wires hummed. Outside the call-box a woman holding up an impatient queue was arguing with a bespectacled harridan behind the Registered Letters counter.

"Are you there?" the voice queried finally. "We assume you can safely pick up in Blackpool centre?"

"No problem."

"The car park behind the Tower Ballroom, then. Three o'clock this afternoon. FordV8–22. Maroon. Registration GGT 617A. Keys in usual place. Return car to Lightburne Avenue, next street to safe house."

"Noted," Hart said. The line went dead.

He left the post office. The woman was still arguing with the angry clerk.

Beyond a butcher's shop announcing *Registered Customers Only*, there was a motor car saleroom. Since none of the three shiny, unused models on display could be purchased without special permission, the main display arranged to interest passers-by was a veteran ERA racing car, which had been driven with some success immediately before the outbreak of hostilities by the Siamese ace Prince Birabongse – notably in the Manx Tourist Trophy and a Grand Prix road race in Jersey. Behind the louvred cowling supporting the tiny windcreen, an excited ten-year-old boy was being lowered by his father on to the padded cushions of the high single-seat cockpit.

Studying the Riley-engined special with its slender body, unguarded wheels and silver outside exhaust, Hart felt something of the child's envy as he stared at the controls. No match perhaps for the 4CLT Maseratis and the team of Alfa Romeos run by Enzo Ferrari, a performance such as the ERA's would nevertheless have been a boon, in the country-wide road odyssey he was obliged to undertake the following day! Even Webster, though, had to have his limits.

Hart crossed the road, went into the dingy railway station bar, and lunched off a pint of bitter and a dried sandwich containing a leathery substance alleged to be ham. Later he took a train to Blackpool.

The sky was clear but there was a chill northerly breeze skimming white froth from the waves breaking far out across the expanse of pale sand. Groups of weekenders huddled here and there near the breakwaters and there were several dozen couples, hugging their clothes to themselves, promenading between barrows selling roast chestnuts, ice cream, chips and carnival favours below the railed esplanade. Hart fancied he could discern low-tide hardies actually bathing, out there in the distance. Suppressing a shiver, he turned away and headed for the huge, ornate ballroom building beneath the spiky ironwork of its tower.

The miracle, surfacing earlier only as the most fleeting idea, was as always astounding in its impact when it did in fact occur.

Searching in the crammed car park for maroon-coloured Ford V8s, Hart abruptly froze. Against all odds, he really had regained contact with Hunzinger!

The man was no more than twenty yards away, being handed into an Austin 16 taxi.

The 'usual place' for keys supplied with counter-intelligence transport was taped to the inside of the offside front mudguard. Hart had located his Ford, snatched the taped keys away and unlocked the driver's door before the taxi driver was back in his seat in the Austin, fiddling with the ignition and the manual choke beneath the dashboard. By the time he left the car park and turned right, away from the sea front, the maroon V8 was close behind him.

Once in the town's eastern outskirts, Hart allowed a light delivery van and two army three-tonners to come between him and the wide black Austin, following along the country roads a discreet distance behind. It wasn't a very lengthy trip, two or three miles at the most.

Masked by tall hedgerows around a tight bend, they came to a broad macadam drive-in. At the inner end of this were wide gates patrolled by blue-uniformed sentries, a brick-built guardhouse, and a big white noticeboard – almost a hoarding – on which, below the familiar laurel-wreathed crest, Hart read: **RAF WEETON – No.7 S of TT**. And then, in smaller letters: *All Passes to be Shewn.*

The taxi had stopped outside the gates. Hunzinger, very spruce in Hart's facsimile uniform, was strutting towards the sentries.

Hart accelerated past, his head turned away from the entrance. Two hundred yards beyond the next corner, he found a space at the edge of a wood and pulled the Ford off the road there. Locking the car, he walked warily back towards the gates. He knew there was an RAF station at Squires Gate, on the Ribble estuary, not far from the safe house, but Weeton was a new one on him. S of TT, he remembered, stood for School of Technical Training – anything from a Spitfire to a ten-cwt van. Presumably the place was an Air Ministry equivalent of those naval shore installations still known as HMS this or that: an air station without an airfield.

Hunzinger was still in view, a hundred yards inside the camp, walking towards a low, hangar-like workshop beyond a block of brickwork and white-painted shutters which was obviously the Station Headquarters. Presumably he had used the uniform and one of the very special intelligence passes left by the lamplighters to bluff his way in. The passes would admit the holder, whose photograph was attached, virtually anywhere without question.

Hart, who was in civilian clothes – a raincoat, a sober suit and tie – had a similar, though not identical, pass; ministerial rather than military. He withdrew before the sentries had seen him, went back to the car, turned around and drove to the gates. Parking outside behind the Austin, he marched up to the sentries waving his pass. "Ministry of Works," he said importantly. "Just a word with the Duty Officer in the guardhouse there. I don't want to go inside the camp."

"Very well, sir," the sergeant in charge of the sentries said dubiously. "Afraid I'll have to come with you just the same. You understand, sir – orders."

"Quite right, Sergeant," Hart said crisply. "Won't take a minute. Let's go."

One of the sentries, wearing an RAF Regiment flash, Hart noted, which meant the station was a high security risk, opened the gates to let him through. The sergeant unslung his rifle and accompanied him into the guardhouse orderly room.

The officer who saw them was an SAS major. "Very well, Sergeant," he said when he had scrutinised the pass, "you may

wait outside the door and escort this gentleman out when he leaves
. . . How can I help you, sir?"

"Ministry of Works," Hart said again. "Just one question, Major.
We are updating our records on official installations – you know
the kind of thing: fire risks, emergency exits, ARP access, salvage
possibilities."

The officer nodded curtly. "And your one question?"

Hart had produced a notebook, riffling through the pages. He
glanced through the window. "That low building there, beyond the
Station HQ," he improvised, nodding towards the hangar into which
Hunzinger had now disappeared. "We don't seem to have it on our
books. Could you just fill me in on its use, purpose, category as a
fire risk?"

"Certainly," the officer said, looking at a chart on the wall. "It's
a new installation. Hardly surprising you don't have it." He glanced
back at the chart. "Maintenance course in the upkeep of infantry
and tank-landing craft – amphibians and suchlike. Six hundred
square yards. Fire category A-3 because there's petrol and diesel
fuel involved . . . Any other questions?"

Hart had been scribbling. "No thank you, Major. That's all. And
much obliged." He closed the notebook. He dare not risk penetrating
furrther or staying too long: the risk of Hunzinger seeing him was
too acute.

Whoever it was that the German was contacting would have to
remain a mystery. It was enough for now to know that there was
a suspected traitor buried in a recently formed unit clearly directly
concerned with the preparation of equipment designed for use in a
seaborne invasion.

Exactly the kind of hazard Hart's mission was expressly created
to suppress.

Perhaps a further, more intense screening of the RAF personnel
staffing the unit might help identify the weak link. Meanwhile, Hart
thought, that was enough corroboration for one day. Best not to tempt
providence by pushing things too hard!

He nodded to the officer, rejoined the NCO, returned to the gates
and regained the Ford V8. He reversed behind the waiting taxi,
turned on to the main road, and drove back to Blackpool.

Approaching the Preston LMS railway station from Blackpool and
St Annes, the route climbs a fairly steep gradient (a bridge, an
embankment?) with the tracks down in a cutting on the left. Past
the brick balustrades on either side of the crest, it slopes more gently

down towards the station yard and the grimed glass arcade arched over the platforms. Fifty yards along the main road passing the exit from the yard, a side street led away towards the river. It was along this, a corner shop at the first intersection, that Hart's first sleeper could be found.

The immediate neighbourhood was run-down, the shop itself dingy. Children were playing football in the street. Hart parked the Ford as far away from the goals as possible and walked past the daily newspaper posters on the pavement (FAR EAST MASSACRE CONFIRMED . . . *BIGGEST RUHR RAID YET!* . . . NO SLACKERS HERE! says Mill Town Mayor) and into the interior of the shop.

It was the kind of place that sold candyfloss, boiled sweets in jars, Woodbine cigarettes in open packets of five and lurid fourpenny paperbacks of the blood-and-thunder variety. Larger paper-covered books without cover illustration hinted from the top shelf at more exciting titles in a back room.

Hart had been told to ask for a Mr Saul Kaner, adding that he was a representative for a midland company specialising in the modernisation of shop-fronts. At a reduced price, he was to say, his firm could easily turn the newsagent's single into a double front, with, consequently, a much more inviting display. To which the shopkeeper was to reply that, unfortunately, his premises were too narrow even to contemplate the opening of a second front.

In fact Hart was spared what seemed to him a fairly transparent allusion to the sleeper's forth-coming activities, for the grey-faced forty-year-old with thinning hair who sat behind the scarred counter leaped upright with a pleased exclamation the instant Hart appeared. Clearly taking him, as planned, for Hunzinger himself, he cried: "At last! We had heard hints that you might arrive. But what a relief actually to see you in the flesh, my friend."

Feeling faintly absurd – it was the first time he had actually had to play the role for real – Hart started to trot his prepared spiel, but Kaner cut him short.

"Forget all that rubbish," he cut in urgently. "I know who you are; you know who I am. Do you have a message? That's the important thing; that's what we are all waiting for, after all this time!"

"I have," Hart said. "It is short and it is concise. You are to contact Ajax and Mercury and Icarus as soon as possible – but only after four o'clock in the afternoons. With the usual prepared codes. They will brief you on what units, sites and concentrations they want surveyed. End of message."

"Admirable," Kaner breathed. "It has been a long, long wait

– but finally we have a chance to act, to play a part, however small, in the establishment of the New Order!" Stepping out from behind the counter – Hart saw with a start that he had a clubfoot – the man stood deliberately at attention and clicked his heels. Ridiculous in the shabby premises, he raised an outstretched right arm, the fingers of the hand extended, and began to declaim: "*Heil*—"

"Don't even say it!" Hart interrupted hastily. "Security is everything now, and one never knows." He glanced through the open doorway into the street. The charade was beginning to make him feel uncomfortable.

"At least, *mein Herr*, you will perit me to offer you a schnapps? We have been keeping a bottle – the real stuff: a genuine Doornkaat! – for just such an occasion."

Before Hart could reply, a football, accompanied by a shout from the street, bounced up the steps and into the shop. Kaner kicked it angrily out and back across the road with his good foot. "Always the same!" he shouted. "Keep your damned kids' games out in the open air where they belong and leave off bothering your elders and betters!"

Hart heard a derisive cry and an unintelligible insult from the youths outside. A smaller boy came into the shop with coins clutched in his grimy hand. He approached two open boxes at the front of the counter, each containing halves and quarters of broken, unwrapped chocolate bars, some damaged, some discoloured, all of them the worse for wear. "What is it, sonny?" the newsagent asked testily. "Can't you see I'm busy?"

The child was staring hungrily at the fragments of paler chocolate. "Off ration, innit?" he asked. "I'll have two ounces of the milk and me da's *Standard*, please mister."

Breathing heavily, Kaner picked up a long, claw-like pair of confectionery scissors and began fragmenting the broken bars into smaller pieces. Weighing these on an old-fashioned machine beneath the jars of sweets shelved behind him, he dropped them into a paper cone, handed this to the boy along with a folded copy of the evening paper and took the proffered coins. "Now run along, there's a good lad," he said not unkindly. "The gentleman and I have business, see."

He turned to Hart as the child left. "Football in the street," he said disgustedly. "Stuffing themselves with stale chocolate! I don't know what this damned country's coming to. Discipline, that's what we lack, a sense of *order* before the bolsheviks take over and anarchy reigns! Forgive me, I was asking: might I grant myself the pleasure of offering you a glass of schnapps."

"That's kind of you, sir," Hart said awkwardly. "The offer is appreciated. Alas, though, I have far to go, more messages to deliver, so I must regretfully decline. I wish you . . . courage in your . . . chosen struggle." With what he hoped could be taken for a friendly smile, he left the shop.

South of the cathedral town of Shrewsbury, Hart drove the Ford V8 into a world as different from the embittered bleakness of the back streets of Preston as it was from the mindless devastation of the London docks. It was a warm day, with white clouds floating high in an azure sky. Hedgerows on either side of the country roads blazed in the bright sunlight with valerian, rosebay willowherb, golden rod and the white umbels of cow's parsley. The scent of newly mown hay drifted in through the Ford's open windows.

In fact he would have preferred the bigger, more powerful thirty-hp V8 to the twenty-two model with its slender radiator grille in a sharp vee rather than a broad shield. But the smaller saloon was agreeable enough to drive, with useful acceleration, although one tended to get shifted sideways along the bench seat on tight corners if one used all of it available.

There was hardly any traffic. Hay wains and tractors monopolised narrow streets between the thatched roofs and half-timbered facades of the villages he passed through.

Nearing his destination, Hart wondered what combination of disappointments, reverses and set backs in life had angled the sad little cripple towards an appreciation of the Nazi brand of 'national socialism'. Was he married? Did he have children himself? Had he been let down by a woman because of his disability? Perhaps his own childhood dream had been to play football for Preston North End. Clearly, whatever had caused the chip, it still lay heavily on his shoulder.

A crossroads with no signposts. They had all been removed, of course – because the government was convinced German parachutists were unable to read maps! Hart ran the car on to the grass verge, switched off the motor, and took one of his own maps from the glove compartment. He got out to stretch his legs, and spread the map across the Ford's hot bonnet. Yes, another three or four miles should do it if he turned right here: the building was actually marked on the map. Chartwood Court.

He became aware suddenly of alien noise disrupting the early summer silence – a distant stuttering, interspersed with louder reports that could almost be . . .

The Ford was parked in the shade of a large elm. Hart moved out into the roadway, the sun warm suddenly on his back, and stared up into the sky.

Beyond the tree, eastwards above the leafy branches, smaller white puffballs punctuated the blue between fleecy clouds – some of them streaked with brown or an orange glare.

Anti-aircraft fire!

Even here, almost in Herefordshire, above the sunbrowned corn-fields, the mooing cows, those thatched roofs! The noise intensified, spread. A fresh group of puffballs peppered the sky.

Straining his eyes, trying to squint out the glare, Hart could locate the gunners' target: a thin, stalked cross moving in apparently leisurely fashion through the teased-out detonations. His aircraft recognition was good. He identified the plane at once: a Heinkel, the model known as 'the flying pencil'. Almost certainly an observation plane, probably sent to photograph the damage wreaked last night in some raid he hadn't heard about. More houses spilled into the street. More ambulance bells, steel-helmeted salvage crews sweating in the dust. More blood splashed over broken stone and weeping women being served hot, sweet canteen tea.

An alarming whoosh, a multiple scream of high-powered, high compression machinery. Hart jumped, swinging around to his right. A flight of five Hurricanes catapulted into sight above a wood crowning a rise in the rolling pasture-land. Streaking low down above the road, the fighters began climbing steeply, arrowing towards the east.

Hart turned back towards the bursting shells. But the Heinkel had vanished behind one of the drifting clouds.

Ten minutes later, he coasted to a halt, parking the car among a dozen others in a gravelled courtyard just beyond a gatehouse, presiding over two immense brick pillars crowned with rampant stone lions. No gates, of course: they had gone, with the safe house's garden railings, to be melted down and transformed into the tank landing craft maintained at Weeton!

Beyond the car park, flights of steps cut into a shaven grassy slope led up to the big house which had been transformed into a boarding school for young ladies evacuated from the home counties.

Chartwood Court was a pretentious red brick Victorian pile with two battlemented towers, its many windows gleaming in the afternoon sunlight. It lay stretched out between two low, wooded hills with playing fields on either side and long swathes of ripening oats and barley bordering the road below.

The gatehouse seemed uninhabited, the door closed, its windows shuttered. Hart shrugged. He had telephoned for an appointment with the rector, Doctor Avian Somerville, reputed to be an historian of some note. He raised the Ford's bonnet, removed a distributor head from the engine block and dropped it into his pocket. Another government must for the military: immobilize your vehicle every time you leave it, even if it's only for a few minutes. Those parachutists again!

He began climbing the steps to the main entrance. Girls in dark blue gym slips and white shirts were playing hockey in one of the playing fields, supervised by a tall, thin, stern woman in heavy tweeds. Further away, girlish cries drew attention to another group practicing netball. Down below he had noticed Italian prisoners-of-war, in their brown battledress with bright yellow patches, working in the fields. A temptation towards other kinds of games, he thought, for some of the older girls!

Hart had given the name used by himself and the real Hunzinger in Fleetwood: Hartzmann, the manufacturer of optical instruments. An elderly female secretary showed him directly into Dr Somerville's study.

The historian was very tall – heavy featured, with a great bald dome of a head decorated by wispy tufts of white hair over each ear. His voice, almost too mellifluous, emerged from thick lips in a drawl that seemed somehow virtually insinuating. Not really a man, Hart thought fleetingly, to whom he would care to trust his daughter if he had one!

Standing behind a wide desk himself, the rector did not invite Hart to take a seat. The room looked and smelled very male: leather armchairs, furniture polish, a hint of cigar smoke and glass-fronted bookshelves covering three of the walls. Hart wondered if there was – he supposed there must be – a Mrs Somerville. It seemed an odd place, anyway, to be talking of shop-fronts!

When the two men had exchanged their ritual recognition signals, pronounced with a certain distaste by the rector, he said: "I fail to see why we have to be embarrassed by this rigmarole. Childish tomfoolery in my view. I recognised you from your photographs anyway."

Hart raised slow shoulders in what he hoped might be taken for a teutonic shrug. "When our masters issue orders . . ." he said.

"Yes. Well." Somerville sounded irritable. "I understand you may have a message for me. Be so kind as to give it to me at once. I am a busy man, and time is precious."

"I do have indeed, Doctor Somerville." Hart's eyebrows were raised. "It is short and it is concise," he said for the second time that day. "You are to contact Ajax and Mercury and Icarus as soon as possible, but only after four o'clock in the afternoons. With the usual—"

"Nonsense!" Somerville interrupted crossly. "How can I possibly get down to Bristol at that time of day when my wife and I have this damned place to run? They will have to come to me."

"Since clearly you must know how to get in touch," Hart replied, controlling his own irritation, "I am sure that I may safely leave such minor details to you, sir." He completed the text of the message and said no more.

Somerville nodded. He pressed a bell on his desk. The secretary appeared. "Yes, Doctor?"

The historian glanced down at a notepad by his telephone. "Thank you, Mrs Kay. Will you please show Mr – er – Hartzmann out."

And that was all; that was it. Message delivered, message understood – and Hart was out in the sunshine again in less than five minutes!

All he had learned of interest to Webster was that one or all of the code-named agents rated by Hunzinger as important could be contacted in Bristol. That was already indiscreet of the rector. Hart wondered what on earth there could be of military importance that such a man could spy on. And immediately in his mind he heard Nichols's voice: *Any and all information possible, old boy . . . every slightest, tiniest detail, perhaps insignificant in itself . . . can combine with other apparently insignificant details to form a global picture . . .*

Returning to his car after such a cavalier reception, Hart was amused to spy out an insignificant detail of his own. Behind the unused gatehouse, one of the Italian POWs was indeed courting a nubile protégée of the rector's in the shade of a haystack – her gym slip around her waist, one of his sunburned hands hidden within an unbuttoned white shirt!

A long time later, having passed through the newly created industrial zone of Abergavenny, where the Hartzmann Brothers were supposed to have their illusory optical instruments factory, Hart crossed the border into Breconshire and headed for the county town.

Abergavenny was old, it looked as if it had grown organically out of the hills aeons ago; the zone was very evidently new: low concrete workshops; saw-roofed modern factories; light engineering works producing components for aero-engines; chocolate manufacturers; canning plants established among the Welsh heights to keep them out of reach of German raids – many of them in fact owned or staffed by refugees from Hitler's Europe.

Brecon was something else again in its nest of rounded, woody hills. No more than the fling of a long-distance stone from The Valleys, that mythical Welsh mining heart, the place nevertheless retained much of the solid nineteen-century gentlefolk calm of such cities as Exeter or Salisbury. The Beacons, gentle domes of misted green now but celebrated more for the russet and amber of autumn, provided the ideal undulating, leafy landscape in which to set a town, far from the bursting of shells, where an antiquarian bookseller could still be found after nearly four years of war. And the premises of Arthur Fordyke (Rare Editions, Fine Art Publications, Early Prints) supplied no discordant note within the harmonious whole. The leaded, bow-front window of the narrow shop was at the back of a tiny flagged courtyard that actually boasted geraniums in pots.

Fordyke had been well cast in his role. He was tallish, stoop-shouldered, about seventy, with thick-lensed spectacles pushed up on to the high forehead crowning his lean grey face. The shop, sunlit at the entrance, reaching back into a gloom alleviated by a single oil lamp, was an ideal enough setting for Hunzmann-Hart's introductory spiel.

The bookseller, poring over an atlas of ancient maps buttressed by walls of leather-bound tomes, showed neither surprise nor pleasure at his controller's unexpected appearance. He recited the necessary response in a high, slightly wavering voice, waited for the message, nodded his acceptance of its instructions, and said: "My dear sir. A pleasure indeed. Please do sit down." He indicated a wooden swivel-chair standing beside an angled draughtsman's table with more maps spread across its tilted width.

Hart glanced around the ceiling-high ramparts of old, shelved books, at tables piled high with dusty volumes, at shallow drawers crammed with etchings, daguerreotypes and prints. There was nobody else within the depths of the shop. He sat down in the swivel chair.

"It is late in the afternoon, but not too late, I hope," Fordyke said, "for a cup of mint tea? Accompanied, perhaps, by a chocolate biscuit from the OP factory at Abergavenny owned by a Czech friend and, er –" a sharp, dry laugh – "fellow conspirator!"

"That would be . . . a pleasure," Hart said. Was it possible that he might be able, if the man wished to talk, to quarry out something of the motivation stimulating at least one of these three disparate traitors? Something that could conceivably interest Colonel Nichols? He had passed a very big military training camp in the hills. There was a huge RAF maintenance unit at St Athan in nearby Glamorgan. He had seen tanks, armoured personnel carriers and mobile artillery manoeuvring among the chewed up slopes of a restricted area not far from Kidderminster. But what was the connection between such obvious targets and this elderly bookworm?

Fordyke had vanished into a back room. Now he reappeared with a tray bearing two small glasses, a plate of biscuits, and a small silvered pot with a long curved spout from which aromatic steam curled lazily. Raising the pot high in the air, he allowed a thin stream of the hot, pale green liquid to fall expertly and accurately into the two glasses.

"Bravo!" Hart smiled. "And not a drop spilled. That takes years of practice, I guess?"

"I spent some time – in my youth, you know – in Greece and the Lebanon," the bookseller said apologetically. "One tends, as they say, to do in Rome . . ." He left the phrase unfinished.

He did wish to talk though.

But it had nothing to do, as Hart had hoped, with the minutiae of military equipment, the performance of specialised vehicles, the logistics of modern war. It had everything to do with the thinking and theories underlying the unleashing of a mid-twentieth-century conflict.

He was of course totally familiar with the works of the great German thinkers of the late eighteenth and early nineteenth-century. "It was naturally Kant who postulated the concept of a moral law which should pre-suppose 'the highest good of all human beings' as its aim," he said.

Hart nodded. The mint tea was very good.

Fordyke pushed the glasses higher up on his forehead. "But Kant was intelligent enough," he continued, "or cynical enough, if you like, to see also that this highest good cannot be realised unless the course of the world is itself guided by moral law." A significant pause. "That is to say by a Moral Master of the universe, whose existence we are driven to assume."

"Or create?" Hart suggested, thinking of the man in Berchtesgaden.

"Exactly, exactly. Naturally *you* would understand. But Kant's philosophy leaves, just the same, an essential dualism unrealised, don't you agree?"

Peter Leslie

"Absolutely," Hart said.

"Nature opposed to spirit, object opposed to subject, the outer world composed of isolated, unrelated substances whose nature is beyond the reach of knowledge." The spectacles had fallen to the bridge of the bookseller's nose, then slid towards the tip. Irritably, he pushed them back up above his eyebrows. "It was Hegel, of course, who bridged the gulf," he said triumphantly, the thin voice climbing the scale with each point made. "Hegel who succeeded in reducing duality to unity. Hegel shows us that all difference implies a unity, that a definite thought cannot be separated from its opposite, that the idea of fulness, for example, cannot be separated from that of emptiness."

"Rather like the motorist's dilemma," Hart said irreverently. "The petrol gauge registers *Half* – but is the tank half full or half empty?"

"Er . . . yes, I suppose so. If you care to put it like that." Fordyke's expression said clearly that, for him, 'like that' was synonymous with 'vulgarly'. But he regained his composure, poured out more mint tea, and continued resolutely.

The long drive had tired Hart. The stress of continuing his impersonation had begun to tell. As the Fifth-Columnist bookseller's voice droned on, his consciousness started to fade; the dusty, sunlit bookshop darkened around the edges; the voice grew fainter, increased again in volume. But little by little the drift of the argument became distilled, meaningless. Only isolated sentences, unrelated terms and phrases filtered through.

Hart tried desperately to stay awake, but the struggle was a difficult one.

"We are driven by the nature of our minds to see design in nature and man as the centre of this design . . . Good will can be construed as an habitual controlling consciousness of membership in an ideal community of rational beings . . ."

Yes, yes, Hart thought hazily. And membership of the Master Race.

"An endless aggregate of essentially related and transitory existences, each of which exists ony as it determines, and is determined by, the others . . . A world of objects, each and all of which exist only insofar as they exist for intelligence, and insofar as intelligence is revealed in them." The words droned on, relentlessly, inexorably. From time to time Hart jerked almost awake to murmur "Quite" or "Understandably" or "Are you sure?"

"The self exists as Oneself only as it opposes itself, as object,

108

to itself as subject – and at once denies and transcends that opposition . . ."

Half drugged with fatigue, Hart found himself in the middle of this Gothic manifesto recalling a waspish comment in the Beachcomber column of the *Daily Express*. The celebrated Walter Savage Landor's romantic comment ('Nature I loved, and, next to Nature, Art'), the humorist snapped irritably, was eternally being misquoted. "What the poet actually said was *'Nietzsche* I loved, and, next to Nietzsche, Art – Art of coure being Arthur Schopenhauer'!"

Many Nietzschean gems on the pathetic inefficacity of Christianity with its compassion for the weak, on the exaltation of 'the will to dominate' and suchlike, may have passed by Hart that increasingly hazy afternoon. But never afterwards was he able to remember precisely how he had managed to excape the mental clutch of the bookseller and his superman theories. Or for that matter how or when he had contrived to regain his car and drive away.

Fourteen

Axel Hunzinger's day had been busier, perhaps more dramatic than the anodyne southward peregrination of his supposed brother. He too had a lot of ground to cover; he too had urgent need of a fast, reliable car and as much fuel as might be necessary. He also, as it happened, possessed in his memory a telephone number – though not a secret one – through which he hoped to obtain such transport. Which would have suppported Colonel Nichols's belief that the sleepers Hunzinger was expected to awake might not be the only pro-fascist elements known to the (genuine) German secret services and still at large in the country.

But for Hunzinger it wouldn't just be a matter of picking the car up from a parking lot. It was only his second full day alone after the break-out from the internment camp, and since he had been imprisoned there since 1940 there would doubtless be new rules, regulations and wartime restrictions with which he was unfamiliar. He would have to take great pains not to raise the slightest suspicion by any untoward action or behaviour until brother Zoltan was at hand to put him right – especially in a country morbidly traumatised, so he believed, at the thought of 'foreign spies'.

He had already taken what he considered an unjustified risk, hiring a taxi to take him to the RAF maintenance base at Weeton. For all he knew, drivers might be obliged by the security people to log all journeys, together with time spent at destination if any, and description of the passenger.

He had no idea if it was still possible to hire a car – and, if so, what documents or justification he might be expected to produce.

Until he could get Zoltan down south, nevertheless, where transport would be freely available, it was essential that he remain mobile until he had contacted the more important members of his ring who happened to be in this wretched area offered to him by fate. Essential, then, to contact Dr Marcus Newman, the most deeply buried of all Hunzinger's hidden company.

Newman, who wouldn't have known an armoured personnel carrier

Blitz Harvest

or a tank landing craft from a grocer's delivery van, was not even among the sleepers to be activated. A brain surgeon, consultant at famous hospitals in London, Edinburgh, Manchester and Bristol, Member of the Order of the British Empire, and respected Justice of the Peace, he was being held in reserve, as liaison between the right wing pro-German politicos and the military government, when Britain was finally occupied. Before Hunzinger had been incarcerated, he had been warned by Berlin: "This man is among the most valued of all our hidden friends. His political views remain secret even from his family. Now that King Edward is no longer available to us, he is, along with Mosley and two others, perhaps the most vital inside ally we shall have when the time comes."

And, the security chiefs had added: "He is not to be disturbed, and his telephone number – which we shall give you – is not to be used except in the most extreme emergency."

Well, this was an emergency, wasn't it? Denied the access to his Embassy in Dublin he had been counting on, marooned in the godforsaken industrial north of this rainswept land, with police and military already after him in his Hartzmann role, surely, for once, he was entitled to ask for a helping hand?

From a public booth in Blackpool station, Hunzinger dialled the number.

"I am afraid Dr Newman is unable to accept new patients at this time," the cool voice of a receptionist told him. "I cannot give you an appointment for at least three weeks. If the matter is urgent—"

"It is extremely urgent."

"—I can give you the number of his senior partner or one of the assistant registrars at Saint Mary's. In the case of an accident however, the Emergency Out Patients—"

"It is a case Dr Newman has treated already," Hunzinger interrupted harshly. "Tell him—"

"Really? I am not sure that I can trouble the Doctor. He is a very busy man, you know. He—"

"Tell him," Hunzinger almost shouted, "that the Schiller Syndrome has reappeared. Mentally."

"Very well, sir, if you insist." The voice was noticeably cooler. "And the name?"

"Captain Hart," Hunzinger said at once. The name was unimportant. The Schiller line was the code introduction, with the word Mental added as confirmation of the urgency. He was in uniform and carrying Hart's papers anyway.

111

The line had gone dead. Hunzinger checked a railway timetable he held in one hand.

"Captain Hart?" The voice was now less Arctic; hardly tropical, but a long way further south. "Dr Newman will see you at five o'clock."

"Five thirty," Hunzinger said, with another swift glance at the timetable. "I am calling you from Blackpool." Newman's surgery – and indeed his home – was in residential Chester.

"Very good, sir," the receptionist said. "First floor. Suite 3B, left of the lift."

"I'll be there," Hunzinger said. He left the booth and hurried towards the ticket office.

The train of course was crowded. All the trains were crowded. Always. Long queues formed outside the gates at the entrance to each platform, waiting for the ticket collectors to unfasten the locks and let them in once the carriages arrived. People stood between the seated passengers in each compartment. The corridors were impassable, jammed with a crowd of soldiers, sailors, airforce men, elderly civilians and women with fractious children, many of them sitting – or even sprawled asleep – on suitcases, trunks, folded perambulators, kitbags, paper parcels and cartons tied with string. The railway class system no longer applied, the air of every coach was thick with tobacco fumes and all the windows were steamed up. Outside, black smoke whirled back past the train to subside beneath the overcast sky and roll away across the flat grey landscape.

The specialist's office was a welcome relief – deep leather armchairs on a fitted carpet, flowers arranged tastefully in Etruscan-style vases, that week's magazines neatly squared up on a polished table. Somewhere, a faint electric humming stirred the calm – airconditioning perhaps, Hunzinger thought. He straighted the shoulder straps of his uniorm and picked up a magazine.

The secretary was about thirty, blonde, quite pretty, with faultless make-up. Presumably Newman – whose father's name had been Neumann – had pulled strings to have her qualified as being in a Reserved Occupation. She would be equally qualified, Hunzinger was sure, for certain other occupations, not specifically itemised but evident when she came out from behind her desk and one saw her full length. The desk was behind a frosted glass partition and bore nothing but a ledger, a crocodile appointments diary and two telephones. The young woman emerged to greet each patient in the waiting room personally – and indeed it was clear, so well-ordered was the consultant's surgery, that there were never more than two clients, at the most, expected to be found waiting in those leather chairs.

The blonde wore high-heeled black court shoes with real silk stockings, slightly dark. Her legs were superb. She was slender-hipped, slim waisted and – judging from the full curve thrusting out the top of the crisp white knee-length laboratory coat she wore – well endowed elsewhere.

She took Hunzinger straight into the consulting room the moment he arrived. No other patient came out of it first and the waiting room was empty. Excellent fieldwork, he noted, following the faintly suggestive sway of a starched backside: nobody had seen him arrive, nobody would see him leave, and he would lay money on the fact that the waiting room would have no other tenant while he was there. He wondered how many times a week the receptionist, who had smiled very sweetly when she greeted him, had to make her own way home at the end of the day.

Anyway, whether or not she was his mistress – and he would be a fool if she wasn't, Hunzinger reflected – the good doctor's cover was safe: there was nothing whatever to connect him with the escaper from the Isle of Man, even if the twins were nabbed and publicly exposed.

Newman looked like an Austrian arch-duke – the broad, fine brow, the immaculately waved silver-grey hair, curling slightly at the nape and over the ears, the proud nose and firm mouth. His voice was very deep and measured. A real crowd-puller all right, Hunzinger approved.

"I assume you are from the Wolf's lair?" Newman asked, citing the indication the spymaster had used before he was picked up under the 18B regulations. Hunzinger nodded.

"And I trust your . . . emergency . . . is vital enough to warrant this serious breach of security?"

"I wouldn't be here otherwise," Hunzinger said. "I need a car for twenty-four hours. Not more."

Newman had been lounging in a wide, leather-padded swivel chair. Now, suddenly, he pushed this back from his empty, glass-topped desk and rose to his feet, pacing to and fro in front of a window that was already blacked out although it was not yet dark. Good fieldwork again, the German noted: he wouldn't ever have been seen in the specialist's presence, not even from a window across the road.

"Cars," Newman said at last, "are difficult. And dangerous. They can be traced. The ration cards for petrol coupons are numbered. If the coupons are forged black-market items, the numbers on those will lead security to the black-marketeers: most of them are known to the police but allowed undercover to continue operating – precisely because they can finger, unawares, bigger fish in the underworld. Hiring, though theoretically possible, is excluded for the same reason."

"I had considered that," Hunzinger said. "Naturally. But since I am ignorant of the latest regulations, documents required, and so on, I thought it best—"

"You were wise to refrain," Newman cut in. "There could be danger there too." He paused, shaking his leonine head. "It is very bad security anyway – abysmally bad – having you come here at all. In fact the only reason I decided to was because . . ." Another pause.

"Because?" Hunzinger prompted.

"Because, frankly –" a short, dry laugh – "it was the best way I could think of to . . . ah . . . get rid of you fairly quickly! And I am bound, I gave my word, to help if it is absolutely essential."

"It is."

Newman had stopped his pacing. He had come to a standstill beside a shaded electric lamp on the desk – a resplendent figure in an immaculate clerical grey pinstripe. The trousers weren't even creased at the knee, Hunzinger noticed.

"Perhaps," Newman said, "if you could give me some idea of the . . . of the *urgency* . . . that is to say of the *scope* of your particular task . . . ?"

"I am of course, sir, not able to reveal any details whatever of my mission," Hunzinger said stiffly.

"No, no. Of course not. Very proper."

"Let me just say," the spymaster began carefully, "that there are other people, less well covered, perhaps, than yourself, but nevertheless unsuspected, here and there in the country. These people could be – what shall I say? – operatives, waiting to be called into action. The call has to be personal. It must be issued to all of those involved in the shortest possible time. And that time is now. I cannot say more than that."

"I see. And you require the car simply for speed and mobility? Because public transport, for instance, used to contact your . . . operatives . . . one after the other, would cause too much delay?"

"Exactly. *Any* delay is unacceptable. All of the people I mention," Hunzinger said untruthfully, "must without fail be alerted, and certain plans correlated, tonight and tomorrow before dark."

Newman sighed. He was fingering the dark-blue and red tie of an exclusive military club known as The Highland Brigade. "In that case," said he, "I shall have to place myself – even if only slightly by comparison – at risk."

"I should not wish in any way," Hunzinger began awkwardly, "in any way at all, to compromise your own highly important—"

"No, no. I have decided." The specialist leaned over his desk, scribbled on a notepad, tore off a page and handed it to Hunzinger.

"Here is my address, and how to get there. Memorise what I have written and give me back the paper." He sat back in his chair again. Decision taken, for better or worse. So back to normal. Positive man with the reins in hand.

"You will take my wife's car," he said when the paper had been returned. "It's dubious – but safer than my arranging anything myself at short notice. It will be in the open garage behind the house, a Vauxhall tourer, blue. The tank will be full, a jerrican in the boot. You must enter the property as soon as you can after dark – the gates will be open – and drive straight away. I will give you until nightfall tomorrow – at which time I shall report the car stolen. Is that clear?"

"Admirably," Hunzinger said with relief. "And the fuel will be sufficient without coupons?"

"It will have to be," Newman said.

"Where would you like me to leave the car . . . afterwards?"

"Any public car park that is convenient. It doesn't matter where. The police will eventually find it. If I urge them to pull out the constabulary finger, I shall doubtless be asked, don't I know there's a war on?" A wintry smile. "Now, here are the keys." He slid open a drawer, took out a small chamois pouch fastened over a ring and handed it to Hunzinger. "Throw them away when you have finished with the car, my wife has others. And if you have time . . . some attempt to make it look as though the ignition, the starter, or whatever, had been tampered with would help."

Hunzinger nodded. He put the keys in his pocket. "You will not hear from me again," he said. "I am very grateful."

"You should be," said the affable Doctor Marcus Newman, OBE.

The Vauxhall was a coach-built, fourteen-hp drop-head convertible in duck-egg blue, with a streamlined body by Salmon and a Tickford head. It was not precisely the most unobtrusive model on the road, even in affluent Chester, but it was a beautiful little car to drive. Hunzinger was at first a little puzzled by its registration number – DZ 1922 – but then he remembered: all vehicles which included the last letter of the alphabet on their licence plate had originally been registered in Ireland. The good doctor must surely, at one time or another, have been wined and dined at the German Embassy in Dublin, discussing with Ribbentrop or Hess the role he would play in the establishment of Greater Britain. Perhaps the pretty little convertible was a gift from a grateful Third Reich to a useful Fifth Columnist's pretty little wife – a gracious acknowledgement for favours yet to come?

The driveway to the Newman house – Georgian of course, sheltered by cedars – was gravelled. But light from a moon now rising earlier filtered enough through the tall trees to show Hunzinger where there was shaven grass to muffle his footsteps. The blackout was total. Newman – prudently enough – had taken his wife to the theatre in Liverpool. The maid had been given the night off. The Vauxhall's engine was warm. The engine started at the first twist of the key.

Hunzinger drove carefully past scented rose gardens with the top down and warm wind ruffling his hair. The uniform of course would help, but there would naturally be the odd roadblock once the night was well advanced – and an officer on a course from Northern Ireland, even if he was driving an Irish registered car – an unexpected bonus – would be expected to have his personal transport in the dun camouflage khaki colour.

Too bad, Hunzinger thought, leaving the tree-shaded outskirts of Chester and heading southeast. And if it came to it, he could always junk the car and run for it, using the Walther as a dissuader if any of the unarmed police decided to play the heavy.

Meanwhile, it would take all his expertise to thread his way correctly through the unsignposted maze of the industrial Midlands and arrive in good time at his destination.

It wasn't a very long journey – something over two hundred kilometres, a hundred and fifteen or twenty miles at the most. But the route led through Newcastle-under-Lyme, Stoke-on-Trent, Uttoxeter, Derby and the outskirts of Nottingham, and an officer too often stopping to scrutinise maps in the feeble light of a dashboard lamp could arouse suspicion. Unwelcome questions anyway.

Hunzinger's first call, unannounced, was at a village called Sutton Bonington, not far from Loughborough, in Leicestershire. His intention was to arrive before dawn and be within his contact's property before the household was awake. Strangers seen in an English village could stimulate, he well knew, a flood-tide of speculative gossip within minutes of an intruder's first sighting – and it was vital that no whiff of intrigue drifted even in the vague direction of his first, possibly most important, sleeper.

Professor Iain Ludham-Lyle had held the Nottingham University chair of German History and Central European Ethnography for twenty years before his retirement in 1938. He was now gain-fully employed as a counsellor to the Allied Psychological Warfare Department and adviser on propaganda campaigns at the Ministry of Information in London. More importantly – essentially for Hunzinger – he was much sought after by the Army Educational Corps as a lecturer on current topics connected with the war in Europe, the forthcoming Second Front and its likely effect among the peoples concerned. He was too, naturally enough, an intimate of many AEC officers actually concerned with the logistics and forward planning of that very operation. Invaluable too, the spymaster had thought when he first met the man, for the jigsaw analysis and later assemblage of the innumerable snippets of apparent trivia funnelled in by the other sleepers.

Some way beyond Stoke, he stopped the Vauxhall and erected the canvas top. A long way south, beyond a bank of clouds blowing up from the coast, he had seen the fitful pulses of summer lightning momentarily illuminating the sky, and he had no wish to be caught unawares in another storm.

Ten minutes later, stopping to relieve himself behind a clump of bushes, Hunzinger realised that he had been mistaken. It wasn't sheet lightning he had seen, but the reflection of anti-aircraft gunfire and bursting bombs. The Luftwaffe must be mounting a big raid, probably on Birmingham.

He braked again, pulled off the road, cut the motor and switched off the lights.

Yes, it was plain enough now. What he had taken for the mutter of distant thunder was the continuous cannonade of erupting high explosive – a menacing groundswell whose rise and fall was punctuated by the thudding of larger bombs and the harsh rattle of defence batteries. As he watched the sky above the leaves and branches screening him from the road, the underside of the cloud front slowly reddened, faded to orange, became fiery again, then settled into a steadily quivering glow. A long way further east, a livid green flare bloomed suddenly against the dark, spread rapidly, sank earthwards, died.

Hunzinger could hear the raiders now. The unmistakable, wavering drone of synchronised aero-engines ebbed and flowed among the stars. Once – a pinpoint of red flame, a low down shooting star – he thought he saw a shot-down bomber far to the south, but it was from the corner of his eye and he could have been mistaken. Then, with shattering abruptness, batteries to the left, to the right and straight ahead opened fire with frightening effect. The shock to the ears was intolerable, deafening, assaulting the skull behind the eyes. Muzzle flashes stabbed into the sky from every side. The gunsites couldn't have been more than a couple of miles away. And now the sky above was peppered with fresh constellations throbbing and twinkling between the Great Bear and the Little Bear, around Cassiopeia and along Orion's belt. But still the planes, ever-present between the salvos of gunfire, remained invisible.

Hunzinger was climbing back into the convertible when a passing jeep braked suddenly, reversed until it drew level again, and stopped. An MP patrol. Two snowdrops, a driver and a tin-hatted subaltern. The officer and the two cops approached. The subaltern saluted. "Sorry to trouble you, sir, but there's a bit of a panic on. Jerry's having a go at the Brummies. I have to ask for the usual – departure, destination, reason for trip, so on. And of coure the jolly old papers."

"On a course from Ulster," Hunzinger said. "Going to Sutton Bonington to see a boffin for the AEC chief in my sector." He handed over the documents, which would of course verify all he said. "If you want to know why I'm here," he added, "I stopped to take a leak, that's all." He grinned. "I have no flashlight, and I have not been beaming coded signals to the aviators, helping them to locate the city of Birmingham!"

"As if they needed it!" the subaltern snorted. "Jerry's supposed to be the maniac for details, the wooden-head who can't see the wood for the bloody trees, everything by the fucking book . . ."

"Jerry?" – and then, hastily slip-catching as soon as possible – "Ah, yes: the Teutonic reputation for being over-thorough".

". . . but, Christ, this country could do with a bit of a clean wind too. All this rubbish about fooling the parachutists when they come. If they come. I mean, tearing down every road sign in the country; blacking out the name of every damned place, *wherever* it occurs, even if it's part of a shop name or something! My people live in a village called Hampton-Chutney. The local pub is called The Hampton. Or was – bloody word's been painted out on the inn sign!" The young man shook his head. "You talk of Birmingham, sir. The BSA works on the outskirts. Birmingham Small Arms, that means. They make guns, motor cycles, probably shells and bombs too now. And . . . you won't believe this . . . there's a bloody great sign proclaiming the company's name along the wall below the factory roof, and they've obliterated the word Birmingham there! I mean, I ask you. Do they think parachutists don't carry maps? That foreign spies can't ask directions in English?"

"Oh, one has to agree," Hunzinger said. "All these wartime regulations, probably based on a sound idea originally, become absurd if they're carried out to the letter."

"Go too damned far, if you ask me," the subaltern said. "Take your car, for instance. Beautiful little bus: super line, wizard colour. But you're lucky she hasn't been daubed all over with that ghastly camouflage muck, chrome radiator included"

"She has to go into the paint shop the day I return to Belfast," Hunzinger said.

"Lot of damned nonsense. Do they believe the sunlight reflected off an SS 100 radiator grille or a pair of P-100 headlamps will lead all the Heinkels and Dorniers in the Reich to a military target or Winston's weekend hideout? God!" The young man's wrath was searing.

"We have to do what our masters tell us," Hunzinger said resignedly.

"Too right, old boy. That is to say, sir . . . Sorry about that . . . And talking of orders, I'm sorry to say that I have to ask you to remain here until these local batteries stop firing. There's not a great risk of falling sharpnel, but there could be some. You know: better to be safe, and all that. Plus of course leaving the King's highway free for ambulances, salvage crews, fire engines and whatnot." He turned back to the jeep. "Won't be long anyway. Probably not more than half an hour. Jerry doesn't like risking his expensive merchandise during the whole bloody night."

"I promise I won't move until the show's over," the German said, sliding into the driving seat.

"Righty-ho. My love to the pretty colleens!" The officer and his companions wedged themselves back into the jeep. The patrol drove away. Hunzinger breathed a sigh of relief.

Professor Ludham-Lyle wore a suit of bright-blue and white striped pyjamas when he came into his kitchen at six-thirty that morning to make early tea for himself and his wife. Hunzinger was hunched up in a wooden chair cradling a mug of Camp coffee he had just made for himself. Steam from the kettle was still eddying around the bottle of black concentrate.

"What the devil . . . ? *Hunzing—!* How the *hell* did you get in here, man? What are you doing in my house?" Astonishment, anger and alarm warred on Ludham-Lyle's face, but he remembered to keep his voice low.

The German's teeth were chattering. It had been a long, chilly night. "I couldn't find the sugar," he complained.

"What are you *doing* here?"

"We have to talk. Urgently. But your wife must not know I am here."

"She most certainly mustn't!" The Professor opened a cupboard door, slid a cup full of sugar lumps across a scrubbed table toward Hunzinger. He was a very tall man, thin, with a prominent nose in a spiky face. An absurd enough figure in the stone-flagged kitchen with his bright nightwear and his sparse hair dishevelled, he nevertheless retained, despite his exasperation, a certain air of schoolmasterish authority.

Hunzinger fed sugar into his mug; sipped the hot liquid with a

119

grimace of distaste. "Not quite as bad as our own *ersatz* muck," he said, "but you have my sympathy if this is all you can get!"

"How did you get here?"

"I drove across from the northeast. Icarus lent me his wife's car."

"My God! Not that open blue thing? Where is it? Where did you leave it? Not parked outside here, I hope! There must on NO account be the slightest connection between Newman and myself. Ever. Or at any rate not until—"

"All right, all right." With a visible effort, Hunzinger shook off his fatigue. His voice hardened and his manner regained it customary decisiveness. He sat up straighter in the chair. "We must on no account be seen together," he said. "It was not light when I came in—"

"How did you get in?"

"We have . . . ways . . . to infiltrate your homes." A tight smile. Jokes were rare in the Hunzinger vocabulary. "As I was saying, nobody could have seen me arrive. There are enough bushes and fruit trees in your long garden to give me cover in the half-light—" he glanced at the window – "if I leave at once. I shall climb the fence and leave through the cornfield behind."

"Where did you park that car?"

"There is no call for hysteria, Professor," Hunzinger said sharply. "Nobody will have seen me. Nobody shall see us together. Or not in the normal sense. I shall visit the village church. As soon as you consider it a proper time to enter yourself, we shall meet there. It will take me no more than ten minutes to give you your instructions – and in any case there should be no churchgoers there early in the morning."

"And the car?"

"I am not a beginner, *Herr Doktor!* The conspicuous car is behind a spinney off a farm track, invisible from the road, half a mile outside the village. I entered your exclusive domain on foot."

Ludham-Lyle smiled. "Forgive me, my friend. Like many academics, I tend not to become fully *compos mentis* until the sun is high in the sky. An heritage from the Greeks perhaps!"

Hunzinger nodded. He swallowed coffee, set the mug back on the table. "Make your wife her tea," he said. "Nothing untoward has occurred since you left your bed. Behave normally. By the time the tea is consumed, there will be no trace here of my visit."

"Normally?" The Professor permitted himself a frosty smile. "You ask, my friend, that I should pursue a course of action logically impossible, quite impossible, to define – and thus, *ipso facto*, equally out of the question precisely to follow! A behaviour considered by common consent normal under certain specific circumstances could arguably –

under an equivalent common scrutiny – be regarded as abnormal were those circumstances radically to be altered. Similarly, in quasi-identical circumstances, the parameters of normalcy for Subject A may well differ axiomatically from those of Subject B. As vulgarly expressed in the proverb, one man's meat is another man poison, eh? One thing common to the corpus of those wise men, Kant and Hegel . . ."

Hunzinger had risen to his feet. As a man of action, he was familiar with that great social fault shared by so many academics – the conditioned reflex. Too often he had found it virtually impossible to conduct a true conversation, a debate with an academic. Mention the key word relative to a subject, and the professorial type, obediently as Pavlov's laboratory dogs, will supply – not a point of view, an opinion which could be agreed with or argued against – but the standard second-year university lecture on that discipline . . . in its entirety!

In this case, probably a one-hour dissertation on *Normalcy as a Concept in a Multi-Cultural Society.* With no possibility of interruption either!

Hunzinger, though, was himself a post-graduate in the positive, no-bullshit approach. "I have to leave you, Professor," he interrupted abruptly. "I shall brief you on the analyses we require of the elements to be supplied to you by the sub-groups working in this area. Bring therefore a pencil and a sheet of paper – which you will, of course, at once destroy when the contents are memorised."

Without another word, he turned about, silently eased open the back door, and stepped out into a fragrant garden world of fruit blossom and pre-sunrise mist.

Ten minutes later, smartly upright in his officer's uniform, he was striding openly along the stretch of the Loughborough road that was in fact Sutton Bonington's main street. Passing the rows of neat houses standing back in their well-tended gardens, he approached the church, navigated the tiled gate, and vanished within the entrance porch.

Before he drove back to St Annes, he had to call, unexpectedly again, on a Scottish osteopath living in the east coast residential preserve of Southwold and a supposedly left wing – but in fact violently anti-semitic – union leader in Bradford.

Settling himself in a pew at the western extremity of the nave, Hunzinger sighed. The silence hanging, tangible as a dusty, invisible curtain, in the chill atmosphere between the high arched windows of the church was a relief that he felt he badly needed.

Fifteen

Two hundred and twenty miles to the northwest, Webster had witnessed from the heights of Cavehill on the outskirts of Belfast a spin off from the Birmingham air raid. It was a minor attack – perhaps fifty planes – aimed mainly at the Harland and Wolff shipyard and the Short Brothers flying boat factory, but it was spectacular enough from the Ballysillan Road area, where Webster found himself when the sirens began wailing. That was after the second attempt on his life – with an unsilenced, large-bore handgun, probably a 4.5-calibre revolver, judging from the amplitude of the detonation. The first, a much closer shave, had involved a silenced automatic-pistol firing 9mm Parabellum rounds – or, arguably, 7.63mm slugs from a German Mauser: three close shots on rapid fire which splatted against a wall inches from Webster's head and lacerated his cheek with stone chips. The evaluation of the weapon had been his own, simply because he had seen the gun, and the hand holding it, and had jerked his head back a millisecond before the trigger was pressed.

Colonel Nichols had sent him back to Northern Ireland on a fact-finding mission not directly concerned with the Hart-Hunzinger operation – but in search of a connection which might well, later, prove at least to have an incidental relationship with Hunzinger's sleepers.

On the surface, though, it was an IRA affair. Since the outbreak of hostilities, the sporadic bomb attacks by clandestine Army activists in Liverpool, Manchester and the North had ceased. But in Ulster the 'Sinn-Feiners' as they were called, remained active at least in a political sense. Young men wearing cavalry macks and slouch hats held forth luridly on the subject of 'occupation troops' and 'imperialist colonialism' in pubs safely within the Catholic areas of the city. It was all rather romantic, really, persuading a girlfriend doing first-year Arts at the university to do part-time war work at the Food Office so that she could fiddle stacks of ration documents and blank Identity Cards destined for the hard men up from the South. But although United Ireland remained the talking point, the sacred target, there was no danger to life and limb threatened in the Six Counties and little damage to the war effort. Let them play their games, Army Security and the RUC had decided: we know how to lay hands on them if we want to. Meanwhile the theoretical conspirators provided a useful line to those who might potentially be dangerous.

Until, that was, the number of those in the latter category, who secretly entered England, was shown to be significantly increasing. And the increase was shown to parallel the hotting-up of plans relating to the opening of a Second Front in Europe.

At which point Webster was told: 'Breeze over there, old man, take a shufti at the deep end of the low-life pool, and see if you come up with anything interesting. We shall be listening.'

Two murder attempts after only a couple of days of questions was interesting enough, Webster thought, for him to have a third go. Enough anyway to answer the poster question posed above every railway station ticket-window in the country: Is Your Journey Really Necessary?

Affirmative, old lad, Webster told himself, shaving carefully around the cuts on his face the following morning. Let Fearless Frazer ride again!

Nevertheless, he thought it prudent to persuade the depleted staff at the Grand Central Hotel to serve breakfast (dried egg, strong Indian tea, Ministry of Health orange juice) in his room. And to leave early via the dustbins outside the tradesmen's entrance.

The dramas had started two days before. Informed local gossip had alerted him that almost all underworld grapevine news would be channelled through a gentleman known as Tucker Connolly – the early Ulster equivalent of London's Richardson gang, the Krays or the Maltese Messina Brothers. Mr Connolly's precise role in the shadowy precincts of crime was less evident than that of his counterparts in the capital. If his large hand lay heavily in the realm of vice, it was difficult to prove in a province crawling with American enlisted men, amateur brass-nailers and mothers prepared to unleash their daughters for the price of a chocolate bar (preferably a Hershey one). Protection activity was unlikely among clubs forbidden to sell alcohol, although there was certainly an opportunity for a modest amount of repartition of the limited amount of fire-water available in the public-house sector. The strongest rumours had it that, in the absence of horse racing, Tucker Connolly and his boys 'ran' the dogs.

The presumed gang boss was an elusive quarry to track down, however – and possibly an evasive one as well, Webster discovered once he had sewn a few tempting seeds with which he had been provided among hotel porters, cab drivers, minor police officers and doormen.

Connolly, it emerged, was a staunch Protestant, born in the staunchly Protestant town of Omagh (or maybe, as some had it, Magherafelt, in County Tyrone). He was thus, despite his trade, a ferocious loyalist, King and Country, boyo, and to hell with the bloody papists! No Catholic teller of beads could be found among his henchmen.

Webster's seeds, therefore, on the assumption that the Connolly persuasion would not be inimical to an anti-IRA approach, had concerned the veiled offer of fingering certain activists, of early release for friends unjustly behind bars, the promise of means (without police complicity) to circumvent a number of inconvenient wartime restrictions. And suchlike.

It was, however, the doorman at the Four Hundred Club – the man who had found Webster and Hart that convenient nearby hotel some time before – who was the first to come up with what Belfast's transatlantic immigrés would term 'pay dirt'.

Tea in the lounge at four o'clock of an afternoon – when Ernie Hicks and the group were rehearsing Pauline and Attracta, the two resident dancers – might prove to be a positive appointment, Webster was told.

He was there five minutes early, in civilian clothes – very tweedy – the chevron of moustache for once removed from his hawk face.

A nightclub in the middle of an afternoon, even a no-alcohol nightclub, is possibly the bleakest, most dreary setting for a profitable encounter yet devised by civilised man. Light intruding past the ragged blackout turns the low-key electric illumination yellow. The red plush is worn, ropey backing showing through where a thouand arses have shifted impatiently, hopefully, lustfully, furtively throughout a thousand and one nights. Cigarette burns engrave hieroglyphics across the fitted carpet. Coffee stains blacken the tables, the scarred reception desk.

Webster found himself facing a large, red-faced man of about fifty, sitting at a low round table laden with tea things. From behind padded double doors the discreet strains of a medium foxtrot (*There'll be a Hot Time in the Old Town Tonight*, Webster thought) were accompanied by the rhythmic tap-taps of dancers' feet. Otherwise there was no sign of human activity.

The man in the chair nodded. Webster sank into the empty seat on the opposite side of the table. "Mr Connolly?" he enquired politely.

"Best not to use names, Mister." The voice was low, almost guttural, with a thick Ulster accent. The man sat completely immobile as he spoke. He was very big indeed, Webster saw now: more probably than six feet when he stood, extremely heavily built – not in any

124

sense athletic, but solid all the way through; the kind of bruiser from whom a single short-arm jab could drop any adversary to the floor. "They say you might have interestin' . . . news," he continued, "that could be of interest to certain friends of mine. What would you be wantin' in exchange for such information? Supposin' it was found to be interestin' enough."

"Information," Webster said. "Of another kind."

"Ah." An arm reached out from the monolith body, lifting a teacup from its saucer. He was actually, Webster saw with something like horror, going to *drink* the tea! "Give us a wee example, but," the man said, raising the cup to his lips.

Webster leaned forward. "Routine stuff," he said. "But stuff your people probably know better than ours. We'd like to save the time and effort needed to find out for ourselves."

"Come to the point, you. What kind of stuff?"

"The Boys," Webster said, "our friends from the Army, are paying us visits more frequently than they were. More of them are doing it. We'd like to know exactly how and why. For example."

Heavy shoulders shrugged. The big man sucked air in noisily along with the tea as he drank. "The most obvious way," he said. "The way they get to bleedin' New York. Fiddle a job as steward along with the boats. Then jump ship on the other side. Use papers the Papish whores flog from the Ministry to give their fuckin' student bedfellers. Students, they call 'em!" A snort of derision. "Traitorous fuckin' brats as'd sell their fuckin' grand-dams for a round of bloody applause in a Papish pub!" The cup rattled back into its saucer. "Will you not be takin' a cup of tea, Mister?"

"Er – not for the moment, thank you. There will, though, be other ways no doubt, less obvious but rather more . . . discreet?"

"Certainly." More tea from the chipped, brown china pot hosed darkly into the cup. "And names to go intil the files along with them. If we will be doin' business together, but."

The band had swung into a slow-drag *Sleepy Time Down South*. "Let me fill you in a little," Webster said. "Here's a brief run-down detailing exactly what's on offer."

Twenty minutes later he left the club. A meeting had been arranged later that day. Whether or not with Tucker Connolly – indeed whether or not he had been talking with Connolly himself at the Four Hundred – Webster had no idea. Progress in any case, he felt, had been made.

He was on his way out when he almost collided with a blonde girl coming in. "Goodness, my mistake! Awfully sorry – clumsy of me . . ." he began, stopping suddenly when he realised the blonde was

June, the dancer from the Empire Theatre who had so attracted Nick Hart on his last night in Belfast – indeed at the very club Webster himself was now leaving. "June!" he exclaimed. "By Jove, what a piece of luck, running into you here. I was just on the look out for a partner to share an aperitif! What about a rendezvous at the Grand Central? At least the bar serves drinks there."

"I'd love to," the girl said. "The only thing is, I'm doing a spot of overtime, working out a one a.m. threesome for a cabaret spot with Pauline and Attracta. And I have a date with them –" she glanced at the entrance – "to work out routines."

"So breeze along to the GC when you're through," Webster said cheerfully.

"Well I don't know if I can . . ." She looked doubtfully off to her right.

For the first time Webster noticed a second young woman, equally blonde, equally well-stacked as June, who was standing a few yards away on the pavement, Clearly they had been about to enter the club together. "Excuse me," June said. "This is a friend – Deirdre O'Shaugnessy. Dee, this is Lieutenant-Colonel – er . . ."

"Webster, at your service." He held out his hand.

The girl, who was perhaps five years older than June, nodded briefly. She made no attempt to take the hand. Oh, all right, Webster thought: one of those! Nevertheless he said breezily: "Better still, old thing: bring Deirdre with you. I reckon the GC barman can run to three glasses!"

"No thanks," Deirdre said sharply. "Kind of you, but I have other things to do." The tone of her voice indicated clearly, just the same, that she meant she had *better* things to do.

"From the South, is she, your friend?" He asked casually in the lounge bar an hour later. "A Catholic, anyway. A united Ireland and God damn the English. That kind of scene?"

"Dee? Oh, she's all right really. She'a sweet girl. It was silly of me to mention your army rank. You know these Nationalists: quote the wrong word and they're up in arms and at you!"

"Well, it takes all sorts," he said easily. "How about your other friend, Zelda? She still here?"

"Zelda? No, no. She's back with her hounds and horses in Kent. I don't know what strings she must have pulled to get the travel permission. Some people have all the luck!"

"I thought she was here officially," Webster said, "representing her husband at some government conference at Stormont. Something to do with farming, I believe."

"Stormont? The local parliament? First I've heard of it." June shrugged. "I thought she was here to see a friend up from Dublin." A smile. "An old boyfriend, if you ask me! But it's none of my business. I don't really know her very well, anyway."

"It's of no importance," Webster said.

Soon afterwards, regretfully, he had to make his excuses and leave the girl. His meeting was in the parlour of a temperance hotel behind the City Hall. The place had an unenviable reputation. It was said that the B-Specials – the part-time paramilitary arm of the local police force – took suspected Nationalist suspects into the back room there to beat them up before they were handed over to the official RUC. Outwardly, though, the atmosphere was of suffocating gentility: plush furniture, antimacassars, a potted palm in the hallway, bottles of ketchup on the tables visible through a half-open dining room door. There was even an elderly, bespectacled lady wedged into an armchair near the reception desk, knitting.

The front parlour, already blacked out, was dimly lit. An outsized engraving of the coronation of Queen Victoria hung above the empty fireplace. Four men sat on hard upright chairs around a table hidden by a brown baize cloth. There was beer to drink.

The individual who seemed to be the spokesman of the committee wore a checked cap pulled well down over his eyes; the others sported felt hats with the brim turned down. Each, despite the warmth of the evening, was belted into a showerproof trench coat.

Webster began to feel as if he had mistakenly wandered on to the set for a rejected scene from the Carol Read Belfast movie *Odd Man Out* Still, finding the atmosphere faintly unreal, he began dealing out the intelligence details he had been fed in the hope that they might stimulate in return at least some material relating to the IRA incursions in England. When this started to emerge, he took notes. Tucker Connolly, if that was the man he had met at the Four Hundred, made no appearance.

The meeting lasted an hour and a half. Webster left the hotel and went in search of a taxi.

In Belfast, the gas-powered, black and yellow Morris cabs didn't cruise. You phoned to make a date, or you walked to the office-garage and hoped the dispatcher might fit you in between reservations as the cars called back to refuel. The gas – butane, was it? – was unrationed and relatively cheap. But the bloated overhead gasbag, running the entire length of the vehicle, had a maximum range of no more than twenty miles when fully inflated, so there was a constant coming and going, day and night.

127

The base was opposite a public ballroom which had been transformed into the American Red Cross leisure centre, a block and a half from the City Hall. Webster walked that way.

It was as he paused to cross the street towards the pale, greenish rectangle of the garage entrance that the first shots were fired.

A cab with its gasbag almost flat had braked in the middle of the roadway to let a refuelled car, bursting with its twenty-mile load, drive out before it manoeuvred itself into the dimly-lit entrance. The low beams of the second cab's masked headlights swept across the macadam as it turned towards the city centre, crossed the pavement, passed over the dark entrance to an air-raid shelter . . .

And momentarily illuminated the long-barrelled firearm, the hand holding it, an arm and a shoulder projecting from the black interior.

Webster was down on the pavement, flat on his face, one hand snatching out the .22-calibre Beretta automatic, before the snout of the silencer had jerked for the third time. He fired twice, whipcrack shots unnaturally loud after the subdued plops from the subsonic muffler, but the taxi and its headlamps had accelerated away, the entrance to the brick-built shelter was empty, footsteps pounded away along the concrete floor inside . . . and out at the far end, then across the rubble strewn bombsite behind.

Webster sprang to his feet and gave chase. The Beretta, the only gun small enough to remain invisible in the pocket of a tweed jacket, was still in his hand. But he knew, rounding the far end of the shelter, that it was no use. The footsteps, scattering the smaller chunks of rubble, avoiding the larger in the dark, were already twenty yards away, moving fast – the footsteps of someone who knew every hump and declivity on the bombsite, an impossible target for the small handgun at that distance, even if it had been daylight. He heard boots scrabbling on brickwork, an explosion of breath, a heavy thump. More footsteps, smoother this time. A door slammed.

As he had thought, the gunman had scaled a wall, run through a garden, and into a house in the next street. He could be a block away before Webster was halfway across the bombsite.

Warm blood trickled down his cheek. The slugs that missed him must have ploughed chips from the wall of the house at the corner of the site. Webster dabbed himself with a handkerchief and crossed the street to the taxi office. A radio from the American Red Cross was blaring out an Artie Shaw swing speciality called 'Nightmare'.

Webster had been given the use of a jeep while he was in Ulster. But he had preferred not to use it in the centre while he was in civilian

Blitz Harvest

clothes and in touch with the underworld. Blonde Catholic girls were not the only ones to be suspicious of the British military!

He had to wait half an hour, but eventually he found a driver – on his way to pick up a theatregoer from Finaghy – who agreed to drop him at a cinema in the Lisburn Road where the jeep was waiting in the car park.

There was also a lightweight motor cycle in the car park – a 250cc Velocette with a driver and a passenger riding pillion. The machine had not been there long. Slightly less time, in fact, than Webster himself, for it had followed his cab all the way out from Corporation Street.

Webster was aware of it only as a crackle, rising to a roar, of exhaust audible over the idling engine of the jeep as he bent down to retrieve a briefcase from under the pasenger seat.

At that instant the Velocette swerved up, speeding close to the stationary jeep as the pillion rider sat up and blazed a single shot from his .45-calibre revolver straight into the utility's covered cab.

The jeep's windscreen shattered, showering wicked shards of glass over Webster's shoulders and back; Webster's head jerked up, ears ringing with the echoes of the shot; the motorbike skidded out on to the granite setts of the Lisburn Road, turned towards the centre and shot away.

Webster was already behind the wheel, foot flattening the accelerator pedal to the floor. The jeep, tyres screaming, raced after the would-be murderer's machine.

Webster's mouth was set in a grim line. The Beretta lay on the seat beside him. The hell with it: two separate attempts on his life within the hour was a bit much! If the biker had watched him go into the taxi office while the first gunner was a block away, then followed his cab out to the cinema, he must have been tailed by at least two separate people in the first place. Which meant things were hotting up to the point of being serious! So who, why – and from where? Perhaps the motor cyclist or his mate could help?

Webster drove like a man possessed, eyes flinty in his bloodied face. Traffic was light. The roads were dry. The jeep was faster but the bike more manoeuvrable.

The chase led him downhill and then out across the wastes of Shaftesbury Square, skating crazily over the slippery, shining web of tramlines criss-crossing in the centre, left into the ultra-loyalist cauldron of Sandy Row. Difficult here. There were children in the street, people sitting on the doorsteps of the low, mean little houses. He was obliged continually to brake, to slow, allowing the bike to increase its lead. It was the same thing above the Smithfield Market, behind the Grand Central Hotel, where there were still genuine slums – not the tenement kind found in Glasgow but again miserable one-up-and-one-down hovels where the children walked the street barefoot because they didn't actually have any shoes. And the housewives shouted abuse simply because you possessed a vehicle. Louder, more vituperative, if it was military.

The Velocette was between three and four hundred yards ahead when they spilled out into the long pull-up of the Shankill Road, reduced to one-fifty as they crossed the Catholic Falls district, then increasing again through traffic outside the Royal Hospital, and a plunge to the Antrim Road. The rider was doing his best to shake Webster off – but so far he hadn't been able to get far enough ahead to turn off into an alley or an entry without being seen.

Now, suddenly, he was climbing once more, left, right, left again through a maze of narrow, shuttered residential streets, the jeep slewing wildly as Webster hurled it through right angles.

And then, finally, they were on Ballysillan, long, straight, south-west to northeast, the highest built-up area in the city, overlooking Belfast Lough from beneath the stone crest of Cavehill. Two hundred yards between them, small, middleclass villas with gardens on either side, and a good modern road surface that encouraged Webster to keep his foot well down.

The distance between jeep and bike shortened. One hundred and fifty yards . . . a hundred . . . seventy-five . . . sixty . . .

Webster gripped the wheel, preparing to flip the nose of the jeep in an attempt to tip the bike over and throw the rider to the ground. They were drawing level. He picked the Beretta up from the seat.

And suddenly there was no road. It ended abruptly at the level of Number 358 or 360. A fence, trees, a noticeboard on a post – and a narrow, open gate leading to a footpath undulating across the steeper, scrub-covered slopes below the crest.

The Velocette was already through the gap, bouncing, rocketing along the sandy path, the exhaust rasping, red rear-light dwindling between clumps of gorse and broom. If the pillion rider had not visibly turned to hold up two derisive fingers, it was easy enough to imagine he had.

Webster braked the jeep yards from the fence and said something ungentlemanly.

Down in the city below, sirens wailed. Within minutes there were aircraft overhead.

Flame lanced upwards from anti-aircraft gunships in the lough.

Batteries on the airfield at the head of the wide inlet, outposted around the shipyards, thundered searing salvos skywards.

The night was cloudless. Light from a three-quarter moon silvered the swollen flanks of tethered barrage balloons floating high above the shores of the lough as the demonic chorus, uniting gunfire and bursting bombs, swelled to a single hellish crescendo.

Fires started by showers of incendiaries raged in a dozen parts of the city. Bursting bombs – flashes from the small ones, strange slow-burning effusions of crimson and orange from the giants, the land-mines – carpeted the outlines of the blacked-out town. Across the water, in Hollywood, Craigavad, Merino, houses and shops burned. Away in the south a targeted refinery belched out a holocaust of flame marbled with black smoke.

Webster waited for the All Clear to sound. There was no point driving down into the inferno: there was nothing he could do; the jeep would only hinder the passage of fire engines, ambulances and salvage crews' and the police would stop him anyway.

It was an odd situation to find himself in just the same.

Immediately below, a long way down, the Antrim Road, residential quarter of the well-to-do, ran out of town parallel both to Ballysillan and to the waterfront. Theoretically it was a quarter well protected by the barrage balloons and their cables. Unfortunately, though, the city's defence planners, instead of staggering or zigzagging the sites, had planted them in two straight lines, one on either side of the road. And the German pilots of the lighter bombers, well briefed about this, were using the balloons as markers – almost as a protection – zooming in between the two rows of cables at roof height to flatten the rich villas one after the other.

It was the only time in his life, Webster realised, that he had witnessed an aerial bombardment from a viewpoint higher up than the machines delivering it.

"It was a pretty dicey show, just the same. All of it," he said to Nichols the following afternoon, having hitched a lift to Heston in an RAF Anson from Aldergrove.

"But who was trying to write you off anyway?" Nichols asked. "And why?"

Webster shrugged. "You tell me. Too many questions in too many of the right places, for a start. The obvious answer, bearing in mind time and place, would be the Connolly mob. Profit from the bait I laid out for them . . . then rub me out so they could get back and destroy the notes detailing what *they* had given to *me*. But I think it's more complicated than that. The IRA could just as well be eager to squash the material I had – if there had been a leak and they knew I had it. Equally, we don't really know – outside of the political overtones – what's on and what's not on in the Ulster underworld. There could be very big noises concerned with the black market."

"What was the other point you laboured in your report to C?"

"About this woman Zelda," Webster said. "It might be no more than a coincidence – though one with a longish arm, one would have to admit – but clearly she had known Hunzinger at one time or another."

"Or known his brother?"

"Don't even say that, Adam! Whichever, that put her in our court for a start. Then there was my drink with the dancer and that story about a boyfriend from Dublin. Remembering that the lady was – like certain rulers I could quote – of Austrian origin . . . Aha! I said to myself. Aha! Could there possibly be something here that it might pay Fearless Frazer to investigate? A possible Dublin-IRA tie-up with the Hunzingers, for instance? So I decided a few more questions here and there might not altogether be out of order."

"Congratulations on the double negative," Nichols said. "There's a rhetorical term for the usage but I cannot at the moment recall—"

"Litotes," Webster said. "If you wish to be specific, the expression of an affirmative by the negation of its contrary. I would not be averse – just for instance – to another whisky."

Nichols pressed the button on his desk. "Mason – you had better bring in the bottle."

He turned back to Webster. "And the result of your questions?"

"I'd put a word about here and there. I took a butchers at the in-and-out logs at Stormont and suchlike. And what do you think?" Webster shook his head. "Not only had she never been near the place; there never was any conference on wartime farming there at that time; and not a soul had ever heard a single word about her husband. Didn't even know the bloody man's name."

"Whether or not there's anything in it," Nichols said. "Hart must certainly be rowed in on this."

Webster nodded. "Ask me," he said, "there's something rum going on somewhere here. Something very rum indeed."

132

Part Four

The Hart Line

Sixteen

I had not realised, of course, what the most irritating – and at times the most irrational – of problems would be. The continued preservation of my counterfeit identity, I had imagined, would present me with the most acute of the difficulties I had to face.

Not so. Not at all. The sixty-day period of brainwashing I had suffered under Webster had so soaked me in the childhood and early adult life of Zoltan Hunzinger that I was ready to react as positively and with as much conviction as I would have been when questioned on my own early days. Once brother Axel had certified the substitution by his unqualified acceptance of me as his long-lost, my quasi-automatic development of the role became as predictable – and, I hoped, as convincing, as the behaviour of those Pavlov dogs.

It was in relation to my own earlier experiences – rather than those of Zoltan – that I found myself most dangerously at risk. Pretending to *be* Zoltan was in fact less traumatic than the fear of revealing that I was *not* Zoltan.

And exposure was menaced through the most banal, the most trivial of everyday events.

Axel, for instance, had been inside since 1940, so it was reasonable that in the matter of the escape from Douglas it should be Zoltan – supposedly briefed by the fictitious Korsun and his team – who took charge of the details and showed himself familiar with British wartime life *at that particular time*. But on existence in Britain as a whole it was Axel, lying low in the country for many years, who must be the knowledgeable one; Zoltan, freshly arrived from Australia, must at all costs suppress any familiarity with systems, customs and behaviour foreign to a man in his position. Especially because of Hunzinger's know-all-trust-nothing professionalism.

A typical case almost caught me out before we even left Lancashire. It was the stupidest of nonsensical nothings. We were in a pub on the seafront at St Annes, with an hour to kill before our train left for the south. Hunzinger was anxious to re-familiarise himself with day-to-day life and so we had started one of those desultory saloon bar conversations with a couple of building workers employed on some highway clearance scheme by the local town hall. And old lady had been knocked down by a truck and killed the previous day and eventually – the way such meaningless encounters rumble on – one of the men made the point that, war or no fucking war, despite the reduction in traffic due to bleeding petrol rationing, it was getting to be even more dangerous to cross the bloody road than it had been before.

Too bloody right, mate, the second man said; fucking maniacs allowed to take the fucking wheel because driving tests have been abandoned until perishing Adolf has been fucking dealt with!

The absence of a police presence, Hunzinger offered, tended to encourage the drunk driver, and what were they going to have? No, no: this time it was on him.

I was about to put in my bit, but I waited while he went up to the bar with the glasses. The wartime restriction on street lighting had maybe played its part too, I was going to say. Belisha Beacons – those orange lollipop globes on black and white posts that marked pedestrian crossings – no longer blinked on and off day and night like the new direction indicators on some of the more modern cars. Which made it more hazardous to set foot on the striped passageways painted across the roadway.

A minor point, not exactly worthy in its profundity of Einstein or Sir James Jeans.

Except that Zoltan Hunzinger had never been in Britain before the war: he couldn't possibly have known that the orange globes used to be illuminated, and blinked on and off!

Zero effect on the road workers if I'd made the remark. But Brother Axel was a trained professional; it could have proved a disaster if he'd picked up on the lapse.

I drank my mild-and-bitter rather quickly and remained quiet until it was time to leg it for the station. Watch it, Hart: remember to let *him* fill you in on such Anglo-Saxon peculiarities as pub opening hours, looking *right* before you cross the road, and the London 'bottle party' night-club system for evading the law.

It was dark when we arrived at Euston – only an hour late – and the sirens were already howling. No raid had developed by the time we left our Inner Circle underground at Victoria, however, and the electric Brighton train pulled out on time beneath a sky speckled with nothing but stars. "Just one of the Dorniers, probably, on an observation tour," Hunzinger told me.

We were going to stay, at least temporarily, with a woman who was a close friend of his – and had once, I suspected, been his mistress. His voice certainly softened slightly from its usual crisp impassivity when he spoke of her. She appeared to be some kind of lady of the manor, for the address was Fortune Hall, outside a village somewhere between Pulborough and Rye, in Sussex. Mrs Fortune's husband, a Colonel in an armoured brigade, had been taken prisoner in Malaya by the Japanese. That was all I knew: Hunzinger had made all the arrangements himself, in a series of short calls from different phone boxes in Blackpool and St Annes.

In fact that was practically damned near all that I knew about anything. Hunzinger was a taciturn individual, given to long silences – presumably concentrating on the job ahead of him, which could have been wearing since he had none of the time-and-place detail written down. It was all, as they say, in his mind. And, professional that he was, he didn't intend to tempt fate – and endanger security – by committing it all to paper at this crucial stage.

Or by committing it to me either. Clearly I would be filled in totally on any operation I was to share with him phyically, but the rest was on a need-to-know basis.

I knew about the osteopath in Norfolk, the anti-semitic syndicalist and the professor who lived near Loughborough. But he had confided neither their names nor the addresses. Nor had he given any hint of their personalities or views; no indication of how or why they should have been sufficiently frustrated, angry, embittered or politically brainwashed as to offer clandestine help to the enemies of their country. The only sleeper he talked of in a personal sense was a sergeant-rigger in the maintenance unit at Weeton – and he, apparently, was the only one doing it for money. He had twice been passed over for a promotion he was convinced that he deserved. And the grudge this had engendered, plus a temperament of deep pessimism – Hunzinger revealed with a rare smile – had earned him among his mates the nickname of Rigger Mortis.

His personal catch-phrase, Hunzinger told me with relish, was: 'Mark my words, no good will come of it!'

I had of course made a full report on the three meetings I'd had, though the FordV-8 naturally appeared in none of them. He had asked indeed how I had managed the round trip. "By train and taxi," I replied – having carefully verified every possibility via my timetable – "and a double ration of exaspertion at the damned inefficiency of everything!"

He hadn't smiled that time. His only comment at the end of my report was: "Good. Well done."

He was equally brief when I ventured – permissible for a brother, I reckoned – to ask casually how he himself had contrived to visit people in places as far apart as Suffolk, Leicestershire and Yorkshire – as well as issuing a detailed briefing in each case – all in little more than a day. "I borrowed a car," he said.

So far all I had to contribute to the list Webster and Nichols needed so badly was a crippled newsagent, the principal of a girls' boarding school and a Welsh bookseller. Unless I was going to be able to accompany Brother Axel in the near future, the list was liable to remain short.

Unless or course Intelligence had been really on the ball. In which case the lamplighters keeping watch on the safe house might conceivably have tailed him when he took off on his own. But I thought that unlikely; they would have had to be in on the Fleetwood dockside brawl to have alerted the team on time. No – it was all down to Zoltan Hart. That after all was what I was being paid for; this was why so much time and money had been spent preparing me for the job.

Hunzinger as a person I was still at a loss to explain. I knew him hardly any better than I did when I shoved him into the tunnel.

He posed virtually no questions on my life in Australia. I was his brother. We were working together. That was enough. He had no curiosity, no interest in matters unrelated to the task in hand, not the slightest desire to talk about his life on the Isle of Man. Discussions – of any kind – were a waste of time. Only one thing was important: what we were doing here, now, this moment.

In one sense this total compartmentalisation of our relationship was an advantage to me: it lessened the risk of my making mistakes, of being caught out. On the other hand it increased the strain: my actual *consciousness*, ever present, of the false position I was in; the chance, every minute, every second, of the fatal error that could bring the whole stack of cards tumbling down – and me, of course, with it. The ferocious concentration this required, I felt, might well be alleviated by an occasional spot of what I call pub conversation – like who was going to win the King George V Stakes at Ascot tomorrow, or would it be possible to wangle an invite to the Bob Hope show at the American Red Cross in South Audley Street next week, or what the hell are Bolton Wanderers thinking of, dropping Smith for the match against Arsenal? That kind of thing.

One had to remember, after all, that this was something more than a jolly game of cops and robbers, a variation of I-spy-with-my-little-eye. Axel Hunzinger was a dedicated professional, OK; a man with a mission, a cause. And in the little chess game we were playing –

that he didn't know we were playing – the odds so far were stacked on my side of the board. But as well as a dedicated man, he was also a dangerous man. And he was carrying a gun.

There was never any doubt in my mind that he would kill if necessary to preserve his cover.

A minor point this time . . . but it was an example of the kind of detailed perfection used as a matter of course by the professional covering his tracks.

I had been told the house we were to stay at was 'outside a village somewhere between Pulborough and Rye'. It was only after we had left the train at Lewes and were waiting for the transport Hunzinger had been promised that I happened to glance at a local map that had been left on the wall of the station waiting room. And it was only then that the penny dropped.

Pulborough is approximately thirteen miles northeast of Bognor Regis; Rye is on the coast, northeast of Hastings – fifty-five miles away as the crow flies, considerably more if you follow the road. Not exactly a precise definition of our destination if anyone happened to be eavesdropping! In fact Fortune Hall was outside the village of Hawkhurst, nowhere near either of them.

Nobody was eavesdropping, of course. And I don't believe Hunzinger would have done it just to fool me: I wasn't supposed to know Sussex anyway. It was simply automatic: good fieldwork.

The transport, when it arrived, was something of a surprise – at least for someone reputed to be a lady of the manor and a big noise in the neighbourhood. It was a ten-cwt Ford delivery van, covered in khaki camouflage paint, which had been transformed into a YMCA mobile canteen.

It was driven by a young man wearing corduroys and a polo-neck, who couldn't have been more than eighteen years old. "Ma Fortune's apologies," he said cheerfully, "but she had to go up to Ashford to see some bigwig about government assistance for turning the rose gardens into vegetable allotments for the locals. You know – Dig For Victory, and all that!"

"No problem," Hunzinger assured him. "Anything's better than walking – or trying to raise a cab with fuel in deep country!"

There was only a single seat behind the wheel of the ten horsepower van, so Hunzinger and I piled into the rear and sat on moveable stools between the fitted shelves crammed with buns, chocolate bars, hairnets, kirby-grips, razors, deodorant sticks and bottles of hair oil. Two huge urns – one of tea, the other of coffee – swashed and gurgled on either side of a built-in sink loaded with china mugs as the van rattled and tinkled and slewed and shook around the narrow country lanes.

Hunzinger filled in the time by explaining kindly to his ignorant brother the wartime system of mobile canteens.

"YMCA . . . ?" I made Zoltan ask.

"Young Men's Christian Association," Hunzinger explained. "Not quite like our Strength Through Joy, but . . . well, they do hostels for hikers, beds for penniless students, good work for the homeless. That kind of thing."

"And shops on wheels?"

"Not exactly. The idea was theirs. They lend it their blessing, underwrite it, if you like. But mainly the actual day to day running of the scheme is something like a double charity."

I looked puzzled. The van took a right-angled turn at forty miles per hour, throwing me against the partition separating us from the driver. About fifty packets of cigarettes – Gold Flake, Woodbines, De Reszke, Capstan Full Strength – slid off a shelf and showered to the floor. "Sorry, chaps!" a voice called faintly through the partition. "Roadholding a shade below par."

"A double charity, yes," Hunzinger said, fitting himself back on to his stool. "You must know, of course, that the Englanders protect their big cities, military targets, airfields, docks and war factories, first by patrolling fighter planes, and, after that, by outposted rings of anti-aircraft batteries and barrage balloon sites. With the hope of destroying or deterring those of our raiders who get through before they reach the targets, these are usually distributed on estuary wasteland, among coastal dunes, on heaths, moors and reclaimed land not under cultivation. In what you would call the outback! The crews, gunners and women from the ATS and WAAF, are billeted under canvas on these sites. And since they are naturally remote, far from a town, village or even bus route, the personnel are particularly isolated during their tours of duty, deprived of the small social necessities."

There was a sudden squeal of tyres. The van shuddered, abruptly lost way, throwing us forward again, slewed almost broadside-on, then resumed its breakneck pace. *"Brakes!"* the voice from the front yelled.

"It was," Hunzinger said, "to – what shall we say? To mitigate? – to alleviate this situation that this mobile canteen system was formed. Psychologically positive, you see. Apart from offering the kind of nonentities one would normally buy at a village shop—" he gestured in the direction of the shelves – "the canteens also provide social variety.

You know – chats over a cup of tea. That sort of thing." He paused, permitted himself what could have been a half smile, then added: "By chance, by good fortune, they provide in addition a very useful service for *us* – and for our rather special team!"

"I am beginning to see" I said. "Naturally the crews get to know the canteen staff. Naturally they chat about their work, the other postings they have had, shop talk in general."

"Exactly."

"Yes, but . . . well, how do we make ourselves, as it were, a party to such exchanges? How do we get on the inside of the canteen organisation?"

"In the simplest way possible," Hunzinger said. "We offer to help."

I stared at him. Cards wound with coloured elastic ribbons vibrated on a shelf behind his head.

"I used the word charity," he explained. "The lists of sites to be visited, the passes to let the canteens in, are decided by the War Office or somesuch, then passed to the YMCA. But the vehicles themselves are privately owned. Most of them have been bought secondhand by well-to-do, well-meaning ladies all over the country, who pay for them to be converted into motorised shops, buy the materials with which they are stocked, and organise a daily round of visits to dispersed sites in their locality. The stuff is sold at cost. The ladies recuperate what they have paid for it, but make strictly no profit."

"Very well. It's an official service – but run by charity. You said a double charity?"

"The personnel who staff the canteens. Usually a driver and a woman serve for each one. They are volunteers. They are unpaid; they get no expenses. Sometimes a single pair handle all the work done by a particular canteen; more often there's a team, working on a rota – students, youngsters waiting to be called up, married women whose husbands and children are away. A lot of kids offer because it's the only chance they have to actually drive anything at all."

"And anyone can offer? There's no particular . . . screening?"

"All help is welcome. I never heard of anyone asked a single question."

"Well!" I said.

"The simplest way of gathering information on troop concentrations," Hunzinger said, "is to make one's way to the places where they concentrate. The rule applies also to gunsites and balloons. This is only peripheral material, of course, of far less value in itself than intelligence on munitions, troop movements or armour – but it will prove invaluable when the time comes. Just one more series of elements required to complete the global picture."

"Talking of the canteens," I said, "you emphasised the phrase 'good fortune' when you pointed out how useful to us this YMCA organisation could be. Am I right in thinking . . . ?"

"You are acute, Zoltan," he said approvingly. "That is good. I do not often permit myself to essay a play on words in the language of our hosts . . . but, yes, you are right: Frau Fortune, the well-to-do, well-meaning lady with whom we are to stay for a few days, whose husband, the colonel, is alas a captive in the hands of our far-eastern allies . . . Frau Fortune is herself the patron, organiser and indeed owner of no less than three YMCA mobile canteens!"

Seventeen

The house was built on a slight rise, with a ring of trees behind it and a gravelled drive curling up to the main entrance from a gatekeeper's lodge. It was a big place – a long two-storey central block with an attic floor behind a crenellated parapet; a tall, square tower, equally battlemented, at each end. Built entirely of red brick, it looked like one of those minor public schools endowed in the sixteenth century by a local baron or knight, but dated almost certainly from the middle of the pretentious nineteenth. There must, I discovered later, have been between twenty-five and thirty bedrooms off the long second-floor passageway traversing the central block. With a dozen more for servants plus boxrooms behind the attic tiles.

There can't have been many kitchen maids and scullions tramping up those last flights of stairs now. An aged, toothless housekeeper, who looked as though she had been there since the hall was built, had a sitting-room behind the kitchens. Two young women from the village – probably the wives of farm workers – handled the cooking. And the rest of the personnel, such as it was, seemed to be composed mainly of students of both sexes about the same age as the boy who had collected us at the station. At any rate, having served the food, they sat down to eat with us at the long refectory table beneath the rafters of a fake baronial banqueting hall. There wasn't actually straw on the floor, though I half expected it.

The flagstones, in fact, were largely covered by genuine Ispahan rugs.

The canteen benefactress, the rich and elusive Mrs Fortune, had not returned from Ashford by the time we went to bed. She was fortunate indeed, I reflected, not to have had half a hundred children evacuated from the danger areas of Portsmouth and Southampton billeted on her.

The appearance of Hunzinger and myself had naturally occasioned a stir of interest, politely suppressed in the British manner. But the unexpected manifestation of two military-age civilians, apparently in perfect health, each of them tall, with the same build, the same thatch

143

of pale hair, and identical square chins, wide mouths and prominent noses, could hardly be expected to pass unnoticed!

Papers supplied by the indefatigable and mythical Korsun (aka Lieutenant-Colonel Webster, DSO, MC) identified us as brothers – how could we be anything else? – in fact the Hartzmann Brothers, importers of precision optical instruments, of Abergavenny in South Wales. Hunzinger in fact was playing himself . . . at a safe distance from a region where it would be known that he had been interned and sent to the Isle of Man. Documents dated more recently indicated that our war work was related to the YMCA and that we were at present engaged on a factfinding see-how-it's-done tour evaluating the different activities of that organisation. Including, of course, the efficiency and effect of the mobile canteen scheme.

One of the slight pleasures I derived from this was the fact that Hunzinger – perhaps because he thought it make him look more like an official – had grown a moustache in the past few days. And that, thus ornamented, he looked in my opinion rather more English than I did!

In truth, though, this astonishing likeness – without which the operation could never have existed at all, either from the British or the pretended German side – was one of the greatest obstacles to the smooth running of the missions, both Hunzinger's and mine.

"Face it, Zoltan," he had said while we were still at the safe house at St Annes, "there is no way whatsoever of escaping the fact: we are brothers! Twin brothers at that. The hell with the papers. Any time we appear togther this is self evident. When we are together, therefore, we are *obliged* to accept this fact, there is no avoding it; we muct continue to play the *role* of brothers."

Too bloody right we must . . . brother! I thought. But I didn't say anything.

"Nothing can hide this fact," Hunzinger said. "None of the usual disguise stratagems, even the more subtle ones – a stoop, a limp, padded out cheeks, spectacles, different hair – would be of the slightest use. The likeness is too obvious."

"Well, of course, I can see that," I said. "I mean it limits us – especially if the Manx escape has been reported – and then linked up in the north with the escape of two suspected German spies from the Fleetwood docks!"

"Together, then, we must be twin brothers, with credible reasons, explanations, for such brothers to be together, at any given place at any given time. Plus proof if possible."

"This is mainly a question of working out a convincing scenario before we go out together, every time we do it," I said. "Surely?"

"Of course, of course. But carefully, Zoltan: the situation is delicate; it could be dangerous."

"Well, naturally. That's why I have to play a minor part. But Korsun believed—"

"If we have a base where it is acceptable for us to be seen together," Hunzinger cut in, "it is of no importance whether we leave or return together or separately. The only thing we have to remember when we work apart is that the work must be chosen *geographically* some distance apart. That way, should any individual travelling here and there chance to set eyes on each of us at different times in the same day, the resemblance could be put down to coincidence, to the fact that the witness was simply mistaken, or to the explanation that he had not in truth seen two different men, *but the same man twice* – because by coincidence their paths had crossed again."

"That could be a reason for us to dress identically when we work apart," I said,

"True. But there are as many reasons, equally valid, for us to dress differently, to emphasise the manifestation of *two* men. And if necessary, for once, adopt those slight disguise ploys – carriage, posture, walk, vocal delivery – we reject when we are an obvious couple. In the one case to underline the resemblance, in the other to minimise it."

"Yes," I said mendaciously, "you are of course quite right, Axel. As always."

As a matter of pure convenience, I would have welcomed – at least during this initial stage – the opportunity to work alone for a day or so. It was essential that I contact Webster, in part to report progress but much more importantly to ask for guidance.

My original orders were twofold, the choice between two alternatives obviously being Hunzinger's rather than mine.

In the first case, I was to allow the German to re-enact his pre-war odyssey and himself regain contact with those former agents still at liberty – leaving the great web of British counter-intelligence operatives to follow up and note who and where. Or, in the second case, accompany the spymaster, if he so wished, and secretly note down the names and addresses myself. The details subsequently to be confided to Webster or Nichols.

But in neither case was any official action to be taken, and no arrests made, until the entire ring was exposed. Sleepers hastily snatched immediately after a visit from Axel would simply blow the entire operation for good.

My immediate problem now was to ask a simple yes-or-no question.

After the unforeseen sea disaster and the lack of information from me because of the Fleetwood cock-up, was the aforesaid counter-intelligence network in fact in place and ready to put Hunzinger under permanent surveillance if and when he decided to go it alone? If the answer was affirmative, a second problem arose. How was I to alert them when he set off on his own? And how could I tell them where he would be starting from – the superbly arrogant four-word address: Fortune Hall, Hawkhurst, Kent?

For all I knew, everything was one hundred percent under control, and half the student helpers at the hall could be MI5 or Special Branch trainees already in place. But I had to know.

And before I knew I had to reach one or the other of the dead-letter drops distributed here and there throughout southern England . . . because only from them could I discover the current routine – which changed every week – for contacting my masters.

I had no idea whom he had contacted – or who might have contacted him – but Hunzinger already had a plan for the day worked out when he came down the next morning for breakfast – urn tea spiced with Ministry of Health baby-milk, laboratory orange juice and scrambled (dried) egg.

"Today, my friend, we take a short trip," he told me. "A round trip, in fact. We accompany the Number Two canteen on its visits to balloon sites, batteries and radar installations at Peasmarsh, Winchelsea, Rye, Romney Marsh and Dungeness."

"Hoop-de-doo!" I said, somewhat rashly.

"What was that?"

"An English phrase that I learned in Melbourne," I said. "Signifying pleasure."

"Ah. Well, let us go and see how the day starts for our benevolent volunteers, eh?"

The day started in the stable yard, which was behind the house. The three canteens had been manhandled out from the long building which had once housed fifteen or twenty horses. They were now being tanked up from jerricans by an elderly man in overalls who could have been an odd-job retainer or a one-time gardener. Half a dozen of the students were wheeling out trolleys loaded with the stock to be sold; a youth from a baker's in Hawkhurst was emplying his van of trays packed with sausage rolls and currant buns; in each canteen a middle-aged woman checked off items on a clipboard list as the young driver handed them up through the let-down hatchway at the rear of the vehicle.

The three models were very different visibly. The ten-cwt Ford
which had collected us from the station we knew already – an over-tall,
overhung van body which threatened to capsize the light-weight
chassis, cab and motor. Our driver from the previous night was
leaning over the open bonnet, his bare arms greased black as far as
the elbows.

Behind this was a Bedford three-tonner, apart from the camouflage
paint, much as it had been when it was handling small-quantity
removals. The original cargo compartment had been modified so
that one entire side now opened and let down to form a kind of sales
counter not unlike a bar. Two deep windows let in light through the
rear doors.

The third canteen – the one we were to accompany, labelled Number
Two – was different again. Much the largest, it had evidently been
designed as a motor-caravan, with a generous living space redesigned
as the shop premises, a tiny spare room used for stock and kitchenette.
A ladder led to the box-like front end which projected over the
cab and had been structured exactly to accomodate the king-size,
coil-spring mattress on which, athwart the width of the caravan, the
occupants slept.

The woman who appeared to be the permanent helper with this
canteen was a pleasant fifty-year-old; grey haired but well made-up
and still rather pretty. Mrs Alice Cooksie by name. Her husband Phil,
who had been invalided out of the Navy after a hair-raising escape
from Singapore, helped the Fortune Hall staff with the maintenance
of the three canteens.

Mrs Cooksie's driver, a Welsh youth called Taffy Morgan –
although the name on his pass and identity card seemed to be
Huw Spearpoint – was passing up the contents of his trolley to the
bar counter.

"Sausage rolls, one gross . . . cream buns, three score . . . choc-
olates: four dozen Fruit and Nut, four of Milk Flake, six of the Caramac
– very popular that new one! – and, look you, Mrs C, Robbins the Milk
says he's sorry but he's fresh out of the Rowntrees; not a single packet
left! Says he's put in two cartons of Mars Bars instead, and will that be
all right?"

"Not to worry, Taffy," Mrs Cooksie reassured. "I'll tell the girls at
Dungeness it's my fault, remind them there's a war on, right? We must
press on regardless."

"There is an angel you are, Mrs C," the boy said fondly. "Now,
cigarettes. The usual of Navy Cut, Gold Flake and Woods. Only
a couple of dozen Passing Clouds and Three Castles. Some of the

sergeants think smoking them makes them feel like officers. Can you imagine! But those Du Maurier with the cork tips sold right out last week . . ."

Ten minutes later, the engine of the caravan burst into life with a throaty roar, Hunzinger and I climbed into the back and found two armchairs, Mrs Cooksie sat next to Taffy in the cab and, waved off by the students left behind, we followed the other canteens down the driveway and out on to the A268 leading south to Peasmarch and the coast.

It was an agreeable enough journey, much smoother and quieter than the trip in the Ford, with sunlit views of the South Downs unrolling behind the rear windows. The only discordant note was the pervasive odour of the tens of gallons of unholy fluids sloshing around inside the two heavy metal urns.

Hunzinger, rarely for him, was finally obliged to filch a packet of cigarettes from a shelf and light one with a grimace of distaste. De Reszke Turkish, I noted with amusement. A beginner!

By the time we left, there had still been no sign of the benefactress, Mrs Fortune.

The meeting, as it happened, was to be a pleasure not too long delayed. First, though, there were several dozen clients in five different localities to be fed, watered and jollied along.

We had of course exactly the same system in Northern Ireland, most evidently around Belfast and in the neighbourhood of the RAF station at Aldergrove – proudly displayed by the locals because recently it had actually been favoured with the laying down of a real runway in *concrete*! "Fifty yards fuckin' wide, boyo, with acres of like wire mattresses intil the insides of it."

So far as the sites were concerned I'd never paid them much attention. They were there. Part of the décor of everyday life, like the blackout and no railings and mud-coloured cars, they were the business of the sappers, the gunners and the RAF Regiment. I'd never been inside one.

The security at the first one we visited in Kent could hardly be described as tight – a lance-corporal with a slung rifle, lounging by a five-barred farm gate, with a cigarette hanging from his mouth. Mind you, this was just a balloon site, on a stretch of marshy wasteland between a stream and a meadow with horses. The war material on view was hardly top secret stuff: equipment for deflating the bloody things, for re-inflating, with mechanical winches for feeding them up into the sky and hauling the down again. Around the second balloon site there were cows.

Blitz Harvest

The batteries were different. Very brisk, very efficient, very Royal Artillery. *All Passes To Be Shewn* – just like the War House, and proper sentries at the gates.

Wherever we went, we were greeted with pleasure, almost with joy in the more isolated areas. The crews crowded around with laughter and badinage. Trade was brisk. Mrs Cooksie, clearly very popular, was a dab hand at passing out mugs of tea and coffee, transferring cigarettes and chocolate bars to the forest of outstretched hands, answering questions and manipulating change for the flood of pennies and shillings and the occasional pound note. She was quick with the repartee after the occasional pleasantry, and she knew many of the outposted crew by name.

Behind her, Taffy was kept busy turning taps on the urns, reaching for stuff on the shelves.

Hunzinger and I, downplaying the YMCA officials, got out of the canteen and walked here and there among the men and women, nursing their hot mugs and chatting together or examing their new purchases. We had been introduced as Inspectors, so we asked the occasional anodyne question – Were they happy with the service? Could they suggest improvements? What did they like best? – though this was more for the benefit of Mrs Cooksie and Taffy than for the crews.

Their actual meals of course, breakfast, lunch, supper, were provided officially – by NAAFI trucks, I supposed. What was important about the mobile canteens was the contact with life 'outside' and the fact that for once there was choice – what they bought, which delicacies they chose to nibble, when they did it.

The gunsites, evidently, were far more 'interesting' for Hunzinger. Some of the batteries were concealed beneath camouflage nets strewn with brushwood; others were dug into bunkers or buttressed with earth and turves like prehistoric barrows. Of those revealed in the open air, I could see multi-barrelled, fairly lightweight material of the Oerlikon and pom-pom type, and a number of more serious dissuaders I took to be seventy-five mm or eighty-eight mm models. Naturally, we made no attempt to approach the batteries. Hunzinger was certainly evaluating the anti-aircraft artillery mentally, but he wasn't there to make a run-down himself – simply to judge what possibilities there would be for his sleepers once they had been accepted into the YMCA's pool of volunteers

Nearer the coast, I knew, there would be far more powerful weapons aimed at possible land and sea targets, dug into clifftop bunkers facing seaward or sheltered by bomb-proof concrete strong-points. But I doubted if the canteens would be permitted to come anywhere near these.

There were five different sites for us to visit, for example, among the great shingle wastes of Dungeness. But all of them were very much outposted, three balloons and two batteries – both anti-aircraft rather than land-sea defences. "Don't the lads and lasses with the sea view ever get a go at the Fruit and Nut or the Brylcreem?" I asked Mrs Cooksie, with a glance at the distant pylons and pillboxes glittering in the sun.

"Lord bless you no, love," she laughed. "That's all top secret down there. Very hush-hush. You know: RDF masts – radar they call it now – those great shallow bowls and buried dugouts galore. You've got to have a special pass autographed by Winnie and countersigned by the king even to get close to the barbed wire there!"

The canteen rounds, such as they were, would nevertheless be valuable enough hunting grounds for sleepers – even if what they came up with did no more than add confirmatory detail to the picture as a whole. Apart from which, for those who happened to have an interest in the precise emplacement of batteries and balloon sites, and who happened to find time to make surreptitious notes on the canteen's round, there could be an additional advantage, especially in the sensitive southeast. The concentration of huge and ever increasing numbers of troops, together with their artillery, armour and logistic apparatus, cannot be hidden behind a single barbed wire enclosure or among clifftop bunkers. Such operations require a great deal of space – and a sizeable amount of time to develop.

It's all very well to have cardboard, timber and drainpipe mock-ups of tanks, aircraft and armoured vehicles dispersed around the countryside. ('It's just to fool the Jerry observation planes about the disposition of our forces, you know.') We had noticed quite a few on that day's round already. But if half the passers-by who see this happen to be German agents . . . and if there happens to be a coordination centre . . . and if there happen to be other agents noting the position of genuine dispersal sites – well, a ten-cwt Ford Anglia mobile canteen on four worn tyres is as useful a tool as any aerial camera at ten to twenty thousand feet.

Whatever. We passed the rest of the day doing what the conductors call 'Once more, with feeling', and we were trundling back up the driveway to Fortune Hall a few minutes before four-thirty in the afternoon.

Not, on my part, without a certain backward glance – at a balloon site in Rye, as it happens – towards a certain brunette of maybe thirty who had very definitely, despite the shapeless, baggy other-ranks WAAF uniform, given me the impression that anything to do with feeling what lay within the confines of that blue-grey jacket and skirt would not be repulsed with the indignation so often characteristic of the Anglo-Saxon female confronted by the physical.

Why the green light had glowed so positively in my direction rather than Axel's puzzled me at first. Perhaps it was because he was German?

And this deplorably racist thought prompted another reflection somewhat more profound.

For Axel, all the brunettes and blondes and redheads with whom we were joking and exchanging risqué wisecracks, all the earnest, cheerful young men politely answering his subtly posed, never-too-pertinent questions, were to him 'the enemy'; his life was dedicated to their destruction and the destruction of all they stood for. Amongst them on the human scale, how did he feel about this? Could he visualise this blonde, that brunette who had just offered him a cigarette, on the train to Dachau, to Oranienberg, to Ravensbruck? Could he see them, naked and cold, watching Mum and Dad on the way to the ovens?

And that of course prompted the spin of the coin, my heads to his tails. For me Axel Hunzinger was equally the enemy; my mission encompassed the destruction of everything that *he* stood for. How did I feel about this?

Simply that the maximum he faced, even if he was a war criminal, was a prison sentence.

Could that have been why we were fighting?

Never mind. We were back in the stable yard. Taffy and his lady were stretching their legs. The student helpers were unloading what remained of the stock and packing it away in the stable block. A large Armstrong-Siddeley limousine was parked in front of the double stairway that led to the hall's main entrance, and there were dogs baying somewhere behind one of the towers.

Mrs Fortune, back from Ashford, would be happy if we could join her for an aperitif in the library.

The library curiously enough, was full of books. And brass-buttoned leather armchairs and a full sized billiard table. Axel went in ahead of me with outstretched arms. After all they were old friends. Or more than that.

"Axel! My dear one – a delight, a joy! How did you manage it, what happened, tell me all. But later, not just now. Let me look at you – and savour this reunion with a glass of champagne!"

151

The voice was low, melodious, with the slightest trace of an accent. I knew at once that it would belong to a self-assured woman, probably between thirty and fifty, almost certainly chic and well-dressed. If we were lucky, someone mature and voluptuous as well, conceivably on the fleshy side? Personal preferences you understand; wish father to the thought, and all that!

I scored ten out of ten for that – but no thanks to my conscious mind; the unconscious was holding the reins at that particular moment of time.

"My brother Zoltan," Hunzinger said. "Just . . . arrived . . . from Australia."

She was sitting in a high-backed chair, invisible until she rose to her feet with an outstretched hand. "Zoltan!" she smiled. "Of course. What an extra pleasure for me!"

I saw auburn, shoulder-length hair, a superbly cared-for forty-year-old face, exquisitely cut and pressed tweeds with a crisp ivory-coloured shirt. I took in full breasts and superb legs. The accent of course was Austrian.

I had the devil of a job stopping my jaw dropping the way hers had the first time. I was staring at Zelda, the woman we had met at the Embassy Club in Belfast – and with whom Webster, as it happened, had spent the night in the hotel behind the City Hall.

Eighteen

I suppose I should have known. Or maybe guessed. Perhaps my subconscious didn't rate the ten out of ten score every day. *Zelda Fortune*, by God. But of course! The woman we met in Belfast hadn't given her surname. I hadn't thought to ask. On that date she had simply been Webster's girl. The indications had been there, though. Most importantly, she had known one or other of the Hunzinger twins. She was Austrian, married to a British officer in the Allied Control Commission after the Great War, now something of a local big wheel in southern England, the husband a prisoner of the Japs.

But by chance nobody – neither Hunzinger nor any of the staff at the hall – happened to have mentioned the oh-so-charitable Mrs Fortune's Christian name. Or not in front of me anyway.

In my mind there had been two entirely different women, separated by time, by geography and by situation – the sexy night-clubber in Ulster, packed neatly away in the past; and the mobile canteen benefactress in Kent, no more than a question mark in the future. I had known the married name of one, the Christian name of the other: a case, as it turned out, of two different halves making very much less than a single whole!

But the single whole was now here – and it was the present.

It was in fact offering me a flute of 1928 Hiedsieck Dry Monopole . . . and it was likely to prove a considerable headache, though not because of the champagne.

My mind, as they say in the novels, reeled. The problem, naturally, was not one I could share with Hunzinger. But problem it could be.

I would be accepted as Zoltan. No doubt of that, since Axel himself had presented me as such. But Zelda herself was sure to mention, at one time or another, that she had run into this astonishing individual, this amazing coincidence, while she was in Belfast a week or two ago. "My dear, a dead ringer as the Americans say – it could have been either of you, I swear it! A British army officer, can you imagine!"

I could imagine all right. Did you really? But how extraordinary!

You mean *exactly*, unmistakably like us? Identical, you say? Good God, don't say there's room in the world for *three* Hunzingers! And like that. Big joke, of course.

Except that it wasn't quite that simple.

An extraordinary coincidence, fine. And I was thankful that Webster had had the presence of mind, although I was in plain clothes, to introduce me as myself; he hadn't dared to risk saying I was Zoltan, in case it was the Australian brother she knew.

Well, she hadn't known Zoltan. But the genuine introduction, in a way that couldn't have been foreseen, had carried with it a load of possible trouble in the future.

We had in fact been a little too clever-clever, a shade too proud of our smartness.

For one of the cover identities we (in our role as Korsun) had provided for Hunzinger was that of an infantry captain from Northern Ireland – a certain Nicholas Hart. The uniform, which he had already used once, during his visits to Sutton Bonington and Bradford, was packed in his valise upstairs!

And if he used it again while we were based at Fortune Hall – or, worse, if he ordered me to wear the uniform and assume the Hart identity . . . well, that would be tempting fortune (in every sense) a bit too much.

But the worst, the catastrophe scenario, would be if Zelda happened to recall the name of the British officer – the Christian name might be enough – and Hunzinger happened to quote one or the other if he used the cover again!

Did I hear someone say 'What's in a name?' Brother, I didn't even want to think about it.

Zelda did in fact mention the 'coincidence' during dinner. It would have been hard not to, faced across the table with already two of us. The dialogue went roughly as I thought it would. Axel, thankfully, didn't show signs of pursuing the story; he dismissed it as the coincidence she said it was: amusing, but let's get on with life. There are more things in heaven and earth, Horatio . . .

One of the things – it should have been evident from the start, I suppose – was that Zelda herself was totally in Hunzinger's confidence. I don't know what he had told her of his escape during the phone calls he made, but it was clear not only that she knew his task was to reactivate sleepers but also that she was in all probability one of those agents herself. What better cover, after all, with a husband safely away, than a team of mobile canteens swanning around the corner of southeastern England nearest to continental Europe?

154

Much of the conversation that evening revolved around the mechanics of infiltrating some of the sleepers among the volunteers staffing the Zelda Fortune and other canteen circuits in the area. That was not the subject that kept me awake half the night. Suppose, I thought, that Zelda was not a sleeper but an *active* German agent – one who would be able to help Hunzinger but who was in fact already working for a genuine Nazi intelligence team? Suppose her visit to Belfast, which was while he was still interned, was in reality connected with that work – making contact with the IRA for instance? It would be no wonder that she was staggered to find herself dancing with a Hunzinger sosie on that very visit.

In which case . . . but no; it was too much, it wasn't possible! Yet if Hunzinger himelf did, off his own bat as it were, suddenly appear as the sosie – name and all – of that same army officer . . . how in hell could any sane individual dredge up a credible explanation for that?

At the very least, every single person concerned would be utterly convinced, as Webster would say, that something very rum indeed was going on!

Meanwhile it seemed to me that the best thing I could do – another impossible chore – would be in some way or another to get rid of, make vanish, destroy or otherwise volatilise that damned uniform and the papers that went with it.

Is there a magician in the house?

Nineteen

Hunzinger had already left when I dragged myself up the following morning after a belated couple of hours uneasy sleep. A slip of paper beneath my door stated simply: LONDON URGENT BACK TONIGHT. CHECK ODD STRUCTURES APPARENTLY FLOATING SHIPYARDS RYE CAMBER.

There was no signature. I flushed the paper down the lavatory and hurried to his room. There was no sign of the uniform or papers in his suitcase. I swore. I don't know what I could believably have done to get rid of them without blowing my cover, but now there was no choice. Fortunately it was raining and he had worn a lightweight showerproof which would hide the telltale pips and flashes at least while he was outside. Once again there was no sign of Zelda, and the parking bay reserved for the Armstrong-Siddeley was empty.

Mr Axel, one of the village women told me, had received a telephone call very early, and Mrs Fortune had driven him to the station at Haywards Heath.

I hitched a lift in the small Ford canteen, whose round penetrated further into Rye than we had been in the caravan yesterday, and walked the rest of the distance to the Mermaid Hotel. This was one of the more fortunate coincidences: the Mermaid happened to be one of a dozen drops I had been alerted to in the extreme southeast.

It wasn't a drop in the normal sense: no tiny wads of paper crammed into a crack; just a polite question to the barman in the Snug as soon as they opened. Had a Mr Nichols by any chance left a message for Dr Watson?

Indeed he had, sir. A small envelope with the name of a local hospital printed on the front. I thanked the man, bought a beer, and took it to a corner table. I slit open the flap as I drank.

A squared page torn from a notebook. A single line of pencilled figures.

The drill was to ignore the first seven and then dial the rest. I found a public phone and dialled.

Blitz Harvest

The phone was lifted after the third ring. A woman's voice: "Listening."

"Doctor Watson," I said. "Is Holmes by any chance available?"

She read out a list of figures, repeated it, and hung up.

I found a public callbox, fed in money, and dialled out the numbers. Sigh of relief: it was Webster himself who answered.

"Not to worry," he said when I posed my vital question. "We know where you are. We're with you all the way. Your man took the 10.43 for Victoria. We'll be looking after him in London – and on the way back. We only haul off when you're together."

"Splendid. The names and addresses, can you keep them yourself – I mean your actual self? At the moment my secretary's on holiday and my filing cabinet is rather limited."

"Wilco."

"One other thing: could I have a direct number for you, one that I can call at any time without going through Madam Listening? Only in case it's really urgent, of course."

"I may not always be there," he said, "but I'll give you my private line at home. Nell Gwynn House in Chelsea."

I jotted the number down, memorised it, chewed up and swallowed the paper. "Mind you," Webster said, "you have to realise – the line may be bugged."

"Piss off," I said.

I walked towards the boatyards. It's an odd little town, Rye, deliberately preserved as it was in Jane Austen's time and earlier – all oak beams and diamond-leaded window panes, with steep cobbled streets that still boast two strips of stone inset to make the grade easier for carriage wheels. It was originally added to the mediaeval Cinque Ports between Hythe and Hastings, but the sea receded and now it's inland with only the Camber estuary linking it to the Channel. Winchelsea, it's sister port, is two miles from the sea! The boatyards that remain deal in pretty small stuff today – launches, cruisers, yachts and suchlike – but there were certainly 'odd structures that floated' on the seaward side of the town: the larger ones like small aircraft hangars without roofs. I knew what they were too: tank landing craft. I had seen some of them being tested on Belfast Lough, along with Churchill tanks built by Harland and Wolff, whose factory was at the head of the lough, by the river Lagan.

There were also a couple of APCs under camouflage nets and, a rare enough sight, an LVT-4. This amphibious ship-to-shore 'vehicle' (the letters stood for Landing Vehicle Tracked) was driven through the water by its caterpillars and could ferry huge quantities of

157

troops, heavy artillery and supplies. With 12.7mm armour, it weighed 27,000lbs empty – but it floated all right! I could see two of them, the white American star on their raised ramps, in an artificial basin which had been carved from the banks of the Rother on its way to Camber and the sea.

Well, that was something for Zoltan to report to his brother – although hopefully Axel would be back inside before he could make use of it. I walked back into town.

It was a relief to have Webster's confirmation that he knew where we were, and that all the necessary tails to keep Hunzinger under surveillance were in place. Interesting too to have certain deductions of my own verified.

"Hardly surprising, old boy, to find you and your bro shacked up with your present hostess with the mostest," he had said when the initial exchanges were over. "Matter of fact, the seductive Zelda is top of one of my lists – the one headed Don't Forget to Tip Off Hart."

"Listening," I said in the most feminine voice I could manage.

Webster permitted himself a cackle of laughter. "I'll quote you a number all right," he said, "but it's something of a specialty number. Even if it has to do with – er – figures."

"Meaning?"

"Happened to be back in Belfast on another job, and I ran into your girlfriend June – the blonde bombshell dancer. We sank a jar together at the GC."

"Lucky you," I said.

"Yes, well, the fact is I asked for news of the sexy Z for Victory, and June came up with a couple of items which gave Mrs Webster's boy, as our Allies say, furiously to think. Item: June knew nought of any conference at Stormont, farming or otherwise. She thought Zelda had pulled strings to get there because she wanted to meet a boyfriend from Dublin. Oh-ho, I thought."

"Oh-ho, indeed!" I echoed.

"Remembering the lady's surprise when she saw your face – astonishing enough, I admit, but indicating that she must have known at least one of the Hunzingers – I thought to myself: Dublin? Not by any chance a boyfriend connected with a certain illegal organisation? So I put out a few feelers here and there."

"With two girls like that, I'm not surprised," I said.

"June was right, of course. Zelda had never been near Stormont. They'd never even heard of her. Which brings me to Oh-ho Number Two. Scarcely had I posed the final question when miscreants – two different chaps, with two different guns – did their damnedest to kill me."

"Christ!" I said. And then: "Did they succeed?"

He let that one go with the tide. Rye is as good a place as any. "Bearing all of which in mind," he said, "Adams and your obedient reckoned it would be as well to warn you. Just in case you ran into Zelda again. But as you've literally been hurled at her, I daresay you've already sussed out something along similar lines yourself, eh?"

"Funny you should say that," I replied. "The lady happens to be top of one of my lists too: the one headed Don't Forget to Tip Off Webster."

So. Things were under control so far as the Adams-Webster line was concerned. My Mrs Fortune reservations were justified. I had a telephone number. But the Hunzinger-Hart headache – it was something more than a reservation – remained a constant danger.

There was only one thing to do. The canteen wasn't due to pass by again and pick me up until half past three. I went back to the Mermaid Hotel and had lunch.

Hunzinger changed into civilian clothes before he saw Zelda that evening. I thanked God for that. His panic call to London had been the result of an unexpected intelligence windfall. One of his sleepers – a friend of Zelda's who was a nightclub entertainer – had just acquired a new boyfriend, an ultra-Conservative politician who was Parliamentary Secretary to a cabinet minister in Churchill's wartime coalition government. And she was fairly convinced that she could persuade – or perhaps subtly blackmail – him to talk freely about official but still secret plans concerning the invasion of Europe!

Invaluable, of course, to the analysts coordinating the snippets of information culled by the other sleepers. But a situation so sensitive – and so liable to be wrecked by a false move or too strong a push in the wrong direction – that the spymaster had thought it vital to see the girl immediately and brief her in depth on the kind of approaches to make. And, perhaps even more importantly, to reject.

"A most alluring young woman," Hunzinger confided over dinner. "You were quite right, Zelda, to describe her as – er – seductive." And then, to me: "You shall meet her, Zoltan, the day after tomorrow, when we have several other friends to interview in London."

"And tomorrow, Axel?" It was becoming increasingly important to me to find time to make some kind of record of what I knew already

– and encypher or encode it surreptitiously, preferably with the help of a seemingly inoffensive novel or guide book.

Not tomorrow though, Josephine or no Josephine. "Tomorrow," Axel said, "I want you to come with me on a small sightseeing tour of Surrey, Hampshire and possibly even the coast of Dorset. Zelda has kindly and unselfishly offered to lend us the Armstrong." He smiled fondly at her. "A little fresh air from the counties before we brave the foetid vapours of the capital after dark!"

The trip, which was limited by the range provided by the limousine's full tank, included stops in Reigate, Camberley, Salisbury, Petersfield, Ringwood and North Camp – a suburb of the army centre of Aldershot. The cross-section of professions involved – and the variety of non-professional spying concerned in each case – was interesting. And very professionally selected.

Camberley of course was the watering-hole for officers from Sandhurst; a pub landlord there was a natural for picking up informed gossip. A retired colonel at North Camp thought the modern army "Too damned soft, by God! Hitler's common as dirt but we should be fightin' on his side: at least his army is run by bloody professionals!" A territorial officer who had lost a leg on the Somme – and considered his country had ill-rewarded him for the loss – was naturally fascinated by the armoured corps manoeuvres on the restricted sectors of Salisbury Plain that he could see from the windows of his 'gentleman's farm'. In Petersfield, a Superintendent railway signalman was in charge of a junction directing trains – many of them munitions specials – either to Portsmouth or Southampton. Two call-girls sharing a house at Ringwood, in the New Forest, enjoyed – so Axel told me – a fruitful series of liaisons with senior army and navy personnel organising military traffic through those two ports. And finally there was a doctor in Reigate. He was a therapist, most of whose psychiatric work was in Greenwich, among naval patients psychologically damaged on Arctic convoy and other perilous routes.

But we never did get to the Dorset coast. "We're lucky to make twenty to the gallon on these country roads," Hunzinger said. "And these British guages are notoriously inexact. Pity they didn't think of fitting Bosch or Weber electrical equipment."

I hadn't actually met any of these people. Axel had been a bit cagey about it, in fact – the first time I'd seen him in any way discomfited. "It's a little awkward," he said. "I want you to know who these people are. And where. But, for the moment at least, I'd prefer . . . well, you see they only know me. As me. And I'd rather not complicate matters,

160

at this most critical moment of their service, by introducing a double. If folks start asking questions . . . well, one never knows where it may lead. At the moment, you see, everything's cut and dried, everything in it's place, and . . ."

"It's all right, Axel," I said. "Don't worry. I understand. I'll wait outside, in the car."

"If you would. There's a – um – a chauffeur's cap, one of those things with a shiny black peak, in the glove compartment. If you wouldn't mind . . ."

"I'll pull it down over my eyes," I said. "Sir."

"You'll meet them all later," he said. "But at this very delicate moment for them . . . You know . . ."

"I know," I said. "Boats that are rocked can easily be capsised. I shall sit very still."

London, he promised me, would be different. And indeed it was.

Especially if one was being introduced to it for the first time by a supposed Welsh factory owner named Hartzmann and one was oneself believed to have lived in Australia since the age of nine.

Even more so when one's real father was a country vicar only fifty miles away and one had passed one's schooldays at Bedford with Graham Greene.

I had in fact been contemplating an engagement on my next leave with a red-haired tennis player named Maureen, the daughter of one of my father's churchwardens. They had all been informed that I had received an unexpected posting to Alexandria – some very hush-hush infantry training job – but that I should probably be back within two months. Meanwhile that I was in good health but temporarily unable to write because of the nature of the posting. No post offices in the Sahara, I supposed. In any case after more than four years of war, and all those posters warning of the dangers of Careless Talk, they knew better than to ask questions.

London itself, of course, I knew pretty well. Better than Alexandria anyway (I had done a year at St Martin's before I was called up, with the vague idea of a career in advertising). I had been anxious that I might risk revealing by some inadvertent error that I knew it too well. Like knowing that the Morden-Edgware tube split itself into two different routes traversing Central London – one through the City, the other via Leicester Square.

I needn't have worried. You needed to check with the chalked up notices at every station if you wanted to get anywhere. For London was in a mess. The night raids had been stepped up during the past few days (the Hawkhurst area had been on practically continuous

Peter Leslie

alert), and apart from pulverising the dock areas, the previous night's blitz had put two of London Transport's main signalling circuits out of action.

Chaos, therefore. Roads closed. Salvage crews mountaineering over huge slants of rubble spilled into the street. Fires still burning in the East End, and tin-hatted ARP wardens standing guard over roped-off notices advising: *Danger – Unexploded Bomb!*

We walked from Victoria to Soho, threading our way between the crowds of office workers carrying the obligatory square cardboard boxes supposed to contain their gas masks – but more frequently packed with sandwiches, cigarettes, powder compacts or notecases. Nobody really believed any more in the secret-weapon scares involving gas bombardment. On the other hand, no pickpocket or sneak thief was going to risk arrest against the possible gain of nothing but a pig-snout rubber face-mask.

"There's a place called the Coffee-Ann," Hunzinger told me, "mostly frequented by artists, out of work actors, failed painters – Bohemians if you like – which used to be in a basement somewhere between Soho Square and Tottenham Court Road. It's a kind of club; people play chess there and criticise the government and drink coffee all day. I'd like to spend a couple of hours there this morning: there's someone I want to see who's an habitué – and it's the only address I have for him."

I nodded. "If the place still exists, of course," he added. "I've been . . . away four years after all."

Of coure I knew very well the Coffee-Ann still existed. But I was – quite literally – in no position to say so. I allowed him to make several casts around the Oxford Street Corner House, including a false start near an intellectuals' pub called the Bricklayer's Arms and another in Denmark Street – Tin Pan Alley to the music business, because most of the publishers had their offices there. Finally, however, he vectored in on the right building and we went downstairs.

I have to say that I was apprehensive. I'd been something of a regular when I was at St Martin's, only a couple of hundred yards away. To put it another way, I was shit scared that someone I knew would recognise me. Especially as there were two of me now!

We had in fact toned down the resemblance as far as we could without being obvious. Hunzinger remained himself – the naturalised businessman evacuated to Wales: dark suit, sober tie, even a furled umbrella to go with the gas mask case. Liberties had been taken with me. My hair was dark again, we had found a convincingly bushy moustache at a theatrical costumier's, and I wore horn-rimmed spectacles.

162

Blitz Harvest

To complete what difference there was, I wore a roll-neck sweater with corduroys, adopted a hunched, rather round-shouldered stance and a slight stammer to support the diffident, not-too-self-assured role I had adopted.

And this was where Hunzinger displayed another aspect of his professionalism. The double bluff routine, you might say. Having minimised the likeness as subtly but definitely as possible, he then made a point of drawing attention to what similarities remained by introducing me as his cousin. In this way he automatically answered and explained any questions or reflections before they were even framed. Attack is the best means of defence, as they say.

My clothes and stance, equally automatically we hoped, might underline the implication: for cousin read country cousin!

From Hunzinger's point of view this would cover any non-metropolitan gaucheness a real Zoltan from Down Under might reveal.

The Coffee-Ann was crowded. It was always crowded, day and night. Boris, the monolithic Russian who seemed to own it and knew everyone by name, moved easily from group to group. Quite a few of the people I knew by sight myself: Tambimuttu, the creator of the 'Poetry London' imprint, Dylan Thomas, Louis MacNeice and JF Hendry, Mr Freedman of the Zwenner avant garde bookshop in Shaftesbury Avenue, John Lehmann with a circle of contributors to his 'Penguin New Writing'.

And of course the three most regular regulars: Nine Hamnet, the renowned artists' model and author of 'Dancing Torso'; Colin, a tall young man with a wispy beard who would publicly recite an interminable epic poem called 'The Eddystone Light' at the drop of a half pint of beer; and the indefatigable Mac.

Mac was a professional busker who entertained theatre queues. He was reputed to know the entire works of William Shakespeare by heart. Nobody had ever caught him out. With his fine Henry Irving voice he was quite capable of running through half of the First Folio, punctuated by a handful of the sonnets, to astonish three or four hundred people waiting in the rain to scramble into gallery seats for 'Dear Octopus', 'Mr Bolfry' or the Mona Inglesby Ballet.

Everybody in London knew Mac. His speciality at the Coffee-Ann, much applauded, was to select at will couplets which he would loudly declaim by way of a satirical commentary on clients arriving at or leaving the club premises.

As we trod down the dusty staircase, he looked up from a table, stared briefly at Hunzinger, and roared: "Behold a certain lord, neat and trimly dressed, fresh as a bridegroom. Yet his chin, new reaped, shows still like

163

stubble land at harvest time!" The gaze swung towards me. And at once he continued in the same breath: "But here a devil haunts thee in the likeness of thyself: a tun of man is thy companion."

There was laughter from below, and some applause. We went up to the bar. Hunzinger ordered two beers. Eventually we'found a tiny corner table.

Mac, however, had not been the only one to take in facial features.

Behind us, I heard a stumble of feet, a slurred voice I didn't at first recognize.

A slightly drunken voice loudly calling out "Nick! By all that's holy, bloody Nick!"

I froze. Panic. The catastrophe scenario.

The owner of the voice lurched past me – a tall, gangling thirty-year-old in the uniform of an RAF flight-sergeant; a face I vaguely recognised – St Martin's? Aldergrove? Bedford?

But the face *he* was recognising wasn't mine: it was Hunzinger's.

Swaying a little, he halted by the table and punched the spymaster lightly on the shoulder. "Who the *hell* would believe I'd run into you here, of all places!" he hiccuped.

Hunzinger's face stiffened. "I am afraid you are mistaken, Sergeant," he said coldly. "My name is Hartzmann. I do not recall ever seeing you before."

"Oh, Christ! Terribly sorry, chum. My mistake an' all that. No offence, I hope. But I could have bloody *sworn* you were my old mate Nicholas fucking—"

I knocked over my glass of beer before he could get the surname out.

Smashing of glass on the tile floor. A cascade of liquid. Hunzinger springs to his feet. The barman hurries up with a cloth. Confused apologies from me. Stupid of me . . . clumsy oaf . . . take more care next time. Meanwhile, let me get you . . .

Conversation, temporarily halted, resumed. It wasn't a fight after all. Shamefaced, the drunken NCO had made himself scarce amid the confusion. Yours truly breathed a sigh of relief. A heavy one. There were enough things that required to be taken for granted in this charade already. But to have Hunzinger addressed by name, by a total stranger, as a fictional individual *who was in fact no more than one of his own cover identities* . . . God, no: that would really be asking too much!

A spare man with thinning hair had brought a vacant chair to our table. His name was Diego, Hunzinger said. He was a fishmonger in Frith Street – and indeed there was in fact a whiff of cod emanating from the navy-blue and white striped apron he wore.

Diego was perhaps forty-five years old. Maybe fifty. He owned a refrigerated van, and he had a petrol allowance that permitted him, legally, to go twice a week to the fish markets at Grimsby and Lowestoft, driving the supplies he bought back each time to the capital.

Hunzinger spoke very fast, fairly quietly. In the brawling din of the lunchtime crowd now cramming the Coffee-Ann, over the stentorian declamations of Mac, it was impossible for me to catch more than half the exchanges between the two men.

Diego, it was clear, was the character we had been waiting for. He was to take particular note, any time he was within twenty miles of the East Coast, on each and every trip, of all military convoys he came across – and, if possible, their eventual destination, number of units and armour if any. That, in general, was about all I could make out. I did, however, hear what turned out to be the pay-off line. "After each journey south," Hunzinger said, "you will summarise what you have observed for Hyperion, in Finchley, and leave the paper for him the following morning, before you open the shop. And the shop must open on time. Is that clear?"

Diego grinned. Yellowing horse teeth in a weathered face. "Whatever you say, guv!" A scarred forefinger touched his right temple. "Orders is orders – even if they don't come direct from the bleedin' Reichstag!"

"Don't ever say that!" Hunzinger snarled. "Ever. It is not funny and it could be dangerous."

Diego's grin became crooked. He shrugged. "Whatever you say: you're the boss." He gave a second mock salute, nodded to me, and slouched away.

"Damned Cockneys!" Hunzinger growled. "Never any sense of when!"

"Could it for example," I suggested, "be a case of the celebrated British sense of humour?"

He shook his head. "I have analysed this. For the Englander, to call a lean man 'Fatty' is funny. Everyone laughs, including the lean man. But so to call a man with a beer belly, that is impolite. Nobody laughs, it is a breach of good manners. And the man with the belly is offended. Similarly with the vice versa. Call this belly-man 'Skinny', and he laughs along with everyone else . . . But for the thin man this would be an insult and he is enraged. Nobody laughs. You see?"

"Are you saying, Axel, that for the British to laugh, the proposition must be untrue?"

"Er – not exactly. It is more complex than that. The mores of the culture have to be taken into account. The socially acceptable and the unacceptable. And this in turn revolves around behaviour and the class system. Very specific affirmatives and negatives; rules that are unalterable yet nevertheless never actually stated or expressed. I tell you – what is in and what is out, this is a constantly changing yet curiously immutable . . . yardstick they call it. Something against which agreed behaviour, speech, comportment is measured."

"It sounds a little like the fashion business," I said. "What is the acceptable length of a skirt? You only hope you have got it right; you only *know* if it is in fact wrong."

"Perhaps." He finished his beer and held up the empty glass to signal the barman.

"Does Diego really have to go all the way out to Finchley to contact your analyst?" I said. "I mean before he opens his shop here in Soho?"

"Not at all. That would be noticeable. No – there is a drop in Covent Garden Underground Station, less than a quarter of a mile from his shop. A loose tile in the corridor, near one of the lifts. And since it is a very old station, the passageways curve a great deal, so it is no problem to manipulate a section of the arched wall without being observed."

"I see," I said.

What I saw a great deal less clearly was the relationship between my mission and the appearance of the third and last person Hunzinger and I encountered at the Coffee-Ann.

This one, like Diego, was a rendezvous. It was in fact the cabaret artist whose new boyfriend was Parliamentary Assistant to a cabinet minister. She was Canadian, she was a singer and her name was Estelle. It was evident that Hunzinger had great hopes for her as a possible inside ear.

Mac, who had saluted the departure of Diego with the porter's line from *MacBeth* ('A very ancient and fishlike smell,') was in fact now celebrating the descent of this important lady:

Lo, here she comes! Fie, fie upon her!
There's language in her eye, her cheek, her lip;
Nay, her foot speaks; her wanton spirits look out
At every joint and motive of her body.

And indeed the svelte, full-breasted brunette who undulated up to our table with a welcoming smile was a delight to the appreciative eye.

Except that my particular eye had seen her before. Dammit, I had spent a whole night with her!

Only that time she had been blonde rather than brunette. She had been neither Canadian nor a cabaret singer named Estelle. She had been a dancer at the Empire Theatre, Belfast. And her name at that time was June.

Twenty

I could say: Consternation! Panic! Plain, simple surprise!
But frankly I had progressed a little beyond the stage of mere
astonishment in this particular caper. Especially where the female
roles were concerned. To find out later that *each* of the blind dates
Webster and I had bedded that night in Belfast were already – or had
subsequently become – involved in the Hunzinger ring was stretching
the arm of coincidence a shade far. Asking one, as the theatre folks
say, to suspend disbelief a little too long. Yet the alternative – that the
whole thing had been a set-up; that the meetings had been engineered
precisely because the good lieutenant-colonel and myself were known
to be in our turn setting up Hunzinger . . . Christ, that made no
sense whatever, from anyone's point of view. Who after all would
it profit?

From this aspect of the affair, however, I could draw at least one
logical confusion. Zelda had been genuinely amazed when she saw
me because of the resemblance to Hunzinger, whom she knew. June,
on the other hand, had showed not the slightest reaction later that same
night. Ergo, *she had not at that time met the spymaster.* It followed
therefore – after all, the two of them were friends – that it was
Zelda herself, afterwards, who rowed June into the ring. Some other
contact in London must have found out about the politically sensitive
boyfriend and phoned Fortune Hall. It was a reasonable assumption
therefore that the Canadian singer Estelle was a recent fabrication.

Panic, you ask? Well, not for me. I was Zoltan, Hunzinger's brother,
vouched for by the man himself. The only person who might have
experienced panic – or for that matter consternation – was the girl
herself, and then only if she knew the man she faced across the
table was Captain Nicholas Hart, her Belfast bedmate, and *not* a
Hunzinger twin.

OK, so we were a Canadian cabaret singer, a Welsh manufacturer of
electrical goodies named Hartzmann, and his country cousin from that
rube antipodean region originally colonised by deported ex-jailbirds!

And what plans did we have for the rest of the day?

We were going to have lunch at one of the best small restaurants in London that still served edible food – The Akropolis, in Percy Street, less than two blocks away. "A treasure house, as far as I recall," Hunzinger said, "of shashlik, pilafs and individually prepared mousaka in small china bowls!" Afterwards, it seemed, there was to be a night on the town.

All Hunzinger wanted to do, so far as Estelle was concerned, was listen – at least in this initial stage. Briefings could wait. He wanted to hear everything – every tiniest detail – the girl could recall about her lover. What kind of person he was, how he dressed, what tastes he had. Was he a sporting type, did he play golf, squash, tennis? Who were his closest friends? More importantly, seeded amongst all this, were the casual questions about his work. What meetings did he attend? Did he ever go to Downing Street, to the SHAEF miltary conferences at the Ministry of Information? To what official minutes did he have access? Could he have sight of the Press Censorship's daily list of *Dead Stops* – subjects it was forbidden to mention even in passing? What opinions did the Minister have on this subject, on that one?

For the rest, Hunzinger wished to establish a routine of occasional appearances with the girl – as a family friend rather than a rival or putative lover. Often enough for her to appear familiar, rarely enough that no one would raise an eyebrow.

After dark, Axel told me, in the small hours when it had seemed prudent for Estelle to return decently to her love-nest, there were other contacts he hoped to make in less salubrious places at addresses supplied to him by Zelda.

And Zoltan? I was only too happy to string along. After that first shock in Adam Nichols's office – of seeing the photo of Hunzinger that I was convinced was me – nothing, I was determined, was going to shake me that way again! Not, at any rate, during this particular mission.

It would be a change, anyway, from the atmosphere of over-brewed tea and canteen coffee.

It turned out, in fact, to be rather more than that, in every possible sense.

The lunch, exactly as advertised, was a dream to one perforce acclimatised to the rigours of *La Cuisine Ulstérienne*. A cosseted atmosphere of well-mannered garlic spiced with the subtlest hint of pimento. Subdued, indeed respectful, conversation among the discreet tinkle of cutlery and the drawing of a Retsina cork. Then vine leaves wrapped around a Dionysiac confection of olives, sultanas, chopped basil and you tell me; the savoury inverted domes of mousaka –

multi-layered aromatic strata of aubergine, macerated lamb, pepper rings and paper-thin potato slices etiolated beneath their secret, soft-crust soufflé tops; small cakes of marzipan in its most ephemeral form.

Delicious.

We drank Bardolino. Pity. Especially as there was Barolo on the list. But it was Axel who was ordering. I felt his choice might more profitably have been attributed to an Australian brother.

Nevertheless, a special occasion. Quite a lot of which I spent eyeing, with lascivious memory, the generously swelling outline of the recent brunette, visible above the starched white tablecloth. There was no doubt about it whatsoever, dark or pale, June or Estelle, Parliamentary Secretary or no Parliamentary bloody Secretary, I would relish a second innings on that particular pitch!

Not tonight, Zoltan.

If only because we were to be faced later with something *not* exactly as advertised – the heaviest, most damaging night raid on London for more than two years.

The club where Estelle was singing was called The Surrogate (in the sense of substitute, I imagined, or through-lack-of-anything-better). In the sub-basement of a modern apartment block off Berkeley Square, it was not exactly in the class of the Colony, the Astor or the old Café de Paris, destroyed by a direct hit a year or more ago. It was moreover one of those peculiarly English the-law-is-an-ass institutions euphemistically known as a 'bottle party'.

There were several dozen of these establishments, created to circumvent the absurd licencing regulations in central London, in varying degrees of squalor.

On the way there – we had actually grabbed a taxi! – Axel Hunzinger kindly explained to his bumpkin brother the principles on which such places operated. "To sell alcoholic liquor here," he said, "you have to do so from premises licenced for that purpose – from an off-licence or wine store or suchlike if the liquor is in bottle; from a restaurant or hotel if it's for consumption on the premises. On-site licences are difficult to get, especially if the stuff is to be drunk late at night, after the pubs and shops have closed. There has to be a local demand; there may be opposition from rivals; the police, whose advice is asked for, may object."

"Why?" I asked.

"Oh, the usual reasons. Might lead to the association of undesirables, so forth. So – since folks are going to drink at night anyway, especially at times like these – ways must be found legally to get

Peter Leslie

around the law. Are you familiar with . . . that is to say, are bottle parties on in Australia?"

"Bottle parties?" I echoed. "You mean you phone around, saying we're having a bit of a do on Saturday. Love to see you. Do come and bring a bottle. So each guest brings what he or she can afford and everyone gets stinking. Sure, everybody's doing it."

Hunzinger nodded. "The law in this country," he said, "acts like the fond mother who says to her husband: 'Go and find out what Johnny's doing – and stop him!' But it can't stop people drinking as much, and as often as they like, with as many friends as they wish – provided they're in their own homes. And provided they don't take money for it."

"You mean . . . ?"

"I mean – and here's the loophole – a club, with a properly constituted membership, is a private institution. Legally, so long as its own rules are followed, it's as untouchable as home sweet home. Provided always – as it would be at home – that no alcoholic drinks are charged for."

I nodded. It was my turn. The cab was at a standstill. A traffic jam halfway round Hyde Park Corner as far as I could see in the diffused light from all those masked headlamps. We seemed to have been there some time. Hunzinger said: "Theoretically, the places we're talking about are simple social clubs. People meet there because it's a place to get together, maybe dance a little. For a modest fee, a generous management will provide members with glasses and soft drinks . . . but there's nothing to stop a guest bringing his or her own bottle of liquor. And drinking it there."

"Very well," I said, playing it dumb, "but what's in it for them? The management, I mean. Like why bother?"

I heard Axel's chuckle beside me. He didn't do it often. "Theoretically again," he said, "the poor member happens to have forgotten his bottle. Stupid of him. Put it out earlier. On the hall table. Then clean forgot, can you imagine! Deuced inconvenient. Now he'll have to go out and chase up some place where they sell stuff late and legally."

"Not to worry, sir," the MD says smoothly. "One happens to know such an establishment. To save sir the trouble of actually leaving and bringing back the bottle personally, one could send out a waiter to carry out the errand for him. If sir would be good enough to advance the price . . ."

"Which is, of course . . . ?"

"Not more than twice what one would normally pay. The dialogue I just quoted never, of course, actually takes place: the implication is that it did! So a bottle is brought up from stock, the client's name is duly marked on it, the level of spirit remaining noted if there is any,

170

and the bottle stashed away until his next visit. If any. At which time 'Mr X's bottle, please', is demanded of the sommelier, and the bottle – or one closely resembling it – is duly placed on the table again."

The cab jerked forward suddenly. Engines throbbed. Warm exhaust fumes drifted in through the open window. "The Englander sense of hypocrisy is highly developed," I ventured.

Another chuckle. A high score for one day. "The system has entered its decadent phase," he assured me. "All that will change when we take over."

I imagine he jerked his head upwards. Over the traffic noise, sirens already wailed the alert.

As Hunzinger had implied, The Surrogate – like all the other 'bottle parties' – was no more, and sometimes rather less, that a second-class and second-rate nightclub. The décor – worn red plush, low-key bracket lighting, tawdry drapes and decrepit tables hidden beneath white cloths – would, I was sure, prove to be as unappetising in daylight as any I had seen. As if I didn't know!

Shades, I thought as we ducked in under a grimy striped canopy, of the Embassy and the Four Hundred, of Hall's Hotel in Antrim. Shades of night-life the world over: everything promised and fuck-all given, when you came down to it. The British had no corner in hypocrisy!

We didn't, in any case, have to go through the rigmarole. There was already a bottle on the table. We were guests of the star attraction – Estelle de Caunes, late bill-topper from Montreal, Ottawa and the French Can-Can in Quebec. Theoretically in both cases.

Maybe half the tables were occupied. Half of that half, too, could well have been members not only of the club but also of the undesirables whose association the police wished to prevent – bulky, unsmiling men in wide-shouldered suits with black shirts and white or silver ties. With, of course, the usual frizzy blondes. High heels with ankle straps. You know.

Hunzinger and I had filled in membership applications when we arrived. "I thought you couldn't just get membership cards over the counter, like a pack of cigarettes," I said.

"You can't," he said. "The law requires a delay. Otherwise it's not a proper club. Twenty-four hours minimum." A sly grin. "To allow the Committee time to consider, accept or reject you!"

"And so?"

He glanced at his wrist watch. "Today's the twelfth. We handed over the membership fee – anything from a shilling to a quid – together with a dated, but not timed, application, at twenty-three hundred hours and forty-five minutes. At midnight-five, it will be the thirteenth of the month. Our membership cards should be with us at any moment – dated the thirteenth, but again not timed. Twenty-four hours, like time in general, can pass quickly. When it's necessary!"

The club band, unlike the décor, was modern, inventive and rather chic – a tasteful quartet lining up a piano, bass and drums behind the clarinettist Frank Weir. Mainly slows, dreamy, a trifle smoochy, by the masters: Cole Porter, Hoagy Carmichael, Berlin; mood pieces from Ellington.

Estelle-June made her appearance at one o'clock wearing a floor-length silk dress – bottle green, what else! – which looked as though it had been sprayed on her in a Rolls Royce paintshop. It was so low-cut that you could almost see her belly button.

Her voice – a little buzzy, warm honey with gravel – was agreeable enough. But it was clearly a chorus-girl voice rather than a curtain call show-stopper. Wisely, she restricted herself in the main to declaiming, almost a recitative, rather than actually singing full out – such slightly risqué point numbers as *Let's Do It, Miss Otis Regrets, Anything Goes, It's Tight Like That* and *Won't Some Kind Gentleman See Me Home?*

The act as a whole was nevertheless quite impressive, mainly because she traded on her not inconsiderable skill as a dancer. It was evident that she wore nothing beneath the skin-tight green sheath. Indeed, so close was the fit that the subtle bulge provoked by the lightweight pressure of her pubic hair became almost obtrusively evident each time she swivelled her hips. That, in fact, was the secret of her success: the alternation between the overt, almost vulgar sexuality of the words she sang and the diabolically restrained illustration of them provided by the ambiguous handling of that insolently voluptuous body.

It was almost as though she was attempting to *prevent* the swelling weight of her full breasts bursting into full view as her torso twisted lithely from left to right; as though she had been taken unawares by the indecency of the dress top, which was scarcely more than two slightly wider shoulderstraps. As if she repudiated the heavy fall of the silk skirt, dropping sheer as a knife blade between the quivering cheeks of her buttocks as she writhed and heaved.

She was halfway through an exuberantly improper number entitled *I'm a WAAF Named Fanny Adams . . . But They Call Me Sweet FA*, when the first near-miss exploded between Curzon Street and the Park and shook the block to its foundations.

All the lights went out. From outside we heard the clatter of pulverised bricks and tiles shower-back into the street. For an instant there was dead silence in the club. Nobody screamed. A population in fear of nightly extinction, busy drinking and dancing its insecurity away, wasn't going to create over the one that missed them. "Jesus, I knew this was a hot number," June said into a dead mike, "but this is taking it a shade too far!" People laughed. The lights blazed on again.

Frank Weir stamped the quartet in with four, and they swung the girl into a fast version of *Roll Me Over, Lay Me Down, And Do It Again*. Another stick of bombs rattled the cutlery.

Before the end of the number, a third started to march across the rooftops towards us. One . . . two . . . three . . . Wait for it! *Christ* – That was close! Then a fifth, further away on the other side of the block. They must have dropped a shower of incendiaries on the neighbourhood, which the bomb-aimers were using as a fiery target. But they bloody missed us again!

It's an extraordinary sensation, finding oneself in a building very close to a direct hit. First of all, almost insidiously, the ear-drums are blocked by the blast wave, although there is no actual effect of *noise*. The floor seems to rise up and pummel, ferociously, the soles of the feet – a scarifying drubbing that transmits itself upwards throughout the entire body until it explodes white lightning behind the eyes. This lasts in fact probably no more than an instant, but it is only after it that one is aware of the sound, the colossal, fracturing impact of the detonation.

At The Surrogate that night the whole structure was shaken as busily as a rat seized by a terrier. Glass smashed somewhere in the kitchen quarters. Water splashed noisily to a tiled floor. A cupboard full of crockery detached itself from a wall and thumped appallingly down behind the bandstand.

It was a moment before I realised the music had ceased and all the lights had gone out again. Then, bit by bit, I registered real life. Whistles shrilling. Voices, close by and far away. In the distance, the clangour of fire-engine bells, men shouting in the street.

I was sitting on the dance floor in the dark, legs stretched out in front of me and one trouser leg steaming with hot coffee. Somewhere above, beyond the ceiling, much higher up, a heavy metallic something rolled and thumped, and clattered and rolled, interminably bloody *rolling*! Could it have been a dustbin careering down a concrete stairway? Whatever it was, it was too damned much; it was driving me crazy.

A voice in the dark. Presumably the manager or the MD. He was frightfully sorry, Ladies and Gentleman, but the ARP had informed him that Hungerford Court, next door, had been badly damaged. There was a risk of collapsing walls affecting this building; a more serious risk of fire if gas mains had been fractured. The wardens had decided that the basement should be evacuated at once.

173

Regretfully, therefore, he had no alternative: he must ask patrons to leave the premises – as quickly and as quietly as possible, please.

One by one, matches flared, cigarette lighters glimmered in the blackness, the wavering flames of candles multiplied, illuminating half a hundred ghosts in evening dress trooping shakily towards the area stairs that led up to the street.

Like myself, Hunzinger was undamaged apart from a soaked shirt-front – whisky in his case. So we collected the girl and made for the exit. "But I can't go out like this!" she wailed. "There are street clothes in my dressing room: it won't take me a minute to—"

"Sorry, Miss I have to ask you to leave immediately." A blue uniformed man, wearing a tin hat and a yellow ARP brassard, had materialised beside us.

"Oh, come on," I protested. "The poor girl's half naked! You can't expect her to . . . I mean, she's not going to change: she just wants to snatch up the stuff and she can change outside."

"Sorry, sir." He was blocking the doorway leading to the rear of the club.

"Oh, do be reasonable!" June cried. "What difference is thirty seconds – fifteen seconds – going to make to the damned war effort, for God's sake?"

"It's you I have to ask to be reasonable, Miss," the warden retorted. "I have my orders. Clear this basement PD-bloody-Q. I'm urgently needed elsewhere – places where there's folks maybe totally naked. With an arm or a leg missing too, I daresay."

I took off my jacket and draped it over her shoulders. "Come on, love," I said. "Let's do what the man says and get out of here."

A waiter – it might have been the MD – stood at the foot of the stairway. "Terribly sorry," he apologised as we began to climb. "Not exactly our fault. But we hope to be open again tomorrow night. If not very soon after. Your bottles will be waiting for you anyway . . . Estelle, darling: call the office tomorrow, will you? Just in case."

The street was unrecognisable. Rubble strewed the roadway; feet crunched over shattered glass on both the pavements. At the far end, steep slants of roof and a forest of chimney stacks etched themselves darkly against a furious orange glow, rising and falling beneath the stars.

Behind us, floodlit salvage workers were already picking over the the chaos of fallen masonry and beams and smashed furniture cascading across the entrance drive from the pulverised facade of the apartment block which had been hit. Brick dust fogged the radiance of the salvage arcs and dimmed the interior lights of ambulances with open doors. Silently, small groups of people, mainly in nightclothes, stood on the far side of the street watching firemen hose down the smoking stonework, searching for survivors.

Along with most of the nightclub patrons, we headed east. West-wards, the fires were flaming – and we probably wouldn't have got through anyway.

There were flames too in the distant east, probably beyond the City, among the docks. But Piccadilly, once we got there, was relatively quiet – quiet, that is, except for the ever-present, all-pervasive drone of aero-engines above and the crackling, echoed detonations of the anti-aircraft batteries which had been withdrawn from the centre and re-located at a safer distance around the Thames estuary.

We walked slowly, supporting the girl from time to time. High heels and a long, tight skirt are not the most practical gear for a night-time hike.

I was astonished at the number of girls still lurking in doorways, seated on balustrades or simply strolling the Stygian wastes of the blacked-out street.

A mathematically-minded friend of mine – a one-time fellow OCTU cadet – had once taken note of the number of times he was accosted after dark on a walk between Piccadilly Circus and Hyde Park Corner during a London leave. Two hundred and thirty-seven different approaches, he reported – although the actual number of girls might be slightly less, since he suspected several might have crossed the road in the blackout and tried a second time. It was a moonless night and it was before midnight.

Tonight, however, it was well after two. And trade appeared still to be brisk.

I recalled, as we limped down the slope past Athenaeum Court, the result of subsequent researches carried out by this public-spirited friend – let us honour his fieldwork: he is a sapper captain and his name is Chamberlain! His is the quasi-scientific type of mentality which realises instantly – while reading a cheap paperback thriller – that it is *mathematically impossible* for one of the miscreants therein described to sport a *three*-day growth of stubble *more often than not*.

Work it out for yourselves.

For a civil engineer whose professional life is spent considering such subjects as the Theory of Structures and Strength of Materials along with arcane calculations of Shearing Stress and the more banal elements of statistics in general, it was normal enough that Chamberlain should show a fraternal interest in the facts and figures of a brother – or rather – sister profession.

The 1943 wartime price, he logged, was two pounds for 'a short time', five for the night. In the circumstances, with transport problems and the near-total lack of hotel accommodation, most punters took the night. Although the physical services rendered differed little from the two-quid trick, often enough the client was only too happy to have a bed!

An unwritten rule among West End prostitutes – Chamberlain discovered – a rule as inflexible as any trade-union embargo, was that girls patrolling Bond Street, Curzon Street, Grosvenor Square and Mayfair in general were strictly confined to their accepted beats. But if they had not clicked by one o'clock – not a second earlier – they had the right to move 'down to the Dilly' and compete with any of the class trade still operative.

Those unattached later still – or clocking off after a busy night – passed the remainder of the dark hours gossiping with their ponces, black marketeers, small-time crooks and other Bohemian small-fry at the Lyons Corner House in Coventry Street, which was open all night during the war.

After a few hundred yards of honeyed voices offering unparalleled sensual delights from the dark – and one lady full of initiative in a doorway, who shone a pocket torch on the swell of a naked breast, the areola purplish in the artificial light – it was Hunzinger who posed the question.

I had observed him smiling approvingly at the evidence of bomb damage. Now, suddenly, he was all at once a trifle irritable. For once he didn't know exactly where he was. "So where the hell do we go now?" he asked.

It was Estelle-June who replied. "I'd ask you back to my place," she said, "but it's in Kensington, on the far side of those fires. God knows if we'd get through. But judging from the trade still flourishing to our left and right . . ." She paused. We were outside Green Park tube station. Down below, the hundreds, thousands of bombed-out, or marooned or fearful or simply shelterless, would already have bunked down for the night with their rugs and their paper bags on the deserted platforms. Across the road, beside the Ritz Hotel, the Park – now that its railings had gone – would be an anthill of lubricious sexual activity beneath the early summer trees.

"Judging from the amount of activity here," the girl continued, "there should still be room for a trio of the godly—"

"Don't tell me," I dared to interrupt. "I've heard tell of this place in Melbourne! We're going to spend the rest of the night in the Coventry Street Corner House, right?"

"Too right, sport!" the non-Canadian non-singer said.

Twenty-One

B y the time we had reached Piccadilly Circus and skirted the people sleeping rough on the steps surrounding the boarded up statue of Eros, the roofed horizon was ringed by an almost continuous circle of fire. As I had thought, the fiercest concentration was in the east, where actual flames could from time to time be seen leaping hugely into the sky. But a pulsating glow more to the north indicated some kind of incendiary firestorm ravaging the heights of Hampstead and Highgate. South of the Thames, the evidence was intermittent, but one vast crimson stain bloomed abruptly as we watched, spreading across the dark sky to boil redly on the underside of a towering column of smoke. I wondered if perhaps the raiders had scored a lucky hit among waterfront refineries or devastated the spider web of railway arteries at Clapham Junction.

Since we had left the club, our ears had become accustomed to the ceaseless cannonade of bursting bombs and exploding anti-aircraft shells – a groundswell of disagreeable, no-longer-frightening noise punctuated by ambulance and fire-engine bells, the whistles of ARP wardens and occasionally the shouts of firewatchers positioned on the roofs of higher buildings, directing salvage teams to the sites of direct hits. But for some time the uneven drone of marauding aircraft had been considerably reduced.

Now, all at once, it was increasing again. A fresh wave must be making its approach. The detonations of the bombardment became more frequent, seemed more violent. Overhead, the sky was a carnival of incandescent lights, scarlet, orange, green and livid white.

Unconsciously, a conditioned reflex influenced by habit, late-comers still loaded with bedding and prized possessions accelerated their pace as they approached the open entrances to Underground stations at Piccadilly and Leicester Square, scurrying to safety on the crowded platforms far below. I glanced over my shoulder as we waited to push our way through the double blackout screens inside the Corner House entrance. Above and behind, picked out of the dark by

Peter Leslie

the sickly light of a flare floating down towards the river, brave Nelson stood proud on his fluted column.

The all-night section of the Corner House was in the basement, beyond the great row of lavatories, toilets, washrooms and whatever, where the nightbirds retired to shoot up, snort up, tank up in secret, or simply wash up throughout the dangerous hours.

It was exactly as I remembered it during the phoney war, when I was a cadet before the blitz began: crammed to the ceiling with a brawling, laughing, chattering crowd, the majority of whom could have been hired on sight as extras for a gangland musical or Soho denizens in a documentary on the London underworld.

The noise was deafening, with laughter and giggling as prominent as anything. We found a table, jammed into a corner next to two girls with frizzy perms, sticky make-up, short skirts and stockings (with seams) painted on their legs. Each of them was accompanied by a young man with brilliantined hair, sideburns and a five-o'clock shadow although it wasn't yet four. The subject of conversation, quite openly, was the behaviour, demeanour and demands of 'clients' winkled out from the dark in the shadowed wastes of the unrailed Green Park.

". . . standin' on a bleedin' mound, bent forward against the trunk of a bloody tree," one of the girls was relating, "and still 'e couldn't fuckin' make it! Old dodderer he was, must've been at least fifty. And you know what? For every punter with the girls in there, there was at least a dozen dirty bastards simply watchin'. We was silhou – silhou—?"

"Silhouetted," one of the young men supplied.

"That's right. Against the light from the fires, see, and the traffic in the Dilly. And there was these buggers 'aving a free show! You could see 'em, in amongst the trees – well, not them but their bloody ciggies. Dozens of little red points of light, brightenin' as they drew on them. Fishin' out JT to jerk off, I reckon."

"What they call a silent fuckin' majority," the second ponce said. "Disgustin', I call it."

Hunzinger had seen a face he recognised, down three steps to a lower level. A long-haired, studious type with spectacles, sitting with four or five overalled men – printers homeward bound after the swing shift at one of the newspapers in Fleet Street. Axel waved, muttered an excuse, and threaded his way through the crowd to join the man. When I asked later who he was, I learned that he was a Press Censor. "Passionate admirer of Rilke," Hunzinger said. "Not to mention Goethe, Schopenhauer and the Rhine Maidens! Also, by chance, someone professionally *obliged* every day to familiarise himself with the *Dead Stops* – the secrets that can't be published."

"I see," I said. And see I did. A useful pro-German who would know through his work which way the military wind might be going to blow.

While Hunzinger was away, I noticed a girl staring hard at my companion – a brunette of maybe thirty, very *soignée*, very subtly made-up behind a pillbox hat with a veil. She was wearing a severe black barathea suit with real stockings and small, tight ankle boots. She was sitting with a large, trousered and sweatered young woman, clearly a lesbian, probably from the Gateways Club in Chelsea. After a third or fourth glance, the brunette murmured something and came over to our table. Nodding to me, she spoke directly to June. If she was brass, I thought, she would be a great deal higher up the ladder into the carriage trade than the two girls beside us.

"Don't know you by sight, dear," the brunette said. "I don't think you're a business girl, or I probably *would* know you. But if you were, you'd knock the rest of us for six, wearing that simply stunning gown! Dare I ask: where or how did you get such a man-eating show-stopper?"

June smiled, but pulled my jacket slightly closer around herself. "It's no secret," she said a trifle self-consciously. "That boutique – Dover Street, I think – the Rahvis Sisters anyway."

"Beautiful," the brunette said admiringly. "And you're simply gorgeous in it!"

I sat breathing in her Chanel Number Five while the two of them talked clothes. Around me, I heard:

"Bastard promised me a forty-eight at the end of the month, and what d'you think . . . ?"

"I promise you, thirty seconds earlier and it would have fallen *right on my bloody head!*"

". . . if he wanted it that bad, he'd have to learn that he must bloody well pay for it!"

". . . smashed to pieces, absolutely pulverised! I can't understand how she managed . . ."

"If you're going to stand me up, I said, for a red-headed NAAFI tart, you can bloody well—"

"Four fuckin' quid he offered, and he wanted the full bizarre bondage treatment! I ask you."

"If you was to go with a jerrican and ask behind the church – not St Michael's, St Joe's . . ."

"And if ever you're stuck, Nick, just ask Mama. Always a warm bed waiting, right?"

I stiffened. I froze. The voice had come a few inches away from my left ear. The voice was undoubtedly June's. Estelle's if you prefer it. Warm honey with gravel, I'd thought. With the honey in the ascendance now anyway. Slowly, I turned my head her way. "How did you know?" I asked.

She was looking at me hard, very direct, very serious, the blue eyes intense. "If you've spent a night with someone, a whole night," she said, "and if it was fun, a joy . . . then a simple change of names isn't going to wipe the entire blackboard clear. Not if you're a woman it isn't."

"I don't understand," I said weakly. This time it really was total surprise, consternation – and, yes, the temporary *frisson* of genuine panic.

"It's all right," she said softly. "Nothing to do with me. I won't ask; I won't tell. But I know." I was still staring at her. The woman in the pillbox hat and her friend had left. "Put your hand behind your left ear," June said. "There. A bit lower. Nearer the lobe . . . Right! You feel a tiny lump, a hardness in the skin? A mole in fact. A dark brown mole." She shook her head. "Calling yourself Zoltan won't make that mole go away," she said.

"I can't explain," I said. "I'm sorry, but it's out of my hands: I can't—"

"You don't have to," she said. "I can't explain . . . Zelda . . . either. But just remember. If you should ever need me . . ." A scrap of paper was pressed into my hand. "Here's my address and phone number here in town." Hunzinger was approaching the table. "If you . . . like someone," June said huskily, "nothing else matters. Right?"

"Nothing," I said bemusedly. "I won't forget."

"It will be light soon," Hunzinger said. The Corner House still shook from time to time, concussions transmitted through the earth and rock buried below. "We must be at Victoria in time for the first train. If there is one. I'm supposed to check out a different canteen circuit on the other side of Romney Marsh today. Estelle, my dear, do you think . . . ?"

"I'm on my way," she said. She left the table and headed for the public phones beside the loos.

I looked at Hunzinger. I was too shattered by the absurdly simple, incontrovertible, logical, bloody *human* fashion in which the personage of Zoltan had been summarily destroyed to find any words. I raised an enquiring eyebrow at my newly lost brother.

Christ! After all those months work, after the tunnel, the sea voyage, the escape from the docks and the ferocious bloody concentration subsequently to maintain the credibility of a lie . . . after all that: Bingo! She had noticed a mole behind my left ear!

Something I didn't even know the existence of myself.

Meet Captain Zoltan Hart, master of disguises; now you see him, now you don't!

Hunzinger was explaining. "One of the basic truths of modern life. As long as you know someone, as long as you even have a name, you are, as the Englanders say, all right, Jack!"

I must still have looked puzzled, for he continued: "She's gone to call her inamorato. Even if he is no more than a Parliamentary *Secretary*, the man must have influence."

He was right, too. Waiting outside the Corner House as the All Clear screamed relief into the smoky, sulphurous dawn, we were picked up by an official car flying a pennant. An obsequious chauffeur deposed Hunzinger and myself at Victoria before he drove the girl back to her Kensington home.

We only had to wait two and a half hours for the first train south. Throughout the delay Axel Hunzinger smiled quietly to himself.

Twenty-Two

Hunzinger's Romney Marsh fact-finding mission concerned a mobile canteen circuit – four separate vehicles in all – subsidised by Lady Fewtrell-Farrowby, Justice of the Peace, organiser of the local Hunt Ball, whose husband, a rear-admiral, retired, of the same name, was not only MFH but also the Conservative Member of Parliament for that sector of the Southeast.

The Fewtrell-Farraby Round – four superbly equipped caravans converted from Chrysler shooting breaks – had nothing whatever to do with Zelda Fortune's group. Apart from being foreign, she didn't even have a title. Nobody remotely concerned with it betrayed the slightest hint of sympathy for the Nazi regime. And yet – Hunzinger reasoned – a couple, no more than two, operatives accepted as voluntary workers and working on those canteen rounds could contribute invaluable intelligence on the build-up of pre-invasion forces in the Dover-Hythe-Dymchurch area which was so suitable for the assembly of a seaborne armada.

Wearing his YMCA inspector's hat, Hunzinger – unprepared for the interest aroused by the appearance of twins – was intending to spend the day alone, evaluating the intelligence possibilities of the round, and the chance of infiltrating two of his sleepers in amongst the canteen volunteers.

He had borrowed the Armstrong-Siddeley again for the day, marooning me, together with Zelda and the Fortune Hall staff, with nothing but routine chores to occupy us.

For me, nevertheless, routine was the most pressing of priorities.

A fairly considerable mass of factual material was building up in my mind, all of which must at some time or another be confided in detail to Webster, none of which could safely be jotted down on the backs of envelopes or in a simple notebook – but every single word of which must be readily available to the intelligence operatives waiting to roll up the sleeper network when the time came. The information, in brief, which it was my job to uncover and subsequently transmit.

But how to record it all in a fashion meaningless to the casual reader,

182

even less obvious to Hunzinger or Zelda, but available to those for whom it was intended?

A code, a cypher, evidently. I had discussed this with Webster. But incorporated in a single document that was not in itself obviously a message or a means of information of any kind. A book was the answer, we had decided. But a book that would comprise *within itself*, without reference to any subsidiary key or clue, the information required. A matter therefore of prearranged annotation, underlinings, pencilled marks and numbered references agreed between Webster and myself but suggesting nothing more than a tediously academic reader to a third person who happened to pick up the volume.

I rather prided myself on my choice: a Penguin paperback manual entitled *Modern English Usage – A mid-century guide to slang expressions and informal communication.*

Just the kind of book, I thought, that a foreigner, already an English speaker but unfamiliar with the country, might be expected to buy. I had indeed already made a number of underlinings and queries, but these were all in green ink. And it was accepted that, for the purposes of coding, anything in that colour was to be ignored.

Today, though. was my first opportunity to free my mind of the material already amassed before it risked a confusing surfeit of additional material from later sources. I pleaded fatigue after the sleepless night in the blitz and retired to my room.

Technically, the encoding was relatively simple, inasmuch as the intelligence material was mainly a list of names and addresses with only an occasional comment. So what did I have to offer so far?

My three solo contacts – the crippled newsagent, the rector of the girls' school near Shrewsbury and the antiquarian bookseller in Brecon. The lamplighters would have noted Hunzinger's visits to the Bradford unionist, the Scottish osteopath in Southwold and the Army Educational Corps professor who lived in Sutton Bonington, but it was up to me to alert them to the anonymous RAF sleeper at Weeton – the disgruntled NCO, passed over for promotion, known to his fellow maintenance workers as Rigger Mortis!

Although I hadn't actually met them, I could add here the addresses – and some of the names – of the Camberley landlord, the retired colonel from North Camp, the legless Territorial farmer on Salisbury Plain, the Reigate shrink, the signalman at Petersfield and the two call-girls in the New Forest. Plus Diego the fishman and his contact in Finchley known as Hyperion.

There were other important sleepers with classical pseudonyms – Ajax, Mercury and Icarus in Bristol – but these would have to be identified through interrogation of the minor agents to whom I had passed messages on Hunzinger's behalf.

That left Zelda and June. Two comely question-marks.

Enough for one day, I thought. I'd add the names if and when I knew something a little more specific about the mysterious activities of these two voluptuous nymphs.

I am by no means certain that specific is the right word, but I was certainly to know rather more of the activities of the older of the two in a shorter time than I had imagined possible.

I'd spent some time laboriously adding the dots and squiggles and underlines which would direct a decoder to the Penguin pages wherein I had concealed words adding up to the first two or three entries in my list when there was a knock on the bedroom door.

One of the girl students who seemed to be using the hall as a kind of youth hostel. Luncheon would be served at one-fifteen. Mrs Fortune would be pleased if Mr Zoltan would care to join her for an aperitif at a quarter to.

The hell with it. And I was just getting into the swing of this double reference routine. Never mind. To refuse would be churlish as well – perhaps – as in some way suspicious. You never knew. Mr Zoltan would be happy to oblige. No, no. Watch it. Not oblige – accept.

The lunch was not in the baronial-style refectory but in a private sitting-room Zelda had on the first floor of one of the towers. It was cold, already laid out on a small gate-leg table: fillets of salmon trout – poached doubtless from a nearby stream – potato salad, horseradish sauce. A bowl of dressed watercress. Cheese.

The students had taken one of the canteens not in use that day – one of the Rye batteries was being re-sited – and driven away to spend the afternoon on the South Downs.

The sitting-room was chintzy, hunting prints on one wall, Hogarth's Rake and a Goya engraving on another. Zelda sat in a low chair, criss-crossed with thin bars of shadow as the midday sun streamed through the diamond panes of a mullioned window by her side.

She was wearing a smoky red blouse, soft, loose trousers of the kind known as beach pyjamas, in a darkish camel tint, and white patent sandals. Razor-edge creases as usual, cutting now across the lozenge pattern cast over her generous curves.

"My God," I blurted out. "That's spectacular! You look like a stained-glass window in a modern church."

She laughed. I remembered the laugh very well. Low, verging

towards the musical. "Not The Virgin, I hope! Marie Madeleine would probably be more my type!"

"Before or after?" I dared to reply.

"For that," Zelda said, "you'd have to read up on your history!"

There was a small individual oak table by her chair. Cigarettes, an ashtray, and two tall, stemmed glasses rested on a silver tray on top of the table. An ice bucket, cradled in a tripod, stood beside it. Zelda reached inside this and withdrew a slender green bottle frosted with moisture.

"Whisky and gin," she said. "One does get a little tired of it all the time, don't you think?" She held up the bottle. Sunlight, green and gold, glinted through the hoary glass. "I found this in a forgotten corner of the cellar," she said. "It's a Grüner Veltliner, from the slopes of the Kamp valley, between Langenlois and Krems. A tributary of the Danube in fact, not far from Vienna. I thought it might be a refreshing change."

"It's not often one has the chance to taste Austrian wine these days," I said. "How truly special!"

"The vintners who make it," Zelda said, "describe its late-gathered finesse as 'marvellously high-flavoured and fiery in its performance'. Let us hope today that we shall not find them wrong!"

She poured wine, handed me a glass. "Do sit," she said. "I discovered a Rhine wine for the trout, but I thought it would be good for our souls to drink this first!"

The wine was indeed excellent. I had passed several weekends in Vienna during the three years I was based in Munich; I had been introduced to the five wine-producing villages which lie actually within the city limits – holding their own in the heart of residential areas, spilling across the surrounding hills and up into the Vienna Woods. The new wine, which can be bought and taken away in barrels and bottles or drunk on the premises, is sensational, spirited, sprightly stuff that goes straight to your head. The atmosphere in the leafy taverns where these elixirs are dispensed varies – one connoisseur noted – from the idyllic to the hilarious. In most of them Beethoven wrote at least a concerto.

Zelda's find was as heady as any I remembered – fruity, slaty; its dry finish recalling the soft fruits of spring against a background of sparkling cascades.

Well, I told you I'd lived in Germany, didn't I?

The bottle was already a couple of glasses short when I came into the sitting room. By the time I was ready for a refill, it was down to the halfway mark and my hostess was prettier than ever.

Peter Leslie

The smoky red blouse, buttoned almost to the neck, was fashioned from some kind of Shantung material, silky to look at, very slightly rough to the touch. It was severely cut, with a turned down collar, draped shoulders and three-quarter sleeves turned back at the cuff just enough to contrast a heavy gold bangle with the fleshy smoothness of a forearm and wrist.

She sat smiling at me, the eyes shining, a glass in one hand, a cigarette in a long ebony holder between the red-nailed fingers of the other.

I don't recall the conversation. Zelda had already posed all the usual questions about Australia when we were together with Hunzinger. We talked about Vienna, I suppose. I know we both had fond memories of the *Südbahn* day-trip south to the splendidly named village of Gumpoldskirchen where the great Hungarian plain nibbles at the last fringes of the Alps – and where, as it happens, the spiced finesse of the Gewürztraminer rivals anything produced by the vineyards of Alsace!

Neither Zelda nor Hunzinger had been able to disguise the fact that they had been intimate companions for many years – certainly at least at one time lovers, and definitely retaining now that tender complicity the French term *amitié amoureuse* – amorous friendship (with at least the hint that physical attraction may yet remain a possibility, if only for sentimental reasons).

All the tiny signs had been there – the four fingers laid flat on the sleeve, the automatically straightened tie, a hand resting momentarily on a curve of thigh, in the arch of a back, the level glance and the We-know-don't-we? smile.

I said they hadn't been able to disguise this. But there was no reason why they should have wanted to.

It must have been odd for Zelda just the same – if not downright intriguing – to find herself alone with a double, a mirror image, a perfect counterfeit of the humen being she had known and loved for so long. . . and yet, apart from that one fact, to know nothing whatsoever about him, about the way he thought, felt, reacted, behaved. Would these unknowns in any way parallel those of the identical brother?

Surely some part of her, overtly or not, would be fascinated to find out?

Quite apart from the banal exchanges occupying our voices, the conversation continuing between our eyes led me to believe that question in itself implied an affirmative answer. My own hands in any case dwelled like my supposed brother's – if hands can dwell – on a curve of thigh.

Zelda was sitting with her legs crossed, the right slung over the left. The weight of that right, displaced by the upward pressure of the left, was compressing the flesh of her thigh, flattening it slightly against the thrust from below. And because the caramel jersey of the beach pyjama trouser was loose, not clinging to the precise shape of the leg, the softness, the shifting, sensual weight of that boneless flesh, implied if unseen, subtly emphasised the carnal quality of the entire fleshy female frame – the full breasts hidden by the out-thrust shirt, thighs emerging from the tight curve of belly and the heat between them, buttocks spread by the cushions of the chair. The lot.

Yes, no doubt about it: I had quite a buzz on by the time we took our places at the table.

Zoltan too. But he had to keep Hart sober, to stop the real counterfeit making an appearance.

The Rhine wine, from the Palatinate, was an Annaberg Scheurebe – Annaberg being a village southwest of Kallstadt, Scheurebe the local name for a grape that was a cross between Reisling and Sylvaner. The mixed marriage was a great success. The wine was dry, aromatic – almost gravelly at first – but with an aftertaste as heady, as stimulating as the Veltliner. And infinitely more . . . insidious, I think, would be the word. That is to say you didn't realise it was likely to knock you for a loop before it had.

An hilarious lunch, as the Viennese would have it. And idyllic? Well, like me, it would be better if you could wait before finding out.

She had made coffee on a gas ring, splashed in a measure of schnapps. The top three buttons of the smoky red blouse had somehow become undone, revealing the soft upper slopes of a superbly swelling pair of breasts. It wasn't me, sir! I never touched her. Honestly. Perhaps she had laughed too much?

She moved across to the fireplace to make more coffee. As she passed me I heard the sibilant swish of silk on silk as legs crossed within the loose sheath of the beach pyjamas' upper half.

We drank the coffee. I was walking on a sheet of plate glass about a foot off the floor. If it had been after dark, the stars would have been scything about my head. But Zelda was radiant with sunlight. She was standing very close to me. "Sometimes, Zoltan, I like to play games," she breathed, warm breath winey against my face. "I think, in fact I am sure, that this may be one of the times. Would you do something for me? If I asked you very nicely?"

"Just ask," I croaked. The afternoon had taken hold of me; I was adrift in the current.

"Close your eyes," she said. "Don't open them until you have counted thirty. Quite slowly."

"And then?"

"Just do as I say. Wait . . . and see."

I counted, holding carefully on to a chair back. I opened my eyes. She had been tearing waste paper – envelopes, bills, circulars – into small pieces while we waited for the coffee to brew. Now I saw a small trail of these leading to a door at the far end of the room. No sign of Zelda. I opened the door. A small, rather feminine bathroom. The paperchase led to a further door. I opened that.

A small bedroom, even more feminine – shuttered windows, chintz curtains again, a tub chair, a bedside table, one of those dressing tables with frills. Perhaps a bolt-hole she used when the house was full of guests. Or in case of evacuees?

A silk-shaded lamp on the bedside table suffused the room with a pleasing amber glow.

In the low-key illumination my eyes followed the scraps of paper across a fitted carpet to a plush divan against the far wall. The trail stopped between the heels of a pair of white sandals.

The sandals were occupied.

Zelda stood beside the bed, feet slightly apart, caramel pyjama trousers rising sheer to a tightly belted waist. And on either side of that, completely unbuttoned now and in freefall from those prominent breasts, the smoky red shirt-blouse. Acting now as a lightweight jacket to cover the nipples but reveal that the rest of each breast was nude.

There was a slight, faintly challenging smile on Zelda's face. By the foot of the bed, a lacy red brassiere hung from a brass-tipped post supporting the dressing-table mirror.

I read signs. She had plenty of time to stuff it into a drawer, but the bra had been left there as a signal, an indication that she had only just taken it off. She didn't *happen* to be wearing no foundation on her upper torso: she was telling me there had been but she was now partly undressed.

Well.

It didn't take a Nobel laureate to work it out. If one twin is very attractive – and clearly attracted – to a sexy, sensual woman, why not his sosie? Or at any rate why not find out? Unless it was no more than a fortuitous equation. Curiosity over Veltliner, multiplied by the distilled juice of the Scheurebe grape equals . . . what?

Positive action was the sole solution I could suggest. After all that lunchtime awareness, the eyeball to eyeball conversations, the silly game and now the bra – what more did I want or need?

I wanted this woman. Now.

Red-haired tennis players named Maureen? Never heard of her. Nuptials with one of the old man's churchwardens? Forget it. Blonde Canadians with wizard upperworks? They were as well shaped as my hostess's, but maybe smaller. And they weren't here.

Words, any words in view of the above, in any conceivable circumstances at this stage of the afternoon, were going to be not only superfluous but a strict turn-off.

The cards have been dealt. So play, Jack!

In three strides I was across the room. I dropped to my knees between the white sandals. My hands rose as if pulled by unseen wires to hook fingers under the waistband of the pyjama trousers. I dragged the caramel jersey slowly but decisively down. Down past a subtle swell of belly, past springy hair and over padded hips, pulling the material below the taut thrust of buttocks until it was almost at knee level between parted thighs.

Above me I heard a slight catch of breath as my eager hands rose again to cup the cool flesh cushioning those hips, to clench over the twin curves quivering behind.

It was then, drawing her towards me, that I sank my face between the sheer wings of smoke-red Shantung, pressing my lips to the immaculate downward swoop of belly; then that the heart thudded most forcefully at the joyous first-time alternation between the cool and pliant caress of the outer frame and the vibrant inner heat throbbing against the skin of my cheek from the core of a woman's body.

And then again that the first words spoken broke the silence of the shuttered room.

The head bent down, hunched over my kneeling figure, a little throaty: "My lover man!"

One out of two, I thought; a fifty-fifty chance – not bad odds for a beginner! But my mouth was too busy to reply.

Far away to the south, an air-raid siren sobbed its rising and falling alarm. It was echoed almost at once by another. Then again, much louder – probably from Hawkhurst village – and a great deal nearer, to be followed by a fourth, further inland this time. Reconnaissance, I thought, checking out the damage inflicted on last night's London raid, the observation plane flying steadily northward from the coast. If what we had seen on the way to Victoria was anything to go by, the German photographers would have to reload their cameras a few times! A flight of fighters – Typhoons perhaps – flew past lowdown overhead, but I didn't hear any gunfire.

We were on the bed by the time the last moan of the most distant warning groaned into silence, the long, soft heat of her body – naked now – crushed against me, melting against the hardness of my own. It was the two mouths smashed together now, working together, opening to allow the hot, wet tongues to probe.

Zelda was breathing fast; beneath the shifting swell of one heavy, resilient breast I could feel the pounding of her heart against my chest. Her hands clawed my back, dragging the open shirt down from neck to waist. Something tore then as she flung the shirt to the floor, arching up strong hips to meet the pressure of my own. A hand was trapped between us, clenching on my loins.

I could hear my own breath hissing between my teeth as she ripped open the buttons of my fly. Cool fingers wrenched aside underclothes, knuckling the base of my belly to wrap around me.

Her free hand cradled the nape of my neck as I twisted sideways to take the hard, hot, swollen nipple of one breast between my teeth, teasing the tip with my tongue.

Small cries escaped from her throat. "Oh, God!" she panted. "Now . . . yes, now!"

We didn't have time to get what I was still wearing further down than my knees.

She had both hands grabbing me now, the splendid legs drawn up, the belly heaving. And, Christ, it was urgent, it was compulsive, it had to be.

And indeed it was. Guiding me, teeth clenched on her scarlet lower lip she rolled from side to side, achieved a final frantic squirm . . . and all at once there was sliding moisture, a graze of hair, and the fiery, heated clasp of inner flesh as we thrust and strove.

It was later – the sobbing gasps had died away but her legs were still scissored over my back – it was later that I really looked for the first time steadily into her eyes. She was smiling, the same challenging, slightly secretive smile. "Well, what do you think?" she said softly.

I shook my head. "I think your priorities are absolutely right," I said. "Far better than whisky or gin!"

Twenty-Three

Z elda herself took out the Number One canteen – the converted Bedford three-tonner – the following day, with Hunzinger as a passenger as far as Lewes. He was off to London again, hoping to correlate – so he told me – material from Diego and others with the man code-named Hyperion. It would then, presumably, be forwarded to the history professor analyst in Sutton Bonington for incorporation in the famous 'global picture' of invasion preparations that he was building up. "It will doubtless have to be modified later," Hunzinger told me, "probably several times. But it's essential that the OKW general staff have at least a rough to work on as soon as possible."

"I'm sure you are right, Axel," I said. "It was for the same reason that Korsun was so anxious for you to be liberated from the camp in the Isle of Man."

Since both the principals were away for the day, I took a risk. I called the home number Webster had given me from a phone in Zelda's private sitting-room. I wanted to make a definite date, preferably here in the country, for the handing over of my encoded Penguin paperback. If any other names surfaced, I'd buy another copy and add them there, but it looked as though the actual activation of the sleepers was in a terminal stage: what information they were going to supply now they were at work was something else – something as brief as possible if I did my work well.

There was no reply from Webster's number.

Too bad. Well, I'd spend the rest of the day checking out the codework and perhaps adding a couple of reflections. I was pretty certain the elderly man who fuelled the canteens and helped with maintenance had known – and worked with? – Axel for a very long time. He'd been with the army of occupation, in the Signal Corps, after the Great War. This could well have been an innocent explanation of why, once, I'd heard him talking to Hunzinger in German. Or not.

And the lady of the manor herself? The same considerations applied. It was certain that she had for many years been – and

191

probably still was – his mistress. And colleague? Almost equally affirmative, I reckoned.

So how to interpret her seduction – for that's what it was – of her lover's double? Was it just that she was sexually curious, a randy semi-nympho with a taste for a certain type? Or had Axel been in on the whole thing, put her up to it in fact – a double-check on the authenticity of a long-lost bro? Find out how he ticks, *Liebchen*; get him to talk.

You tell me. One thing only was certain: as machismo Webster might coarsely have put it, she was a bloody marvellous fuck! Yes, alas, we did know there was a war on.

Ungentlemanly therefore, in the circumstances – and ungallant – but worth a brief mention, along with the signalman, in the coded alerts.

They said all was fair, didn't they?

In fact there were repercussions from the Zelda affair that I hadn't even imagined. If we had been characters in a novel . . . you guessed already? . . . she would have turned out to be a double agent, working for British intelligence all the time. And the film of the book would have faded out with our marriage in the old family schloss near Vienna from which the tell-tale wine had come.

It didn't turn out that way, though.

There was an unforeseen twist nevertheless. As usual from the least expected direction.

Not through one of the characters, however. One of the canteens itself held the clue.

But I had to wait several days before I could follow through the initial tip-off.

That first post-Zelda morning, as I thought of it, was sunny and warm – intense blue sky with high white clouds and a flight of twin-boom US Lightning pursuit planes arrowing seawards. The students billeted at Fortune Hall and helping with the canteen rounds were away behind the trees, working on the rose garden that was to be turned into pea and bean and potato and cabbage plots. Alice Cooksie was preparing lunch with the village woman, and her husband had ridden into Hawkhurst on a motorbike for supplies. The stable yard was empty except for the big Number Two motorised caravan-canteen, which was parked in the shade of an elm.

I'd come out of a side door and walked to a seat near the drive with a copy of *The Guardian*. There had again been a particularly heavy raid last night – with a particularly high death roll. Most houses had now been equipped with individual shelters – either the original Andersons, corrugated steel arches halfway sunk into the earth of a garden, or the later Morrisons, each named after respective Home Secretaries. The Morrison was in effect a reinforced steel table with steel angle irons at the four corners and a steel floor. It was usually positioned by an outer wall, and it was said that those who dived under it in time could survive a direct hit which brought the whole building down on top of them. People unable to reach these home shelters used Underground stations or the improvised refuges formed by reinforced cellars in offices or apartment blocks. But there still existed examples of the original street shelters erected after the Munich crisis when public buildings began to be sandbagged. These were rectangular constructions maybe forty or fifty feet long, with brick and mortar walls and a flat roof of foot-thick reinforced concrete laid on top.

They had one unfortunate disadvantage. Blast from a heavy bomb exploding nearby blew all the bricks out sideways, like the drawers from a giant chest of drawers, allowing several tons of flat concrete to drop in a single block on those sheltering below. One such shelter had been destroyed in this way the previous night, with the death of sixty-five people. No survivors.

Twenty-eight German bombers had been shot down by night fighters and anti-aircraft fire. Carrier-based American fighter-bombers had pulverised Japanese fortifications on Wake Island, in the Pacific. Allied ground forces trapped between the German X and XIV Armies were trying to break out of the Anzio beachhead. There had been ugly scenes in Bristol when police were forced to quell a near-riot due to the non-distribution of a cargo of non-rationed bananas salvaged from a beached freighter from Jamaica torpedoed in the Irish Sea.

I put down the paper. For some time I had been half-consciously aware of a persistent noise, not loud but not far away either. A kind of soft tapping, like someone working with a rubber hammer. It could have been coming from the motorised caravan. What drew my attention now was simply that it had stopped. I switched my glance that way. In the open rear doorway of the vehicle, the elderly signals man appeared. He saw me sitting there, hesitated, then walked down the three steps and away into the stable block.

It was the slightest thing really. God knows why I should have registered any of it. But I did.

I hadn't seen him go into the canteen, though he would have crossed my field of vision. He must already have been there, remained there all the time I was reading the paper.

That was odd. He never went inside any of the canteens, not in the back part. His work was with the engines, the controls, the steering and the wheels. And of course the fuelling. His name was Jay; the students referred to his jerricans of petrol as Jay's Fluid.

But what was even odder was that he emerged with a quantity of material. A hammer with a rubber head, certainly. But also a fistful of bunched electrical wires: red, blue and brown; several unidentifiable bakelite shapes – miniature looms? spring clips? a knurled wheel? – and a pair of extra-long-nosed pliers.

As I say, it was absolutely of no importance. As if he had been doing some kind of rewiring in there. Altering the lighting perhaps. I didn't follow-up anyway. It was just that I wondered.

I went back into the house. Reading the paper – aircraft losses, casualty figures – had made me think of the press censorship: what could be published, what couldn't. And the *Dead Stops* on the latter that the young man Hunzinger was cultivating would see every day.

Unforgivably, I had omitted to add him to the list of sleepers. I had no name, but the description should suffice. I hurried upstairs to modify my Penguin handbook.

The hell with the Number Two canteen at Fortune Hall. The following day two things much odder came my way during the course of another, rather hasty, visit to London with Hunzinger.

The first in fact was at the station in Lewes, while we were waiting for the London train to arrive. Among the passengers on the crowded Up platform, I noticed a rather pretty young woman who seemed to be glancing our way a trifle more frequently than necessary. She was a brunette, slender, very upright, in the uniform of an RAF Nursing Sister – severely cut straight skirt, immaculate officer's tunic, dark, seamed stockings of real silk, her neatly waved hair almost hidden by a black three-cornered hat.

The train's imminent arrival had actually been announced on the station intercom when, apparently with sudden decision, she hurried over to us. "Do forgive me," she said to me, "but didn't I see you in Mrs Cooksie's mobile canteen the other day? On the Fortune Round at Rye?"

"Why yes," I said, "with Mr Harzmann here. On behalf of the YMCA."

"I thought so. I wonder, then – it's awful cheek on my part – but I've been called unexpectedly up to the Air Ministry and I was wondering, would it be too much to ask for you to pass on a message to Mrs Fortune when you get back? About the canteen timetable, I mean."

"Well of course," I said. "We won't be back until tonight, but—"

"That would be marvellous. Thank you so much." The train was clicking over points, rumbling alongside the platform. "It's just to ask: could she possibly delay the visit to the Wrayfield Farm gun-site, between Rye and Winchelsea, until tomorrow afternoon. There's new equipment being installed and it wouldn't be convenient in the morning."

"Of course," I said again. "Wrayfield Farm in the afternoon. No problem. I won't forget."

Doors were opening, banging shut. A guard's whistle blew. "Awfully kind of you," she smiled. "Thanks again." She held out a gloved hand. I shook the hand. She nodded to Hunzinger, swung up on to the footboard of a First Class compartment, slammed the door and waved.

Hunzinger and I found room in the next coach.

I said it was an odd encounter. For one thing, there was a telephone at Fortune Hall and she could easily have phoned through the message. OK, she was rushed; it was a sudden call. Or it had slipped her mind. Whatever. This, however, did nothing to explain the fact that I'd seen the girl before. On a balloon site in Rye indeed. I'd even suspected she'd been giving me a spot of the old come-on to tell the truth. O vain and conceited Hart!

But that time she had been a member of the balloon crew. And she was wearing the baggy, shapeless uniform and stripe of a leading-aircraftwoman in the WAAF.

There was just one other thing. Shaking hands just now, she had secretly pressed a tiny wad of compressed paper into my palm. I had dropped it into the pocket of my uniform tunic as we boarded the train.

Yes, uniform. Because Hunziger had insisted: it was my turn to obscure the trail a little and impersonate the mythical Captain Nicholas Hart who was one of the equally imaginary Korsun's cleverly contrived covers!

And this, speaking personally, was the oddest thing of all. To be wearing my own uniform, or one exactly like it, while pretending to be a foreign spy making a pretense of being me – and at the same time making every effort to subdue the real me, to whom this uniform did properly belong . . . man, it was like being accused of sobriety when you were smashed and vice versa at the same time!

I unrolled the paper as soon as I could find a corridor lavatory vacant: the message read:

Urgentest require sleeper list now, even if only interim. Please call W home soonest.

I sighed. So the girl in fact must be one of Colonel Adams's lamplighters, one of the many keeping tabs from afar. It hadn't been the come-on at all: she simply had a message to deliver. Similarly, the sudden call to London was fictitious, the message to Zelda unnecessary. She had been following us and improvised the first opportunity that came her way to make contact.

A slight fieldwork error: it was risky 'recognising' me as a canteen helper when I was in an army officer's uniform: I had been wearing formal civilian clothes in Rye. Otherwise bravo: ten out of ten for initiative and no reproaches!

I tore the paper into very small fragments, jerked down the toilet lever and allowed the Southern Railway to distribute the damp pieces among the cinder ballast somewhere between Haywards Heath and Crawley.

Just another paperchase leading to the pot of gold?

Only time, as they say, would tell. Meanwhile, it was more imperative than ever to get that damned Penguin paperback to London.

Twenty-Four

Hunzinger was summoned to the private sitting-room the following morning to have a conference over breakfast with the chatelaine. I couldn't help posing myself a wry – and somewhat ungallant – question as I went downstairs to the refectory to have mine with the students and Mr Jay and the Cooksies. Would there be Veltliner or Annaberg with the artificial coffee? And in which of the two rooms would the 'conferring' be done in? Unworthy reflection, Hart. If anyone was to be criticised here, surely it would be yourself as much as Zelda. And she, at least, was one of the few people who knew one of us from the other. Who didn't confuse us, that is.

Except of course for June. But there was no confusion there: she simply knew I was me.

Zelda – another stage in my mental rake's progress! – had had a similar opportunity. But not during an entire night. And in any case she didn't know me as anything or anyone *but* Zoltan.

I began to be thankful that I didn't have any close friends to confuse in the Hawkhurst area.

As it happened I passed Hunzinger in the entrance hall, each of us on his way to his respective breakfast. He seemed unusually ill-humoured that morning. Perhaps he didn't like Austrian wine. "Why the devil, Zoltan, is your nose always buried into that damned book?" he challenged, eyeing the Penguin that I was carrying. "This is the second or third time I've seen you with it. Your English is perfectly good, for God's sake!"

"My English is Aussie English, don't forget," I said mildly. "I just want to make sure I don't slip up with some out of date slang or make a reference that's square or laughable. Especially when I'm wearing a British officer's uniform."

"Well, you won't be wearing it today," he said ungraciously. "Zelda is taking Captain Hart down to Poole Harbour. Those two whores in the New Forest have come up with some interesting gen on armoured craft assembling there, and I want to check it out more precisely myself."

"Interesting gen," I repeated, hastening to turn his attention away from the book. "That's exactly the kind of phrase I mean. Would you like me to come with you? Maybe I could take notes or something?" "No," he said shortly. "You stay here. Go out with the canteen on the Rye-Winchelsea round. See what you can find out about this 'new equipment' on the Wrayfield Farm site. You did give Zelda the message?"

"Last night," I said. "Of course."

I had done nothing of the kind, naturally. There was a site at Wrayfield Farm. I remembered it very well. It was a balloon site. There had been no sign of any preparatory work there when I passed by in the canteen a couple of days previously. In any case what kind of 'new equipment' could be installed there, even if the girl had referred to it as a gun-site?

Clearly, seeing Hunzinger and myself on the station platform, she had simply improvised the story as a means of getting the message to me without arousing Hunzinger's suspicions. And possibly quoting that site because that was where I had seen her before . . . and the different uniform should remind me of this and at the same time tip me off that she was an Adam Nichols agent.

Well, it had done that all right. But I still believed there was a green light in there somewhere.

In any case, with hundreds of Nazi planes flying overhead every night, and guns firing at reconnaissance flights every day, who the hell was going to notice if one canteen out of dozens in the area served tea and coffee at a particular balloon site in the morning or afternoon of one day?

What was infuriating me was that we had actually been in London the day I received the message, but I hadn't had the Penguin with me. It would have been tough to work out a credible way of absenting myself long enough to deliver it to Regent's Park, but not impossible: Hunzinger was interviewing a couple of Soho desperadoes in the bar of the White House apartment block, and that was no more than a few hundred yard away, across the park itself.

Now – after all, twentyfour hours ago already I had been told it was 'urgent' – I had to find the means of returning once more to London to deliver the list so far as it went.

And if, in so doing, I risked blowing my cover?

Hunzinger, for example, would ask for a report on the Wrayfield Farm installation. Earthworks, I could say; possibly for an AA battery. But he might go down there to see for himself; he could find out, easily enough, that I hadn't even gone out with the canteen.

OK, so what if I came clean: admitted I didn't go. What then? Explanations please.

I reckoned it was a risk I had to take. One way or the other. My turn to improvise. If I was blown, I was blown. The important thing was the mission. And they wanted what I had found out so far – even if it was 'only interim', that is to say incomplete.

Very well, it was up to me. Hunzinger had already told me he had been to London to correlate details with Diego and others. If I assumed that this implied the reactivation of his sleepers was already at the tidying-up stage, then it followed that there might not be many more names to add. The list already encoded in the phrase book should therefore comprise at least the majority of his traitors. If one or two remained, certainly the majority would be in the net.

In other words, what I was delivering, incomplete though it was, was a great deal better than waiting for a hypothetical grand slam.

So I went to London.

The nearest station, not on the express Brighton line, was at Robertsbridge, only a few miles to the southwest, with a connection through Tunbridge Wells to Waterloo. I made a hasty check of the timetables. Robertsbridge to Waterloo, something over fifty miles. Probably stopping at every station. Allow an hour and a half each way. Very well, two hours. There's a war on, after all. An hour maximum for a taxi – Waterloo to Regent's Park and back. Five hours max in all. Was it possible, with the trains there were, to make a round trip and be back before Hunzinger and Zelda? They left at ten thirty, the canteens soon afterwards. We'd have a damned good try!

The students were digging for victory. I took one of their bikes, without permission, and pedalled off to Robertsbridge. Explanation: It was sunny. I felt like a day exploring the countryide.

In fact it was necessary neither to explain the bicycle nor the affair of Wrayfield Farm.

For once – for once! – everything fell so neatly into place that it was scarcely believable. It must have been one of the fastest day-trips to London ever achieved since the age of steam commenced!

There was still no reply from Webster's home number, so I did the best I could in the time available. Leaving the book, in a tight brown paper parcel, firmly taped and sealed, addressed to the Lieutenant-Colonel himself, 'Personal Only', at Nichols's address. The bike, the train, the taxi; a dash up the steps to the commissionaire and the girl in reception . . . and back. We were lucky. The night raid had been heavy but there had been little damage in the west end. And the cab driver who waited for me was a combination of Nuvolari and

Peter Leslie

the W-196 Mercedes driver Rudolph Caracciola. Because of the lack of traffic he landed me in Waterloo in time to catch the mid-afternoon Hastings train by the skin of my teeth – and I was back at Fortune Hall before the bike had even been missed.

When the canteens were back, I asked Mrs Cooksie if she'd seen anything at the Wrayfield Farm site that looked remotely like work in progress. Nothing at all, she said. So I could safely say to Hunzinger – if he asked – that the installation, such as it was, had been postponed for a week.

As it happened he didn't ask. They were late back from Poole (and in fact, I discovered later that they too had made a considerable detour by way of London).

Before that, however, something very much more vital – something that was to cause me to rethink yet again the entire mission – had unexpectedly burst upon me.

I was on the way back from the stables, just after I replaced the bicycle, when I passed the big caravan canteen standing in the yard. Evidently it wasn't in use that day.

God knows why I should suddenly have thought of it, but for some reason I remembered the curious behaviour of the man Jay, going inside with all that electrical gubbins the morning I had been reading the paper outside the yard. What could an outside mechanic be doing in there?

There was nobody about. The other canteens had been put to bed in the stables, the stock checked and put away, the urns emptied and cleaned. Taffy had gone up to join the students; Mrs Cooksie and her husband had gone into Hawkhurst for a beer in the pub. The door of the canteen was ajar.

I pushed it open and peered inside. Nobody.

I stepped into the rear part, glanced around. There was no sign of any electrical work. The bracket lamps were where they had been, the ceiling light still firmly screwed to the false timber ceiling. Neither showed the slighest sign of recent work, of unscrewing, of rewiring.

I shrugged. Mystery. What the hell anyway. Who cared?

I was about to step down to the yard again when I saw, from the corner of my eye, a short length of that coloured cable, blue this time, hanging down from the closed compartment over the vehicle's cab. This was the space, when it was used as a motor caravan, which was designed exactly to accomodate a double bed mattress and covers for the owners to sleep in – with just enough head-room left to scramble inside without too much discomfort.

200

The hatchway closing it off was shut. I assumed the wire had dropped down in one corner and got closed in without anyone noticing.

Without really thinking, I turned the key operating the patent lock, thinking simply to shove the wire back up there and close it in when the compartment was shut once more.

The hatchway swung up on a counterweight, exposing the entire interior.

My hand was stretched out towards the fallen wire. I froze with my mouth open.

There was no mattress in there, double or single, no bedclothes, nothing to do with sleep at all.

In the brightly lit interior, Jay squatted down on a heavily carpeted floor-space, his head bent, his ears covered by sophisticated headphones linked by a chromium arch. His hands were busy above a combination keyboard and morse transmitter. And beyond that the cubbyhole was crammed with valves and winking pilot lights and rheostats and wired looms on metal chassis. Needles flickered across illuminated dials, a battery of keys and switches stood guard above a row of circular tuners with calibrated scales. It's absolutely not my scene, but it was clear in a twentieth of a second that I was staring at an advanced and highly technical transmitter and receiving complex in perfect working order.

In the instant that I registered this, Jay himself was as taken aback as I was. I had just time to recall that this was in fact his scene – he had been a radio expert in the Royal Corps of Signals after all – when he snarled: "What the fuck are you doing here? What the hell you think you're bloody doing?"

Another bat's blink of time. Panic. Hart discovered where he shouldn't be by the Jerry spies! Then relief: I was after all, as far as Jay was concerned, not Hart but his boss's bloody brother! I mean like, even if a trifle indiscreet, at least on his side, for God's sake! I said mildly: "Sorry. I didn't mean to disturb you. Didn't know you were here. it's just " showing him the wire – "that this had dropped down below the hatch and I thought maybe it should be put back out of sight."

Making, you see, as if I'd known about the installation all the time. Axel, my confidant, right?

It worked. For the moment anyway. Mollified, he muttered: "Thanks," snatching back the wire, "I'll put it away. But nobody's to come here. No one at all. Not bloody ever."

"All right," I said. "All right. Only trying to help. Forget it." I turned and left the caravan.

*   *   *

Peter Leslie

To say that this unexpected information completely up-ended my priorities so far as the mission was concerned is an understatement.

I had already got rid of all the intelligence so far acquired – and the express wish of Webster and/or Nichols had been based, like my own I assumed, on the belief that there would be little more that was serious to come. Hunzinger himself was already speaking of 'tidying up'. Better therefore to get cracking on what we had rather than holding on for what could be minimal interest material. There was, after all, a lot of preliminary background research to be done before any arrests were even thought of. And in a state of national emergency there was no question of actual proof required. Just enough to put them out of circulation until the panic was over. After which, if they hadn't actually committed any offence yet, they should be free to go again. But all our thinking, every aspect of the planning, the eventual roll-up, all of that, had been based on a single premise.

This was the assumption that the analyst's jigsaw puzzle – this 'complete picture' to be assembled laboriously from the fragments collected by our sleepers – would eventually be transferred to Berlin via the German Embassy in Dublin. Probably via IRA sympathizers contacted by Zelda in Ulster, or clandestine agents already in Britain and in touch with Hunzinger or the analyst. The attempts on Webster's life were indeed thought to be because he might be in danger of getting too close to this IRA-Berlin axis. In other words we had a certain amount of time in hand.

But if the stuff was capable of being beamed direct, if the sleepers' researches were transmitted as soon as they were discovered – perhaps to an analyst *already* in Berlin – then we were, as our transatlantic allies would say, in a whole different ball game.

It had been thought that radio transmissions from German agents still here, if any, were virtually impossible at this stage of the war. Detection techniques were at such a stage of refinement that the possibility could almost be dismissed.

But a new and highly sophisticated station apparently ready to transmit (I had even spotted a collapsible aerial beneath a tiny trapdoor in the canteen roof) was a very special danger, I reckoned, simply because of the speed involved. And because, although eventually the transmitter would be discovered, by that time the damage in this case would largely be done.

That was the cleverness, the simplicity, of the ruse here. A mobile canteen, always on the move, rarely in the same place for more than a short time, with the installation secretly incorporated in the vehicle

202

itself, should stall the inevitable crackdown for at least enough time in this one specific case.

And if 'tidying up' was already under way, surely every day must count.

In other words, so far as my particular mission was concerned, it seemed to me that the location and identification of the sleepers so far uncovered, important though this was, was now perhaps less important than the vital intelligence that a means existed whereby their work could be transmitted direct to the OKW in Germany.

So what does A do?

I could see no choice. The secret must be passed on at once.

No chance to get another phrase book, no time to encode. What I had discovered must be added immediately, unequivocally, to the stuff I delivered earlier today.

The first time I found myself in London with an order to deliver – but without the bloody book.

Now the book was in London and I had the information down here!

So I had to get the book back PDQ, Webster still being unavailable, and add the sensitive material to what was already in it.

Even if it meant I was blown, that I could never come back, I had to go back to London at this very minute and get that damned book back in time to modify it and repackage the parcel before – hopefully – it was delivered to Webster when he got to his office tomorrow morning.

I reached for the railway timetable. I was beginning to think it was about time that I invested in a season ticket.

Part Five

Sleepers Awake!

Twenty-Five

D iego Maroni Konstantin, Commonwealth citizen of Maltese origin, known simply as Diego the Fishman from Grimsby, through Nottingham, Leicester and the A6 as far as the Coffee-Ann in Soho – Diego, for the first time in his life, had fallen foul of a police trap! His expensive refrigerated van – crammed with cod, hake, turbot, halibut, brill and even sole for the starving masses of southern England – had been held up in a lay-by, near the village of Irthlingborough, by a black Wolseley with a blue light on its roof while he stopped to swallow a sandwich soon after dawn. Now there was a uniformed superintendent, silver bars and all on his shoulderstraps, and an ordinary bobby making themselves a nuisance, asking silly questions and making notes.

Unfortunately for Diego, he had been taking notes himself on the way up to Grimsby – plus the little detour by way of Bradford on account of something he heard from a fellow long-distance driver at a greasy-spoon fish and chip shop on the Humber.

The notes had been scribbed down on a pad of tear-off invoices bearing the name and address of the Konstantin fishmonger's in Frith Street, with a smaller, wholesale enterprise listed among fruit and vegetable sellers, butcher's suppliers and 'Italian warehousemen' in Covent Garden.

Diego's pad was balanced on the wide dashboard above the central housing of the diesel motor beneath his cab. He had been checking out a few entries while he munched his sandwich.

There were, however, two slightly unusual characteristics about this business document.

First, although there was not yet a single order entered, every single invoice on the entire pad already bore the typed name of the same client – a Mr Fredl Hyperion, at an address in Finchley, North London. Secondly, such scribbled annotations as the first two or three leaves on the pad did reveal had nothing whatever to do with fish, fisheries or the products of the sea.

"Better take a shufti at these, Diego, don't you think?" the Super enquired from his perch inside the van's high cab. "Better copy down what we find, Constable, in your own notebook. You never know when the Beak's going to demand sight of the originals in this kind of case, do you?"

"No, sir," the policeman agreed. He turned a page of the book, pushed back his tall, domed helmet and removed a pencil from behind his ear. He licked the point of the pencil.

"So let's see, then," the officer said, holding the pad up to the light in the cab roof. "Doing a spot of train-spotting in our old age, are we? Some of these kids' games don't half stick, eh?"

"Come off it, guv, for Chrissake," Diego protested uneasily. "What are you on about then? You must know bloody well if you're Ag and Fisheries: everything I fuckin' touch is straight up and above board. Every damned thing is logged out as it should be, accounted for, paid the legal price and shipped in via the rationed foodstuffs boys in the smoke. You want to look in the freezer, check the documents? I don't touch black market, and you should know it. It's not worth the aggro for the small trader: there ain't enough difference in the take – shall I say? – between the white fish and the bloody 'black' variety, and that's the truth."

The superintendent didn't smile. "Actually," he said, "fish is not a subject that interests me." He tore off the top sheet and deciphered Diego's handwritten squiggles with some difficulty:

Southbound convoy to bypass L'don – 20 Stuart Mark III (Lease-Lend US) light tanks; 250-hp + 37mm cannon. Plus 50 Mathilda MkII Infantry Support Vehicles (twin 95-hp diesels).

Twenty-five miles further north – still southbound – Sexton motorised heavy artillery (93mm and 140mm) mounted on US Sherman tank chassis. Too fast for accurate count but at least five, six composite batteries.

Following day: Humber estuary. Concentration in 'park' (fields) several acres containing many squadrons Crusader Mark VI 19-ton 340-hp Main Battle Tanks (57m AA) plus Oerlikon (20mm), Bofors (40mm) and main AA (94mm up to 20,700 feet).

"My goodness me," the Superintendent said. "What a busy little fishing bee we have here, Constable! You get all that down . . . ? Right. Next page, please." He tore another sheet out. This time he read the few lines of the entry aloud.

"Anti-tank six-pounders – hundreds of them, it seems. Long range

Blitz Harvest

guns – fifty-thousand feet, it says here, with one hundred and forty mm rounds. Big stuff indeed, Diego."

"Come off it, copper," Diego said. "Not everyone can wear uniform. There's still some of us, just the same, keeps up an interest in what goes on. There's some, like you say, train-spottin'; others – you must of heard of 'em – crazy for aircraft identification. They even use 'em, down on the South Downs, passin' on the info when the spotters see Jerry crossin' the coast. Some like to suss out the makes of cars, or boats even. With me it's armour, that's all. It's me passion. Kids collect models; I like to see it for real – writing it down, for the memory, like."

It was pretty weak, and he knew it. This time the super did smile.

"Rather depends, I should imagine," he said quietly, "who's privileged to share those precious memories of yours. Do you have many close friends, Diego?"

Diego thought it better to say nothing. He didn't understand what the hell was going on. So far as his business was concerned, he was in the clear: his papers were correct, he declared what he was supposed to declare, all his transactions were legal. There remained solely the fact that he amassed information on troop formations. If this was something that he happened to *notice* and kept mentally to himself, that was one thing. If he wrote it down, codified it, that was something else again . . . but then again it would be, legally, a matter of whether or not such codification was passed on to another person or persons. And if so, who.

This of course was at once dangerous material – verging indeed on the treasonable in time of war – and he preferred at least for the moment to say nothing more. The policeman said nothing more about friends. He detached another page from the pad.

"Just look at this, Constable," he said. "You'd better take this down direct. Now it's not just armour he's after, but bloody boats as well! A man of many parts, you might say."

On the half-sheet of invoice paper, the words – in capitals now – read:

LANDING CRAFT INFANTRY (LCI) – 182 MEN + CREW + EQUIPMENT. LANDING SHIP TANK (LST) – 5,000 TON STEAMER + 18 30-TON TANKS AND 217 MEN. CONCENTRATIONS HUMBER MOUTH AND OFF LOWESTOFT FROM SCOTTISH SHIPYARDS.

Below this again was the final entry on the invoice pad:

Watch this! Long distance drivers report very special giant size

209

Peter Leslie

low-loaders booked next month plus police motorbike escorts from Vickers-Armstrong factory Barrow-in-Furness to Gosport. Cargo reputed two P-19 SERAPH submarine hulls complete six 533mm torpedo tubes, 3 port 3 star. Exact date of convoys to be fixed.

If Diego had been more familiar with police procedure, he would have known that a uniformed superintendent would never occupy himself with a banal routine check accompanied only by a single constable – and certainly not with all the regalia on a dress tunic. Less still, even in wartime, would such an officer produce a Walther PPK automatic pistol with a silencer screwed to the barrel as a means of persuasion in the case of a suspect not even cautioned.

But Diego was frightened. He didn't like guns; he didn't want to be mixed up in anything political. It was one thing to help out a mate, a superior type, and feel you were contributing to the New Europe they all talked about, looking forward to the day when you were a Section Leader or something else important; quite another when the bloody law turned stroppy over fuck-all, waving *pistols* around, if you like! Christ, what did a few notes on military bleeding convoys matter, after all? It wasn't even as if he was being *paid* for it!

In a very short time, therefore – after a few "We got you bang to rights, chum!" and "Would you say five or ten, sir?" – Diego began to talk.

"I didn't mean no harm, honest," he whined. "There was this geezer, kind of a pal of mine, see; we used to hang around together in the BUF, keepin' the jewboys in their place in Brixton and the Mile End. You know. So on account of because I was like travellin', I mean with a straight petrol ration an' all . . . Well, to do him a favour, I like promised to keep me eyes open. That's all."

"And who exactly," the superintendent said, "would this so comfy and companionable superior mate be? I don't imagine, Diego, that you happen to remember his name – his surname, that is – by any chance? Do you?"

" 'Course I do," Diego said readily. "I said a mate. Cove by the name of Hartzmann. He's Welsh. Got a factory there an' all."

"How *very* interesting," the officer said. "You could have saved us a good half-hour if you'd said that at the beginning. Because, you see, Mr Hartzmann is a friend of ours too. We share an interest, a close interest, in – er – military history."

"Oh, well, that's all right then, innit?" Diego said thankfully. "Kind of lets me off then, OK?"

210

"Right off," the superintendent said.

The gun barrel, and the black hole penetrating the silencer, canted upwards, the trigger hand supported by the left wrist.

"*Christ . . . !*" Diego said.

It was the last thing he ever said. The impact of the 9 mm slug, even though it was now subsonic, slammed him against the door of the cab and the body slid down out of sight on the far side of the central engine housing. There was very little blood on the cab window.

"Well, let's hope he was a Catholic, then," the man dressed as a police constable said. "He'll be all right then, won't he!"

The man in officer's uniform started the engine. The big van shook as the diesel rumbled to life.

"You don't think he could still have been useful?" his companion asked.

"Not that kind of material. Until we find out what exactly the hell goes on, it's better to eliminate every single damned element which might prove meddlesome or obtrusive. Clearly there's a lot of work to be done, some kind of mess to be cleaned up maybe, before we can go ahead as planned. Until then, the less people in the way the better."

"Whatever you say," the other agreed.

"Get behind the wheel now, Kunz," the officer said. "I'll look after the Wolseley and junk the blue lamp. He'll be missed of course. But for the moment I want you to drive down to the North Circular, run her a few miles west – somewhere between Brent Cross-Hendon, say, and Ealing – then find a *tankstelle* – a filling station – with a big parking lot and abandon the truck there. RDV at the Willesden safe house midday."

"What do you want me to do with the body?"

"Put it in the refrigeration compartment, of course. I doubt we'll have time before he's found, even so . . . but I'd give a lot to know the difference between his Hartzmann and mine before that happens."

"They'll find him soon enough when the refrigeration unit runs out of gas!" the man with the bobby's helmet said.

The night had been cloudy, almost chilly, but the downpour didn't start until well after daylight. Weather conditions over most of northern Europe, however, had grounded the heavy bombers and raids were restricted to a few coastal airfields and sporadic attacks on shipping in the Channel.

Early on that rainswept morning in central London, quiet except for the drone of a single reconnaissance Dornier checking out the havoc wrought two nights before, a taxi pulled up outside the Cumberland Terrace quarters of Colonel Nichols in Regent's Park. The fare, Captain

211

Nicholas Hart, Oxford and Buckinghamshire Light Infantry, temporarily seconded to CO(S)E and very smart in service dress uniform with polished Sam Browne, tapped on the glass partition. "Wait for me here, cabbie, would you?" he called. "I have to collect something, that's all."

The driver nodded, switching the flag to the *Waiting* position. Hart splashed across the pavement and ran up the steps to the building's elegant porticoed entrance.

The ATS receptionist had just come on duty. She was fixing her hair with her back to the desk. Hart rapped lightly with his cane on the shining surface. "So sorry to intrude!" he said.

The girl swung around. "Captain Hart! Hallo again. What can I do you for this time?"

"A code-book, ducky," he said. "Can't have been delivered by the War House courier more than twenty minutes ago, what! All wrapped up like a Christmas present. Let's have it back a tick, would you? There's something frightfully important I have to add."

The girl rummaged on the shelf beneath the desk. "Yes, here we are, sir," she said. "It's addressed to Lieutenant-Colonel Webster, but it hasn't been sent up to his office yet." In fact the man happened to have a hangover and he hadn't even shown up, but she wasn't going to reveal that, "If you would just sign a release, sir," she said.

The officer nodded. "Let you have it back within the hour," he promised.

Taking charge of the wrapped Penguin, he smiled his thanks and ran down the steps to the waiting taxi, swinging his cane.

A motorbike with a man in khaki riding pillion pulled out from behind the vehicle as Hart was about to climb in out of the rain. There was an unfamiliar type of sub-machine-gun in his hands. Flame belched from the muzzle as the bike accelerated past and the pelting of the rain was momentarily drowned by the hammering rasp of automatic fire.

The young officer dropped to the roadway as abruptly as a marionette with its strings cut, his chest smashed open by a hail of nickel-jacketed 9 mm Parabellum high-velocity shells. The motorcycle roared away, Hart's packaged Penguin code-book in the gunner's free hand.

Rain lancing down from the leaden sky diluted the crimson tide welling out across the macadam from beneath the corpse to an insipid mauve as it lost itself in the swirling gutter.

Twenty-Six

"There's no doubt about it," the Special Branch forensic man said. "No doubt whatever. Blood group O, Rhesus Positive. That could account for a lot more than half the population; doesn't mean a damned thing. We don't have Bertillon Measurements, the way they do in the United States. But the fingerprint types are formal: so, too, are the dental people in Army Records. There's not the shadow of a doubt. The dead man is not your Captain Nicholas Hart."

"Well, where *is* Hart then?" Adam Nicholas demanded. "Clearly, the victim was *supposed* to be Hart. The dead man himself was pretending to be Hart; the girl downstairs in Reception recognised him. He asked her to give him back a package he'd left in earlier for Webster. Wanted to add something, said he'd let her have it back in an hour."

"The signature on the release isn't Hart's, of course," Webster himself said. "Not remotely like it. You can check it with the genuine article – on the chit the real Hart signed when he handed the package in. I questioned the girl very carefully – and the faker made a slight slip. He said the package would have been delivered by the War House courier, and in fact Hart handed it in personally. But unfortunately she didn't remember that until later, when it was all over."

A second Special Branch man, a superintendent, cleared his throat. "So we have this army officer on special service," he said, "handing in a package for the attention of the lieutenant-colonel here, apparently at some time very early in the morning."

"I was expecting it," Webster said. "Unfortunately I wasn't at home."

"Subsequently then, not long afterwards it seems, a person closely resembling the officer and dressed exactly like him appears here and asks for the package back, evidently on a pretext."

Adam Nichols nodded. "The resemblance is . . . was . . . more than close," he said.

213

He opened a drawer in his desk and took out two photographs, one of Hart, the other the original Hunzinger print that Hart had been shown at the start of the case.

The policeman whistled. "As you say, sir. Quite remarkable" he said. "So the bogus officer fools the girl, takes the package, and is about to get into a taxi when he is shot. Am I right?"

"As right as anyone can be in this caper," Webster said in a subdued voice. The hangover was making his eyes hurt, even though the day was dull.

"So where is the packet at this moment?" the superintendent asked.

"With the killers," Nichols said. "Either the killer or his rider snatched it out of his hand as he fell. The cabbie can't remember which. It all happened too fast."

"So somebody, not entitled to it, badly wanted to get his hands on this package – and was helped to succeed by this . . . shall we just say this . . . likeness? But somebody *else* also wanted the package – wanted it badly enough to kill for it. Now I've just two questions to put to you gentleman at this moment. I'll leave aside for a second why the contents are of such value. State secrets no doubt." He cleared his throat again. "First question: have you any idea of who this merchant so closely resembling your officer could be? And question Number Two: Would the killers who snatched the parcel have known they were hijacking the thing, as it were, from someone who'd already stolen it – or would they have believed it was the original, genuine officer?"

There was a slight pause. Rain drummed on a canopy above the bow window. "Those are very good questions, Superintendent," Webster said.

"Here's the most ridiculous damned thing about the whole mess," Nichols said uncomfortably. "We're pretty sure, you see, that we could put a name to an indiviual resembling our man – someone anxious to grab any parcel left by him if he knew it existed. We could also hazard an accurate guess as to the identity of someone organising the killing – if he believed the man leaving this building with the package was not an impersonator but the genuine article . . ."

Nichols was silent for a moment. "Well, sir?" the Special Branch man said.

"Well, the devil of it is, you see," the colonel continued, "that it happens to be the same man in each case! Which doesn't make any sense at all."

Blitz Harvest

"The same man in each case," the superintendent said heavily. "I see."

"We know the dead man isn't Hart," Nichols said. "So it would be reasonable to assume that it's Hunzinger, his double. But why? He'd already filched the packet he wanted. Who would kill him? Equally, the only shooting that makes sense is a case where the victim in the taxi is *mistaken* for Hart. And although at a pinch I suppose Hunzinger might have organised such a thing, that's even crazier, since Hunzinger damned well knew he was already posing as Hart himself!"

"Excuse me, sir!" A detective-inspector who had so far taken no part in the conversation spoke directly to the superintendent. No truck with these amateur dilettantes in the cloak and dagger game – like a load of kids with charades! Just let's leave it to the pros, eh?

"Yes, Chalmers – what is it?"

The inspector was sitting at Nichols's desk. He had been speaking quietly into the telephone. Now he was shuffling together a sheaf of pencilled notes. "Beg pardon, sir. The identity of the suspect, name of Hunzinger, thought to have escaped from internment under 18B on the Isle of Man. Special Branch requested the Douglas authorities to supply a set of dabs PDQ. The prints arrived at Heston in an Anson a half hour ago."

"Good, good. And the results, Chalmers?"

"Negative, sir. No question. The dead man is not the internee Hunzinger either."

"My God," Webster said, "it looks more and more as if what the superintendent's questions imply must be somewhere near the truth. Like there must be *three* separate elements involved here!"

The Special Branch man sighed. "Three separate elements," he said. "Just so."

It was a few minutes later that Webster himself was called to the phone. "Just a small matter of confirmation," he told Nichols. "Negative, of course."

"Meaning?"

"Jill Chandos. One of our lamplighter girls swanning around the South Coast trying on different uniforms here and there. A Naval VAD today if I have it right. She's been keeping an eye, as Hart will know."

"And she confirms?"

Webster shook his head – then hastily stopped before he had gone too far. "Mr Hartzmann," he said, "could not conceivably have

215

visited Cumberland Terrace early this morning, ridden a motor cycle, been shot to death, fired a gun himself or sequestered a package from this building. Following a visit yesterday evening from the local vicar and several neighbours, which lasted almost until midnight, the subject spent the night with his mistress Zelda Fortune and – at the time of this call – was still enjoying a late breakfast with the same at Fortune Hall in the county of Kent. It is therefore geographically impossible for him to be considered in any way at all as an element in the enquiry under discussion."

"Christ!" Nichols exploded. "First the bugger's in three or four places at once – now he isn't anywhere at all, at any bloody time! How big is the cast in this damned thriller anyway?"

The intercom on Nichols's desk buzzed discreetly. "Yes, Mason? What is it?" he asked curtly.

Suave as ever, the batman's well-modulated voice replied:

"Forgive the interruption, sir. There is a person at reception giving the name of Hart who appears to be in an agitated condition. He insists on seeing you and seeks the return of a package lodged for the convenience of Lieutenant-Colonel Webster."

"Spooks," Webster said to Nick Hart, "behave like people. To everyone his own microcosm. Mankind reviewed as the epitome of the universe, as the OED has it."

"Yes, great chief," Hart said, "but if the people—?"

"Exactly. One continent hates, reviles, misunderstands another. Countries ceaselessly bicker over territorial advantage or economic favouritism. Families split up over imagined slights. This pussycat is jealous because that pussycat found the warmest cushion first."

"I don't doubt it," Hart agreed. "Read the papers, listen to the news."

They were sitting in a quiet corner of The Volunteer, between Baker Street station and the entrance to Regent's Park. The police were taking statements. Special Branch were trying to eliminate the impossible in the hope of discovering something, anything, however improbable, that made sense. Nichols had a superior to report to. The girl named Jill Chandos was probably changing her uniform.

"One might suppose," Webster said oracularly, "that the secret services of a given country would find enough material to squabble over and contest within the secret activities of another country. But not a bit of it."

"Ah."

"Confusing the trail, distributing red herrings, playing it close to the chest . . . I tell you, old boy, our gallant allies are the champion mixers in this game! The Chekha, the NKVD, the Deuxième Bureau of the BCRA, the CIA, the FBI and various other allegedly under-cover agencies are the champions in this not-in-front-of-the-children game. But closer still to home, the runners-up come perilous close. The coppers, the Special Branch, the Secret Intelligence Service, MI5, MI6 and Military Intelligence between them share a jealously guarded system of *Dead Stops* the poor bloody censorship boys never dreamed of. You want cooperation? We've got it – and we're fucking well keeping it well beneath our spooks' hats!"

"You mean like: This is our patch. Keep off the grass!"

"Well . . . that's another way of putting it."

"It's shorter," Hart said.

Webster grinned. "Must be time I sampled another hair of the dog," he said. "Barman – two of the same, if you please."

"Large ones, sir?"

"You must be joking," Webster said. "To tell you the truth, young Hart, the reason I have grown this monumental hangover is because I happened to have been sent back to your old stamping ground for a couple of days. Ulster no less. And that's why you couldn't raise me on the blower, for which my regrets. There simply wasn't time to fill you in."

Hart waited patiently. He sipped his whisky. Webster had never heard of vodka.

"Given that the left hand doesn't know what the right is doing," Webster said, "it was lucky that a mate in the Royal Ulster Con-stabulary broke the law of silence and tipped us off that there were a couple of bods from the SIS arsing about over there, pretending to be IRA activists. Activists with a pressing necessity to make frequent visits to Dublin. So . . . well, fortunately, I happened to know one of these lads. A drinking companion, you might say. And, what with one thing and another, I persuaded him – with a modicum of official leaning – to reveal all."

Webster shook his head. "SIS, as you well know, haven't a clue about your particular mission – That's *our* show, God dammit! – so there was no especial reason at this time to share their own spook results. Except that it just so happens – surprise, surprise! – that what they are uncovering is *another* Nazi spy ring about to be installed in this sceptred isle. And the new organisation, spirited in by the Dublin Embassy and genuine IRA types, has as its specific objective – wait for it! – the reactivation of the old Hunzinger sleepers who have been waiting doggo all this time for The Big One to arrive!"

"Christ!" Hart said.

"It's not only the SIS, you see," Webster said. "Berlin too has yet to learn that Hunzinger has been sprung. And why and by whom. For them he's still behind the barbed wire in Douglas, IOM.

"And this new network is already operating over here, in the UK?"

"So it seems. At least in partial activity. With a certain amount of overlapping which is puzzling the hell out of them. The word is that the spooks running it have already sussed out that there's, at the very least, something uncommonly rum in the undercover state of this particular Denmark!"

"So this second ring is already starting, unknown to us and *our* spies, to activate . . . no, it's simply not on," Hart said. "There's only a certain amount the long arm can take!"

"On the contrary," Webster said, "infernally complicated though it may seem at first, this does in some way help to clarify things."

"I should dearly love to learn how! Clarify, he says?"

"You only have to wait. What we have been discussing this morning, for instance. Not by any, not by the remotest, wildest chance could some of the manifestations believably be put down to coincidence. But add a second subversive organisation, unknown to the first and vice versa, and certain phenomena begin to suggest at least the possibility of reasonable explanation."

"Like people being in three separate geographical places at one and the same time?"

"Exactly that," Webster said.

"You can get away with two – but only then when the two of them share an uncanny resemblance. Certainly not with three."

"You could if all three shared this uncanny resemblance."

"Oh, come on, Webster! Come off it. Three identical figures, three ringers as the Yanks say – that's really a fucking sight too much to swallow!"

"An intellectual game," Webster said. "Suppose we were to play Let's Pretend. Given that a Nazi spy-master, released from internment by a pretend Nazi intelligence group, is set to work activating a ring of sleepers here. Let us then suppose that a genuine Nazi intelligence group, unaware of this and not wishing to waste such valuable material, decides itself to free a spy-master from internment and set *him* to work activating the ring here. And let us suppose, however, that in this case, the internment camp happens to be in Australia. What then could be more logical to choose as second spy-master than the twin brother of spy-master one?

218

For a moment Hart was silent. And then: "Are you telling me," he said, "are you saying that Zoltan Hunzinger, the real Zoltan, is here? Doing that?"

"It would supply believable answers to a number of impossible questions," Webster said. "We have asked Sydney if he's skipped camp. We have asked for his prints and his dental record to be flown here top priority if he has."

"Well, if that were the case . . ." Hart paused in mid-sentence. It was too much to take in.

"If that were the case, the irony of the situation would rival the proportions of a Shakespearian tragedy. Let us suppose again – and try this for size. The genuine Nazis are more on the ball than we think. They know a British agent – you – is swanning around London pretending to be Axel; they know you have some kind of incriminating document concerning the ring. *But they don't know that Axel himself is at liberty.* And Axel himself has no idea his brother is here."

Webster signalled the barman again. For some reason his throat was dry. "A few details remain to be filled in," he said, "but basically the position is this: if it is easy enough for an English officer to pose as a German look-alike, it follows that it would be equally simple for the German plausibly to impersonate the officer – and take possession of the latter's document."

Hart said: "The real Zoltan in this scenario, I imagine, assumes that any sighting whatever, either of Hunzinger or myself, must obviously be me. And that I am posing as Hunzinger and never at all as Zoltan?"

"Yes, of course. Now, for the other half of the premise, we have to assume – always a possibility – that you yourself are blown. And Hunzinger knows about the coded book. So . . . lights, camera, action: Zoltan calls at Nichols's office, pretending to be you. The impersonation is a success and he gets away with the book, intending to find out what or who the hell you are. Change of scene. Exterior. Determined to avenge the insult, Hunzinger – having secured for himself a watertight alibi – hires a couple of professionals to eliminate you. Once again the impersonation is successful. The gunman, too, takes the real Zoltan for you. And Hunzinger effectively is responsible for the murder of his own brother."

"You should be writing books," Hart said. "Only nobody would believe them."

"Think of a better explanation, then."

"How long will we have to wait for the gen from Sydney?"

"Probably not before the day after tomorrow. You know how the authorities work."

Hart sighed. "So all we can do, right now, is sit on our arses and wait?"

"Not you, you don't!" Webster said. "You, my son, had better get the hell up off yours and go find that bloody book!"

Twenty-Seven

H art in fact was blown all right. By two separate elements – the second only by chance, since it was stimulated uniquely by the unexpectedness of the first.

It was during the Poole Harbour expedition, when Hunzinger was in fact wearing the Captain Hart uniform, complete with Hart ID, hoping that this would stave off unwelcome queries in what must presumably be a highly sensitive military area. Zelda, alone in the front seat of the Armstrong Siddeley, made a nubile driver in ATS-commandant khaki.

The spy-master had no intention of tempting providence by an in-depth analysis of the various craft which would be identifiable from a waterside reconnaissance; he had far too high a respect for British military security to venture suspiciously close to what must be 'special pass' territory. This initial sortie was simply to glean an overall picture: categories of vessel, some idea of numbers, types of armament, and above all relative concentration of ships, large or small, in active use or merely assembled, waiting to be called.

The details could be supplied by others later. For the moment Hunzinger was content to remain on the higher ground nearer Highcliff and Bournemouth and use – as discreetly as he dared – a pair of high-powered Zeiss binoculars originally issued only to U-Boat commanders. Canford Cliffs overlooking the Solent on one side and the jagged, irregular inlets of the inland waterway on the other were precisely what he needed.

The concentration was far higher than he expected. There was an enormous variety clearly visible, even from this far away. Nothing bigger than a Sloop or a couple of Corvettes, but a bewildering display of MTBs, minesweepers, cutters, air-sea rescue launches, high-speed rocket batteries and barges among the flotillas of infantry and armoured-vehicle landing craft.

When he had taken in as much as he could from that distance, Hunzinger suggested a trip around the northern extremities of the lake and a pub lunch in the town of Wareham – from which, if they

221

chose the right window, they would have a view of the ancient ruins of Corfe Castle on the Isle of Purbeck.

But Zelda's sights were trained on something nearer home. At first she had not broached the subject because Hunzinger had seemed off-colour and ill-humoured – particularly with regard to Zoltan and his wretched phrase book. But now – the shepherd's pie partially abandoned, a glass of Algerian wine refused with a grimace of distaste – the subject could be kept at bay no longer.

"Axel," she began defensively, "I know there are things on your mind. But there is something I have to tell you . . . something I have got to tell you."

"Can't it wait?" he said absently, scrawling notes on the back of an envelope.

"No it can't. It may be important." Zelda plucked up courage. "I know it's important. It concerns you personally anyway . . . you and your brother."

He looked up from his notes, suddenly smiling. "Don't tell me: you got randy the day I was in town. You tempted him into your bed! Am I right . . . ? You always were a sexy little slut, Zelda. So very well; that's you. But was he any good? Was he better than me? Could you tell the difference?"

Zelda swallowed. "All right. I'm oversexed. I love to make love – especially to new partners. You never minded before. As long as I told you."

"I'm not saying I mind now. But you haven't answered my questions. I mean . . . my brother!"

"There is a difference," Zelda said. She hesitated. It was a thing so simple, almost banal, so virtually unworthy of mention to some – yet so disastrous to others. It was a practice adopted by far the majority of middle-class, Protestant parents, certainly between the 1920s and the war; a ritual commonly handled at the same time as a boy's Christening. But, automatic though it might be for those particular English, it was not normal for the Austro-German Zelda or her anti-Semitic lover.

"So what's the big difference, then?" Axel was chiding. "He has horns *and* a tail?"

"It's personal. Kind of, well . . . private," she faltered. And then, suddenly blurting it out: "Your damned Zoltan! He may not actually be a Jew, but he can certainly be no brother of yours! The man is *circumcised*, Axel, by all that's holy!"

And, as the spy-master's jaw dropped in disbelief, abruptly, overwhelmingly, the doors of memory slid open. "That uniform!"

she cried. "I *knew* the name seemed somehow familiar . . . but there was no reason for it to . . . I believed, of course, because it was you who said it was your brother . . . there was no reason to doubt. But now I know this can't be true, the other things fall into place."

"What things? What are you talking about? What about the damned uniform?"

"Not the uniform: the papers, the name with them. All at once I remembered – the extraordinary likeness of this man in Belfast. He was in civilian clothes, but he was introduced as a British army captain. You remember: I told you about him. And just now it was *I* who remembered. The man's name was Hart."

"Are you telling me . . . my brother Zoltan . . . are you suggesting this is an *impostor*, not my brother at all? Are you – *Gott im Himmel!* – are you saying that everything, the tunnel, the escape, everything since is as false as this . . . this barbarian himself?"

"It's the only answer, Axel."

Hunzinger's face was very white. "And you allowed him . . . this bogus Jew . . . this impure . . . you permitted him to touch you, to dare to defile a racially—"

"Axel," she cried. "how was I to know? When a man is excited, with an erection, there is virtually no difference visually. One isn't a professor with a magnifying glass! It is only later, when the person is relaxed, at rest, asleep even – only then that the . . . difference . . . is noticeable. In any case it was you yourself who said it was your brother!"

Hunzinger's lips were a thin, tight line, no more than a crevasse in his face. "And all this time I have stupidly, idiotically been sharing my closest professional secrets with a . . . with an individual I must suppose to be some kind of cunningly substituted counter intelligence agent, profiting from a gratuitous physical resemblance?" He spoke through tightly clenched teeth, his whole frame shaking with fury.

"We shall return to London immediately," he said harshly. "Somebody shall die for this."

Twenty-Eight

"Such SIS intelligence as I have been permitted to share," Webster said, "confirms that the genuine Nazi undercover unit, infiltrated via the Dublin Embassy, is limited to three agents: the real Zoltan Hunzinger and two others. Zoltan is not a professional. He is there solely because Jerry hopes he will lend authenticity to the operation – in other words that the sleepers will take him for Axel, whom they trust, and come out into the open to begin work on their original briefing – to collect information on D-Day preparations."

"And the other two?" Nick Hart queried.

"A heavy who seems to be known as Rawlins – possibly of Irish origin. And the man in charge, who is a very dangerous character indeed. Known in the haunts of spookery as Cosmo. Probably one Demetrios Cosmos, of Greek parentage. A professional killer."

"Will this unit be aware that the real Hunzinger has been sprung? Indeed has started to reactivate the ring?"

"We think not. But only for the moment. They'll soon enough cotton on once they contact people Hunzinger's already been to see."

"And will they know that their own man, actually standing in for him, has been killed?"

"Good God, I hope not. There's been a dead stop on the murder: no papers, no wireless. The roadway hosed down by the lamplighters, the body straight into the morgue without passing through a hospital DOA transfer. But they'll realise soon enough once himself fails to show."

"You are not, I hope," Hart said, "proposing that I should construct a *second* impersonation of Zoltan, in front, this time, of hostile natives?"

Webster laughed, shaking his head. "Even we impose certain limits!" he said.

"I think maybe I'd better drop by Burman's and invest in a false moustache, just the same."

"Something like that," Webster agreed. "One of Nichols's men could advise you. Better in any case to keep a low profile for a couple of days – at least while there are two separate groups of nasties out for your blood, most of them looking for you with three different names and faces!"

"That should leave me, statistically, with a one in six chance of being rubbed out," Hart said. "But seeing that half the faces they come across might be Hunzinger's rather than my own, what difference to the odds might that make in your view?"

"I'd hurry off to Nichols's man, if I were you," Webster advised. "We gather, partly from SIS sources, partly from our own, that the unit follows a fairly ruthless course. What you might call a too-many-cooks-spoil-the-broth approach. Specifically, and a broth of a boy he is, Cosmo has orders, like other clandestine bosses, to liquidate all previous operatives already active in his particular field. On the principle, we believe, that they might have been turned or were already double agents. Kill 'em off and save yourself the trouble finding out!"

"Bit of a waste, just the same," Hart said.

"Saves time, my boy. There are always more where they came from. With Hunzinger, you may have met a character known as Diego the Fishman, probably in the Coffee-Ann. His body was found early this morning in a car park on the North Circular Road. Stuffed in the freezer compartment of his van along with a consignment of Grimsby haddock. He'd been shot with a German automatic. Or the long-haired young man working at the MOI. The lamplighters reported that you met him at the Coventry Street Corner House, along with Axel and the singer. Unfortunate accident coming home from the Censorship night shift. Run over and killed as he crossed the street. Hit and run driver. No witnesses."

"I'd better get that bloody code-book back to you soon," Hart said, "or there'll be no sleepers left for you to roll up and put away!"

The information on the mobile canteen transmitting station he had, of course, already passed on to Webster. Detection vans hurried to the area had so far recorded nothing but one-two-three and over-and-out checks transmitted by signalman Jay. But Webster was certain that once enough sleeper material had been amassed, regular transmissions to Berlin would continue until the radio security snoops fell on them – and the hell with that old-hat Dublin Embassy crap. "No doubt about it," Webster said. "The Fortune Hall round is destined to form the *centrale*, the nub of the entire pre-invasion intelligence service as long as the sleepers remain awake."

"Better get a move on, then, hadn't I?" Hart said. "I'm off to see the wizard – the wonderful wizard of facial transubstantiation!"

"And don't be late: they close at ten-thirty in this part of town," Webster said.

Webster and Hart, of course, were still in The Volunteer. But by one of those freaks of geography, causation and Heisenberg's Uncertainty Principle, each of course unknown to the others, four of the people they had been discussing were at that moment less than three hundred yards away from them. The first two, Zelda and Axel Hunzinger, were seated in Emberson's Wine Bar, a free vintner specialising in fine sherries and madeiras just off the Marylebone Road: the second, the man called Cosmo and his helpmate still dressed as a police constable, were in Baker Street Underground station.

"You're sure the two Soho types, the guns-for-hire you entrusted with the job, will work, shall we say . . . honourably," Zelda said. "I mean, they won't just pocket the fee and take off?"

"They are well spoken for," Hunzinger said. "They have a team reputation to keep up."

"But they haven't contacted you. There hasn't been a word. Nothing in the papers; not a word in the news."

"Well, there wouldn't be, would there?" Hunzinger rejoined. "Not if my dear brother was in reality a counter-intelligence officer. They'd wrap it all up tight, wouldn't they? I just hope they did the job at the right time – between the hours we'd arranged the alibi for. Because if this . . . this traitorous pig is who we think he is, his superiors will certainly know by now that I am in London, on the loose. And clearly then a prime suspect in the case of a murder enquiry, even a secret one."

"I wonder where they tracked him down," Zelda said, "and where eventually they did it."

"We drove up from Poole immediately after our pub lunch – the moment you told me . . . what you had to tell. We were in London by the end of the afternoon, where I had to make a couple of phone calls, then go to the White House to . . . arrange . . . things. By the time we returned to Hawkhurst, he was no longer there. According to Jay and Cooksie, he had gone up to London himself. Twice in the same day!"

"That's the part I never could follow," Zelda said. "Why would he . . . ?"

"He didn't go on the Wrayfield Farm canteen round, the way I told him to. Apparently one of the girls saw him borrow a bicycle and ride towards the station. He was carrying a small packet, about the size of that damned book he always had his nose in. He was back long before we were – with no packet. Then, still before our own return, he had gone up to London *again*! This time he stole a bike – it was found in the station yard. But he had missed the last train. He had to wait for the milk train, which has included a couple of passenger coaches since raids started. So I called the two operatives at the White House again and told them to pick him up at Waterloo. By which time you had organised our little . . . social evening."

"What's this about the book – if it was in the package? Did he forget it there?"

"Be your age, *Liebchen*. If it had been my brother, such a thing could have meant anything. Or nothing. But since it was a *scheiss* of a secret agent there was clearly a delivery to London involved. A delivery of what, you may ask. So you tell me what information, probably coded, there must have been in that damned book! I told the executioners to recover the packet at all costs."

Zelda sighed. "Some people choose complicated lifestyles, don't they?" she complained.

Had Nicholas Hart, who was at that time crossing the road between The Volunteer and Regent's Park, chanced to overhear the remark, he could well have echoed the American comedian and said sourly: 'Lady, you ain't seen nothing yet!'

Determined to visit Nichols's disguise specialist in Cumberland Terrace, he had decided to go via the White House, which was just outside the southeastern corner of the park. As long as he remained outside he was fairly safe from recognition. It was raining again, and this had given him the opportunity to wear a raincoat with the collar turned up and a cloth cap pulled well down to hide the distinctive hair, nose and jaw. The White House was a hunch, but when, together with Hunzinger, he had met the men he thought of as 'the Soho desperadoes' he had formed a definite opinion that they were resident there. The place was a block of self-contained one-room flats, including a swimming pool, squash court, dance floor and a bar and restaurant open to the public. It was a convenient base for transients, foreigners anxious to keep a London *pied-à-terre*, and such no-strings itinerants as journalists, musicians, film people, rag-trade salesmen and Naval officers on leave content to find a bed – and if possible a partner to share it. It was the kind of place where one could easily pass an unobtrusive hour or two without being specially remarked upon in the constant ebb and flow of anonymous humanity.

Hart, all of whose energy was concentrated on the location and, if possible, recovery of his vital phrase book, was convinced of one thing. If Hunzinger had gone to the trouble of organising an alibi involving several different groups of people, it was reasonable to suppose that he would row in dubious characters he knew already to do any dirty work there was to be done.

If, that was, they were right and it was indeed the spy-master who commandeered the Regent's Park assassination of the man he believed to be Hart himself.

If, indeed, they were right again and Hart's Zoltan impersonation had in truth been blown.

This was not in fact a verification Hart was eager to confirm via a personal meeting.

The one proof they had, nevertheless, the sole incontrovertible fact that could not be denied, was that it was the killers on the motorbike who had taken possession of Hart's book in its package.

Did they have it still? Had they any idea what value it might have? Had they simply chucked it once they saw that it was nothing but a banal, dog-eared paperback? Or had they in some impenetrable way actually been instructed to steal the book? In which case, crookedness in certain cases proving contagious, were they holding out for more loot before they delivered?

One way or the other, Hart thought – nose buried in his upturned, sodden collar – the White House could at least be on the way to the answer. To some answer. To any answer.

He turned the corner from Baker Street to Marylebone Road, head ducked against the stinging rain. Cosmo and Rawlins, by the newspaper stand at the top of the steps leading to the station's main entrance, saw him thread his way through the crowd waiting by the traffic lights, heading east, towards Great Portland Street. "There he is!" Rawlins shouted. "Where the fuck have you been, you prick? What the hell's the idea, keeping us waiting this way? Zoltan . . . for God's sake, Zoltan . . . !"

"Pack it in!" Cosmo said angrily. "No sense drawing attention. The fall-back at Madame Taussaude's – it's only a couple of hundred yards away. We'll follow him and meet up there." He seized Rawlins by the arm and propelled him hastily down the stairway.

Hart was some way ahead now. If he had noticed the shouts – or even recognised the name Zoltan – they had passed him by in the hubbub of the busy crossing. He passed the arcaded entrance to the world-famous waxworks museum, skirting the low wall which had once supported the railings bordering the park, accelerating his pace as the rain gusted across the wide roadway.

"He's passed the bloody waxworks!" Rawlins exploded. "Christ – what the fuck's he at? Hey, Zoltan!"

"Forget it," Cosmo said. "We'll find out." He quickened his own footsteps.

Hart crossed Albany Street opposite Great Portland Street station. He ran up the steps to the side entrance of the White House and in through the swing doors. Cosmo and Rawlins were temporarily halted when the lights turned red, then hurried after him.

Hunzinger took a telephone call at Emberson's and returned to his table. "They want us to meet, now, at a place called the White House," he told Zelda. "It seems it's not far from here. Do you know it?"

"Of course," she said. "It's just down the road. You met them there before, with . . . him."

"I remember." He drained his glass of sherry and rose to his feet. "Let's go then. Right?"

Webster, who had never actually seen Hunzinger in the flesh, came face to face with him at the Albany Street crossing. "Look out there, Hart," he called. "The armoury closes at seven, man!"

Not surprisingly, Hunzinger made no reply. He might not even have heard. The rain was falling heavily and there was a lot of traffic.

Webster paused on the wet pavement, frowning. He had been on his way back to Cumberland Terrace, hoping to catch the disguise expert while Hart was still there. Now, after an instant's hesitation, he recrossed the road and followed the couple into the main entrance of the apartment block. "Something," he said under his breath, "whispers that soon it may be time for Fearless Frazer to strike again!"

Twenty-Nine

Several members of the local police force called urgently to the White House late that afternoon – together with agents of the security organisations less evident in their presence – were unable to agree when formulating their reports on the exact chronological sequence of events once the action started. The barman behind the reproduction oak counter of what the management chose to call the Tudor Lounge was so nonplussed by the speed and drama with which the scenario unfolded that his statement to the police contradicted itself four times in the first three pages, and the Special Branch interrogator eventually dismissed his evidence as 'lacking credulity' and 'the result of an overactive imagination'.

But then he, of course, was trying at the same time to memorise the orders of half a dozen waitresses and pacify a score of regulars baying for drink along the edge of the bar itself.

It had started quietly enough. There were a lot of people jostling this way and that, trying to find a table, hoping to retain a chair for a friend who hadn't arrived yet, hurrying to pack in a final double before the sirens sounded. It was after all the rush hour. But nobody was creating, there were no quarrels or bad temper, no one shouted.

Hart saw the 'Soho desperadoes' at once. They were squashed into a niche dark with fumed oak and at the same time glittering with pewter and horse-brasses – two wide-shouldered men in striped suits with pale ties and heavy-lidded eyes. Hart passed the niche without turning his head or checking his stride. From the corner of his own eye he registered the two chairs jealously guarded on the far side of the table. He went through a pass door to a passageway leading to toilet facilities and, eventually, the squash court and pool. Through a frosted glass-pane in the door, he could observe, without being seen, the two men in the niche. There was a row of open phone booths along a wall beyond the door. He took up position in the nearest, lifting the receiver and pretending to flip through a directory.

Hart kept watch, miming now an animated conversation with the handset. Hunzinger and Zelda threaded their way through the press

230

around the bar, nodded a rather perfunctory greeting, and installed themselves on the two vacant chairs. It was clear that a fairly heated discussion started at once.

Webster, who had followed the couple in, had snatched a dry martini from the barman with the ease that only an experienced barfly can achieve. Now he was leaning against a pillar nearby, picking his teeth with an olive stick.

Nobody paid him any attention; none of them had seen him before. Two factory girls in tight dresses and platform heels drifted past, giggling. "Flynn!" one of them crowed with a saucy grin. "In uniform and ready for action already. Watcha doin' tonight, Errol boy?"

"Fancy a spot of jitterbuggin' down the Lyceum?" the other girl winked. "It's Harry Roy!"

Webster leaned his hawk face down towards the couple. He lanced a shifty sideways glance. "Actually, girls, I'm on duty," he confided in a low, solemn tone. "You know – secret service stuff. Somewhere in this crowded bar there's a nest of dastardly spies plotting to kidnap the King!"

"Oh, you!" the first girl retorted. Arms linked, they melted away in the direction of the bar.

Rawlins and Cosmo had halted at the entrance, confused by the disappearance of Hart, then doubly taken aback by the appearance, with a girl now, of *second* man they took to be their own Zoltan. For once Cosmo seemed momentarily ill at ease. "The fuck's going *on*?" he muttered angrily.

And it was precisely at this moment that voices rose also in the niche.

Hart pushed through the pass door in time to hear the end of a furious exchange.

". . . told you, deliver that damned package at the same damned time." (Hunzinger.)

"If it's that fuckin' important, it's worth maybe a sight bleedin' more!" (One of the striped suits.)

"Any case, you ain't come across yet with the second half. You promised—" (The second suit.)

"I promised half in advance, half on completion."

"So where's the bleedin' loot?"

"It's safe. But no money until I have the package."

"Sod the package. Cost you even more if you try to hold out on us. Shit – we done the job!"

By this time, his face well hidden between the cap and the collar, Hart had passed the table, hesitated, started towards the bar as though it was too crowded, then half turned as if deciding to return through the pass door. On the way he had exchanged susprised glances of mutual recognition with Webster at his pillar. Apart from a raised eyebrow on Webster's part, neither made any sign. Hart caught the tail end of the argument.

"Unless I see that book – that package – which is mine any-way—"

"I told you. No cash, no see. No extra cash, no package."

"Where is the damned thing? You do have it? You try and cross me and it'll be worse—"

"It's safe. And don't try steamin' in to play the heavy with me, mate," the first suit shouted, "or you and your fuckin' tart'll be sorry!"

"At least show me package. Then we can talk," Hunzinger fumed.

"For Chrissake, Don. Fetch the bleedin' fucker and show 'im," the first suit growled angrily. "But pay first, touch later, eh?"

Hart was back through the pass door before Don, scowling, pushed his way out past the table and left the bar. Hart's first wild impulse was to follow him, but he checked it.

He was tenths of a second too slow, it would look too obvious – to Hunzinger as well as to the remaining suit – and he wasn't one hundred percent *certain* either that these thugs were the killers or that the 'package' was the one he so desperately needed. The snatches of argument had not been quite specific enough for him to act immediately. And in any case it was too late now: the man had vanished among the crowd thronging the apartment block's entrance foyer.

He was away perhaps three minutes. During that time, sirens sounded the air-raid alert. At first blasting in from some local high point, then further away, nearer, in the distance, until the whole universe seemed to vibrate with their sobbing screams.

A few people left the bar. Some couples drained their glasses before they hurried out. Most of the drinkers stayed where they were, and there was a rush of fresh orders. "God, he's early tonight!" someone shouted. "Didn't even have the time to down me second pint!"

Hart had to think quickly. He was armed; he had carried 'Zoltan's' German gun since his first London visit to deliver the code-book to Sunderland Terrace. But the bar was still crowded, and the foyer too. The use of firearms in such conditions was unthinkable. Quickly, then, he made up his mind. Past the pay phones, along the corridor, branching to the right to take a passageway linking the pool with the reception area, he emerged breathless in the foyer just as Don came out of a lift and turned back towards the bar. The package gripped firmly between his right hand and his left elbow was Hart's all right.

Hart followed him through the crowd, the gun, cocked, concealed in the right-hand pocket of the raincoat, hand curled around the butt and a finger on the trigger.

Don shouldered his way through. Past Cosmo and Rawlins, non-plussed by the manifestation of two Zoltans in the same bar, neither the one they expected. Past the languid length of Webster staring into his martini by the pillar. Up to the niche and the anxious trio at the table. He had been told to be ready for an attempt on Hunzinger's part to snatch the package, so he moved behind Zelda on her side of the table, sliding into a seat opposite her and diagonally across from the German.

It was precisely at the moment that he lowered himself to the oak settle, just as his companion sidled aside to make room for him, that Hart acted.

The only real weapon he had under those conditions, the only effective one, was surprise.

Hart swooped between Hunzinger and Zelda, thrusting the woman aside. Using his right hand, he fired two rapid shots into the ceiling of the alcove, at the same time seizing the slender parcel from Don's grasp.

The roar of the two unsilenced reports in the crowded bar was deafening. Pandemonium was immediate. Hunzinger shouted, the suits yelled, Zelda screamed. Women in the bar screamed. A glass crashed to the floor. There was a confused scramble away from the bar. People near the alcove flung themselves to the floor.

Before the echoes of the gunshots had died away, Don – attacked from an entirely unexpected direction – had loosened his grip and Hart, package in hand, had crashed through the pass door and into the corridor.

Hunzinger's chair crashed over backwards. He sprang to his feet, furious anger for once overwhelming his professional caution and instinct to play safe. Drawing his own automatic, he emptied the entire clip, firing blind through the panels of the door at the zigzagged, sprinting figure of Hart glimpsed through the shattered window-pane. At the same time, in an attempt to avoid a total panic, Webster had fired two more shots into the ceiling from his own small Browning automatic. But things in the bar had already gone too far and his calming voice was swamped in the general hysterical uproar.

By this time Hunzinger had recovered his sense of reason and realised that it was senseless shooting through a closed door at a moving target. Crashing through himself, he slammed in a fresh clip as he pounded after the fleeing Hart. Two snap shots at the man with the package failed to score, and then Hart was around the corner and racing again for the crowded foyer.

In the bar, the two suits had leaped over the table, knocking Zelda to the floor, and fought their way out, preferring to cut their losses rather than risk getting involved in what could be a murder investigation. For similar reasons – and fearing perhaps that one, or both, their Zoltan look-alikes might have lost their minds – Cosmo and Rawlins had also thought it prudent to withdraw.

Webster was the man who drew the short straw. He was still there. He had been seen to fire shots. He was now surrounded by an angry crowd refusing to listen to the explanations he was unable truthfully to give anyway. He was also, it seemed in some quarters, being held responsable for the fact that – curiouser, and curiouser! – there appeared to be no dead and no injured.

Hart hared through the reception area, knocking bellboys, guests and porters left and right. He dashed through the swing doors, down a semicircular flight of steps and up to the first cab waiting at the head of a taxi rank outside the White House entrance. Hunzinger was not far behind.

"Quick!" Hart panted, jerking open the door. "This is urgent."

"Where to, sir?" the cabbie asked imperturbably, clicking down his flag.

Hunzinger was running down the steps.

"Kensington. Rosewall Gardens." Hart slammed the door and glanced through the small, round rear window. Hunzinger was approaching the next cab in line.

The taxi moved out into the traffic heading west. It was dark already and the air, laden still with a fine drizzle, was heavy with the throb of aero engines. Far away behind them, in the Thames Estuary Hart supposed, the murderous stutter of anti-aircraft gunfire could be heard.

As they crossed Baker Street into Marylebone Road, bright flashes of fire, orange, yellow and incandescent white, stabbed the night southwards, and seconds later the earth shook with the reverberation of the first high-explosive assault from the sky.

Thirty

It shouldn't have happened that way, of course. It was against all the forecasts, Allied as well as German. It played hell with the blitz routine people almost felt they had the right to expect. But a rogue depression spiralling down from Iceland upset all the calculations furnished by metereologist boffins on both sides of the North Sea and spread havoc everywhere.

Arctic convoy PQ-37C – twenty-seven merchantmen scheduled to leave Reykjavik at 0100 hours en route for Murmansk – was retained in port. The destroyer flotilla was ordered to stand off and the main task force covering them instructed to stay north of Bear Island.

A raid on Bremen, by two hundred Halifax and Stirling bombers, was called off. But four times that number of planes destined for the heaviest raid on London so far that year took off in clear starlight from airfields in northern Germany and Holland with a promise of moonlight later.

Once over the Channel of course, it was evident that the Met service had boobed. Again. The ragged streamers of cloud obscuring parts of the east coast had thickened to a heavy overcast by the time the navigators hoped to identify The Wash, and London itself was blanketed with ten tenths all the way down. In such circumstances there was nothing to do but press on regardless, but with no landmarks, no Thames to follow, no fires to pinpoint, the bomb-aimers dropped their loads where and how they could, only too anxious to scramble home.

It was by chance, therefore, that night, that the East End and the docks were relatively spared. This was because a particularly furious fire had taken hold between Fulham Broadway and Kensington Gardens and there was enough reflected light to penetrate the cloud cover with a faint glow. As a result, the heaviest damage was suffered between Hammersmith and the West End.

The first firestorm spread through multiple incendiary attacks which happened to link blazes uniting waterfront gasometers, a chemical factory and a motor works. Nicholas Hart saw the first stick of high explosives aimed through this – some way to the south, not far from the river – as his taxi rounded Hyde Park Corner. A heartbeat afterwards, concussions from the billowing fountains of flame, smoke and debris cracked his eardrums. The blast from the second stick skated the cab halfway across the roadway beyond St George's Hospital, and before they reached Knightsbridge there was no longer any need – or any possibility – to count. Hell was erupting all around them.

Traffic had halted and people were running for the entrance to the tube station, the shelters. Wardens spread across the street, gesticulating. Fire engines already clanged their way past red lights and in the distance ambulance bells shrilled out of the Emergency hospital gates.

Somewhere above, on an upper floor, a woman screamed hysterically from an open window.

"Put out that sodding *light!*" a warden shouted.

The cab angled in to the kerb with brakes squealing. "I'm sorry, guv," the cabbie yelled. "I can't really . . . Any case, the wardens'll have us off the road." He jumped down into the roadway.

"Of course you can't," Hart called. Hunzinger's cab was halted perhaps two hundred and fifty yards behind. He flung open the door, thrust notes into the driver's hand. "Keep the change. Get under cover – and good luck!"

"Bless you, sir." The man was already running for the tube. "It ain't far," he panted over his shoulder. "Coupla hundred, maybe a little more. Right, off Beauchamp Place . . ."

Hart was already running. Impossible to distinguish which of the hundreds of sets of footsteps behind could be following him, but one would be, he knew. He thrust the phrase book, in its wrapping inside the raincoat, between the lapels of his jacket; forging ahead through the glaring, detonating, occasionally floodlit interruptions to the shouting blackout.

He had no conscious recollection of why he had given the cabbie the Rosewall Gardens address; it was the first one that came to him, the only private one he knew in London, in his head perhaps because it had been given to him by the singer, June-Estelle. Perhaps because she had said call me if you need me. In any case because he had to get out of there, fast.

There seemed no limit to the roar of bursting bombs. By the dark bulk of turreted Harrods, tiles, bricks and fragments of masonry showered into the street from a direct hit behind the store.

Hart tripped, kicked away a plaster-covered encylopaedia that was lying in the roadway, and increased his pace. There was now a definite, quite distinctive pattern of footsteps discernible somewhere behind – steadily pressing onwards, emerging from the ragged clatter of background noise, perhaps even gaining a little as the pattern established itself?

He turned into Beauchamp Place, the heart pumping, breath labouring a little now. Glass from the shattered windows of modistes, hat shops and antiques specialists coruscated in the reflections from a nearby fire to flood the whole width of the narrow street in a glittering tide.

There was a church burning on the far corner of Rosewall Gardens. As the flames brightened, he could make out the name of the street. The express train screech had scarcely registered before he was felled by the wall of blinding fire. The ground beneath him trembled to a thunderous detonation and the wall of a house leaned outward, separated into individual locks of stone, then crashed to the ground. The roof caved in, vanishing behind a boiling tower of black smoke marbled with crimson. Hart struggled back upright off his knees, dust covered, checked that the precious package was still tucked into his jacket and ran on.

The footsteps were still there, considerably nearer now.

The number the girl had given Hart was at the end of a short cul-de-sac, where two small Edwardian apartment blocks faced one another on either side of a paved courtyard. Another fire – from somewhere behind, perhaps in Hans Crescent? – was now fierce enough to see fairly clearly: the roof of an entire five-storey block, hit by a load of incendiaries, was now ablaze from end to end, the leaping light from tongues of flame searing out to send sinuous shadows swarming over the flagstones of the courtyard.

And to reveal that one of the blocks, boarded up and evacuated after a previous raid, had been abandoned while the other, still partly inhabited, had been severely damaged at the same time. Checking the numbers, he saw with relief that this was where June should be.

It was evident that the club where she worked could not yet have been re-opened. He had just to keep his fingers crossed that the Minister's PPS was not in a specially randy mood tonight!

Hunzinger's footsteps were still crunching, fast and heavy, over the shards of glass littering Beauchamp Place. Once, now they were in a quieter, narrower street, Hart thought he might have paused to loose off a couple of shots, but he couldn't be sure: 9 mm automatic fire was hard to identify against the hell of thousand-lb high-explosive bombs bursting. In any case, like Hart himself, the man was limited to the two clips of ammunition supplied with his Walther in the escape kit – and he had wasted one of those already at the White House.

It was still raining. The underside of the cloud front heaved redly with the reflection of fires on every side. Between the incessant detonations of exploding bombs, the growling crackle of flames now laid a menacing groundswell beneath the frantic salvage activity of the burning city. Hart dodged through ripped out blackout shields and found himself in a small octagonal hallway floored with marble that was now smoke-stained and fissured.

An old-fashioned openwork lift stood at the foot of a shaft opposite the entrance. The six remaining sides of the octagon had each contained an apartment door. Three of them, undamaged, were numbered. Four, Five and Six. Two of those facing them were blistered and boarded up; the last hung on a single hinge, revealing a blast shattered interior in the dim radiance of the masked hallway light. There was also a light inside the lift.

Hart wrenched open two wooden doors, slid back the concertinaed steel inner gate, and reached for the buttons indicating the eight floors served. Hunzinger's footsteps no longer trod broken glass; they were faster now and harder. He was running towards the courtyard. Did he know the building was where Zelda's contact June lived? Flat Thirty-Two on the fifth floor?

If only, battling against Sod's Law, the bloody lift was in working order . . . if only June was in . . . if only the apartment had a solid, defensible door, stout enough to resist bullets . . . if only . . .

Hart slammed doors with his free hand, stabbed the button marked Five. The footsteps, very loud now, halted momentarily between the two apartment blocks.

The lift car shuddered, creaked, shook itself like a dog coming out of water . . . and moved.

Somebody heavy shouldered through the damaged blackout. Hart shot out the hallway light as the lift rose past the ceiling on its way to the first floor. A voice below cursed in German. Footsteps dashed for the stairway circling the lift shaft, started to scramble upward in the dark.

It was then that chance looked kindly in Hart's direction for the second time.

The blast damage that cracked the floor and sacked the devastated apartment had not been limited to flats at street level. Evidently a whole section of the building's outer wall had been affected, including the premises immediately above. And including that side of the stairway.

In light filtering down from the landings, Hart saw as the lift rose that two entire flights of stairs had been demolished, had dropped out of the spiral and fallen in separate sections to smash in fragments on the basement floor beside the lift mechanism far below. The lift was the only way left to reach the upper storeys.

The car rose smoothly past the second floor landing. There were no more footsteps. Hunzinger tried an off-chance shot, firing up through the rising floor of the lift. For some reason it sounded even more deafening than Hart's own round in the hallway. The slug struck metal, didn't penetrate, was lost in ricochets down the shaft. He didn't try again. There was nothing he could do but wait until the car returned to the ground floor – which it must unless Hart remained inside it!

The girl *must* be there, had to be at home. Yet nobody had emerged from any of the undamaged apartments to demand what the hell was going on. Perhaps they were all in shelters. Perhaps June, the nightbird, was the only one left?

She had to be there because the one essential, vital priority was that he must at all costs stay holed up with the book safe and sound until help arrived. Webster was too late to help at the White House, but he would eventually trace the cabbie and find out the address Hart had given. But it was too much to hope that he could do this before the All Clear. And even then the taxi driver might have gone straight home, lost his cab, been killed or injured even.

It was kind of an uneven conflict, really, Hart reflected as the lift left the third floor behind. Not entirely fair, dammit! He might recall a few of the many details he had encoded, but the book itself must be treasured, protected, kept undamaged, intact, until it was delivered – whatever happened to Hart himself. All Hunzinger had to do, however, was destroy it. Any way he wanted, with or without Hart. He could burn it, throw it in the river, leave it in an undetected dustbin, tear out the pages and eat them or throw them down the loo. And his job would be done. Zero. Finished. End of story!

Odds in his favour then. So far. The lift was approaching the fourth floor.

Automatically, idiotically, the way one did, he ducked his head, hearing the unmistakable advance of a stick, nearer than the others, pulverise the roofs in his direction. The last bomb – and it was a monster – seemed to make the whole city tremble upwards from the ground. Floor by floor the block shook like leaves in a gale. The flash of the explosion was so agonisingly vivid that Hart was temporarily blinded. And it was only after his reeling head had cleared that he realised the incandescence had not been replaced by the wan illumination of the lift and landing lamps. Every light in the block had been extinguished.

The lift shuddered to a halt, blocked between the fourth and fifth floors.

Frantically, Hart jammed his thumb on buttons, rattled the steel cage. No current anywhere.

For the first time, near-panic seized him. After all this! "June!" he shouted suddenly. "*JUNE!*"

Bricks and masonry were falling into the street. An abrupt roar of flames not far away. Nearer still, the heavy splashing from a burst water-main seemed unnaturally, annoyingly loud.

Someone was shouting in the street. And then, unexpectedly, out of the blackness above, the wrenching open of a door. A voice, shakily, hoarsely: "What is it? Who is it? Who's there?"

Magically, blessedly, heart-stoppingly – June's voice!

"The mole!" he yelled, God knows why. "I'm trapped in the bloody lift!"

"We'll get you, you bastard," Hunzinger's voice, thick with rage, floated up from below. "You and your imbecile code-book. A rat in a betrayer's cage!"

June was on the landing. "You're certain there's absolutely no current, Mole?"

"I'd have been out of here before the Romans left if there had been," he called.

"The inner cage can't be moved. But if the electricity's not connected, the two wooden outer doors can be opened," she said. "At least I think so"

"Can't see the point of that if the inner's jammed," Hart said. "One's still stuck here after all."

"I can open them from above you. If it's not too far, I can drop on to the roof. There's a trap. If we can open it, I could help you out. Wait – I'll fetch a flashlight."

"That's my girl. But be careful of the glim. There are men with guns."

The pad-pad-pad of feet on carpet. In the distance a drawer opened. The tiniest glint of light.

Odd how the simplest of manoeuvres can at times seem to take an age of complication while others, seemingly complex, appear to pass in a flash almost before they have even started!

Hart heard the double wooden doors swing open. Hastily dowsed, another brief shaft of light.

From below, Hunzinger fired again. But the angle was too acute.

240

There was a hollow boom as the slug once more struck metal. The lift car tremored.

Hart heard the soft thump of rubber soles above his head. A tearing rasp, as if wood, too long sealed up, had been levered away from its emplacement; a current of cool air – then June's voice out of a space in the centre of the lift's ceiling: "Lying flat, I think I can reach far enough down to touch your hand. Stretch up and try."

Spread fingers groped, touched, clung. Hart sprang; she heaved; he grabbed the framework of the trapdoor and hauled himself up on to the exterior of the car roof. "Good girl!" he breathed.

"The doors are only about seven feet above," she whispered. "The floor, I mean. You can shove me though then use the ironwork of the shaft to climb up."

A one-second flashlight glimpse . . . and after all it was as easy as that. She led him into her flat.

Hunzinger was now shouting, storming from below. "Somerville! Fordyke! For God's sake – are you there or not? What the devil's happened to you? I need help, for pity's sake: the damned lift is blocked and there's a traitor in the top half of the building!"

Another door opened, higher up. "What the hell do you think, we're doing". The voice, hoarse and shaky, sharpened by anger. "We're lying flat under the bloody Morrison shelter in the dining-room, for Christ's sake!"

And then again: "This is no time for histrionics, man! We're the only other tenants in the building, apart from the girl. It's a total holocaust out there!"

Hart had uttered an exclamation of surprise. He knew the names, of course. They were two of the first sleepers he had himself interviewed. The second voice belonged to the renowned Doctor Avian Somerville, august rector of the girls' boarding school near Shrewsbury; Fordyke was the teutonically-inclined antiquarian bookseller from South Wales. Hunzinger, taken unawares by the raid, must be gathering his clans before an all-out intelligence effort.

"You will come out right now," he bellowed. "With guns. Take the staircase down to the fifth. Apartment Thirty-Two. You are to shoot out the lock and take the couple there prisoner. The woman is no longer on our side. If necessary kill them both and secure a package the man carries."

"Well, I don't know if we can successfully—" Fordyke began.

"Be quiet and do as I say," the spy-master seethed. "Is there a fire escape in this building?"

"It is on the damaged side," Somerville replied. "The upper part is secure; you might be able to reach the lower portion through the wrecked flat off the entrance hall, but I am uncertain—"

"I will see if the outside fire escape can breach the gap in the inner stairs," Hunzinger interrupted. "Get into that flat, hold the couple, and I shall join you there."

Hart closed the apartment door. June clicked the lock. The door felt fairly lightweight to him. "What kind of a lock is it?" he asked in a low voice.

"An ordinary Yale. With a mortice lower down: I'll fetch the key for that."

Hart ripped down blackout curtains. At once the fiery flicker of flames from several different directions etched the outlines of furniture from the darkness of the room. Chairs, bookcases, a gate-legged table, a settee. The only heavy piece was a Victorian sideboard with a curved back. "That's the only thing likely to be of any use," Hart decided. "The Yale's nothing. Lock the mortice and we'll have to heave it in front of the door. Even then, once the lock's shot out it'll only be a question of time before superior weight will dislodge it. I warn you: this could be tough."

He touched her arm. Warm flesh through some silky material. Rising and falling, the pulsating red glow sculpted out for him a knee-length housecoat, a swell of breasts. "He did say, the man below – no longer on his side?"

"My boyfriend ratted," June said tightly. "Off to the safe Shires constituency with the boss!"

"That's too bad." He had begun to heave the sideboard away from the wall.

"The hell with it." She was lending her own slight weight to his efforts. "Dear Zelda had begun to get her claws into him anyway. Too good a prize to leave to the hired help!" The sideboard, which was fitted with castors, had begun to move across the fitted carpet.

"I'm a good-time girl, anyway," June said defensively. "I like to have fun. I love to make love. I don't want to get mixed up with all this boys' adventure story rubbish. Especially with politics!"

The throaty crackle of the fire from Hans Crescent, the thud of falling beams, seemed very loud suddenly. Hart, panting as he swung the buffet, had heard a clatter of displaced rubble while Hunzinger forced his way into the ruined flat in the hope of finding a gap in window or wall that could lead through to the outside fire escape. Whatever happened, they didn't have long.

Together they wedged the sideboard across the entrance. "Add the settee and the table," he said. From outside the door, he heard the stealthy tread of feet on the stairs. He went to the window.

"I'd just love to have had you come right back to bed with me," the girl said. "As of now, Mole!"

"Well, I mean, ditto of course," Hart said gallantly. "But preferably without the audience."

Where he was, it was a nine to one chance of out for the count. No point putting the wind up the girl, but with his clip and a bit against two unknown handguns and Huntzinger's remaining rounds indoors . . . Well, it was unhealthy to say the least. To say nothing about the book.

Whereas with what he had seen . . . long odds again, but worth a try, Jack! And at least there was a better chance of getting the book back into the home coop. "Have you ever ridden pillion on a motorbike?" he asked the girl.

"Pillion? Why, yes. You grip with the thighs, wind the arms tight around the pilot's waist . . . and hope, A for the best, B that he knows what he's bloody doing! Best with the head on the shoulder."

"Exactly. Well we're going to have a fast shot at the pillion now – only fate has it, I'm afraid we're going to have to do without the actual bike." Hart nodded his head towards the open window. June approached, looked out, stared at him in the firelight. She looked puzzled.

Hart gesticulated, explained, reasoned the odds each way. The only solution, he said. In the circumstances. "You must be bloody joking!" June said.

Outside on the landing, somebody called something stupid about opening the door. The voice was followed by two shots, then a third. The mortice installation was displaced in its housing. A panel above the door handle splintered and split.

Outside the window, the flaming firelight fitfully illuminated Hart's target.

Twenty feet from the window, at the angle of two of the octagon's faces, iron staples attached to the wall held a thick, heavily insulated electric cable projecting into the void. The far end of the cable, spanning the courtyard, homed in among the twisted pipes and fractured conduits spining the facade of the bomb-damaged block on the far side of the cul-de-sac. Below the window of the octagonal block a string course, a decorative ledge perhaps six inches wide, circled the building – and above it there was a coping separating the fifth storey from the one above. "If I was to stand on the ledge facing the open window," Hart explained, "and you were to climb out on to my back and ride piggyback, you could reach up and grasp the coping to balance us . . . and then I could edge along the string course until we reached the cable. After that you simply adopt the pillion position and I'll lower myself to the cable and transfer us hand over hand until we get to the block on the far side of the courtyard. Then it's no more than a matter of getting out."

"You're out of your mind!" June protested. "I mean like, no way. We're between sixty and seventy feet off the ground, for God's sake!"

"The trick there," Hart told her, "as my old break-and-enter instructor at OCTU used to say, is to imagine you're doing the whole thing at waist level. Only two foot six to fall. After that it's a piece of cake."

"It's not a cake that I'd care to taste," she said.

Three carefully placed shots shattered the wood of the door – below the handle, above one hinge, ripping open the central panel. The door jerked suddenly inwards; the sideboard shifted. Hunzinger's voice was abruptly present. It seemed almost at the same level now.

Hart was astride the window-ledge. Now he was standing on the string course, his hands on the sill, facing inwards. "You pays your money," he said.

June said something unladylike, climbed up, and then out on to his back. The sideboard shook. Hart released a hand, fired a single shot in through the open window, out through the martyred door. For an instant the assault on that was withdrawn.

During the lull, Hart said quickly: "Stretch up for the coping. One hand will do. Grab me with the other." Feeling an arm thrust over a shoulder, knees gripping him between waist and ribs, he began to inch his way clear of the opening.

Hart flattened himself as much as he could, ankles, calves, buttocks tensed inwards, arms outspread. His fingers clenched desperately into every narrow fissure separating the blocks of stonework cladding the wall, his cheek pressed the rough surface, willing himself flatter still, harder against the unyielding vertical face.

He could never have remained there if she hadn't been gripping the coping above. Her weight clamped to his back – nine stone? ten? – relentlessly displaced his centre of gravity . . . away from the median line, outside the hips, beyond the width of the six-inch ledge, threatening to topple them both into the void. He dreaded to think what the effort must be doing to the muscles of her hand, but he dare not risk her using both: if she wasn't clinging hard to him with the other, the relative shifts of two separate bodies could hurtle them to infinity.

Slowly, gently, easing the sole along the gritty, sooted surface; move the left foot away an inch, two inches . . . with infinite care; balance the weight, shift the right up to it . . . slide the left again . . .

The distance to the iron staples and the electric cable was twenty feet – little more than the height of three tall men lying prone. There was no variety in the exercise, the operation; no alternations of relaxation and stress; no change in the rhythm of effort. Muscles, tendons, sinews must be kept at screaming point all the time.

Flames licked the sky. Bombs exploded. Fire engines and ambulances swerved wildly through the desolation below. In the apartment they had left behind, a loud crash accompanied by the breaking of glass and a heavy splintering of wood announced that the sideboard had finally been overthrown and the door burst open. Voices called. There would only be a short pause now before the pursuers discovered the flat was uninhabited. And after that the window.

Slide the foot, search for another crevice, move up the other, slide again; keep the breath shallow in case the expansion of the lungs moves the body away from the wall. In a sense the monotony of the limited movements available could almost become boring in its sameness.

If it hadn't happened to have been the longest journey Hart had ever made in his life.

The cable was almost within reach. "Hold tight, duckie," Hart breathed. "One more move . . ."

He advanced his left foot, his left hand. He advanced his right. Perhaps this time a shade too quickly. Perhaps, overcome with relief, he snatched.

The fingers of the left hand locked into a fissure. But somehow the right skated across the wet stonework and the brusqueness of the movement cast it – and with it the left leg – away from the wall and the ledge. Like an opening gate, pivoting on fingers, toes and June's grasp on the coping above, Hart's body with its human supercargo swung out over the gap.

Then he was frantically swivelling the left foot, exerting pressure with the lacerated fingers of his left hand, to swing them both back facing the wall again.

The stone fringe of the string-course crumbled. Fragments of the ledge dropped away. Hart's left foot slipped into space.

This time he uttered a frantic cry. The entire weight of their two bodies plummeted downwards, wrenching intolerably at June's shoulder, wrist and fingers locked over the coping. For a timeless eternity they were prevented from falling only by the anguished clutch of those fingers.

But for that one moment her reactions had been even faster than Hart's shock of dismay: as the ledge crumbled she had already wrenched her arm away from his shoulder, tightened the knees gripping his waist, and shot the second arm up to help the first support their dual weight.

Agonisingly, Hart scrabbled with bent knee for a foothold, found it, straightened the leg, eased up the other to relieve the load on their two overtaxed sets of muscles – and found himself, still locked to the coping via the girl's frame, splayed forward along the wall at an angle of forty-five degrees. And from here, miraculously, he could stretch out his arms, grab the cable and allow himself to fall – this time deliberately – at full stretch, ready for his hand-over-hand traverse.

He was gasping for breath, his eyes were streaming, the blood thundered within his chest. "Let me off now," the girl panted. "We can go one by one; I'll follow you across."

He shook his head, realising astonishingly that rain was still falling. Their clothes were sodden, hair plastered to their skulls. "No, stay on my back," he decided. "Worst part's over now. Anyway I'm used to this – you know: battle courses and all that!"

"Whatever you say." This time she wound both arms around his neck and again scissored her legs to grip Hart's waist. He could feel his heart pumping against her thighs.

The cable was two inches thick and heavily insulated. It stretched perhaps forty feet to another pair of staples attached to the parapet of the damaged block on the far side of the courtyard. The lower part of the facade was boarded up, but the glassless windows of the upper storeys were open to the elements, and he reckoned they should be able to force an entry here or over the parapet and get away somewhere behind before Hunzinger and his henchmen could lock on to them.

With the girl safe again in her 'pillion' position, Hart began to move out along the line.

To a trained young military man in combat condition, forty feet hand over hand along a wire, even fifty feet above ground, presents no especial difficulty. Not even with a second person slung over the operator's back: one of the reasons they use the technique in battle courses is to help combatants remove a wounded comrade from a battle zone.

Odds however become slightly lengthened if marksmen between thirty and fifty feet away – three of them with semi-automatic handguns – are firing at the travellers as they hang from the wire like fairground targets. And, again, if the wire itself is in danger of losing its horizontal aspect and plunging to the ground.

In the case of Hart and June's traverse, the risk deriving from the first case was minimised, since the light available to the sharpshooters was an undulating glare that varied from a pulsating crimson glow to an abruptly leaping dance of flaming orange, green and even smokey blue.

Once Hunzinger, Fordyke and Somerville had leaned out of the apartment window to locate, sight and aim at their targets, Hart at once swung himself around through 180 degrees so that the girl on his back was shielded by his own body. At the same time, he panted:

Blitz Harvest

"Take . . . gun from right-hand pocket. Spare clip in left. Then . . . the odd shot . . . more to dissuade than score."

Perhaps, at those distances, as moving targets, in that light, danger from the notoriously inaccurate automatic pistol was less of a peril than it seemed. Certainly the blaze of Hart's gun, belching flame two-handed from not far in front of his chin, caused the pursuers to duck and withdraw and move around. Nobody on either side, in any case, seemed to suffer hits. In fact it was the second of the two alternative hazards that provided the real danger that lay ahead.

They were a little over halfway across when most of the questions preoccupying Hart's mind – stimulated by what seemed for a moment a sudden lowering of the wire and a swift glance over the shoulder – faded rapidly into the background. Had he imagined the movement? No, an abrupt resurgence of flames nearer at hand revealed a definite subsidence of the cable lowering its human cargo by several inches. This was followed by a second downward jerk as Hart transferred the weight from his left hand to his right. He turned his head fully and stared at the wall of the octagonal block. There was now something like twenty-one or even twenty-two stone dragging down the electric line . . . and the weight, shifting as it was, had begun to pull the rusted staples out of the weathered, perhaps blasted stonework cladding the wall of the building.

Hart cursed aloud. He dared not try to accelerate his pace: he would risk pulling the old iron spikes completely free. Yet with each precarious move these staples emerged a little more, the insulated wire dropped a fraction lower. The fiery light now highlit a thin stream of plaster, trickling, remorseless as the sands of an hourglass, from the place where the staples entered the wall. Unless they were very near the facade, near enough to grab hold of some projection, they would be smashed against the brickwork of the abandoned block, or shaken off to drop into space, when the cable pulled free and slammed them unerringly as the weights on a pendulum across the remainder of the gap.

The end came when they still had fifteen or twenty feet to travel.

But before the expected lurch there was one more surprise in store. From the gaping window apertures of the wall facing them a fusillade of gunfire spat lethal flame across the courtyard at the window of June's flat, driving Hunzinger and his men inside.

The cable, weighted by its human load, swung down free towards the opposite wall.

Bracing himself for the final shock that would hurl them both into the eternal night, Hart saw in the last hundredth of a second that the impact would smash them not into solid masonry but against a fourth

247

floor window embrasure that was immediately below the second set of staples still securing their lifeline at that end. Clinging frenziedly to the cable, he brought up his legs an instant before the shock. His heels exploded through splintered wood and the grimed glass of a pane still astonishingly in place as the window burst inwards. The human counterweights fell across the sill and pitched forward into the bare room beyond.

Webster was waiting three paces away with a group of armed police at the next window, the hawk face intense in the burning light.

Hart was on his knees. Nothing surprised him now. Jerking the precious code-book out from between his drenched lapels he croaked: "Special Delivery! Sign here, please."

Then he felt an intolerable blow between the shoulderblades and the night went dark.

"That last shot was from Axel," Webster said. "More of a two-fingers-up gesture than anything else, but it winged you in the back. Lucky one for you, though. Missed the spinal column, no organs touched. You've been out for a few days, but you'll be all right."

Hart was lying in a hospital bed. He had a sore back and there was a saline drip in his arm. For some reason he seemed to have a thumping headache. "Rounded them up?" he asked groggily.

"Bagged the lot," Webster said happily. "And the sleepers afterwards. Thanks to you, cock!"

"And June? The girl? Is she all right?"

"Never better, old boy. Badly grazed hands but all the upperworks are fine. She got a job singing at the American Red Cross. No looking back: can't stop her now!"

Hart managed a grin. "I wouldn't be surprised," he said.

"Meanwhile," Webster said, "Colonel Nichols orders complete rest and at least a couple of weeks rehabilitation – the course and the leave following it to be organised by our tame kinaesthetics genius, Sister June Chandos. She really is qualified in 'the study of body movements' too."

Hart turned his head sideways. She was sitting demurely on the far side of the bed – no ATS, WAAF, VAD uniform or RAF three-cornered hat this time; just the crisp dark blue and white Florence Nightingale nurse's rig. "I've been waiting for you," she smiled.

Epilogue

The Hunzinger twins were not perhaps truly identical. Near enough for A to be taken for B if the latter wasn't there. Or vice versa if there were a number of years in between. Or for Nicholas Hart to be taken for either. Or vice versa, as he found to his cost. But such three-way 'ringing' can cut . . . well, at least three ways.

On a troop carrier bound for North Africa and then Sydney just before the Allied invasion of southern France in the first half of August 1944, Hart found himself, posted to an Intelligence unit in Alexandria, face to face one day with his own past.

Or somebody's past. Or perhaps nobody's past at all.

Rounding a corner of the promenade deck, he discovered himself unexpectedly eyeball to eyeball with a military prisoner. It was no less than the captured Axel, exercising under armed guard on deck.

There was a moment of surprised recognition. Hart searched a little awkwardly for some kind of anodyne greeting, perhaps a few words of conversation (they had, after all, in a sense worked together once). But the German totally repudiated the truth.

"My brother Axel was shot down by an unknown assassin in Regent's Park," he said coolly. "I am Zoltan Hunzinger, bound under escort for Australia and the internment camp from which I escaped last year." And then, to his guards: "I am afraid I do not know this gentleman."